MW00756704

THE
AFTERLIFE
OF
EMERSON
TANG

THE AFTERLIFE OF EMERSON TANG

A NOVEL

PAULA CHAMPA

HOUGHTON MIFFLIN HARCOURT
BOSTON • NEW YORK
2013

For information about permission to reproduce selections from this book,
write to Permissions, Houghton Mifflin Harcourt Publishing Company,
215 Park Avenue South, New York, New York 10003.

www.hmhbooks.com

Library of Congress Cataloging-in-Publication Data
Champa, Paula.
The afterlife of Emerson Tang : a novel / Paula Champa.
p. cm.
ISBN 978-0-547-79278-1
1. Women archivists — Fiction.
2. Collectors and collecting — Automobiles — Fiction. I. Title.
PR6103.H3654A68 2013
823'.92 — dc23
2012014030

Printed in the United States of America
DOC 10 9 8 7 6 5 4 3 2 1

The author is grateful for permission to quote from the website
CocteauTwins.com.

To Mike

CONTENTS

PART I

THE BODY

1

PART II

THE ENGINE

131

We declare that the splendour of the world has been enriched by a new beauty: the beauty of speed. A . . . roaring motor car which seems to run on machine-gun fire is more beautiful than the Victory of Samothrace.

— F. T. MARINETTI, *The Futurist Manifesto*, 1909

Do you remember *The Incredible Shrinking Man*? He shrank and shrank, and went from world to world. Finally he's shrunk through the grass and down into the atoms — you don't know where. And on the sound track, you hear, "I still exist."

— MIKE NICHOLS

PART I

THE BODY

I

AM A WOMAN WITH no fingerprints. No patterned ridges to
leave a trace of myself in a waxy coating of furniture polish.
Nothing to press into an inkpad or scan with a computer eye. I
am undetectable, a model of discretion. And I am human. At least
I was during the time in question, with a bellybutton attesting
to my birth thirty years earlier, a first and last name (Bethany
Corvid), and ten fingers that were otherwise so ordinary as to
pass without notice.

But—the ends. This was where the erosion of the self
materialized. And if the ends of my fingers lacked the usual
loops, whorls and arches, my other human qualities must have
amounted to nearly as complete a blankness. That's how it felt
when the whole business started with the car. I didn't know about
my missing fingerprints then. I only sensed the blankness on the
inside. Maybe you know what I mean: When someone you care
for is dying, you can feel the emptiness of losing him even before
he's gone. I had no idea how many ways grief could rob you before it gave you something back. Sometimes I imagined myself
a ghost, like the ghostly figures woven into the carpeting of the
Royalton Hotel in Manhattan, where the artist Hélène Moreau
established her provisional encampment that June of 1996.

If I'd had the talent of ghosts to haunt lobbies and hallways,
to drift freely across oceans and eavesdrop on lives more definite

than my own, I could have spied Hélène a few days before I came to meet her at that hotel, when (as she would later recount to me in frank detail) she was still waiting on a sofa in the office of Manfred Zeffler in Schnell, Germany, world headquarters of the automaker AG, AG.

Ghosts are close. They observe things: how glumly Hélène lifted the mug of coffee Zeffler had set in front of her . . .

I can picture Zeffler's manicured hands tapping his phone as he told Hélène he wished she had called his office first, how he could have saved her a flight from Paris.

"These are what we have." He stooped awkwardly at his desk to read to her from a few sheets of paper, as if those thin pages could have relieved Hélène's obvious sadness. "The car purchased by a Mr. Alto Bianco in Rome was ordered on the ninth of October 1953. Chassis number 39212. *Alto Bianco—*"

"And the color?" Hélène interrupted in German, ignoring Zeffler's neutral choice of English in addressing her.

He consulted the records and replied in his native tongue: "They called it Egg Cream Custard."

"What about the interior, was it red?"

"Scarlet leather, yes."

He handed her the page to see for herself.

"Do you . . ." Her lips were quivering. "I don't think this helps me. I thought you might have something else."

"Of course." With a sigh of futility, Zeffler consulted the second sheet of paper: "The car was one of the last left-hand-drive models manufactured in 1953, road-tested and approved for export to Italy on Wednesday, the twenty-third of December—"

He glanced up. Hélène appeared to be lost in thought, resting the coffee mug against her cheek. Zeffler winced as she moved it to her lips: Emblazoned on her face was the lighthouse emblem of the Beacon Motor Company, the perfect reverse of the logo molded onto the side of the mug.

Was she branding her cheek on purpose?

He must have sensed she was not the type of collector who would be satisfied with anything as easy to locate as some substitute model. No, the drop-ins tended to be fixated on tracking down one particular vehicle, its chassis stamped with an identifying number as unique as a human fingerprint. Ambushed by Hélène's pleading gaze, Zeffler was like a postman whose customer was begging him to open the mailbox so she could unmail an envelope. A love letter posted too hastily, perhaps. They always wanted something back. Something disguised in the shape of an automobile: a memory or a person they knew, a way of life they once had—or never had, and still coveted.

He offered the remaining sheets of paper to Hélène for her inspection.

"But where is the car now?" she asked, blinking wildly, turning over the pages.

"That information is not in our current database."

Hélène's chin sank to her chest.

"When we acquired the Beacon trademark three years ago, we consolidated the production records and archives to form the Heritage Trust," Zeffler explained. "You understand, with Beacon having been dormant since the factory closure in England in 1976, this was an act of corporate generosity on our part. We intend to register the current owners of the classic models as their identities become known to us. That will be phase two of the Heritage Project—"

"But I've come all this way."

"I am afraid we have no ability to locate the current owner," Zeffler said. "Are you aware that our new Beacon Heritage Museum has recently opened to the public? There are some fine examples of the type 135 roadster on display." He reached for the employee map on his desk. "It's just here."

Inside the tiny, well-ordered Beacon museum, proceeding from one wall text to the next like the Stations of the Cross, she encountered among the polished bits of chrome and glass the first motorcar to bear the lighthouse badge. On a wall nearby: a painted portrait of the company's founder, the late George M. Beacon, in middle age. An earnest-looking man with the resolute stance of a wrestler.

> Like many of his fellow engineers who had been children in the First World War, George Beacon spent his second set of wartime years dreaming of what he would build when the fighting was over.

> In 1947, at the age of 44, he formed his own company, with an uncompromising focus on the engine—what he considered the soul of the sports cars manufactured by his fledgling Beacon Motor Company . . .

That boy—

What was it about the child in the photograph? No more than seven or eight years old, he was seated with Mr. Beacon in one of the company's models, not smiling, not posing in any way. At George Beacon's side, the boy was concentrating with great intensity on what was being said. Even the ends of his hair appeared to be standing at attention. The boy wasn't aware of the camera, only the direction in which the older man was pointing: forward, to some unseen splendor.

It was the last image on display in the museum. Still meditating on the photograph, impressed by the bravery she detected in the boy's face, Hélène heard her name and turned to find Manfred Zeffler striding through the exhibits, the panels of his suit jacket flapping like pinstriped wings. In his fingers he held another sheet of paper.

"Well—I found something for you."

With a flurry of words—*not in the database, had to search the files, take my own time to photocopy*—he explained that someone in his office had corresponded with the current owner of Beacon chassis number 39212, purchased the previous June at auction, through Bonhams. He could offer her no further information, but he was pleased to provide her with a copy of the public auction record.

It listed my employer, Emerson Tang Webster, who at that moment was drifting into a morphine dream in his loft in Greenwich Village—four blocks from the private garage on Perry Street where he stored the same magnificent machine.

Hélène wept during a swim in her hotel pool that evening and on her flight to JFK the next morning. As the jet touched down, she reached into her handbag to cradle her souvenir from the Beacon gift shop—a 1:43-scale model car.

And so it started, the race for a car and an engine that ended in a collision not of vehicles but of fates. Emerson's, mine, Hélène Moreau's, the boy's in the photograph—our stories collided so forcefully that they cannot be pried apart. We're like an Ambiguous Figure, a trick image with multiple parts. You might see, for example, the silhouette of a chalice in the center of the page, but when you shift your gaze to the edges of the frame, another image is revealed of a man and a woman facing one another. Their profiles form the outline of the cup, suspended between them, as if to seal a solemn pact they've made. Whether you notice the man and the woman, or the cup, they're all part of the same picture—and more than that, the shape of one is determined by the others.

I can illustrate with a second example, using a paintbrush of Hélène Moreau's that ended up in my possession: Here is what appears to be an old woman. She is troubled by some memory or sorrow, her chin sunken to her chest. But look again and you may also detect the outline of a younger woman there, to one side. The girl is turned away, shy, unwilling to show herself fully. Both figures are present—they're composed of the same lines. What you perceive is a matter of how you read them.

It's the same with the lines here, composed of letters and words, running along page after page connecting one event to the next. In the end, it's impossible for them to reveal the shape of Emerson's afterlife without revealing my own, or the fate of Hélène Moreau or the boy in the photograph, who was a grown man by the time she went off in search of the old car. Our stories cannot be separated, any more than they can be separated from one final image I must not neglect to share here, at the outset.

Look, and you may detect, peeking through the lines, the disquieting face of an Asian woman. At first you can just make out the slight curves of her forehead and nose; her cheeks, smooth but for the scar on one side where she fell to the ground from exhaustion. Here are her eyes, fixed in a hopeful stare, eager to take in their share of wonders. And the red bow of her lips—sealed, like her fate, by famine. She is part of the picture as well. The car brought us together, but it was grief that joined us, really.

2

I HAVE NO RECORDS from the Royalton Hotel from 1996, no way to calculate how many days and nights Hélène Moreau passed in that midnight-blue cocoon before the turpentine fumes that trailed in her wake made their way through the corridors for a final time, alerting the housekeeping staff to a recently departed room. This lack of records is an embarrassing oversight, for during that summer—during the business with Hélène and the car—my life was consumed by record-keeping: I was employed as a professional archivist, contracted by Emerson Tang Webster to manage his photography collection. And by the time his collection was disbursed I had become the archivist for the man himself, the custodian and conservator of one small part of his life—namely, his death.

Years later, as a souvenir, Hélène gave me a Royalton message slip, a crisp study in Helvetica folded once and tucked into a royal-blue envelope. It reads:

MR. EMERSON TANG RETURNED YOUR CALL.

From this artifact I can trace the start of things to the day before, Wednesday, the nineteenth of June, when Hélène phoned Emerson's office from Penthouse B and reached me. I recognized her name, though not as anyone Emerson did business with. It was unusual for an artist of her reputation to contact our office personally, instead of having her gallery or an assistant do it. What was not unusual was for me to tell her that Emerson wasn't available. For the most part, he'd lost interest in talking on the phone the previous autumn, and any gallery or museum people who needed to reach him spoke to me. I asked Hélène if she wanted to leave a message.

"Of course."

"And that is?"

"I just told you. I'm in New York."

It was hard to know if she was being rude or if she'd simply misunderstood.

"To meet . . . ," she continued. "When he's available."

Coffee was mentioned. Her voice was French-accented, but I didn't hear it that way. What I heard was weariness punctuated by a smoker's staccato coughs, like an engine struggling to warm up in the cold.

While Emerson slept on the other side of the loft, fed by a morphine drip, I picked through my mental file on Hélène Moreau. A painter. Postwar avant-garde. Her early canvases in the 1950s had received the most attention: the Speed Paintings, named not for how quickly they were painted, but because she'd used speeding cars to create them. From what I remembered, not a drop of paint had been involved in the transaction. They were gashed canvases, studies in motion—the pure violence of an automobile moving through a medium that could do nothing but record its presence. Large in scale. Primitive. Void of figuration, they presented the unpresentable in negative form.

The Speed Paintings had been celebrated enough to warrant reproduction in art history texts forty years later. I wanted to group Hélène Moreau with the Abstract Expressionists, but I didn't think she was catalogued as part of the school. She'd been young when she made the Speed Paintings. Then? Nothing. No strong impression of her later work. I had barely heard her name since my college art history classes.

I wondered if she was still making art. The possibility made her phone call more curious, since it was known in art circles that Emerson had sold his important paintings eight years earlier, on his twenty-fifth birthday. All the proceeds had been used to fund his current collection, devoted to photographs of Modernist architecture. It was this collection he and I were preparing to dismantle via his Last Will and Testament.

Of the many indicators of my employer's decline (his doctor's records show that by then he was 63 inches tall and weighed 90 pounds), I mark the point of no return by the condition of Emerson's bookcases. Daily, more and more of the books on his bedroom shelves were transformed into a menagerie of medical supplies: boxes of Triad alcohol pads, basic-solution tubes, plastic fluid paths with regulating clamps . . .

It began one night with volumes of Hemingway and Eliot and Woolf, catalogues on Brancusi and Duchamp, tomes on the great buildings of Europe—they all abandoned their former shapes in order to lie down and become finger guards and disposable syringes, boxes of rubber gloves, Sani-Cloths soaked with a patented germicidal solution . . .

What I mourned most was a bound monograph on the painter Edward Hopper, a volume I had not paged through, never even took down, but one I'd always admired for the simply embossed name on the spine in a font that, like the artist himself, had no pretensions. Now that too had disappeared, changed into a heparin flush kit for the Hickman port in Emerson's chest.

It was one of the night nurses, Maria-Sylvana, who led me out into the living area to show me that Emerson's books had not wholly disappeared. Rather, they had journeyed from his bedroom to form a bibliographic Easter Island across the hardwood expanses of his loft.

"I didn't drop any," Maria-Sylvana assured me on the way back to Emerson's bedroom. "I'm making sculptures."

She pulled a thick volume from a shelf overcrowded with tubes and, with its weight distributed across her hands like a tray loaded with champagne flutes, glided out into the hallway, got down on one knee and laid the book in place with the same care she used in handling the wasting parcel of bones and tissue that comprised Emerson himself.

Maria-Sylvana had unearthed a spiral-bound notebook amid the clutter on Emerson's bookshelves. From what I could judge by the dates inside, it was the sum total of everything he had written down in college. In the same spidery hand I recognized from his to-do lists (and his things-done lists, in the manner of Caesar Augustus) were passages he'd copied down in preparation for assignments that he would have punched out later on a typewriter:

Philosophy of the Person   (due 4/5/82)
example: Sartre, War Diaries, notebook 3, page 51

– to be "barricaded within stoicism" = positive
– he is "cowardly," "grumbling" but still a HERO

– a hero who will die "screaming and begging for mercy" but without confessing*

(an attractive idea, to which we can all relate)

* "what they wanted him to confess"

The bulk of the entries dropped off steeply after 1984, his last semester at NYU. It amused Emerson to see the notebook again, so I left it on one of the shelves, along with the battered jewel case of his On Fire CD by Galaxie 500 and everything else in his "Merritt Parkway Driving Music" stack.

Not that he could drive anymore. By the time Hélène Moreau checked into the Royalton that summer, his thighs and calves had begun to show bone—all the more noticeable on days when edema caused his ankles and feet to blow up like balloon animals, the skin straining over them the color of ripe citrus. On lucid days, he would review whatever decisions he had left to make. He kept signing documents until the morphine ate his muscle coordination and the arcs and dips of his signature grew closer and closer, then shorter.

That was how his identity disappeared from him that summer, like the stiff black hairs that would not stay attached to his head. His identity fell in clumps from him—his memories, but also his cares. If he went through denial, anger, bargaining and depression, there were days when he was in a kind of bliss, with one of the home healthcare workers, Brian or Zandra, rubbing his back, or me reading to him from the *Times* while his own blood and waste seeped out of him, dark and metallic-smelling from the meds.

Emerson woke in time for the six o'clock news, refreshed but pin-eyed from the morphine. I gave him the phone message with his evening antacid.

"Hélène Moreau called your office earlier. The artist." I didn't want to be condescending, but sometimes the meds confused him. "She phoned personally. She sounded tired."

His opiate slur was still wearing off. "What'd sesay?"

"She's here in the city."

He snapped his head around to face the doorway.

"She wants to meet you for coffee," I went on, watching him.

"Dishe say when?"

"Do you know her, Emerson?"

His only response was to raise his arms in the air like a child waiting to be picked up. Then, with a kick of his feet, he propelled himself out of bed. He brought his hands down onto the rails of his portable toilet and balanced himself there as he tucked a cashmere lap blanket around his hipbones, sarong-style. I watched him move away from the handrails. Steady tonight. Relatively steady on his feet. Zandra was in the kitchen eating dinner before her shift ended, and Maria-Sylvana wasn't due until

7:30 p.m. There was nothing to do but follow him, follow his deliberate pace through the loft, follow him and try not to step on his blanket as I bent to rescue his morphine pump from the floor. It was a small plastic cartridge, the size of my old cassette Walkman, attached to one of the medical ports in his chest by a length of silicone tubing. Left to its own devices, it trailed behind him like a dropped leash.

"Where are you going?"

The eternal question. One I asked whenever he went mobile without apparent direction. Not that I couldn't understand why he preferred to drag himself to one of the bathrooms in the loft; pissing into Tupperware was unappealing at the best of times, and walking was one of the few forms of exercise he had left. His physician, Dr. Albas, encouraged it whenever she saw him. But that night he wanted to go to his office—even farther.

I tended to his opiate train as we crossed the hardwood spanning his corner of Greenwich Village, a loft space stretched across the second floor of two abutting buildings. The brick façades, facing Charles Street on one side and Bleecker on the other, had been maintained in their original nineteenth-century aesthetic, but inside was a different story: Sometime in the 1980s, Emerson had gotten the maze of rooms on his floor demolished, along with some sections of the common walls. His office and a collections-storage area now took up most of one building, with two bedrooms in the other. A kitchen and living area occupied the canyon in the middle, where moveable screens displayed the custom-made enlargements from his photography collection. On permanent exhibit was a trophy wall of Modernist residential architecture—his fantasy neighborhood: stylish, radical, mechanized and clean.

At the start of one curated streetscape hung a portrait of the architect Alvar Aalto's modest home in Helsinki, along with a photo of a more elaborate villa he'd designed for friends else-

where in Finland. The two residences faced one another agreeably across the polished hardwood. And from this gateway of
sorts, the house photographs continued down the block alphabet-
ically, by architect, in the minimalist frames Emerson used to sur-
round every lot in his personal subdivision—each one fitted with
a picture light sculpted from wire to resemble a miniature street
lamp.

He lingered over a Marcel Breuer house with a cantilevered
wooden deck, then shuffled past a portrait of the travertine house
that the architect Gordon Bunshaft had built for himself and his
wife in East Hampton—the architect's only residential design. As
it is logged in the Accession Register, the photo was taken by the
great Ezra Stoller in 1963, one year after the home was completed.
(This structure now exists only in photographic form; it was
razed some years after Emerson's death.) We continued down the
hallway, with Emerson mumbling to himself.

"Had photosofaces. Once . . ."

Until the meds wore off, it always sounded as if his lips were
stuck together with peanut butter. I wasn't sure I'd heard him
right.

"Faces? Not houses?"

His narrow back and shoulders convulsed in a shrug.

"Sonlyone. Now."

"One—photo?"

"No! Nophotosofaces! Faces uhavtaleave. Only—afacesis . . .
gone . . ."

"Who's gone?" I asked, convinced he was hallucinating when
he answered:

"Whichouse dishegoin?"

"She—who?"

He stopped suddenly.

"Whyermy books outere?"

"That's Maria-Sylvana. She's been stacking them."

I hoped a general answer would satisfy him. If he hadn't noticed the latest surge of medical supplies on his bedroom shelves, I didn't want to be the one to point it out to him.

"Isse readinem?"

"Well . . ."

"Teller to movem out."

"What?"

"Theydon matter."

"They matter hugely! We just used them yesterday to look up that Alfred Parker house in Miami, with the snaky indoor pool."

"Umaybe attachtoem Beth."

"I am not!"

Outside, the days were growing longer with the unfurling greens of summer. But inside, with all the shades pulled down at Emerson's insistence, the progress of the new season was barely perceptible. His speech cleared as we worked our way along the hall. He was in a contentious mood.

"Homes aren't machines," he fumed at a villa by Le Corbusier. "Not castles for defense either," he added, shuffling ahead. "Or symbols of prestige. Ask Schindler—" He pointed down the hallway, in the direction of the S's. "Homes should be capable of flowing with your life—encouraging better living." His pace slowed. "Until your life ends. Then you have to stop. Then you have to pull over to the side of the road."

The trees outside, thick with leaves, cast shadows over the shaded windows, giving the impression that dusk was falling, though the miniature streetlights had not yet come on for the evening.

"This idea of life after death," Emerson said, turning to me. "This legend. You want to believe it. But what if it's a lie?"

It was a conversation we had been having on and off for weeks. His lucidity on the subject was inversely related to the strength of his morphine doses.

"I don't believe it's a lie," I told him. "But who can blame you for not wanting to find out? Your life is your story. Of course you don't want it to end."

He nodded vigorously. "And when you die, do you even know how it ends?"

In the office, he slipped down so far into his desk chair that I had to prop him up with sofa pillows. He got himself settled at the fax machine, positioning his legs on either side as if he were going to drive it, before commencing an agitated transmission.

I watched from my desk behind him. "Can I do that for you?"

Silence.

My head felt heavy. For a moment I mistook the morphine pump beside him for a pack of cigarettes. My eyes were closing.

"Shit."

"What?"

"Busy!" Emerson bellowed. "In the middle of the night."

"It's just past dinnertime now."

"No, in Europe."

"Who are you faxing?"

It made me crazy to see his morphine tube tapping against the fax machine as he punched the buttons.

"I took care of the Schindlers yesterday," I reminded him.

Tap, tap. Tap. Silence.

"San Francisco took them."

"Oh?" he asked distractedly.

"S.F. MOMA."

No response. He evidently had no recall of the bequest I had been working on for two months — one of the last groups we had left to finalize. Or maybe, like the books, he didn't care about his photographs anymore either.

"Who are you faxing, Emerson? Can I do it for you?"

"Personal."

Tap, tap. Tap.

"But thank you, Beth."

I pulled open the sturdy brown-board cover of the Accession

Register and prepared to work on the Transfer of Title documents.

Accession Number: ETW 1992.8.3

Year acquired:	1992
Object:	B/W Print
Photographer:	Hartmut Zeit
Title:	Lovell Beach House
Location:	Newport Beach, California
Date:	1926
Subject:	Residence designed by architect Rudolf Michael Schindler; commissioned by physician Dr. Philip Lovell
Other subject:	(see Notes)
Original print held:	Y
Original neg held:	N
Acquisition method:	Purchase
Copyright:	Hartmut Zeit
Related photos:	Y

NOTES:
– Print depicts the street façade (angle approx northwest). See also: beach façade (west), accession number 1992.8.2. See also: interiors, accession numbers 1991.102.5–1991.102.7.

When Emerson got tired of the busy signal, when he had slumped so low that the fringes of his blanket were splayed out on the floor, he let me roll him back to bed in his desk chair.

I knew Emerson for the same reason everyone in my hometown knew him: He was the first Asian boy we had seen in real life —the only child of Chinese ethnicity registered in the Burring Port, Connecticut, public school system in the 1960s. I was born two and a half years after him, in the same hospital, named for his family, and raised along the same few square miles of New

England coastline. By the time we came face to face, my older brother Garrett had already shared a kindergarten classroom with him. Whatever my brother's impressions were, they are lost to time. I only know that, for me, Emerson was the object of unparalleled fascination, the evidence of a wider universe beyond the one I knew, though I could not articulate it at the time. Was this how the ancients felt the first time they saw a comet?

My family wasn't part of the town's social set. We lived in the outer planetary rings of Burring Port, in a wood-shingled, two-story house built on land that had been subdivided in the 1940s and, after a brief lapse in zoning restrictions, shared ever since with the low brick headquarters of an electrical supply company. At the far end of the property, passing trains shot through the green frame of our back yard, advertising a regularly scheduled temptation of escape in one of two directions, east or west.

But even outside the Websters' circle, some things about Emerson's family were common knowledge. Not long after graduating from Yale in the late fifties, Emerson's father, Lynford Webster, had gone traveling in the Far East and returned with a Chinese wife. The year he met his bride, in the midst of Mao's Great Leap Forward, the race to transform Communist China into an agricultural and industrial power had driven millions of citizens from their remote villages to cities. Emerson's mother had gone farther. Along with a shipment of Chinese cotton, she'd made it to Hong Kong. Mr. Webster imported her to the United States, and Emerson was born in 1962.

In my memory, Lynford Webster is filed as a curiosity at one of my brother's school recitals: a slight man with black, bushy sideburns, and disappearing into them, a pair of eyeglasses with round rims and straight sides, so heavy and geometrically precise that they appeared to my amazed eyes to be fantastically large bubble-blowing wands.

While his son, my brother and the other children did their worst with a collection of antique musical instruments, Mr. Webster sat in the front row of the audience in a child-sized chair like mine, concentrating on each tortured note of plucking and blowing as if enchanted by an exquisite melody. With closed eyes, in some solitary darkness, he traced the pitch and volume, the rising and falling, with the movements of his head.

Mr. Webster wasn't in the music business—his business was related to land development—but photos of him in local newspaper articles archived from that time reinforce my recollection that his wardrobe mimicked that of certain British musicians of the day: slim pants, bright stripes, elaborately embroidered shirts and suit jackets with little mandarin collars. Never a necktie.

Lynford Webster was outstanding not only because he costumed himself so much more flamboyantly than the fathers of our New England town, but because he was a conspicuous civic benefactor in a part of the world that favored discretion and anonymity. At his insistence, the new Burring Port library, dedicated in 1970, bore the Webster family name ("showy," decided my father when it was reported in the *Burring Port Standard*), as did the new regional hospital he had financed, in memory of his deceased parents, when he was still a student in New Haven. But there was another respect in which Lynford Webster was unlike his forebears —people who had sailed from Britain to the New World three centuries earlier and named everything after the place they left: Mr. Webster did not settle. He maintained the family estate on Gray Hill, but his business took him abroad for most of the year.

Before Emerson started school, the primary curiosity in Burring Port had been Mr. Webster's wife, the former Miss Tang. It was not unusual in the early 1960s for the young bride to be sighted on Water Street in the village, doing errands with her translator, enlisted from Great Britain. The inner planetary circles reported that she patronized the bakery and the pharmacy, and every Thursday drove with the translator into Manhattan to get her hair done and shop on Fifth Avenue.

The woman did not occupy the town's imagination for long.

Before Garrett and Emerson started kindergarten, word went around that the former Miss Tang had succumbed to an undisclosed medical disorder. She was gone, but Emerson favored her so heavily that in her place he became our municipal symbol of diversity, christened by Garrett and his classmates circa 1968: the Chinky-Chinky-Chinaman.

But the first time I saw Emerson, I knew nothing of these matters, nothing of his existence. My brother and I were riding in the car with our parents, waiting for the horses we always waited to see in the field after Camel Rock, a roadside boulder so closely resembling a dromedary that, in its honor, the early colonists had included a single-humped "ship of the desert" in the design of the town flag. If the horses were out that day I never noticed, because my eyes swerved to something else instead: On top of a stone wall, sipping a drink through a straw, stood a dark-haired boy squinting into the sun.

No other figure of my youth made such an impression, in his white sneakers on the crest of that wall. It was not the boyness of him, already hopelessly unexotic to a three-year-old girl with an older brother. And it was not what stands out to me now, in retrospect: the absolute domain over wall and field evident in his stance, his asymmetric haircut, or the fact that he was alone, unsupervised—as if he had taken himself, drink and straw, out into that field.

What was there to describe? Nothing I could name. No, it was only my child's mind, shaped by recognizing patterns, and then by recognizing when something is unlike the patterns it has already learned. And by this primitive system, I was alerted to some new information in his expression, something I had not encountered before.

"That boy—"

3

ÉLÈNE MOREAU REACHED the bottom of her pot of Kona coffee. She was easing herself off an acid-green banquette in the Royalton lobby when she was reminded that hotels held more spirits than living occupants. For every traveler who passed through, there were ghosts, for every luncheon meeting and business trip, for every honeymoon and tryst . . .

From all she would later tell me concerning her troubles that summer, Hélène was stalled there herself, suspended in a kind of limbo. And so she was charmed to find that her countryman Philippe Starck had made the phantoms visible in his renovation of the old hotel. A chorus line of ghosts danced along the carpeting underfoot: white shapes on deep blue, trailing the length of the lobby like a wake of Aegean foam and curling into an existential question mark at the end of the corridor outside Penthouse B, where a bellhop placed a copy of *Le Monde* into Hélène's hand.

I imagine myself among the other eavesdropping spirits as she locked the door and paged apprehensively through the newspaper, finally dropping onto the bed with a cry of misery.

"Oh! Just as he said."

She punched at the telephone buttons until the line connected.

"Arthur—the notice—yes, very good. But the photo—I can't look at it."

She pulled a page from the newspaper and held it at arm's length.

"Again. Unbelievable, to run it again! They always want this one. That car. As if no one has made another photo of me in forty years. Oh, that I even tried to smile. What you do at twenty-one . . ."

She hung up, murmuring, "The rest of the paper will be useful, anyway, for cleaning brushes."

She ripped the offending sheet in half and then tore at the newsprint until it was reduced to a cheerless pile of gray confetti.

Emerson returned Hélène's phone call from his bed the next morning, but the line to Penthouse B was busy, obliging him to dictate the message slip I now possess. He tried again after lunch and succeeded in reaching her: a conversation so brief I had barely gotten down the hall before he was yelling for me to come back. On the way, I stopped to pull some art books from the library of Easter Island.

"We're meeting her tomorrow," he announced.

"Oh?"

"Four o'clock."

"What does she want?"

"I don't know." He dropped the phone onto his blanket. "I can't concentrate on the phone anymore. Can you help me roll down my pajama legs, Beth? I'm cold."

I rested the books on his bedside table and bent to reach them. "She's coming here?"

"No, her hotel."

"You're going to wear your food pack up to 44th Street?"

He stared at me, his eyes narrowing behind the silver frames of his glasses. "And can you make us an appointment for tomorrow at Golden Hands? We haven't been in a week."

Hands—always hands on him. His doctors prescribed a bookcaseful of well-calibrated meds for pain, but beyond administering them, there was little the home healthcare workers and I could do to soothe him except to rub his arms and back as gently as we could. In the tiny, immaculate confines of the Golden Hands nail salon, at least he could get a proper massage.

I admit there were times when it might have been natural for me to hug him, but this was difficult to accomplish. Not because he was my employer, but because he couldn't manage it. I chalked this up to his natural guardedness, a reserve he exhibited when it came to anything personal. I'd been shocked when he'd tried to kiss me on the cheek earlier that summer, by way of appreciation, but the most he could do was to rub his cheek lightly against mine. And I suspect even that made him uncomfortable because, at age thirty-three, he still had some lingering acne.

When Zandra finished bathing him the next morning, she dressed him in a soft, stretched-out T-shirt and a pair of British walking shorts he had special-ordered from a men's shop on lower Fifth Avenue.

"I'm going to walk off my hangover on the way to Golden Hands," he announced.

I rolled my eyes for his benefit. The only walking we would be doing was in and out of a taxicab, and he knew it. By that spring, his body had grown incapable of absorbing regular food. The fuel that kept him running was a prescribed liquid-nutrition pack, a miraculous milky elixir sealed in plastic. Each day, a one-gallon bag of protein and other nutrients flowed with the assistance of a mechanical pump into a port surgically inserted in his gut. The manufacturer provided a refrigerated backpack to dispense the fluid into him over the course of eight hours, accompanied by little more than a low-pitched whir. Mobility proved to be liberation: It prevented mealtimes from being new stretches of nothingness for him to fill.

According to Dr. Albas, his digestive tract now functioned more or less like a plastic baby doll's: Feed it a bottle of tap water and almost immediately a stream of liquid would pour out the other end. But while he could no longer digest regular food, she said there was no reason he couldn't taste it—a policy that preserved his sole remaining physical pleasure. The tiniest leftovers became feasts for him: two bites of a hamburger, half a lemon donut . . . The day we were due to meet Hélène Moreau, Zandra had put together a special lunchtime collection of his Greatest Hits: a single cold shrimp, some mushroom soup and a few forkfuls of reheated SpaghettiOs.

"The Chef outdid himself on that can," Emerson said, wiping his lips with satisfaction.

"No, the Chef does the ravioli you like," said Zandra, attempting to clear his fogged mental windshield. "This is Campbell's."

After Zandra replaced his plastic underwear with a fresh pair, I escorted him into a taxi for the brief ride down Bleecker Street to Golden Hands. Our patronage of the salon was an accident of the previous autumn. I needed to find a masseuse after he complained about the way the physical therapists touched him, and I recalled that when I had gotten a manicure once, for my college graduation, there had been some massage involved. At the first shop we'd tried, the Nail Palace on Sixth Avenue, the matron did not appear to be listening to a word I said. She was staring at Emerson's bulging knees. Then I turned and saw a line of faces staring along with her, a row of young women collapsed over their tables like wilted lettuce. An air conditioner whispered hopelessly over the doorway. Something unpleasant bit my nostrils.

"I feel cold," Emerson said.

"Excuse us," I told the matron. "Another time, maybe."

"Tell me, what the hell was that?" he demanded when we got outside.

"I think it's the chemicals and stuff they use to sculpt fake nails."

"They breathe that in all day? And Beth, why do they all perm and dye their hair?"

"I don't know. Different reasons, probably."

"They have pretty hair and they fry it!"

A few blocks away, on Cornelia Street, the front room of Golden Hands was bathed in the sweet, sharp fragrance of fresh-cut limes. A thin stream of sunlight filtered through the ground-floor windows. There, on a bench covered in silk, I'd gotten the second manicure of my life, from a young woman named Mei, who at the time had seemed as uncertain as me. Nine months later, as she confidently led me to her little worktable, I could see I was the one who had lost ground.

"Mani-cure?" a voice sang out as a middle-aged woman named Li, Emerson's favorite, offered him her arm. Li was not a tall woman, but she was elongated anyhow and there was an athletic grace to her elongated form. Emerson lowered his eyes as she placed his hands in a bowl of warm water.

"You work today?" Mei asked me.

It occurred to me that Mei and I both worked about fourteen hours a day, that we were both working at that moment.

"Yes." I smiled politely. "You too, I see."

Over at the next station, Emerson's nutrition pump whirred through its cycles in the silver bag on his lap, just audible over the chattering of birds in their cages. He reminded me of an astronaut getting oxygen. His face in profile communicated exactly nothing.

I usually took him to Golden Hands once or twice a week, more if he wanted. He wouldn't let them paint anything or cut his nails or cuticles, only wash his hands elaborately in a deep clay bowl, then rub thick white lotion into his elbows and arms. If Li was available, she helped him to the massage area behind a bamboo screen.

Mei took my fingers between hers, smiling the distracted smile of a young woman who anticipated a life outside of work that I could not begin to imagine.

"You go to party tonight?" she asked.

It was the question she asked me most frequently, probably every time I sat with her. I supposed this was why most of her customers came to get their nails done—a thought that seemed especially absurd when I pictured the night ahead: Dr. Albas had warned me that Emerson was likely to lose most of the blood from his last transfusion. The hands Mai was manicuring would spend the night dipping in and out of surgical gloves, helping to discard plastic underpants heavy with black metallic slush. Tisa, one of the night workers, had already stocked up on supplies. I didn't need to explain any of this, but I felt lying was disrespectful.

"I'm working tonight."

This seemed to disappoint her.

I didn't want to go to parties anyway, couldn't think what I would say to anyone.

"Who's your boyfriend this week?" I teased her.

Mei's cheeks bloomed bright pink. "You still short nails."

"I use my hands a lot."

She frowned. "Polish don't stay good short nails."

"Just clear, please, like yours. Yours look pretty."

We were due to meet Hélène Moreau at her hotel in an hour. At the next table, Li unfurled her arms with gymnastic precision and indulged in a brief stretch before returning to buffing Emerson's nails. On our first visit to Golden Hands, her hair had been permed and dyed an unnatural shade of eggplant. Now it hung smoothly to her chin, the inky black of a grand piano. At the crown, her part revealed a keyboard of thick, graying roots. The ends swung lightly before Emerson's nose as she moved the buffer back and forth. He raised his eyebrows, and I wondered if he was inhaling the scent of her shampoo. His ears twitched. Then Li put the buffer down and his eyebrows relaxed.

Some days, if I was falling asleep from a lack of caffeine, I would turn my neck to ease the muscles, and study the manicurists' faces. They were stylish, not wilted. Some of them were learning English, and they left their books and magazines in the restroom. If any of them were married, they had no gold or diamond rings to show it. They wore shell necklaces, hoop earrings, thin rubber bracelets. All except Li, who recently, I noticed, had begun wearing a chunky metal cuff—an amassment of gold thick enough to knock someone's teeth out, and expensive enough (if it was real) to finance a good portion of the small salon we were sitting in. I wondered if Emerson had given it to her.

Mei held out a hand to me, bandaged across the soft place between her thumb and forefinger.

"Need some massage?"

It was pretty the way she said it: *Massage-uh.*

The hands slapped at my shoulders and arms, out of control—a windmill of frustrated swipes so fierce it took my mother leaning over the back seat to fend them off.

"He said he'd trade me!" my brother cried.

"That's not your sister's fault, Garrett. Don't take it out on her."

Nothing could console him, falling away from me into the back seat of my parents' car, a Chevy that my father had nicknamed the Green Goose after a model warplane he was building at the time—it must have been the early 1970s. At a birthday party for a boy named Nathan Stirling, my brother had been determined to trade a scratched-up car from his Matchbox collection—a Triumph Spitfire—for one of Emerson's scale models: a golden Maserati Ghibli, as Garrett would continue to remind us bitterly for years. It was to be their second trade, at Emerson's insistence, after my brother complained to anyone who would listen that he'd been fleeced of a Hot Wheels "Classic Cord" on the first round of trading. Yet, in place of vengeance or satisfaction of any kind, Garrett was fastening the tiny hood of his Triumph closed with an orthodontic rubber band and crying because Emerson never showed up.

When school started in the fall, we found out Emerson's father had moved him to a private school in Greenwich—an offense for which Garrett never forgave him. Stories about Emerson drifted back to us now and then: How the house on Gray Hill was visited by a world-class pianist following his performances at Carnegie Hall, not to give Emerson lessons, but to play private concerts to foster the boy's appreciation of the musical arts. Or how, when Emerson turned thirteen, Mr. Webster sponsored a school field trip to the Museum of Modern Art. The class was taken afterward to an art gallery on 57th Street, where each student was invited to choose a lithograph to take home, courtesy of Mr. Webster. (According to a copy of the *Burring Port Standard* from 1975, the businessman had hoped to start the youngsters off as art collectors —or at least appreciators—in his son's name.)

I was a teenager by the time I saw Emerson again, inside a pizza place in Burring Port Village. I recognized him immediately, distracted as I was trying to pick out songs on a jukebox that had all the song titles written indecipherably in ballpoint pen. He pivoted in just long enough to pick up his food order, long enough for me to register his ripped jeans and sweatshirt, his black hair arranged in a Mohawk, except for a shaggy waterfall over his eyes where the tips were bleached orange. By then he'd started driving an old sports car around the course on his father's property —my brother called it a Speedster. Garrett and his friends were jealous to the point of violence, not so much because the car was a Porsche, but because Emerson had a private track to practice on, a full year before any of them qualified for a learner's permit.

Emerson passed me in the car one afternoon that winter, though I didn't see him so much as hear him. I was by myself, as usual, on my way home from the library for dinner, loitering along the Sound with my parka hood pulled up, when a muffled buzz came vibrating through the fabric. All at once the noise cut off. I pulled off my hood to listen, and for a few moments the air was filled with nothing but seagull cries, as loud and raucous as the engine had been.

There was no sound of a crash, and I hesitated before I left the beach road and stepped onto the Websters' property, peering through the trees for a glimpse of Emerson or the car as I climbed farther into the woods. What I came upon not long after was a sight I cannot forget. At first I had trouble making out the driver, as I was still at some distance. There was no road leading to the place where he was parked. The car had been driven straight through the woods to the top of a rise, cutting deep ruts around the trees and through the carpet of rotted leaves. There was nothing around but bare trees, melting snow and parts of some stone walls once erected as boundary markers—no people, no buildings—but it was empty in an expectant way, like the stage of an outdoor amphitheater that had yet to be populated with sets and costumes, only an audience of crows cawing in their mournful way overhead, waiting for the show to begin.

When I looked back at Emerson, I could see it had already begun. He was the actor in a private scene that I sensed I should have turned away from, but couldn't. I was riveted by the strangeness of what I saw. He was seated alone in the open-topped car, stopped alongside a pile of rocks, his hair covered by a knitted cap and his neck hinged back at an angle so extreme that, until that day, I had seen the gesture only in paintings of carnage. His eyes were closed and his mouth was stretched open, but there was no sound coming out. I thought he was laughing to himself, so overcome by a hilarious thought that he'd had to stop the car. Then I thought he was in a state of ecstasy, about to reach the climax of some motorized jerk-off session. I started to turn away when all at once his shoulders heaved, and I recognized that his posture had nothing to do with pleasure. He was wailing, silently, his face to the sky, running with tears. His body began to shake. He raised his hands, fitted with racing gloves, but instead of wiping his face he reached out and gripped the windscreen. He arms shook as if he were trying to tear it off the car. All at once his body sagged. With his arms hanging there, he bowed his head in surrender to some unknown misery.

An odd sensation came over me: It was as if I could feel the force of his suffering. His pain was unknowable to me, though I seemed to taste it then. I feared that he was physically hurt, that he'd hit something after all—what were all those loose stones around the car? He could have a wound or injury I couldn't see. Without thinking, I hurtled up the hill, kicking through the frozen leaves, but within seconds the engine started up and, abruptly, he was in retreat. I stood listening until I couldn't hear the sound anymore, a roaring mechanical chord that rose and fell like a wave through the woods and out to the graffiti-scarred lighthouse at the end of the Point.

When he left for prep school in Lakeville that year, it went around that he had picked the school for its proximity to Lime Rock Park, a racetrack tucked between colonial houses and acres of farm fields in the foothills of the Berkshire Mountains. Of course, everyone said, Emerson wanted a new place to drive. He had grown bored of the private course on Gray Hill.

I reasoned the opposite. He probably never got bored, but that didn't mean he was happy, either. For a while I wondered what had taken him into the woods that day. I'd felt something through him, as if he'd held a match to an emotion that had been shielded inside me. As far as I knew, his life wasn't anything like mine, yet I had been out there by myself, too, and I had felt less alone watching him cry. Even then, I had a sense of myself as a kind of ghost, a feeling of being separated from others in a way I never tried to explain. You can be surrounded by people, a loving family, and still feel alone. It was a subtle but impassable barrier, like coming upon an artifact in a glass vault and expecting that you can reach out and touch it, except I felt that barrier around myself. The sensation only grew worse in my teens. To avoid the discomfort, I chose to sleep, and there was little anyone could do to keep me out of bed beyond my required waking hours. I was unconscious so frequently that the days when I was wide awake stand apart in vivid relief. For instance, the morning when a whole orchard of apple trees rose from the exhaust vapor of a police car, parked with its lights flashing. Someone was taking pictures of a truck jackknifed off the road. It was a cold morning, full of frost and the sickly sweet smell that fallen apples give off when they're crushed underfoot. Our school bus passed some sparkly patches on the road, glass and ice scattered like birdseed, and when the bus inched forward again I saw—we all saw—the station wagon pinned under the trailer. The tingly taste of fresh-picked apples, the cold of such mornings, the question of anyone being alive or not alive entirely overpowered by the abrupt sensation of being very awake.

It was summertime, 1979, when another one of those very awake days happened, courtesy of Emerson. That morning—a Saturday after what must have been his final year at prep school —my neighbor Beckett appeared at my bedroom door with news that Garrett didn't know: Emerson Tang had hired out the track near his school in Lakeville to race. Beckett's family lived on the opposite side of the electrical supply company, but we weren't exactly friends. As with the few kids I spoke to or sat with at school, our acquaintance revolved around the expediencies of carpooling: we were pushed together into back seats so regularly that we shared a kind of resigned familiarity. Beckett had never stepped inside my bedroom before, and I caught on pretty fast that her invitation was motivated by desperation. Her parents wouldn't let her take the car unless she could find someone to ride with her. I agreed when she said her brother Tom was one of the kids racing that day. I had never kissed anyone (though I understood from the other carpool girls that I should have, by then), and I was not opposed to Tom.

Beckett claimed that Lakeville was "nearish"—she had just gotten her driver's license—but it was two hours before we parked and hiked across the property to a hillside where at least a hundred other kids were sprawled. We sat on the grass near a heavyset kid named Cutler, who worked at his parents' pharmacy in Burring Port and didn't ignore us when Beckett waved.

"This guy's just on his practice lap," Cutler informed us, gesturing to the hunk of metal disappearing down the roadway at the bottom of the hill.

"Who is it?" Beckett asked.

"That's Frankie. He borrowed a car from his brother. He's looking pretty quick out there, but we've got a bunch more to go."

The new summer grass felt soft against my bare legs, tickling my thighs under my denim cutoffs.

"When is the race?" I asked.

"Right now. All day."

"But there's just one car out there."

"Each driver is being timed," Cutler explained with a trace of disgust. "Best of five laps. The track people wouldn't. Ever. Let these idiots out there all at once."

I could no longer see Frankie's car. It had become a sound moving like a thick crayon through the air, tracing a curve behind the grassy hill, where the track's irregular shape continued past a stand of trees.

It wasn't long before I spotted Emerson by the edge of the roadway in flat boots and a racing suit. He was yelling up to the top of an elevated platform, where a man in white coveralls stood surveying the track.

The buzz of Frankie's car grew more muffled, then louder as

it reappeared around a bend and sped down the long straight in front of us. The man on the platform waved a green flag and Emerson jumped, cheering, as the car went past.

"All right—here goes Frankie's first timed lap," said Cutler.

I lost sight of the car again almost immediately as the road course curved off to the right.

Beckett got to her feet, pulling me after her, and we stood on tiptoe in the grass, catching glimpses of paint as the car flashed along the ribbon of track behind us. Then she saw her brother and we moved down the hill, settling on a viewing spot behind the pit area, where we watched a few more drivers take their laps. Eventually, Beckett's brother waved to us, not specifically to me. (I knew from experience with Garrett that it was a wave that merely tolerated his sister at such proximity, but did not welcome us any closer.) Beckett identified the drivers as they took off their helmets, and the names whirled in my mind with the colored flags and the blunt smell of burnt rubber. On my tongue and lips I tasted a fine black grit. I studied Tom's lips, now that we were in range. Somewhat thin. It wasn't clear if they would be nice to kiss after all.

Then the hillside came alive with shouts as an open-top car rolled onto the track. Sticking out of the driver's seat was a beefy kid named Horace, who was obsessed with pornography, according to the rumors Beckett enthusiastically repeated to me. His car was low and wide like the others, but with a more exaggerated, curvy shape. Behind each of the front wheels, a bunch of metal octopus legs came together and merged into a fat drainpipe stretching along the side of the car.

Emerson strolled beside the car, cupping his hands to his mouth. "It's a pig!"

Horace's head jerked around, but it was impossible to read his face inside the helmet. He gripped the wheel and revved the engine.

Emerson leaned in. "It's a complete and total pig!"

The driver tilted his head and called out something inaudible.

"*Carpe diem!*" Emerson yelled with a wave.

"When are you up, anyway?" a girl named Kit asked Emerson when he jumped back from the road. But before he could answer, Horace was off on his practice lap with a screech of rubber. Almost immediately, the chattering on the hillside dropped away.

"Oh, God."

Even a person like me, who knew nothing about racing, could see it was odd the way the car was moving as it gained speed. It was accelerating toward the first turn in the track with the back end sluing from side to side, like a mast cut loose in the wind. The car seemed to be fighting with the driver, or the forces of gravity, or both. Roughly, with a struggle, the beast finally followed the track around the bend.

The other drivers watched in silence.

Emerson shook his head. "Where did he get that?"

"His uncle loaned it to him for the day."

"All style and power—no grace," snorted Kit.

"So, which one of your cars are you using?" Tom asked.

Emerson shrugged. "Haven't decided."

"No way! You're not driving one of your own cars!" said a kid named Alexander, who had the best lap time on the board. "You live on this track. No way is this a fair contest."

"Uh, he's paying for it," said Tom.

"Hang on," Emerson said. He jumped closer to his accuser, an expression of amusement lighting up his face. "What if I drive something I've never touched before? You pick."

"Sure," Alexander said. "Except you've been in everything here."

"No. I haven't been in Jeff's Mustang."

"Yes! *Respect!*" A kid with a wiry frame sprang to his feet in front of me and, with a righteous pump of his fist, tossed a set of keys at Emerson's chest.

"And this is a massive handicap," said Emerson, waving the keys at Alexander. "Because, as we've seen, Jeff's car is useless for anything except straightaways."

"Hey—"

"Your cornering was a nightmare, Jeff. You *nursed* that thing around the track."

Then the air filled with an avalanche of sounds announcing Horace's approach. Emerson erupted with laughter as the car roared by, snaking from side to side past the green flag to begin its first timed lap.

"Wait," Emerson yelled, "I haven't driven THE PIG."

He watched soberly as Horace approached the first turn. Again, the car appeared to protest strenuously around the bend.

"I'm driving *that*," Emerson announced, handing Jeff's keys back. "I've never even sat in one."

"I'm not sure that's enough of a handicap for you," said Alexander.

They debated it until everyone turned at the sound of Horace heading into his second timed lap, his arms stiff at the wheel and shaking like a jackhammer operator's.

"Okay, okay," conceded Alexander with a look of dismay. "Drive the pig."

"No—" said Emerson. "Let's make it harder. I'm thinking, let's add some weight."

Kit rolled her eyes. "Are you totally high?"

"Seriously." He jerked his chin in Alexander's direction. "I want him to be satisfied. Not too much weight. Someone about my size."

"Get my sister. She'll do it," said Tom, gesturing to where Beckett and I were standing.

The group of drivers turned.

Beckett waved hesitantly. A burst of her baby-powder antiperspirant flooded my nostrils.

Tom's face contorted with second thoughts. "Nah."

"Oh, thanks!" she yelled.

"It's physics! We have to calibrate the weight handicap."

"What about her?"

I looked up to find Alexander's grease-smeared finger pointing at me.

Emerson glanced over his shoulder. "If she wants to."

Oddly, unintentionally, his four words opened the door to a role I could play. *If I wanted to.* Something other than studying and sleeping.

Did I want to? The blood was pumping hard in my chest, as it had on the winter morning when the school bus inched forward in the orchard and I saw—we all saw—the limbs inside the station wagon, against the windows. Some kids being driven to school by their parents?

"What do I have to do?"

"Hold on wherever you can and try not to die," said Beckett.

"Just feel the glory," said Tom.

Glory or death. Either could be waiting for me, or so I believed with the heightened sense of drama native to adolescence. Was that what had Emerson and his friends piling into these tiny cars —the prospect of some extraordinary sensation? Whatever it was, I'd never felt it. And it came with the very real risk of not surviving the ride. The thrill could not exist without the danger, that much was clear.

I glanced over to where Emerson stood, the ringleader of the day's events, an impresario to the crowd gathered there, not keeping himself separate, not sitting on the sidelines as I was. By stepping into the car with him, there was a chance of joining him in victory, and also a chance that our fates would be joined the way that the family's had been joined with the truck driver's in the apple orchard. If Emerson were to make the slightest miscalculation, if a tire were to blow . . .

The others were waiting for an answer.

"Okay, yeah, I guess."

"Someone find her a helmet that fits," ordered Emerson.

Kit directed me to a bench, where Tom pulled a piece of cloth like a ski mask over my head to line the helmet. I was enjoying his attention, until Beckett wrecked it.

"Watch the ponytail," she protested, defending me from her brother's hands.

"I'm not touching it," he said. "The ponytail's good. It'll keep the helmet on tight."

I wasn't sure. The next two drivers took their laps while Beckett and Tom pulled helmets on and off my head, trying to find one that fit. The insides stank like wet dog hair and other people's nasty sweat, but otherwise I liked being inside the helmet. It wasn't like being trapped behind glass, but taking the glass along with me. Separate, yet adventuring. The astronaut way.

They finally found a helmet small enough, and Alexander opened the passenger door for me. Emerson was already behind the wheel. I climbed over the doorframe and dropped lower, lower, into the car, until I was seated inches over the pavement, shoulder to shoulder with him in the tiny cockpit. As Alexander worked to fasten the harness of seat belts, my helmet filled with the smell of gasoline and gluey plastic. Then the door shut and I sensed Alexander moving away from the side of the car.

My legs tensed.

Emerson yelled to me over the idling engine: "I'm gonna try to do this in less than five laps. For your sake."

I looked for a place to hold on. The interior was stripped out. There was nothing, not even a regular door handle. I rested a hand on top of the little door beside me.

"Keep your hands inside the car!" he shouted.

We were never introduced.

Then my head jerked back, heavy in the helmet, and we were moving forward.

But also sideways. Like a sideways rocket rocking chair.

Each push of the gear shift under Emerson's glove opened a trap door in my belly, where my stomach dropped through.

It was like the tacking of a boat in rough seas. Wave after wave, the gearshift and the trap door did their work. Roar. Push. Drop. At every right-hand turn my knees slammed into the door panel.

I let my body fall into one continuous vibration with the car, with Emerson—the same as the vibration in my ears and throat, the same as the landscape shaking past us.

Was he driving like this the day I saw him crying? I did not feel sadness now, only exhilaration and then queasiness when I caught sight of his racing gloves out of the corner of my eye. I had to look ahead to keep my stomach in place.

A horizon of green and noise, long streamers of trees. The sky was a great ocean, and then we passed under a bridge and back out into bright blue. On the hill, the blur of kids in T-shirts looked like a mountainside covered in flowers.

Emerson grunted.

Roar. Push. Drop.

The road, the sky, the woods, the sounds, they all merged into a single vibration flowing through me like an electric current.

We shot along a ribbony stretch of roadway and under the bridge again, then rounded a turn, running past the cheering crowds toward the man on the platform for the second time. The checkered flag in his hand floated up and down, like laundry drying in the wind.

Emerson slapped the dashboard. The car skidded to a stop, and he jumped out.

Dizzy, anxious to follow him, I found the crude door-release and lifted myself out. The moment my right foot hit the pavement, something ferocious bit into my leg. It wouldn't let go. Something with ice-cold jaws.

"Get her!"

I danced a few steps to the edge of the track, screaming inside my helmet. My face mask steamed up from my breath and I couldn't see ahead of me.

"Over here!"

A shoulder pressed under my armpit, hustling me over to the pit area. Someone pulled my helmet off.

Through the little opening in my cloth hood, I saw Emerson kneeling at my feet, his helmet and racing gloves scattered on the pavement. He was examining my right leg.

I tried to speak, but nothing came out. I searched the faces around me.

Alexander was lecturing: "Cars have shiny bits of metal all over them. The side exhaust pipe is not just another shiny bit of metal."

A rectangular patch of seedless watermelon appeared to have replaced the flesh on the inside of my calf.

"She's lucky," Emerson said, staring at the burned skin. "That could have been *much* worse."

"Are you okay?" asked Tom.

I smiled at him through the little hood, and he looked at me as if I were insane.

"Where can we get some ice? We need ice," Beckett said.

"No. That's actually not how to treat this burn," Emerson said. "It would kill the skin."

While they bickered, Tom's face appeared at the edge of my vision. "There's usually a standby medic, but we waived everything except the fire engine. That wasn't negotiable." He pointed to an emergency crew idling around the truck at the far end of the straight, oblivious to our unfolding drama.

One of the drivers dragged over a first-aid kit as big as a picnic cooler. I tried to meet Emerson's eyes.

"I can treat this right here," he assured me, speaking directly to my leg. "Or do you want me to send someone out to those guys for an ambulance?"

"No, please don't."

Already, kids were starting to come down the hill to look.

"It just stings a little," I lied.

"I can get rid of that really quick," Emerson said.

He asked the others who were standing around to bring him some water, then he reached for his helmet and propped it under my calf. At first the water pouring over my skin made the same biting sensation as the burn, but after his helmet had been filled up and spilled onto the grass, the pain was tolerable. I hugged my arms to myself, shaking, as he wound a bandage around my calf.

"I know it was an accident. Except. You got hurt," he said, training his eyes on the dressing. "Sorry." He got to his feet. "It might blister. If it does, don't pop it, because it can get infected."

"Did we win?"

"That's three inches of leg you won't have to shave for the rest of your life."

He walked off, yelling to Horace to take some laps in an easier car.

I limped back to the parking lot beside Beckett, a current of adrenaline still charging through me—heart rate, pulse rate, blood pressure, all set loose in an ecstatic whir by that uncontrollable hormone of speed. It was impossible to hold on to the sensation, I learned, or to recall it except through that plot of scarred flesh, which I came to cherish as a trophy of the day. As we walked, Beckett confirmed that Emerson and I had beaten Alexander's time on the first lap. That meant the second time around had been our victory lap, but when I turned back to look, Emerson didn't appear to be celebrating.

After he left for NYU that fall, it went around that Mr. Webster had arranged for different cars to be delivered to him during the term breaks. Somebody said he got his after-shave custom-blended in England, even though Garrett insisted that Emerson couldn't possibly have enough facial hair to shave. Instead of Chinky-Chink, Garrett and his friends started calling him Emperor Tang.

My clear nail polish was hardening under a mechanical dryer when the Emperor limped out of the massage room on Li's arm. His clutch foot was still swollen from the excess fluid in his body.

Undeterred, Zandra had expertly wedged it into one of his un-laced sneakers. He couldn't drive anymore, and he hated to be driven by car services. After his feet started turning into water bal-loons, the subway became out of the question. I had no choice now but to hail taxis, an arrangement Emerson accepted on the grounds that a Ford Crown Victoria was not a car he wanted to drive anyway.

Li helped him get settled next to me by the window, where the nail blowers faced a sculpted tabletop mountain, a miniature Eden ribboned by a recirculating waterfall. The stream of water snaked its way past shoots of live bamboo, splashing down onto a striped brown marble in a shallow pool. I watched the magic mar-ble doing somersaults in the water as Mei's fists pressed down on my shoulders and neck, struggling to release the muscles. I tried to imagine that the hands on my body cared about me, that love came through them. When Mei finished her work, I turned my neck to crack it, and I saw that Emerson's biceps had collapsed. What was left of the muscles had slipped down and accumulated in low humps just above the crooks of his elbows—a rearrange-ment of body tissue that rattled me more than the prospect of taking him for his next blood transfusion.

"I'm finishing the paperwork on that group of Prairie Houses going to the Modern," I reminded him in an effort to distract myself from his dislocated anatomy. "I just want to confirm: You know that this group of photos includes the Robie House?"

"Obviously."

He'd told me more than once that the home he'd grown up in on Gray Hill was a copy of the Robie House in Chicago—an imposing brick edifice of dramatic horizontals and overhangs, de-signed by Frank Lloyd Wright in the first decade of the twentieth century.

"Do you want me to do something else with that photograph?"

He avoided my eyes. "No, it goes with the others."

"All right. Just wanted to check."

"Okay."

"I got you something new to replace it," I announced. "Eames and Saarinen's Case Study House number 9."

"Pacific Palisades, 1949."

"Yes."

"That's one I was missing," he confirmed, letting me know I had pleased him.

It was only a matter of time before I would have to give that photo to a museum with all the others, and it had cost me a month's salary, but since I had moved into Emerson's guest bedroom, he had been reimbursing me for the rent on my uninhabited apartment in Chelsea. The way I saw it, there was very little we could do anymore besides read or watch TV. At least we would have a new house to look at.

"I've never been interested in owning a *house* house," Emerson said, testing the temperature of the waterfall in front of us with his outstretched fingertip. "I prefer to live in a multifamily dwelling. Though I always wanted to be on a higher floor."

"Right now, we're lucky you don't have to climb more than one flight."

We were back on Bleecker, running late for his meeting with Hélène Moreau, when he spoke again.

"I saw myself in that fountain, Beth. I was climbing the rock. There's a cave at the top. That's where I'm going after this: the cave on the Golden Happy Island."

"I didn't see a cave, Emerson. I've been staring at that thing since we started going to Golden Hands last year. There's no cave."

"You didn't see it. But it's there."

4

I DON'T KNOW WHY I think of it as autumn when we walked into the Royalton lobby, because the avenues announced summer with a parade of tourists in shorts and sandals, and in any case, the hotel gave no indication of the season, no indication of the outside world.

Maybe it was the way the seasons didn't seem to fit—or that time itself seemed out of joint—that inspired Emerson to insist we exit the taxi on Fifth Avenue (instead of Sixth, late as we were) so he could walk back along 44th Street past one of his favorite buildings, the New York Yacht Club, at number 37. Among the nondescript façades of brick and stone, it was a piece of architecture that never failed to astonish an unsuspecting passerby: a great galleon-shaped building sculpted in limestone, cutting through waves and dolphins and chalky seaweed.

"It's a record," Emerson said, stopping to take in the grandeur of the stone ship improbably floating in the middle of the block. "Every building is a record of some idea about how to live."

"So what's the idea of this one?"

"The whole building's announcing it, Beth." He frowned and pointed. "That's the stern."

I saw what he meant. No matter where you stood, the ship had already sailed past. As we continued down the street, I wondered if the turn-of-the-century craftsmen had sensed the tide of history changing even as the building took shape in their hands. Beneath the club's stately rooms, the Beaux Arts currents were beginning to mingle with the municipal waters, while all around the world the ancient dominance of ships was giving way to ever-faster vessels: trains and zeppelins, automobiles and airplanes. The culmination of thousands of years of civilization—a whole age of adventure and exploration—was entombed there in the departing limestone ship, a monument to a previously unrivaled form of speed; celebratory and defiant, but frozen there just the same.

I was still contemplating the frozen ship when we reached Hélène's hotel, a slender building framed by arching silver handrails and jewel-box windows swept with velvet curtains. At the top of the front steps, we were met by a doorman, his handsome face inexplicably sullen. I could not help thinking Emerson's father would have approved of his uniform: a midnight-blue Nehru jacket and slim pants fitted over dark, square-toed shoes. Revived by Li's massage, Emerson limped ahead of me through the polished wooden doors and into the narrow lobby, which had graciously assumed the public duties of the neighboring yacht club's private rooms. A long wooden wall crowned with softly glowing horn lamps overlooked a ship deck's worth of seating: loungers upholstered in rich velvets and white muslin, the fabric parting to expose silver horned legs. Between columns aligned like the funnels of an ocean liner, gleaming handrails snaked down to game boards set for chess and Chinese checkers. A row of glass fishbowls perched on a shelf behind the games like arcade prizes, sending little halos of reflected light swimming up the walls.

"I spoke to Alice at the Modern about Hélène Moreau," I told Emerson, attempting to do some pre-meeting coaching as we waded deeper into the lobby. "She says the Speed Paintings bridged the dominant schools in New York and Europe at the time."

"But I'm not sure she completed the bridge."

He fell into step with me, our progress reflected in an angled wall-mirror hanging from a pair of oversized tassels, like the world's largest pasties.

"I always want to label her as an Abstract Expressionist," I said.

"I definitely wouldn't go the other way, to Minimalism," he said. "Think of Frank Stella's Black Paintings from the late 1950s, when he was around her age—what, early twenties? The Speed Paintings are raw emotion. You can't get any further from the cool, Minimalist rejection of emotion."

"Apparently she's making paintings of laundry now."

He shrugged. "Stella once worked as a housepainter."

In the tiny elevator up to Penthouse B, I was surprised to see that he was sweating. Even taking into account the afternoon's physical exertion, he was normally so collected, so completely self-possessed. His quiet containment tended to cover for a certain amount of detachment, even snobbishness. But his silence that afternoon was different.

A wave of musk washed into the darkened corridor outside Penthouse B, where we were met by a silvery form silhouetted in daylight from the open doorway. When we crossed the threshold the apparition resolved into Hélène Moreau, a handsomely groomed woman in a silk tunic and capri pants. A crop of platinum hair framed her tiny jaw and wide face, its features blunted to the profile of a Persian cat. Protecting her flat face, like a giant windshield, was an oversized pair of gold-rimmed aviator glasses. The lenses had a purplish-pink tint, I noticed in the daylight of the room. In Emerson's company I had met people with countless eccentricities, and I never ceased to be fascinated by their vanities. I supposed the colored lenses were meant to brighten the woman's eyes, which nevertheless shone dully through the glass.

"Please," she said, pointing us toward the sitting area. The hem of her tunic floated out behind her as she crossed the room to her desk, where she proceeded to rummage for the room service menu.

Across from me, Emerson was attempting to lower himself into a blue velvet chair tilted back precariously on a single metal spike. As he leaned down, the neck of his T-shirt hung open to reveal the deep hollow pockets around his collarbone. But if his wasted appearance unsettled Hélène in any way, her tinted gaze didn't betray it as she offered me the menu.

"I'd love some herbal tea," I said. "Chamomile, mint, anything like that."

She turned to Emerson with the menu, and he waved vaguely. "Nothing."

"The Kona coffee here is excellent," she said. "From Hawaii. Very strong."

"I said no."

I tried to catch Emerson's eyes while Hélène placed the order, but he was busy paging through her copy of *New York* magazine.

Hélène hung up the phone.

"Mr. Webster, I asked my lawyer to find out how I might contact you. On the title, the name is Emerson Webster. On the auction record it's Tang. I wondered—"

"Webster is my legal name. I prefer my mother's family name. It's also the name I use for my business, which handled the bidding."

She nodded. "Have you seen the Tang Dynasty polychrome Buddha uptown at the Met?"

"Can't say I have," Emerson replied.

She turned to me and I shook my head.

"Brush painting flourished in the Tang," she said wistfully. "Also dancing, metalwork, poetry, music. Every form of high culture."

Emerson yawned without bothering to cover his mouth. A fine line of saliva stretched from his top lip to the bottom, then vanished.

"It was the golden age of classical Chinese art and literature," she went on, struggling to make conversation.

Emerson appeared to be ignoring her. Instead of replying, he blew me a stagy kiss.

I was too confused by their conversation to laugh at his absurdity, as I knew he wanted me to. What was she talking about? Some kind of auction. At least that was territory I knew Emerson could handle: buying and selling things. And this alone made me relax somewhat; I only wondered if there was a way to get her on track before my employer sagged with exhaustion.

"We're familiar with your work," I volunteered, hoping to get the ball rolling.

"And I am familiar with Mr. Tang's photography collection," she said. "Though not until recently, I confess. I'm not in favor of photography as a medium. I prefer to imagine a work of art rather than capture something I can already see."

"How do you know?" Emerson asked with some annoyance.

"What?"

"What you're capturing? What a photo can capture. What it holds in its emulsion, versus a painting?"

"I learned this."

"Then you've made photographs."

"Of course. I shoot them. I know how to develop them."

It was pretty the way she pronounced it, *devil-up,* and pretty the way she tilted her head attentively toward Emerson as she chatted with us at her accentuated clip.

"I am very fond of photographs," she continued. "But they are not my art."

We were interrupted by the arrival of the tea tray on the unsteady arm of a room service waiter. He could have been the brother of the sullen doorman, but for the sincerity of his smile. The warmth of it made me think of Oliver, in Chicago. How long had it been since I'd ended it with him? I tried to count back as the waiter arranged my tea with the uncertainty of someone who had taken up his line of work only recently, in between casting calls.

Sheepishly, the waiter placed a silver carafe and a basket of miniature muffins on the desk in front of Hélène.

"That a Rolls?" he asked, presenting her with the check.

She picked up a little model car from the desk and dropped it into his palm. "No, it's a Beacon. Also British. In its day it entirely eclipsed any Rolls."

The waiter pushed the car back and forth on the desk as she signed the check.

"Cool," he decided, parking it back in front of her.

"Most of the early Rolls-Royces still run," Hélène told the waiter as she showed him out, conceding a point in some analysis she was carrying on in her head. "They run well. But then, so do Beacons—they don't stop."

"Rolls are quieter," Emerson said. "But is that a plus?"

He slid open a box of Royalton matches to show me: a row of slender black sticks, like charred wood, frosted with bright blue tips. I gave him the thumbs-up. In apparent agreement with this verdict, he dropped the matchbox into the front pocket of his backpack. I was so surprised by his petty theft that I lost the thread of their conversation. Hélène was staring at me. I stared at Emerson, hoping he would say something, but he was dead still. What had she been talking about? Painting versus photography.

"You have a good imagination," I blurted out.

Hélène frowned. "I trust my imagination."

Emerson was studying his arms at his sides, poking his fingers at his biceps. "You still haven't told me why I'm here," he said.

In the silence, I could hear the low whir of the food pump cycling in his backpack.

He shivered.

Hélène flexed her hands and selected a paintbrush from a pile on the low table next to him. "It's cold in here, *non?* This air conditioning you love so much in America. Maybe some fresh air . . ."

She pushed through a glass door at the far end of the room to a balcony outside. A narrow easel had been set up there under one of the stone arches, and she dropped the paintbrush onto a tray clipped to the front. The spiraling call of sirens followed her back into the room on a gust of warm air.

With one look at Emerson, I could tell that his patience was deteriorating along with his physical comfort. My best course of action was to try to wrap up the meeting as quickly as possible. And yet I sensed in Hélène Moreau a certain frailty of her own: some struggle she was going through that, by summoning us here, she was now at least partly entrusting to Emerson and me. Her eyes, shielded behind the pink glass, seemed to beg: Please give me a moment, one more gesture toward nothing before I have to say it.

And so I asked, "Are you painting the city?"

The lilt in her voice answered me with gratitude.

"Oh! No, I was attempting to find some light! It can be rather subdued in Manhattan. So many tall buildings."

What I could see of the painting on her easel looked like a Tuscan countryside, a blue sky fringed with black cypress trees. Floating in the foreground were some large negative shapes, like bed sheets hung out to dry in the sun. I was about to ask her if she was going to fill them in when Emerson cleared his throat, a hooking sound that grated my conscience. I could see he was fighting to remain composed, but his eyes betrayed an irritation at the small but vital alliance I had just made with a woman who was wasting one of the remaining days of his life.

It fell to me to do my duty and get Hélène to the point.

"Are these paintings why you've invited us today?"

With an almost imperceptible flinch, her fingers came together around the model car on her desk, and she settled down to the business at hand.

"No, the matter involves something quite different from my paintings." She fixed her pink gaze on Emerson. "I understand you purchased the R-135 last summer."

I turned to him. I thought I knew every object in his collection. If she was referring to a house photograph, it wasn't in my Accession Register. But I could see that he knew what she was talking about, and the knowledge didn't comfort him. Rather, he seemed to shrivel, to lose focus. His head dipped down to study the pile of magazines in front of him. I had seen small boys act this way, boys whose mothers had ruined their fun by telling them "no."

"It's an *M*," he said finally. "R-135-M. It was factory-modified for competition."

"Yes," said Hélène. "I was disappointed when the clerk at AG told me that it had been auctioned so recently. I've never had the best timing."

She arched an eyebrow so high it shot up over the rim of her aviator glasses. It struck me as a well-practiced move. I was sorry Emerson didn't look away from the magazines to see it.

"I'm interested in buying the car from you," she said.

He glanced up. "It's not for sale."

Abruptly, she got to her feet. She had apparently been arranging flowers in a vase on the desk when we arrived, and she resumed now with a thick white lily. The heavy bloom tipped back, clinging tentatively to the stalk as she thrust it into the vase.

"That flower has a broken neck," Emerson observed.

With a sigh, she ripped the hanging bud free and disappeared with it through one of the doorways, only to return a few seconds later looking more composed, with the stunted bloom sticking out of a water glass.

"Please forgive me," she said, returning to her arranging. "It's difficult for me to sit still. I need to keep moving. Sometimes I think that's why I make art, why I'm always working. My mother used to tell me I was lucky to be born poor, because it motivated me to work."

Rearranging your own hotel flowers did not seem like work to me. And if she had been born poor, she certainly wasn't now.

"The sale price of the car is in the auction record," she informed Emerson, who was now flipping miserably through her copy of *The New Yorker*. "I can improve on it considerably."

I didn't know how much energy she had, but she seemed prepared to conduct a ceaseless arrangement of flowers, drawn somehow, as everyone seemed to be sooner or later, into Emerson's extraordinary self-possession. Something in him was so solid, you felt as if you would come apart if you moved away from its magnetic pull. Even then, as diminished as he was physically, he still had that power.

"It may not be evident to you," he said, "but I don't have much use for your money."

"There are other means of exchange," Hélène said. "My paintings, for example."

Emerson's lips were hanging open again, crossed with a thick line of spittle. I wanted to walk over and wipe them off, but I knew he would be furious if I did. All I could do was watch the line of liquid quake as he tried to keep from shivering.

"Is the air conditioning still on?" I asked impatiently.

As soon as I spoke, I could tell it was not the right thing to have done by the way Emerson refused to look at me. No doubt my concern for his health was somehow undermining his present advantage with Hélène. I would have said I was sorry, but I knew I had said too much already.

Emerson rolled the magazine into a makeshift telescope and regarded Hélène through one end. "Why do you want to buy it?" he asked.

I was shocked to see her smirking at him over her coffee cup. "Why do you want to keep it?" she countered.

He remained silent, staring at her through his spyglass.

"I have come with a generous offer. You might at least consider it, Mr. Tang?"

He turned his spyglass on me. Rarely did I feel that I should correct his behavior, and I knew it was not my place to do it, but sitting there hearing the rising ache in Hélène's voice as he went on silently studying me through the rolled-up magazine, I shook my head at him. We were in the process of giving away everything he owned, a meticulously assembled collection of photographs that he loved and looked at every day, and he was hesitating about parting with something he couldn't use.

"With respect to your earlier answer," Hélène ventured, "is there any other consideration you would give to the idea?"

"No."

It was the same tone he had used to refuse the coffee.

"But—"

Emerson was struggling to his feet with his backpack. "Beth, I don't want to be late for our next—"

"There must be some arrangement we can discuss. I have come a long way."

Emerson lurched toward the door, his body dragging after his head like a dead weight.

Hélène turned to me. "I'll be staying here in the city for a few weeks. No more than that, I shouldn't think."

The announced length of her stay agitated Emerson immensely.

"Staying for what?" he asked, swaying on his feet.

Hélène stepped forward.

He fought to regain his balance. "What are you staying for?"

"I'm arranging a show with my gallery." She looked to me with a worried, uncertain smile. "Perhaps we will speak again?"

Emerson seized the doorknob and held on as if he were being sucked back into the room. He did not turn his head, but addressed his comment to the polished wood in front of him: "I don't care if you have the engine. I'll get it."

"I'm offering to buy the car from you," Hélène replied, arching her brow again, this time in confusion.

Emerson was curled over the doorknob, unable to pry back the leaden weight. I crowded myself in beside him and pulled the door open, a move that seemed to inspire calm in him. With a firmer footing, he gained the hallway. I followed him out, conscious of Hélène's anxious presence in the doorway, but she said nothing more as Emerson and I retreated together to the elevator.

It was only after the elevator doors had closed behind us that I noticed the paintbrush in Emerson's hand—a long, varnished wooden stick with a cracked tip. When he had stolen it, I couldn't say. Had he slipped it into his backpack while Hélène was calling room service? Now he shamelessly played with it as we descended the floors, twirling it in his fingers like a majorette, stroking the back of his left hand with the stiff bristles. He knew that I saw. What was it that kept me from speaking? The frankness with which he flaunted his kleptomania? I couldn't take my eyes off the bristles rising and falling over a hand that looked more dead than alive.

"What's this about a car?" I asked, hoping the casualness of the question would assure him that I was willing to pretend what had just gone on between him and Hélène Moreau was not as uncomfortable as it had been. Nonetheless, my question got no response except for a variation in his handling of the brush. Whereas before he was painting his hand with the care of a Renaissance master, now he moved in bursts like a conductor, making great flying strokes and dabs and slashes with it in the air.

He was still waving it around as we exited the hotel—waving it at the sullen doorman, who stared at him without blinking, looking him up and down, step by step through the lobby. I don't know what was running through the doorman's mind as he moved aside for the regal and extremely thin man limping his way past with a whirring backpack, but his expression was not one of compassion.

The doorman jogged reluctantly over to Sixth Avenue to hail us a taxi, and Emerson and I stepped out into the confusing autumnal summer.

5

Accession Number: BC 1990.8241

Year acquired: 1990
Object: What Emerson Tang Webster handed me when I asked him for a job description:

SUBLIME—
In the event of an absolutely large object . . .—or one that is absolutely powerful . . . the faculty of presentation, the imagination, fails to provide a representation corresponding to this Idea. This failure of expression gives rise to a pain, a kind of cleavage within the subject between what can be conceived and what can be imagined or presented. But this pain in turn engenders a pleasure, in fact a double pleasure: the impotence of the imagination attests *a contrario* to an imagination striving to figure even that which cannot be figured. . . .
—JEAN-FRANÇOIS LYOTARD, "The Sublime and the Avant-Garde," section III, page 250

This was hand-copied in blue ink on a page torn from a notebook, converted to scrap paper. At the bottom, in pencil, in the same hand, was a list of what I assumed were the qualifications for my job:

- some knowledge of architecture, art, design, history
- able to work independently (in silence)
- an interest in the preservation of artistic works and their related information
- engrossed in the pursuit of sublime organization

I took the position with Emerson not long after the satisfaction of the work I'd known as a college student devolved into an assortment of sensory data that merely signified work: the clicking sounds of the rolling library shelving in the Media Center of the ad agency in midtown where I was first employed after graduation; the slippery coated paper of the magazine articles I clipped and photocopied for forty hours a week plus overtime; the perpetual beeping and wheel-of-fortune smells emanating from the employee kitchen across the corridor . . .

At first the profession of a media archivist had promised some fulfilling and useful application of a native trait: my habit of holding on to things. For among the personal paradigms available to anyone's life (Butcher, Baker, Beggarman, etc.), I self-identified, in part, as a Saver—someone for whom living essentially equaled the ongoing accumulation of souvenirs. And these mementos, in turn, represented the rough outlines of my existence. It was a circular compulsion, more than evidenced by the quantity and variety of objects filling the drawers and closets and storage boxes in my apartment in Chelsea (a one-bedroom in London Terrace), a collection that was always meticulously organized.

I reasoned that my liberal arts education had more than demonstrated the value of archival- and conservation-based work. How could my own studies have taken place if not for the legions of custodians over thousands of years who had gathered, organized and preserved the materials I fed from so hungrily? Not only books, but everything that kept me company: paintings, sculpture, music, countless forms of human creation. And though I created very little myself, I saw that at all points in history people had stepped forward to look after the output of other minds and hands (and just as importantly, to preserve the records of their destruction), for no reason other than that they believed it was a valuable activity.

It was in this frame of mind that I'd left college in Philadelphia and apprenticed myself at the agency in Manhattan under the direction of Louise Jarvil, a discreet coupon clipper with a graying pageboy and a preference for frosted coral lipstick, not only in summer but all year long. She commuted into the city with a brown bag lunch every morning by train from a town near Burring Port, where my parents still lived (though by then my brother Garrett was in London, working for an American bank).

Jarvil's background was in library science, and the fluorescent-lit Media Center she oversaw on the twenty-eighth floor was much like any other library, archive or museum with its professional system of organizing and cross-referencing materials. The world was linked only tentatively by computers then, and we used primitive machines (glorified electric typewriters) to create our records and reports. Beyond a couple of databases, the highest form of technology in the agency was a roomful of Xerox machines, where my colleagues and I stood for hours packaging reference materials for the agency's creative, research and account teams. From the start, I enjoyed the daily work of reading newspapers and magazines. I certainly didn't mind logging and filing. The tasks weren't the problem. The problem was that, despite a continued commitment to my higher calling, I found it difficult to summon any enthusiasm for the commercial products of our labors.

It was then, with nearly three years under Jarvil's wing, that I was invited, along with every other girl from Burring Port, to the bridal shower of my old neighbor Beckett. It was the first shower I had been to, and as I described my job to Beckett, making small talk, I remember staring at her in confusion—she was wearing a bonnet someone had constructed from a paper plate, festooned with all the colored bows from her gifts. She blew some tendrils of curled ribbon away from her face. "Remember the guy you got into the car with? At the track that summer? He started a photo collection. Tom said he's looking for someone to manage it."

Meeting Emerson for the second time amounted to one phone call. I found him standing on the steps of the Public Library, on Fifth Avenue, dressed as he had described on the phone, in a leather jacket and jeans, with a crewcut. It was a look that suited him, and from what I had observed of him in the past, he dressed to suit himself. His appearances in my life were so infrequent and his style so changeable that his choices always intrigued me, but I can't say I ever felt attracted to him in a physical or romantic sense. His was a more mysteriously compelling effect. Something about him made me pull myself up to my full height. I had come awake when I'd driven with him at the track. Unwittingly, even as a child, he'd expanded the narrow margins of my world, and as we stood toe-to-toe beside the stone lion he had chosen for our meeting point (the one nicknamed Fortitude, closest to 42nd Street), I believed that working for him could be a way to continue such experiences.

I detected the remains of his punk scowl as he took in my interview attire. For the occasion, I wore pants to cover the shiny rectangular scar on my right calf. I suspected he wouldn't remember me from the track—my face had been under a helmet and a hood most of the time—but even so, something told me it was not to my advantage to call that particular incident to mind during a job interview.

He sat down and questioned me there on the front steps.

"Why do you want to manage my collection?"

"I'm inclined to organizational tasks," I explained, adopting a formal tone in an effort to override the squealing brakes on Fifth. "Working in the Media Center, managing a collection, we're caring for materials people might need at some future time they can't predict. The way bees fill a hive with honey even though they won't live to consume it."

"And what do you find valuable about that activity?"

"For the bees?"

He nodded.

"A connected point of view, I guess—survival of the group over the individual. But in archiving, in conservation, there are individual benefits as well. The value is in whatever anyone will need to know or use in the future. It's public, but it's also private."

He appeared to be waiting for me to continue.

"You can go back to records maintained by monks and courtiers, lawyers and merchants, documented acts of aggression, family records of births and marriages . . . But also objects, theories, philosophies—it's a kind of collective memory. There are so many uses."

He was watching people pass up and down the steps of the library, seemingly content to let me ramble. I glanced at the unusual job description and told him about the art history and design surveys I'd taken in college.

"Why do you want to leave the job you have now?"

"I'm not particularly social."

I admitted to him that I found it exhausting to work at a big company. I was content—it was almost as peaceful as sleeping —when I was quietly filing, cleaning or polishing things. I didn't know how it was related, but I acknowledged in myself a tendency to keep things ready for something, though I did not know what: the refrigerator stocked, the bed made. As if at any moment it would all be put to perfect use. Though I couldn't say it ever had been.

Emerson demonstrated no memory of me during our interview. To test him, I mentioned that I had grown up in Burring Port and asked him if he knew my brother Garrett, so as not to risk reminding him of the track. He looked at me with an empty, apologetic expression. I was a stranger. But he called a few days later and hired me to create a basic documentation system for his photography collection—an order he expected me to maintain. I proposed to put together a documentation plan for his approval, but he told me not to bother.

"I don't care how you set it up. You're the one who has to use it."

I was pleased to find that the storage areas in his loft were already impeccable. He'd renovated the space a few years earlier with the help of a conservator, Eric Dart. After all the light meters and hygrometers and thermometers passed through, they installed a collections storage area behind lockable panels in the office section of the loft, where I kept his permanent records in a fireproof metal cabinet.

For more than a year I busied myself doing the retrospective documentation on all the architectural photographs he'd acquired before I got there. During those months of logging acquisitions, it occurred to me that if you are an intensely private person, other private people were ideal employers, because the extent of your intimacy was cut and dried: I was hired to create and maintain a system, and to feed that system Emerson bought photographs. Some days he appeared in the office and we spoke. Many days I didn't see him. Whatever dramas may have marked his personal life in those years were not mine to know. I let myself in through a door on the office side of the loft, a formality I appreciated, and he took himself where he needed to go. Among my duties, I paid his monthly bills for a travel agent on Sixth Avenue and a private garage on Perry Street, where he parked his car, an aging Audi Quattro.

It was during that time when I began sleeping with Oliver, who was a client of my former agency and lived nearly three hours away by plane. He'd said the magic phrase: "I won't be in town for long." I learned to rely on such cues, because they meant physical contact without involvement. By then, I'd found that my body was easier to share than my thoughts or emotions, and arrangements like the one I had with Oliver provided the illusion of companionship with the advantage of sounding convincing to parents, brother, co-workers. "Do you love him?" Beckett asked me at her wedding reception, a few months before I broke it off with Oliver. "In a way," I said honestly, relieved to know that in less than twelve hours his airplane would again be ascending to cruising altitude.

It wasn't until one afternoon in July of 1995, when Emerson invited me to join him for lunch at Florent, that I forgot about my easy misconceptions of companionship. I caught the odd tone in his voice as soon as I got into his car for what was, to me, a ridiculously unnecessary drive of five blocks, to Gansevoort Street. I knew Emerson well enough by then to be familiar with his occasional insolence. In his business dealings, he sometimes used aggressiveness to disguise other emotions that he was less eager to reveal. I had seen him behave horribly, sarcastically and spoiled when I sensed he felt vulnerable or uncertain. But until that lunch at Florent, I had never heard him speak so warmly.

"I've enjoyed working with you these past few years," he told me when we were seated at the restaurant, not meeting my eyes but tracking some new arrivals in the mirror behind my head. "Working with someone—I didn't think I would enjoy it, but I have. I wish we could keep things the way they are for a little longer."

I was certain I was being fired. My eyes dropped to the table and traced the lines of a funny postcard—a schematic drawing of a stomach stuffed with French food—propped in the ashtray.

"I wish this wasn't the case," Emerson went on. "But I'm sick."

"What?"

"Sick," he repeated. "And my doctor says I can't count on next year. Which is weird to think about."

"What do you mean, next year?"

"I call it Omega, you know?" He laughed oddly to himself.

"I don't understand."

"They say I'm going to need someone to help me take care of myself. Actually, it'll be more like organizing . . . health things —hiring nurses for me and helping with stuff I can't do." He stared at his fork, then pushed it away abruptly. "Of course, you would be compensated differently."

The changes he proposed to my terms of employment meant continuing publicly as his collections manager and privately assuming duties as his healthcare agent. As he saw it, the amount of time allotted to each of my jobs would shift as time went on, and eventually I would serve as the executor of his will and trusts. He was careful to emphasize that it was a business arrangement that suited him. He may have had no idea who I was when I started working for him, but by then I was familiar to him.

"This . . . event . . . ," I began.

"Just Omega."

I drained my water glass and started again. "In terms of Omega . . . Do you know what it will be like? What kind of things I'll need to do?"

He shook his head. "Just, I'll get sicker, there will be Omega. You'll help me get there."

I immediately fixated on the paperwork, the aspect that struck me as being the most manageable. I reasoned that I already handled so much of it for him—and there was a system. I had a sense of what being an executor involved: When my mother was executor for one of her brothers, she'd wrapped up the business with a morning's worth of signatures.

"My lawyer will take you through that," Emerson promised. "It's all written down."

When his eyes finally met mine I felt a cold egg crack open in my stomach. An icy liquid ran through me with the sickening coincidence: I had a related job qualification. A very specialized type of experience.

To tell the truth, I had experience with death because I had been dead. For a short time, as a child. The resuscitation of my body in a hospital after some acceptable number of minutes was deemed a success, superficially. The problem I couldn't explain was that my brief communion with death seemed to have come with an uncomfortable side effect: For as long as I could remember, I felt something like a woman trapped in a man's body, except the issue wasn't my gender. Some part of my being was in the wrong place. I was maybe transexistential.

Beth—rhymes with death. Why was I here? As I grew older, I kept running across the idea that everyone's life had a purpose, or more than one. Things you were meant to be accomplishing. By that way of thinking, if you were forcibly brought back to life, wasn't the expectation that much more emphatic? But I didn't know what I was supposed to be doing. I felt no shape to my life, regardless of how much I busied myself with studies and tasks. The blankness was there even then, I admit. Must a life be long to have value? By the time I was in my twenties, I suspected that whatever my purpose was, however small, I had obediently fulfilled it long ago, before that night in the hospital. I was meant to have gone off duty then, as scheduled, at the age of four. But through the power of some other force or will, I found myself on a very long overtime shift without an assignment.

Until Emerson's request that day, sleep and solitude had helped me escape the discomfort I felt, but they could only approximate the absolute peace I'd known so briefly. Even more seductive than sleep was what had lured me into the car with Emerson that day in my teens: the possibility of a crash—something that would end my life for me—a flirtation with death that had only left me burned and scarred. After that, I bowed to the tension in my being, the inescapable conclusion that I was simply out of place. I lived in the city with the illusion of closeness that came from being surrounded by people. I dated so-called boyfriends, made almost-friends whom I rarely saw and celebrated their significant events—showers, weddings, births—with the feeling of witnessing it through glass. I tried to imagine myself in the ribbony hat that Beckett wore so excitedly at her bridal shower, a bright helmet marking her official entry onto the marriage and parenthood track, but I did not see myself joining that race. I had experience with death. On instinct, I decided not to tell Emerson about it.

He emphasized his intention to function normally for as long as he could, and then our food arrived, and my own sense of privacy prevented me from asking too many questions about his situation. I admit it took some time for what he asked of me to settle in. I don't recall any formal change taking place. I continued going to work every day for weeks and months, and my duties segued gradually, just as he had described, and it never seemed very different until we were far down the road. It was paradoxical in the extreme to enter into an arrangement to help someone guard against death, and at the same time to be the caregiver who, in whatever small way, eases that death. I didn't know anything about birth, but being a midwife for death was a matter of utmost open-mindedness.

I told almost no one my job had changed. Maybe I felt protective of him after the years of public speculation he'd endured. And ironically, as he must have assumed, it wasn't necessary to announce or explain anything when we were arranging bequests all day on his behalf. He was hiding in plain sight. I confided in my parents and the home healthcare workers. The only other person who might have tempted me was my brother in London, but because he had no idea how sick Emerson was to begin with, Garrett rarely expressed any interest in my employer. He'd long ago grown bored of the Emperor's vicissitudes.

I considered Li and the other manicurists at Golden Hands to be part of Emerson's nursing team, but I didn't think there was anything I could tell them that they didn't already know from observing him week after week.

"I like their sounds," I confided to Emerson one afternoon on the short cab ride home from Golden Hands. "I like listening to Mei. She talks at all strange angles, like guitar strings popping."

"I have no clue what they're saying, but sometimes I feel like they're talking about me," he said.

"That would be natural. I mean, for them to talk about their customers."

"I guess."

"I have to ask—do they make you think of your mother? Or is that presumptive and racist of me?"

"Yeah, no—a little bit." He stared at the filthy plexiglass divider separating us from the taxi driver. "I stopped imagining her, I don't know when. When I was little, she was a fantasy. Then, at Lakeville, I had friends with families, and she was always this thing about China. To everyone else. Not to me. I think she must have put it behind her—because she left . . ."

"I like Li."

"I think she would have liked Li. I have no idea why. I didn't know her, you know? I don't even remember hearing her voice. I have the idea—my father must have told me this—I have the idea we spent some time by a stream before she died. I turned four that year . . ."

I waited for him to continue.

"My father had a portrait of her, done by one of her friends before he met her. Some girly afternoon, I like to think."

"Girly?"

"You know, a picnic beside a river, eating, laughing . . . In the picture, her face was marked on one side by a smudge of paint —or some dirt, maybe, from the muddy riverbank. I tried to lick it off once, and the paper tasted like dust."

6

EVERYONE'S IDEA OF home is accompanied by its own environmental expression of loneliness. Mine is the view from trains in the Northeast. From my window seat on Metro-North, moving east and away from New York City, another summer went by on the other side of the glass. Past Harlem, the silver cars hooked right and the city gave way to steel bridges and glinting water, then the jigsaw sprawl of Westchester, a fortress of stone retaining walls and chain-link fences holding back the encroaching suburbs. The landscape sharpened along the coast, like the cut of the passengers' suits. Everything was painted in primary colors: blue sky, white clouds, green grass and channels of deeper blue bleeding into Long Island Sound. In the long, narrow back yards behind the train tracks, rusted aluminum sheds stood guard over abandoned swing sets.

Emerson was asleep in the next seat.

A familiar melancholy descended on me with the motion of the railcars. During college I'd made the same run on Amtrak more times than I could count, with a cassette tape in my Walkman and my backpack jammed with textbooks and dirty laundry. It was a game for me to pick out figures on the beaches, people walking dogs in the middle of the day or taking a boat out after work. I liked to watch from the window seat, leaning my head against the glass.

Somewhere around Stamford walls of concrete rose up and chattered with graffiti. Emerson was awake and pointing out the window to the edge of an embankment, where the front half of a plastic Big Wheel trike was suspended in midair.

"Some kid's car!" he exclaimed. "How does it just get left there—to tip over like that?"

He hadn't said anything more about the vintage car he owned since our trip to the Royalton the previous week, but I'd been thinking about it, especially after I'd found a message on the answering machine in the office a few days later:

Yes, hello, this is Hélène Moreau. I am trying to reach Beth. I am hoping we might speak again.

There was a long pause, so long that I thought the message was over, until her voice came through again, hesitantly:

I would like to . . . well, it would mean a great deal to me if you would return my call.

The tape was still running.

I have heard you are very skilled in your area of expertise . . . I wondered if you might be able to help me . . .

Then she seemed to lose her nerve—

Thank you.

As flattering as it was that an artist of her reputation knew anything about my professional skills, I doubted this was what she really wanted to talk to me about. Instead of calling her, I called her gallery.

"I spoke to Hélène Moreau's art dealer, Arthur Quint," I informed Emerson on the train, puzzling over the conversation I'd had with Quint and the gallery assistant.

"Yeah?" Emerson asked, perking up at the prospect of some gossip.

"I was curious . . . you know, to see what I could find out."

I'd worked for him long enough to know that he'd never object to any intelligence about a rival. He settled back in his seat and closed his eyes, waiting for me to continue.

"I talked to the assistant, Katya, first, and she said that when Arthur Quint was organizing a Pollock show he wanted some of Moreau's Speed Paintings for context, and they found out she was still represented by her old dealer in Paris. Well, he was dead, but his gallery . . ."

The pump in Emerson's backpack whirred along to the rattling of the train.

"In the sixties, she lived in Copenhagen," I went on. "And she did make photographs, it turns out, but they're not well known. A series of 'obelisk' portraits—highly collectible, apparently. She shot them as if they were people."

"Obelisks?"

I nodded. "Like the one erected at Karnak for Queen Hatshepsut, plus all the 'wandering obelisks' from Egypt that are all over Rome now, and the one that was stolen from Ethiopia by Mussolini's army. A lot of time in cemeteries, you would think. But she found them all over the place—on a beach in Sardinia, on the Thames—"

"What about lighthouses?"

"There might have been a few of those. Katya said some of the photos were blurry. She got Arthur Quint on the speaker—I used your name, I hope you don't mind."

Emerson allowed me a small grin, confirming my hunch that he'd be flattered.

"I was trying to warm up to the subject of that car she wants from you, not to be obvious. I started by asking if there were similarities to Lucio Fontana in her Speed Paintings, but Quint said no, Fontana mainly was forcing a three-dimensional space on the viewer." I made a tent with my fingers. "He wanted them to see paint outside its accepted flatness. The scale, the intent—Quint said Fontana's work had nothing in common with Hélène's, except the gesture of slashing."

Emerson considered this. "Didn't she attach brushes to the wheels of cars?"

"No, well . . . they call them brushes. But he confirmed there was no paint. They were sharp poles, really, welded to what he called 'knockoff spinners' on the wheels—these enormous lances. She had them fabricated from steel, to withstand the speeds."

"Drive-by stabbings," Emerson said, looking amused at the thought.

"She had cages built to support the lengths of canvas, to keep them taut as the cars raced past. He said some of the canvases were practically shredded."

Arthur Quint had said more than that. *Moreau was uncontainable,* he'd said. *Those paintings are rapturous. Powerful and mechanical and brutal . . .*

"The woman Katya said they were very *Futurismo*. Arthur took it up and said the Futurist movement has had an influence on countless artists—how Moreau wanted to express power and sweeping change, and yes, she wanted violence in the paintings, but *Fascism* as a political program was never her milieu."

I could see Emerson was enjoying my impression of Arthur Quint.

"I finally asked if she was using those old cars again in her work. But he said, 'No, no, she has always been on a forward trajectory.' After the Speed Paintings, she did some related canvases—the Pleasure Drive series."

"I've seen those," Emerson said derisively. "They're a bunch of mud tracks glazed with puddles of wine."

"I asked, 'Wasn't there a particular car she used? A Beacon? Weren't Beacons very popular then?' and he said, 'There were countless cars. And now, in her maturity, she is again working with movement through fabric. It's a gentler and more *eco-*

logical expression of motion. Earlier in her artistic career it was speed—'"

"Speed!" Emerson shouted, erupting from his seat in protest. "She doesn't know anything about speed."

"She didn't know anything about it *then*," I agreed, amazed at how automatically his competitive reflex kicked in. "She wasn't from some aristocratic family with fast cars, or flying around in jets after the war. Speed was foreign to her, as it was then to most people, according to Arthur Quint. Unless they were rich."

At this, Emerson turned sheepish.

I didn't say it to him, but I thought I could understand something about how Hélène might have felt.

"Did he tell you why she wants my car?" Emerson asked impatiently.

I shook my head.

A door slammed open and shut behind us, and I heard the click of a metal punch as the ticket taker moved down the aisle. "Darien."

We watched from our seats as commuters stepped in and out of the cars to their practiced choreography, then we were in motion once again.

"Why did you buy it?" I asked.

"I don't know. I know I'll never drive a car again. I might as well be dead. I'm waiting for the arm of the toll booth to rise, and there's nothing on the other side."

"We're on a train."

"I was speaking metaphorically."

He shut down after that.

"What is it about that car?" I persisted.

He dismissed my question with a grimace. "I'm freezing."

I pulled off my sweater and draped it like a scarf around his leather jacket until the doors opened in Burring Port.

"I'm not looking forward to this," he said, limping out onto the platform.

"What are you not looking forward to?"

"Telling him."

"Telling him?"

In typical form, Emerson had never said why I was escorting him to visit his father. It hadn't occurred to me that Lynford Webster might be unaware of his son's condition.

"Phone conversations are always really short with us," he said, surveying the tiny Burring Port train station as if for the first time.

"How long has it been since you've seen him?" I asked.

"No idea."

The air on the platform hit me like a wall, strangely thick and dry. "God, it's like breathing in powder," I said, waving to one of the idling taxicabs.

"I like it," Emerson protested, shrugging off my sweater. He insisted on riding in the front seat of the taxi, where he turned his baseball cap backward and slumped against the window.

"I called him a while ago," he announced when we were a mile or so from Gray Hill, thawing, perhaps, in the powdery summer air. "When he got on the phone I thought: If I tell him, he's going to ask me if I want one of his friends to write me a recommendation letter into heaven."

"What are you going to say?"

"I don't know." He glanced at the taxi driver, who was staring ahead impassively.

A muted sky flickered through the green trees overhead. Emerson's voice drifted back to me over the seats. "More *ask* him, I guess. I want to ask him some things."

"Like what?"

"Personal."

The taxi turned off the country road and passed under a plain stone arch into the Webster estate. The drive turned sharply to the east and continued through a tall allée of trees that I'd never known was there. About a quarter of a mile along, the road branched into a wide trident.

"To the left here, please," Emerson directed the driver.

A noticeable change came over him as we turned on to the secondary roadway. Abruptly, he pulled himself up in the seat and addressed a challenge to the driver, his face lit with boyish amusement: "Okay — let's see what you can do!"

The local drivers all knew the private course was there, to the south, past the empty stables and down toward the Sound. The route continued along the coast briefly before it looped back over some hills to intersect with the main drive. (For all the hospitals, libraries and civic projects funded by Lynford Webster over the years, it was the blind eye he turned to the locals' use of the racing course that remained his most beloved civic gesture.)

The taxi driver was a man of about fifty, with the easygoing air of someone who had nothing to prove. He was ignoring Emerson and driving sensibly, treating me and his obviously fragile passenger to a leisurely tour. We continued inland, where the estate was thick with pines and stone walls. The taxi cruised past flowering bushes and a knoll with a stream running on either side. I was enjoying the sightseeing tour until Emerson complained: "We're not going fast enough."

"What?" I said.

"I want to feel it!"

I shot a look at the back of his head in response, but now the driver was rising to the bait. He was already accelerating when Emerson leaned in.

"Come on, you can select a few gears there. You've got a V-8 in this, don't you?"

The driver nodded.

"So let's use it."

I was instantly thrown back against my headrest. I reached for the grab handle above the door to steady myself as we raced ahead furiously, with Emerson behaving like a co-driver in one of the auto rallies he made me watch with him on TV.

"Okay—you've got a sharp right coming up here," he coached. "Second gear. Yes! Yes! Come on! Don't brake!"

We approached the curving road out to Long Island Sound, and Emerson turned to me with a look of bliss that made me reach protectively for the old wound on my leg. Then, as if suddenly remembering the driver, he resumed his coaching efforts: "Come on—nail it! Nail it! Full throttle!"

I managed to roll down my window an inch when we reached the beach road, letting the dry wind slip in through a crack, enjoying myself a little more now that I wasn't being thrown around the curves. The taxi rattled along the shoreline like a plane preparing for takeoff. Out on the Sound, only a handful of sailboats were tempted by the strange afternoon weather, with its powdery heat and shifting winds. Then we turned from the coast on to a road that climbed back through the woods, running down an unpleasant series of twists and turns that brought Emerson to delighted attention in his seat.

"Okay, you'll get up to third gear on this last stretch. Keep your foot down! Don't brake. Don't brake . . . Okay—*brake!!!* Shift into second!"

I watched the taxi driver making complex maneuvers with the simple gear shifter on the steering column. Emerson appeared to be going off-duty now, satisfied that his intense tutelage had achieved its goal. He was rocking and bouncing in his seat, a frail body connecting ecstatically with the force of speed. I couldn't help wondering what was running through his mind. I understood some of the thrill, the rush, I felt it myself, but I could see it held a stronger power over him.

We passed the old stables again, from the other direction, and then the vast roof of a house came into view. At the sight of it, Emerson drooped in his seat. "So yeah, cool, okay," he murmured. "Please turn in up there."

The taxi rolled to a stop before the architectural oddity Emerson had warned me about: what had once been the home of his ancestors. In the three hundred years since his branch of the family had broken away from the Massachusetts Bay Colony, various descendants had undertaken extensions and updates to the core structure. Finally, Lynford Webster had remade the whole exterior in imitation of the Robie House in Chicago. Frank Lloyd Wright's original design occupied a city street corner—what had once been an open plain. Out of context here, in a wooded landscape, even in crude facsimile form, it didn't look like a house so much as an Asian temple: a system of wide horizontal brick bands stacked and coupled in striking proportions.

Compared to the photo of the original house in Emerson's collection, Mr. Webster's copy may have succeeded as a gesture, but it abandoned all pretense on the inside. Inexplicably, we were greeted by the architectural remnants of a Georgian entry hall —and by Laurel, the housekeeper, a squat woman with a reddish buzz cut and a ruddy face, who I guessed to be in her mid-fifties.

"Hello," I said, silently admiring the pristine white T-shirt tucked into her khakis.

She was busy taking in the camouflage outfit that Emerson had put together with Brian that morning. They had piled him up with baggy sweatpants, the leather jacket and his backpack, but the fine silver frames of his glasses did nothing to hide his sunken eye sockets.

"It's nice to meet you," I said to Laurel, extending my hand. I explained that I was taking the taxi to visit my parents a few miles away, and I would not be gone for long.

She ignored my outstretched hand and instead gestured down one of the hallways for Emerson's benefit.

"Check out the grounds, or whatever, if you get back before I'm done," he called to me as he loped off, baseball cap in hand, in the direction of Laurel's weathervane arm.

• • •

Duty is a robotic emotion. In order to initiate it, the mind perceives the existing elements—place, time, persons, historical variables, intention—and the course of action emerges like the sum on a calculator. In the case of that visit to Connecticut, the elements had come together to produce a vision of my parents' faces, having heard from a mysterious source that I had been in town and not gone to see them—an unwelcome vision, augmented by the creak in my father's voice, dry with disappointment if I gave him any cause to worry. Or any *more* cause to worry. After what I had put him and my mother through at the time of my childhood death, I saw it as my duty not to unnerve them again.

I found my father at the kitchen stove, reheating some soup. He was a short, slender man—as slight as I was—the result of a strict diet after being informed by a specialist at Webster Memorial that he suffered from an enlarged heart. When I was a child, he had seemed so much bigger: Garrett and I had once made a tent out of his trousers.

"Your visit is short, so we're having a simple lunch," he announced, giving the soup a gentle stir. "Even you won't have time to take a nap."

"I hardly sleep anymore," I protested. I refrained from mentioning that this was because Emerson woke up every two hours.

"Not sleeping can't be healthy either," he said.

"Maybe." I glanced around for evidence of his latest model-plane project, which I knew would never be far out of reach. There: On one of the TV trays next to the dining room table sat a pile of colored plastic racks with little pieces clinging to them like seeds—the components of what were no doubt World War Two aircraft waiting to be snapped off and filed down, then painted and glued together. Garrett and I had long ago formulated the hypothesis that, because he had been too young to fight in the war, the period had taken on a mythic immensity in his imagination.

I scanned the room for the model-plane boxes with their crazy-looking airbrushed fight scenes, but he must have left them behind on one of the card tables in his workspace upstairs.

"What are you making this time?" I asked him. "Allied? Nazi?"

"A little of both," he said, enthusiastically waving me into the dining room.

"Where's Mom?"

"On the way." He urgently directed my attention to a thriving spider plant suspended from a metal bracket over the dining room window. "Now, imagine each one of these babies is a Messerschmitt 109 on wires—well, a little higher."

He gestured to the legion of baby spider plants rappelling down from the mother on a series of thin green shoots. As instructed, I tried to picture them as German fighter planes, well aware that this was only the preliminary staging area; after he'd worked out the latest air fight tableau—this time depicting a scene from the Battle of Britain, he informed me—it would be installed in his workspace up in the attic, where the ceiling was painted sky blue and the assembled wings would hang, frantic and frozen, from lengths of fishing line.

The baby spider plants swung back and forth as he brushed them with his fingers. "See, the RAF pilots are going to have all these Messerschmitts in their face before they can get to the Nazi bombers." He pointed to the opposite wall, where a sun-bleached portrait of my parents, my brother and myself stared back at me from the 1970s through a frame of cracked gold leaf.

"So the German bombers will be over there?"

"Right! They're coming to attack, with their fighters out in front to protect them. Over here, the British pilots are going to be picking them off—shooting the fighter planes down so they can get to the Nazi bombers over the English Channel, before they reach London."

I nodded approvingly at the invisible scenario, pretending to understand it.

My father looked over at me.

"You're early," he said, as if suddenly aware of my presence. "Everything all right?"

I shook my head.

He took a seat at the dining room table, and I dropped into a chair opposite him.

"Beth, have you thought about what you're going to do when this is over—job-wise?" He searched my face. "I'm concerned."

I wasn't sure how to answer him. "Why are you concerned about me? I'm not the one who's dying."

We sat in silence.

He turned to the tray full of plastic pieces but restrained himself from reaching for them.

Was there ever a time when we had been close?

He readjusted his chair away from the temptation of the TV tray. "I'm trying to understand," he said. "You got a good education. That job at the agency. Now it's . . . Are you switching to the health field?" He was evidently speaking to himself, or to my absent mother, when he added, "Even before this, she hasn't shown much interest in getting on with her game plan."

I sensed that he and my mother expected my life to have goals or a more developed plot, but I was borrowing one from Emerson. I had no idea what I was going to do when it ended, either.

"What do you mean, 'game plan'?"

"You know, what's your strategy, Beth? What's your plan? Living is a process you can manage. The question is, how are you going to manage it?"

"Right now, I don't know."

Why did it always feel like glass? Like the domed canopy on one of his fighter planes, sealing me off.

"I'm really confused. About a lot of things." I was unsure how to explain that I had been thinking about my own childhood death more often as Emerson's health declined. I shifted in my seat and bumped my elbow into a partially assembled plane.

"Lancaster bomber," he informed me good-naturedly. "That's for the next project." He reached over and set the model right again. "It needs some work before it's ready to—well . . ."

"Sorry."

"It's fine. It's—"

"I feel really flat. Blank."

"You're helping someone who's very sick. You can't save everything, honey."

I wanted to unburden myself. "But, I mean, even before this. I don't feel right in myself. I never feel right."

"Are you sick?"

I was only worrying him.

"No, no." I smiled a little, hoping to reassure him. "Forget it."

He pulled his jaw to one side, contemplating my predicament no more successfully than I had.

"I don't know what to tell you." He looked down miserably at another half-painted airplane on the sideboard, then seized it. "Say you're the pilot of this Spitfire. It's Britain in the summer of 1940. Your allies have all been defeated or occupied, and you're alone against the enemy. Your country is under deadly attack from squadrons of Nazi fighters and bombers, and you are the only force capable of stopping them."

He swept his hand across the dining room. "Up in the air" —he indicated the baby spider plants—"it's dogfighting, one on one, mano a mano. You're up there alone, and it's your skill versus the enemy's. Your own *thoughts* can be the enemy. If thoughts of defeat were to overtake you—no way."

"What am I fighting for?"

"*For everything.*" He tapped the tiny fuselage with one of his glue-capped fingers. "The future is in your hands. You have to stop the enemy at this critical point in the war. You've got the tools, Beth. Your engine is—incomparable. Like the Merlin engines that powered these Spitfires." He shook the plane at me. "If it wasn't for these engines and the skill of the RAF pilots, the world would be a very different place today." He nodded forcefully, as if confirming the truth of this to himself. "And not a good one."

He brought the model plane in for a landing on the TV tray.

"What are you saying?" I asked.

"Where's my Beth?" I heard my mother calling from the front hall. "Is she here yet?"

His eyes bored through me. "They fought."

"Beth?"

"They didn't give up. Like—"

My mother entered the dining room and leaned down to give me a hug. She was pixie-sized as well, standing slightly taller than me in a pair of the low-heeled pumps she wore to her volunteer job at the Webster Memorial Library.

"What are we talking about?" she asked, pulling out a chair at the dining table.

My father smiled. "I was just telling Beth how proud I am of her."

I looked to him in confusion.

"What happened at the Websters'?" asked my mother.

"Nothing—I don't know. I just dropped him off and came here. He's talking with his father about . . . you know."

At this, she became somber: "I hate to think what that man must be going through."

"Not to mention what *his son* is going through," I pointed out.

"Of course, Beth, that goes without saying." She frowned. "But . . . to lose your child, and that man lost his parents, too, when he was young. Then his wife."

"Do you know anything about her?" I asked.

At this, my mother unfolded a memory from the sewing box in her mind, a sighting she'd had of Mrs. Webster one Christmas at Kennedy airport, when everyone still called it Idlewild. The previous spring, the news had gone around that the woman was showing a pregnancy. "I hoped she'd be in the maternity ward with me," my mother said. "Then we heard she had a boy, before Garrett was born. I missed her by a few weeks."

Maybe I inherited my archival instincts from my mother, who proceeded to give an account of Mrs. Webster at the airport in 1962 that was as precise as any Accession Register. I can picture it as if I were floating there beside them: my mother, seated in the smoky lounge, waiting for my father to tire of watching the airplanes take off and land outside, and—from among the clusters of businessmen murmuring over glasses of scotch and beer—an Asian woman materializing out of the cigarette haze, accompanied by a nanny in uniform. The nanny, a redhead, was holding what my mother could only assume was a baby wrapped in a blanket, a parcel nearly identical to Garrett, in her lap.

Immediately, the possibility occurred to her. But this was New York City, with a substantial Asian population, versus Burring Port's near-total void. (Note that the racial data from the U.S. Census of 2010 show only a slight change in the makeup of Burring Port, CT, after more than forty years: 95.16% White, 2.43% Asian, 1.13% African American, 0.47% Native American, and 0.81% from two or more races.) All uncertainty dissolved a short time later, however, at the sight of Betty and Stewart Cutler, the professionally inquisitive proprietors of the pharmacy in Burring Port, stopping to greet the Asian woman on their way into the lounge.

My mother had imagined Mrs. Webster would have red-lacquered lips and be costumed in a skin-tight dress splashed with plum blossoms, or perhaps a dragon phoenix, but what she observed was even more exquisite. The woman was turned out in Yves Saint Laurent—the designer's first collection since leaving Dior. My mother aimed her baby son's eyes to behold what she had admired in magazines: the drop-waist dress in pale gray, its skirt flaring softly like a tulip. The woman's dark hair was tucked loosely into a turban, and draped over narrow shoulders, the un-mistakable coat of ornamented silk brocade.

Then the turban whipped around, and all at once Mrs. Webster was speeding toward my mother.

She stopped abruptly before the plate-glass windows a few feet away. At such close range, my mother was free to admire the fawn-colored gloves bunched elegantly around the woman's tiny wrists. Her gaze followed the gloved hands to a purse, then to a camera, then out the window. There, across a wet stretch of pavement, my mother was astonished to see a set of monumen-tal wings poised for flight: the roof of Eero Saarinen's new TWA terminal, its soaring curves hard against the flat winter sky. She traced the lines with her eyes.

"It looks like . . . a concrete dove," my mother said, reenacting the scene for us at the dining room table.

She let her face go blank and mumbled the words, then showed us how startled she'd been when they were overheard. For Mrs. Webster had turned to her and, as if the two had been conversing about that extraordinary building for hours, said in a tense Eng-lish accent, "But the architect—the one who created it—didn't live to see it."

My mother regretted the fact that she didn't get to say another word, for, before she knew it, Mrs. Webster was sliding to the floor with her camera. She'd thrown her coat down and was fol-lowing with her body, twisting to the floor like an apple peel as she shot the building from increasingly lower angles.

Emerson might have become fixated on the architecture of the period then and there. I imagined his infant eyes following her antics with fascination, immobilized on the nanny's lap as his mother fell into a delirious trance. Even when the buildings that were so pristine in Emerson's photos would grow old and dated, when the concrete would be stained and the joints would leak, they would always be a vision of the new, a promise for the fu-ture. And his mother would always be present there.

"The mood was primal," my mother went on. "Without that coat covering her, it was shocking." She held her hand to her chest. "All bones. So thin."

She'd feared Mrs. Webster would crawl on her belly across the floor, until the nanny intervened with a few words. Back in her seat, Mrs. Webster planted her elbows on her knees to form a tripod and continued to shoot until her film ran out: a barrage of snapping sounds that fanned across the lounge, suggesting to my mother that Mrs. Webster had caught her in some of the frames. She never saw Mrs. Webster again.

She looked at my father across the table. "It couldn't have been easy where she came from. There were hard conditions then, I think. People were hungry."

"They were trying to catch up with the developed world all at once," my father said. "It's only now that historians are uncovering the extent of it. Mao was setting impossible targets for grain, steel, and these people were being pushed. When you're overworked, when there are food shortages, malnutrition . . . It's the law of survival when you have a situation like that."

"She was a survivor, then," I concluded, until I remembered that she'd only lived to twenty-four. "For a while, anyway."

My mother said, "When she came here—they do say you binge after hunger—she had everything new. She brought him along in that way, Mr. Webster. Did you see the house?" she asked, suddenly curious.

"I wasn't inside for long."

This seemed to remind her of the meeting that was taking place there. "To lose your child—I hope you never know, Beth."

"Well, soup's on!" said my father, springing to his feet.

My mother stared somberly after him, exiting the room. "And your spouse. To lose both. I couldn't bear—"

"The thing is," my father called back, "you'd be surprised what you can handle when you have to."

• • •

On my return to Gray Hill, Laurel showed me through the main hall into the study to wait for Emerson. Instead of Wright's open floor plan and built-in furniture, I found myself surrounded by all the unsurprising things we found in one another's homes in Burring Port: nautical objects, colonial sofas and Impressionist paintings (except Mr. Webster's were real). It occurred to me that Wright would have torched the place in a second.

The air felt damp, despite the heat outside. One of the windows was cracked open an inch. I pulled it up and surveyed the room. It was well proportioned, arranged with a fireplace at one end and, along the other, rows of bookcases and a writing desk, where no one appeared to have written much lately, if ever. I stood at the window listening to the rumble of thunder outside, followed by the tinkling of bells—or was it Laurel putting away the crystal with a heavy hand? I thought I heard weeping in the hallway, then I was sure it was the sound of wind chimes in the yard.

From what I could tell, the storm wasn't coming from the Sound, but inland, from the north. I guessed that I might have time to stretch my legs, as Emerson suggested, before the grounds flooded with rain. At the front door, Laurel walked past carrying a vacuum cleaner. I waved hesitantly.

"Where are you going?" she inquired.

"I'm not sure, actually. Which way would you go for a short walk?"

She stood beside me at the open door and swung her weather-vane arm to indicate a route through the woods in the general direction of the Sound. I tied my sweater around my waist and set out, following the driving course past the stables, then cutting inland through a grove of pines, where there appeared to be a roughly made hiking trail.

The narrow path nearly disappeared at some points—the work of some careworn Pilgrims maybe, whose buckled shoes had once scraped the earth as heavily as my sneakers did now. As I walked, I imagined the conversation that had been going on be-

tween Emerson and his father, in parallel to my own. A wave of
anxiety swelled in my gut when I considered what I had been trying not to think about since Emerson limped down the corridor a
few hours earlier: Was everything about to change?

I climbed a gently sloping hill, like an Indian burial mound,
wondering as I went if all of our daily routines would be dis-
rupted by whatever was being discussed or decided between Emerson and his father. I conceded that I had become protective, too.
Not only of Emerson, but of all the intricately calibrated details
of his care.

At the top of the knoll I found that I couldn't walk any farther
on my path. The way was blocked by a pile of rocks from some
crumbling walls that, on closer inspection, looked almost art-
fully arranged. The sensory flavor of the place was familiar, and I
looked around, possessed suddenly by the idea that the rubble at
my feet was the remains of the same stone wall I had seen Emerson standing on when we were children, sipping his drink through
a straw. But that wall had been near Camel Rock, much farther
down on the road.

Disoriented, I sat on a piece of wall that was still standing. The
rain was suspended in visible sheets a few miles off. Above me, a
gust tipped the highest branches of the trees. An ash-gray wave
hung over it all like a question: *Would he replace me?* The question trickled into a gathering stream of other, more troubling
questions: Would Mr. Webster move into Emerson's guest room?
Would I be asked to move back to London Terrace, relieved of
my duties, while someone else took over?

I hurried down the hill and back to the house, unable to out-
run the truth that my father had pointed out: I had no plan. The
thought of being replaced consumed my vigil in the study, until
Emerson shuffled in to tell me he was ready to leave. I looked
past him, expecting to see Mr. Webster entering behind him, but
Emerson was alone. He stood by the windows and watched the

storm hang over the woods, his eyes now partially shaded by his baseball cap.

"It's going to be impressive," he said quietly.

Heat lightning popped in soft explosions behind the trees, but still there was no rain.

"How are you doing?"

"He's traveling all summer, first to someplace called Hainan Island. Then to Taipei, I forget why."

It took a moment for me to absorb the meaning of his words.

"Did you ask him about postponing it?"

"Actually, I don't think the storm's coming any closer. It's going straight east. Let's get out of here."

"What about the window?"

"Leave it."

I gathered my things. On the way out, I thought I heard someone whistling in the yard.

Beth, hello, it's Hélène Moreau. I've extended my stay in New York to take care of some business. I would love to see you again. To meet for lunch . . . if you're available . . . Thank you.

I found her second message on the answering machine in Emerson's office later that evening, after he had gone to sleep. This time she sounded much more composed. It was the last thing I expected: an invitation from her. And one that sounded vaguely social.

I lay awake that night with fireworks in my stomach, folding and unfolding a prescription for ulcer medication between my fingers. The pain in my gut was always there, sometimes dull, never less than dull, alternating on a daily basis between bruised and burning. *You're having sympathy pains in your stomach,* my mother diagnosed at lunch that afternoon. My doctor was confident it was an ulcer. *You're under stress. Your ulcer is mimicking his condition.*

My place at Emerson's side seemed assured after the visit to Connecticut, but while my body may have been struggling to cope with the stresses of the situation, until then I hadn't fully acknowledged the reality of the decisions and unknowns I would be facing with him as his health continued to decline. Awake in the dark, I thought of Hélène Moreau on 44th Street, high above the nightly party in the lobby and the steam funneling out from the underground vents of Times Square. I imagined a life like hers—living in hotels, where there was no reason to pretend you were there for any more than a temporary stay. She was outside the world of nurses and blood transfusions, just as I'd been on the nights I'd spent at the Royalton myself a few years earlier. From the archive in my mind I retrieved one, when I'd ended up in the lobby with a Swiss man who'd invited me to play chess with him at one of the gaming tables, and who'd accomplished each move with the aid of improbably large biceps. It was one night, but in a way it was all the nights I spent with men, even the ones I halfheartedly went on to see for any length of time: secret adventures and their attendant artifacts—matchbooks, cocktail stirrers, complimentary pencils—all filed away in boxes. At one point the chess player had made the inevitable move to the elevator. The door of his room clicked shut and the cool air filled with the wonderland smell of white musk . . .

Uncluttered now of Emerson's recent affairs, my mind roamed with pleasure over the memory of the smudged pale shapes of the man's body reflected next to mine in the polished wooden frame around the bed—the warmth of his skin and the illusion of our togetherness there among the Surrealist postcards, the horns, holes and headless cones . . . a night of blissful escape as curious as the hotel itself.

And now Hélène Moreau had stationed herself there in that curious wonderland, offering a different sort of escape. When I returned her call the next morning, I made sure to do it while

Emerson was asleep. I told myself I could use a few hours away while I still had the chance to take them, and I would find out for Emerson why she wanted the old car.

He had said nothing more about it. But even in silence there is a contract, an agreement between parties. And I understood that such contracts were mine to record and keep. I was in danger of violating my duty to him simply by letting Hélène Moreau think I didn't recognize her barefaced attempt to take me into her confidence. She was interested in acquiring something that belonged to my employer, and he'd told her he did not want to sell it. Still, when she repeated her invitation to lunch, I accepted without hesitation.

7

I T WAS A WARM AFTERNOON in early July when I met Hélène
in Bryant Park, behind the Public Library, a few blocks south
of her hotel. I tried to remember when I had last gone out for
any length of time without Emerson, but I could not think of
one. Putting on my clothes I felt self-conscious, as if I were heading out for a date with fish on my breath.

Whether Emerson sensed that I was up to something, or perhaps because of some less complicated fear, he was reluctant for
me to leave. Fortunately, Zandra was scheduled that day, and she
amused him. I found her in his room with her dreadlocks pushed
over one shoulder, hooking up his nutrition pack.

"Just meeting someone for a late lunch," I told her, enjoying
the casualness of the phrase, the impression it might have given
her that I had a life beyond the walls of our minimalist sick bay. I
knew Emerson would never ask me where I was going because he
loathed being asked such questions himself. I hoped this simple
explanation would put him at ease. "I'll be back in a few hours. I
don't want to have too much fun without you."

"Go ahead," he urged defiantly. "I have fun without you all
the time. I'm going to drink and smoke with Zandra while you're
gone."

"You do that with Brian, not with me," Zandra countered in
mock protest.

"I feel like I've always got an IV going into me," he complained as she zipped up his backpack. "Eight hours for this nutrition bag, forty-five minutes a day for the antibiotic, one hour twice a day for something I can't remember . . ."

"I remember for you," she assured him. "You're covered."

He stared at me in the doorway.

"It may be hard for you to believe, Zandra, but I used to be a very active person."

At Bryant Park, I was the first to arrive at the statue of Gertrude Stein, where Hélène had suggested we meet. I had walked as far as my own apartment in Chelsea to pick up my mail, then hailed a taxi to get to 40th Street on time. Hélène had no more than four blocks to walk, but apparently she was less concerned about punctuality. I sat on the bench next to Gertrude's plinth to wait.

My head felt heavy. Had I nodded off during the short taxi ride? A microsleep? Maybe. For weeks I had been sleeping in two-hour increments. The night nurses were supposed to make that unnecessary, but I couldn't forget that there were essentially strangers in the loft with us every night. Like a new mother, I always heard Emerson when he woke up, and I usually checked to see if there was anything I could do. I was surprised at how often there was. In the months of our growing intimacy, there was no time to think, only to plunge in where a hand was needed. The home healthcare workers taught me how to bolus his morphine pump (Emerson called it a turbo-boost) and prep the syringes to administer meds into the single port in his arm; they showed me which cleaning solutions to use on the floor or the rug when he overshot his portable urinal. From Tisa, who was as small as Emerson and me, I learned a technique for changing his soiled sheets without moving him out of the bed. In between, I dozed off in the guest room only if I had taken a self-prescribed antihistamine, which induced something that felt like sleep at first but turned out to be thick and unnatural by the middle of the night.

On the gravel by my feet was a squashed packet of ketchup, its comet tail of red ooze blackening like blood in the sun. I raised my eyes to study the face of the writer instead. The likeness of Stein was mounted on a marble pedestal with the dates 1874–1946 etched into its shiny surface in the manner of a tombstone. In bronze, as reportedly in life, she was a small mountain of a woman; the narrow belt at her waist barely contained her mass of flesh. She sat like a hunchback Buddha, except her hands were not open. Her gaze was downcast, contemplative. Resigned. Not joyful. The face of a thug or a statesman: a doughty, formidable face. At the base of the statue, a thin layer of water had pooled around her dress. Gertrude Stein had wet herself.

I looked up to see Hélène making her way toward me on the slate pathway. A caftan floated around her ankles, where the laces of her Roman-soldier style sandals were tied. The most curious thing: She was walking between the beds of ivy not with a sword, but with a tree branch balanced on her index finger, the thin end resting on her fingertip, the heavier end four feet in the air.

She was concentrating, keeping the leafy branch upright as she walked. With a flick of her finger, she sent it up into the air and landed it again, still upright, a moment later.

"You try," she said, pushing the branch toward me.

"Oh, no. I have no coordination."

"It does the coordination for you."

She wagged her finger. The branch swayed a few degrees, then balanced again like a butterfly on a leaf.

Reluctantly, I took the branch from her and let the thin tip find a resting place on my index finger. As substantial as the other end was, high in the air, I could barely feel any weight as I set off gingerly over the paving stones. A light pressure rolled around on my fingertip, but the branch remained vertical.

"What's the trick?" I called over my shoulder.

"None! Nature."

I tried running. The branch remained upright with even less effort. Then I took a corner too fast, and it flew off onto the paving stones.

When I bent to pick it up I found myself laughing. I felt light. I felt nothing. No glass walls. No thoughts. A strange sensation then—when I remembered Emerson and everything else.

I walked back to where Hélène was sitting, cross-legged, mimicking Stein's posture. She looked insulted when I offered her the stick back. "It's for you!"

I leaned it against the plinth and sat down next to her. A patch of sunshine was burnishing Gertrude's shoulder, making it glow.

"To me, it's a sad face," Hélène said.

I nodded. "Or it goes sad, anyway, when you stare at it."

"I hate that her eyes are empty," Hélène said. "The sculptor has made her like a blind person, of all things. I do enjoy sitting with this statue, though. In the flesh, I don't know if I would have enjoyed the woman's company."

I tried to picture her together with Stein, an artist whose experiments with words had been an attempt to express a continuous present. From what I recalled, the effect she sought was outside of time and sense, outside of the causal relationships between words—or even between moments. It was ironic: The woman for whom the memorial was erected had no need for memory. Perhaps that was why she looked so sad.

When there is no sense, no causality, there is only the present, only presence. It was how I had experienced death. It was how I had experienced speed. There were no memories and no need for them. There was only the moment, the balancing of the stick. But I didn't suppose that memory was something Hélène was willing to forsake—not when she had traveled halfway around the world to find an old car.

"Why don't we have lunch at the hotel?" she suggested.

I stood behind her in the dark hallway as she worked to fit an odd metal key into the door of Penthouse B. Inside, the space was filled with a perfume I thought I recognized; a heavy, old-fashioned scent. I tried to identify the amber note, but I was distracted by the unsettling feeling that I was smelling someone specific. My elementary school art teacher?

"Would you like some coffee with lunch?" Hélène asked with a junkie's glow as she prepared to call room service.

"Maybe some herbal tea. I have an ulcer."

Hélène Moreau was a person who consumed coffee continuously—a substance I had to avoid for the sake of my stomach lining. This put me at a disadvantage in following her patter through the meal as she praised the state of New York and the naked beauty of the George Washington Bridge, going on to recount her aesthetic conversion to the work of Thomas Cole and his fellow painters of the Hudson River School.

"I see that the pyramid in *The Architect's Dream* foreshadows Cole's own death," she observed. "The man is alone there, gazing at the glories of the past. He made that painting for a patron, but compositionally, the pyramid resembles more and more a mountain to me. He died in his own home, did you know this? Overlooking the Catskill Mountains."

I knew the painting she meant, and it reminded me of one of Emerson's photographs of a Case Study House in Los Angeles: a wistful, solitary man surveying an idealized world that stretched past the horizon. I almost mentioned this, but if she was trying to get me onto the subject of Emerson's collections, or death, or dying at home, it would not work. I surveyed the airy landscape of Penthouse B more closely. A slate fireplace occupied one wall, but in place of wood smoke the room was filled with that musky, familiar smell—turpentine? Draped across the curved metal back of a chaise longue was a chambray shirt splattered with paint, its arms twisted into tiny pleats. A row of canvases had accumulated outside on the covered balcony, but it was difficult to tell much about them from a distance.

"Are those paintings of the Italian countryside?" I asked, recalling the one I'd seen on her easel the last time.

Her face brightened. "Just one of them is Italy. But they do have something in common. They all depict *clotheslines,* as you say in America. Some people do not understand this . . ."

Her voice grew frail and then trailed off. I could see she was sensitive about them.

"My career is not what it once was," she admitted. "The critics like to remind me: My time in the spotlight was prolific, but it was brief."

She stood and picked through a pink suitcase, open like a clamshell on the floor. When she straightened again she was holding an armful of small leather-covered books. Her right hip swung higher than her left as she carried them back, I noticed, now that I wasn't distracted by the stick. The spine will show it if you have carried a heavy weight for a long time. Her gait reminded me of Emerson's, who sometimes gave the impression of a cowboy slinging a gun.

"I could show you some little drawings I did?" she offered. "I was maybe not more than nine or ten years old."

"I'd like to see them."

She sat beside me with the sketchbooks and turned the pages, each one bruised with purplish lines of fading India ink, lines that swooped and curved—crude renderings of sheets blowing in the wind.

"These were 1941, '42," she explained, opening another sketchbook to reveal pencil drawings of shirts hanging upside down, aprons dangling by their strings. "For me, the laundry was maybe a stand-in for people who were absent, the wind animating the empty forms. The sensation of movement already had something to do with my imagination. But at that time, the air was moving past—not me. That changed, being in a car."

I thought Emerson was wrong about her when he said she knew nothing about speed. I wondered if she could help me understand its power over him.

"What is it about speed?"

She closed her eyes. "It was new once. It isn't new anymore. It's not modern—in the best sense."

I could see she didn't understand my question, but I hoped the turn of our discussion would yield some information about her interest in the Beacon. This, I reminded myself, was my only excuse for being there. At the same time, I wondered about her badly disguised vulnerability. She had made a place for herself in the world—a place in art history that few women of her generation could claim—yet as I'd sensed the first time we met, there seemed to be a struggle taking place in her.

"Did you drive the cars yourself when you made the Speed Paintings?"

She cast a glance at a manhandled copy of a French newspaper by her side, then took a gulp of coffee. "At first, yes, I drove them. But as soon as I could, I worked with the race drivers. They understood that we needed to paint them at maximum speed. The truth was creation, yes, but some amount of destruction at the same time. This tension was meaningful to me."

The infusion of caffeine and the recollection of her early artistic aims seemed to reestablish some of her equilibrium. She went on: "When I was young, I was fascinated by the power and the beauty of those machines. Also by the filth—the grease and noise. The canvases put another physical form in place of the car body. Even to your eyes as a car is passing by, the wheels are ghosted by the force of their own speed. What do you see of a speeding car? What do you feel driving it? Speed is the only thing that exists then. But it doesn't exist. I wanted it to exist. To remain in existence."

"Do you still own any of them?"

"Only some of the later paintings." She cleared her throat. "I had quite a few of the early canvases. One day I couldn't look at them—I nearly destroyed them. Instead, I sent them to a museum outside of Copenhagen, where I lived many years ago."

I sensed my moment.

"Did you use the Beacon to make your paintings?"

At my question, her face contracted in a look of horror. She sat paralyzed for what seemed a full minute. Only her eyes moved —racing between my face and the newspaper by her side. Then her expression softened, and instead of answering, she stood: "Beth, would you like a drink?"

I could not say no. We made small talk in the elevator down to the lobby, where she led me behind a curved wall into a hidden bar—a round room with walls upholstered in pale blue velvet. It was an elegantly padded cell, filled with what could have been the amusements for a mythical seaside resort: Under our feet, black and white floor tiles formed a bull's-eye target for a giant's game of darts, and perched delicately on the tiles, as if waiting for a child to climb on for a ride, was a row of silver bar stools shaped like seahorses. Hélène leaned across them to collect two glasses from the bartender.

"This will taste fresh," she promised, passing one to me.

We took a seat at one of the glass tables along the curved banquette and Hélène lit a cigarette.

"I hope my question upstairs about the car didn't upset you," I said. "It seemed like a reasonable assumption."

She pushed her drink aside and leaned across the table. Lowering her voice, she asked, "Beth, is he going to sell me that car?"

Her directness caught me off-guard. I was as thrown by the bluntness of her question as she had appeared to be by mine. But even if I had wanted to answer, I was relieved to discover that I was saved by my own ignorance: Emerson had given me no sign of his intentions.

"He hasn't talked about it since we came to see you that day. Do you collect cars?" I asked, attempting to change the subject.

"Does he?"

"Not as far as I know. I mean, he keeps an everyday car garaged in the Village. That and the Beacon are the only cars he pays storage on."

"He can't drive it, from what I saw."

"He buys and sells things—I just organize them."

"Yes, and I understand you've had a great deal of success finding recipients for the objects in his collections."

So this was the expertise she'd referred to in her first phone message. "Those were all photographs," I explained. I tried to enjoin her with a smile. "Do you mind if I ask why you want the car?"

"It's normal that you would want to know this, I realize," she said, meeting my eyes evenly through the shield of pinkish-purple glass. "I would have liked to explain it to him myself, but I'm not comfortable discussing it."

"Is there something illegal about that car? Because I should tell him if there is."

"Not as far as my interests are concerned."

Her answer sounded too qualified to be reassuring.

"Beth, would you take me to look at it? Perhaps I might just see it one day, when it's . . . appropriate?"

"I don't know," I answered uneasily. "It would depend on the way his insurance policy is written."

"Oh, yes," she said gloomily. When she spoke again, her voice was full of forced lightness. "Never mind. We are here enjoying a drink! Tell me about yourself, Beth. I know you work with his collections, et cetera, but what do you do with your friends? Or" —she glanced at the bare fingers of my left hand—"a boyfriend?"

It was the kind of silly question I usually asked Mei. I could have excused myself to go back to work then, but other than Emerson, I had no one to talk with but medical workers, and most of the time we discussed his care. At least she was pretending to be interested in me.

"The last guy I was with was Oliver," I answered, draining my drink. "I ended it a while ago. It didn't mean anything."

"Nothing?"

I shook my head.

"How often do you see your friends?"

"Oh. Not very often. I'm busy with work. And they're busy themselves, working, having babies . . ."

"Maybe you need some balance, Beth."

"What we're doing requires concentration."

"Your shoulders look very pinched."

It was true. The many months of light massages from Mei had failed to help me in this regard. "Sometimes they won't go down," I said. "I have a lot going on with Emerson. He isn't going to need me forever, but he does right now."

Intentionally or not, I had given her an opening.

"Is he dying?"

The nakedness of her question took me by surprise, but I could not lie, when half the art world might have given her the correct answer. I nodded.

"Cancer?"

"Does it matter?"

I regretted the words when I saw how embarrassed she looked. Then I found myself nervously laughing, and this caused her to look even more uncomfortable.

"Is something funny?" she asked, wrinkling her flat nose.

"It's not funny," I said. "Really." I dropped my gaze to the floor.

I suppose I'd imagined us to be accomplices in our secret meeting. Or rather, I had cast her as a subtle operative, trying to woo me into helping her pry the car from Emerson. But I was alone in my deceit.

"I'm sorry," I said. "I'm so tired . . . It's just that we were at a newsstand a few weeks ago and a girl was staring at him. Really rude, just gawking. He stared back at her, straight-faced, and said, 'It's a Polynesian disease that affects the hips.'"

Hélène raised her glass in a toast and struggled to smile.

"It's not—it's something related to his mother," I said. "Something genetic."

She stared at me, blinking rapidly behind her pink shield.

"To be honest, I don't feel comfortable talking to you about him," I said. "He's my employer. We've always had a formal arrangement. I only moved in with him a few months ago so that, as you saw, I can escort him to his appointments and things."

She bowed her head.

"I don't know what he's planning to do with that car. He won't tell me. That's why you asked me here, isn't it?"

The game was up. I doubted I would get anything else out of her now.

"I'm sorry he's so sick," she said. "I was sick for almost ten years, when I was younger. Heartsick, really, but it had a physical effect. I lived here in New York for some of that time, and being here reminds me of it."

She asked the bartender for another round of drinks, blinking her eyes at a speed approaching that of hummingbird wings. I had seen some pictures of her in Emerson's art books, and as she fluttered her eyelids, her face morphed in front of me, flickering into the Kodachrome images of a young woman walking along the lakes in Copenhagen, surveying the swans in the distance. In every photo, the same disturbing flat smile, the same unconscious air of melancholy.

Now she aimed the disturbing smile at me. "Are you all right?"

"I get unbelievably tired, but then sometimes I get bursts of energy, like I imagine it is when you're taking care of a baby."

"Beth, are you stopping your own life?"

I laughed to myself at her question.

"No?" she asked.

"No. I'm not stopping my own life. Believe me."

"I respect the enormity of what he's going through," she said. "Though in my own belief system, death is not negative."

"Being dead isn't negative to me, either," I assured her. "But the process of *dying* is extremely negative to him right now. I have no problem with being dead, but that's different from dying —that series of events, whether they're violent or peaceful—"

"You sound so certain of this."

"My father likes to tell me that living is something you can manage, but if you're looking at it every day, you see that dying is also something you can manage and learn, if it isn't imposed on you violently or suddenly. If you're given the opportunity—Emerson, though, he's doing everything he can to avoid it. He's one of the most open-minded people I know, but not on this subject."

"Does he talk about it?"

"Sometimes. But mainly it's to convince himself that there's nothing he can believe in beyond this life."

"Others have made this observation before," she said, "but we have lost a healthy familiarity with death. You have to die of something."

Maybe it was because I had not let myself tell Emerson in the first place, or because we were now speaking so matter-of-factly about what he was going through. In any case, something made me answer her as abruptly as I did.

"I know that. I've already been dead."

Her brow furrowed. "What do you mean?"

"Just that. I died. Briefly. When I was little."

"Of what?"

"Of something, as you say."

She stared at me, waiting.

"Pneumonia. My lungs filled up. A priest at the hospital gave me last rites. Then someone named Dr. Forza—a resident—he resuscitated me."

"You were very lucky."

I felt bile running like lava in my throat. "No, I wasn't."

She looked confused. "What do you mean?"

"He had no right to do it."

"Who?"

"The doctor."

"Do what?"

"Resuscitate me."

"What are you talking about?"

The couple at the next table looked over and I lowered my voice. "I'm saying—I died. My story was done, and he changed the ending."

"You're joking, yes?"

"No."

She looked at me incredulously.

Probably because I had never been able to articulate the feeling, I was as unsure as she appeared to be about my words as they came out. "I'm not supposed to be here. I don't have a plot. Like you. Like other people." I paused to take a sip of my drink. "I've been squeezed in here . . . like someone with a broken nail who gets squeezed into a manicurist's appointment book. So it looks like I have a slot when I really don't. Meanwhile, I'm sitting here for a *long time,* waiting."

"But this is an absurd comparison—"

"To you."

She leaned forward and spoke more gently. "With Mr. Tang, you were maybe a little bit attracted to—well, I can see why you might be drawn to his situation. But at the same time, it must be very difficult for you to witness."

"No," I said, wanting to make myself clear. "Getting there is precious. It's an accomplishment, like graduating from school or getting married or having children. It's the ultimate accomplishment, but everyone loathes it."

"Of course, because of our survival instinct. It's only human."

The naturalness of her comment only reminded me of my own strangeness.

"Do you remember being dead?" she asked.

"A little."

"What was it like?"

"It was very different than this."

She said nothing for a few moments. She was staring at my forehead, her eyes lingering on the place where I had a birthmark of sorts: a path of purplish veins roughly in the shape of an *M*. The mark had begun to show by the time I was in kindergarten. It darkened when I got drunk, and disappeared under strenuous exercise. Most of the time I forgot it was there, except in college, when I cut my hair to cover it after my tutor Praveen started calling it my Scarlet *M*, an affection for high Modernism — and melancholy — being something that needed to be defended in the 1980s on a campus with a booming business school. I felt around self-consciously for the soft ridge of veins and pulled some strands of hair across to cover it.

"What if your story, in so many words, included being resuscitated? I think this is part of your plot."

"Maybe," I said, hoping I didn't sound too dismissive of her theory.

"Beth, you are an archivist. You save things. I would think you of all people would understand a doctor's impulse to save something extremely valuable. A child's life — anyone's, there, in front of you."

"Yes, I save things. I collect all kinds of souvenirs because they add up to a kind of story about myself. It's ballast. Like sandbags."

There were other things I could have said, but didn't. As committed as I was to my current profession, I knew storing wasn't living. Nor was I deceived about my temporary place in Manhattan's archival and collections-management community. Emerson's was a relatively contained (if jewel-quality) repository, and soon it would be emptied. But Emerson himself was another matter. He was even more fragile material.

"Have you told Mr. Tang about what happened to you?" she asked.

"No. Something stopped me."

"Oh?"

"Why would my story give him comfort? He keeps saying he doesn't believe anything survives beyond this lifetime."

"But wouldn't your experience help him to see that?"

"Maybe. Except I'm *here*."

"Oh yes."

"Anyway, he's not in a position where a resuscitation could give him the happy ending you think I got. His doctor told him that if he insists on being resuscitated now, he'd most likely be prolonging his life in an even more degraded state. As a vegetable, basically."

I realized too late that she had gotten me talking about Emerson again. But before I could change the subject, she did it for me.

"Beth, you seem shamefully ungrateful about being alive."

"Shamefully?" I asked, puzzled.

Rather than feeling cowed, as I had before in tentative attempts to talk about it with my parents or anyone else, I was emboldened.

"I got home. You don't know what it was like."

"No."

"I got pulled back here so a doctor could convince himself that he was stronger than something that was his enemy, not mine."

"Would you rather be dead?"

I took a gulp of my drink. Was this the second vodka tonic or the third? "For most of the past twenty-five years, yes—the answer would have been yes."

She leaned closer over the table. "Since all these years? But this is depression. This is serious, Beth."

"I don't know what you're talking about."

"You have a wish to die."

"A death wish? No. Not since I was a teenager. Look—I'm not killing myself. I'm here. I'm trying to make myself useful. Death was just—"

I stopped myself from saying *better*. To assign that value to death was to be perceived as devaluing life. It required a different mindset to see that this was not the case. How could I tell her otherwise? To have known something so complete and then to be expelled from it—it was like being forced out of a restricted archive that was heavily guarded, when you already knew it contained everything you needed. I couldn't access it—I had lost my privileges. I sensed this was why we weren't meant to remember it.

"I'm saying, what I feel inside is more like the death you're imagining."

She sighed and said something about young people and alienation.

I fell silent, and she must have sensed that I would not be drawn further. I panicked briefly, thinking I had failed to convince her. But then she shook her head and gave me a sympathetic smile. At last, I had gotten through.

"I can't question your experience. If you say this is how you feel . . ."

"I do. Or I did."

I glanced at my watch. I had stayed much later than planned. I was sweating with exertion and triumph as I gathered my things.

Hélène stood with me. "Beth, I have use of a car here in the city. Why don't we go for a drive up the Hudson one afternoon? Some fresh air?"

My heart sank as I became suspicious of her motives again. I didn't know how to answer her. I had not had so much to drink in a long time, and I was dangerously nearing my limit of clear judgment. The black-and-white-checkered floor was waving in front of me like a racing flag. "That sounds nice," I managed to say. "I don't know. Let me check my schedule with Emerson."

I tried to shake her hand firmly in goodbye, but the vodka-smeared expression on her face told me she was not going to tolerate defeat.

8

THE HOSPITAL JOHNNY was math-paper gray from being endlessly laundered, but Emerson approved of its softness and its faded starburst pattern. The new slippers given to patients in the blood unit were another story.

"Beth, please tell me they do not expect me to wear green foam slippers with happy faces on the toes."

I looked down to where he stood, beside his unlaced sneakers. "Your feet won't fit in them anyway. They're too puffed up today."

"But the floor is cold."

He stood on top of the foam and shuffled his way over to the transfusion bed, one of five arrayed around the room, ringed with curtains for privacy. At a central station, a nurse was indulging in discreet bites of lunch from an aluminum pie plate at her side.

"That smells incredible," I told her.

She waved her plastic fork in the direction of Broadway. "Takeout Ethiopian."

I sipped from my can of ginger ale, depressed to feel the liquid burning all the way down to my stomach, stoking the ulcerous flames there. Emerson hadn't been allowed to eat since midnight, and I expected him to be more interested in her food. But he was busy examining his transfusion bed, a mattress of black rubber covered with a sheet stamped MANHATTAN GENERAL HOSPITAL.

"It's not comfortable," he complained.

"You were fine last time."

"You've probably lost some body fat since your last transfusion," the nurse said.

She brought a portable scale to the side of his bed and helped Emerson swing his legs over and stand up.

"Eighty pounds," she announced.

Emerson snapped to attention. "Did you say I weigh ninety pounds?"

His voice was shaking. His body began to shake along with it as she helped him back down onto the bed.

"No. You weigh eighty pounds," she repeated, glancing over sadly at me.

He sat forward. "That's not good. That can't be right. I want to do it again."

The nurse helped him back onto the scale. I leaned over to check for myself.

"Can you see the number?" the nurse asked.

He crashed back onto the bed and proceeded to stare in silence at a neutral point a few yards away, seeming to rifle through his brain for a weapon to hammer down the reality of the number.

"I'll put some blankets under you for padding," offered the nurse.

His hospital bracelet was little more than a plastic credit card embossed with data. I checked where it listed the attending physician for the name Gary Hertz, and showed Emerson.

He perked up enough to give me an appreciative smirk.

"Excuse me, who is Dr. Hertz?" I asked the nurse.

"Never heard of him," she said, tucking a blanket around Emerson's legs.

"That's disturbing," said Emerson.

"That name is always on his bracelet," I said. "Every time we come in here. But that isn't his doctor. His doctor is Carol Albas."

"Dr. Hertz is the head of the unit," said a resident taking the blood pressure of a woman in the next bed. "They use his name on everything."

"You realize it's a terrible pun?" Emerson asked.

The resident frowned. "It's the man's name."

Outside, the buildings of the Upper West Side stood like dark cutouts against the flannel-gray sky. Every television in the unit was tuned to the coverage of what Emerson called "the Death Watch" for a celebrated socialite going on across town. According to the news reports, the woman's illness was more advanced than Emerson's, and a crowd was keeping vigil on the streets below her apartment on Fifth Avenue.

Emerson was transfixed, his interest no doubt colored by one fact Dr. Albas had made clear to him: By continuing to insist on transfusions, he was also increasing his own pain. But since the new blood was prolonging his life, she could not refuse him. The outcome was inevitable; the choice of how to get there was his.

Emerson shifted his hips and winced.

"Are you all right?" I asked him. "Zandra mentioned that you were asking for me last night."

"Yes. You were out, apparently."

In the fluorescent light of the unit his eyeglasses shone eerily at me, so fine, almost invisible, the frame just a glint of silver around his small face. The fragility of his body made everything else seem so fragile.

I pulled my chair closer to the transfusion bed.

"What's going on?"

"I've been thinking about what to do with that car. The one Hélène Moreau wants."

"The Beacon?"

It was eerily coincidental that he was prepared to reveal his plans now, after being so close-mouthed on the subject. I could not suppress my mild paranoia: Was he trying to guess where I had been the previous evening?

"When I asked you about it before, you wouldn't say," I reminded him, feigning indifference. "So what are you going to do with it?"

"It's personal."

"Oh."

I knew better than to try to drag it out of him, but his tricks and secrecy could be infuriating.

"So—what did you want to talk to me about, if it's not that?"

His misery increased visibly as he remembered. He pulled open the gap in the front of his johnny to expose the tube leading to his nutrition pack.

"Dr. Albas called yesterday while you were out. I was kind of woozy, but . . . she *definitely* said that pretty soon she's not going to give me this stuff anymore. She said I can't have my food, Beth!" His voice began to tremble as more of the conversation came back to him. "You have to talk to someone—another doctor—"

"She's not holding out on you," I said, gently closing his gown. "She explained to us—remember?—at some point your system won't be able to handle the liquid food anymore, just like right now it can't digest real food. It's not that she doesn't want you to have it."

"But—then what?" He pulled miserably on the tube.

"Be careful!" I pushed his hands away. "You still need it now."

He pushed back at me in frustration, then dropped his hands onto the bed. He sat quietly after that, collecting his thoughts as the first bag of blood drained into him. When he spoke again, he sounded as matter-of-fact as if we'd just been discussing the weather.

"Beth, did you know they're developing other things for cars to run on, besides gasoline?"

"Cars? I guess. Isn't there one that runs on electricity?"

"Yes, but that idea is really old—they were doing electric a hundred years ago. They're looking at all kinds of other things now . . . developing things." He frowned at the tubes for blood and food running into him. "Engines get replaced, reconditioned, moved between cars. But people are imagining them now in completely new ways. Completely different." He plucked at the feeding tube. "I wish I could run on something else."

"I wish you could, too."

"I feel like I didn't get to do anything with my life."

I pulled the curtain around his bed.

"You've barely turned thirty. Who has?"

"A lot of people. Alexander the Great."

"Violence and conquest?"

He rolled his eyes. "Which spread classical Greek ideals across the known world. Valuable ideas about city planning, and art, and education, all before he—Omega—at thirty-three."

"So, just a minor act to follow."

He raised his hands and shrugged.

"What do you want to do?" I asked.

"Incredible things! There's so much . . . but I'm leaving."

"What if what you're doing now is one of the things you're here to do?"

He hung his head. "That doesn't seem fair."

I didn't know how to answer him.

I could not say I envied his privileged upbringing per se; it was the ease of being he'd always seemed to possess. He had a slot firmly booked on life's appointment calendar—a sense of what he might achieve—yet he was being forced to leave and I wasn't. The slots were all confused. It made no sense to me either.

A pinkish color came back into his skin on the second pack of blood. On the third, he flushed beautifully with sweat and his eyes grew clear and wide open—it was a remarkable transformation, as long as they kept the blood pumping through. When the last bag was empty he slept for a while with his head propped against the bedrail. As he drifted off, his right hand came up to his chest and made a shaking motion, as if he were salting a plate of food.

I dozed in the chair next to him until the movements of the nurse woke me. Emerson was twitching. A foul smell from his fitted briefs cut the air.

"Urine slightly tinged with blood," the nurse reported.

He was bleeding somewhere internally, she said—most likely his stomach.

"Could you give us a few minutes?"

In the entry hall of Emerson's loft stood a nurse I didn't recognize. Her ginger hair and fair complexion reminded me of an English princess, but there was a brittleness in her bearing, an aloofness that was not royal but merely vocational. I assumed she was there to take the blood samples Dr. Albas had ordered. Instead, she reached into the leather folder under her arm and pulled out a piece of paper, a white sheet printed with bright red ink.

Visiting Nurse Association of New York City
— CONFIRMATION —
DO NOT RESUSCITATE ORDER (DNR)

ORDERS:
THIS PATIENT HAS AN UNREMITTING, INCURABLE
MORTAL ILLNESS; THE PATIENT AND FAMILY, OR
LEGAL GUARDIAN, AND PHYSICIAN AGREE THAT
CARDIOPULMONARY RESUSCITATION IS NOT TO BE
INITIATED.

"Could you give us a few minutes?" she asked again.

I stared at the paper until the lining of my mouth went dry and the husk of a single word fell from my lips.

"Okay."

Even as I left them alone in his bedroom, I could see Emerson was not going to give her an easy time. She spoke loudly, as she assured me she would, so I could monitor their conversation from the hallway.

"What a Do Not Resuscitate order does—a DNR—it's a document you sign," she began. "As your doctor has explained to you, we keep one copy on file, and we keep one here with you. If you're . . . moved . . . for any reason, it travels with you. And it says—in the event that you stop breathing or your heart stops —you *do not* want to be resuscitated."

Silence.

"What this means is, if you don't sign a DNR, medical teams *will* make an effort to resuscitate you. Do you understand?"

I could hear Emerson kicking his legs around on the bed, but he said nothing.

"Do you think you want to sign a DNR?"

There was no sound from the room. As I stepped forward to peek in, I was startled by Emerson's voice, booming through the loft. "You know, I used to be a very healthy, active person!"

To demonstrate his strength or his displeasure, or both, he lifted his arms and propelled himself to his feet in front of her. He didn't bother to pull the blanket around himself as he took aim at the portable urinal. From the doorway, I could see his naked hip-bones shaking.

"I'll give you some privacy," said the nurse.

She followed me to the kitchen, where one of the healthcare aides, Brian, was packing up sheets for the laundromat across the street.

"Do you want a cup of coffee or anything?" I asked her.

"Some water, please."

"Dr. Albas has had this conversation with him," I said. "He may still be processing things. Can you come back another day? He's probably tired."

Without answering, she asked me to direct her to the bathroom. When she returned, she collected her waiting glass of water without comment and carried it back to his bedroom.

From the hallway, I overheard her speaking more patiently to him. "Are you comfortable?" she asked. "Do you need anything?"

"I'm fine," he insisted.

"As I was saying," she began again, "a Do Not Resuscitate order is a document you sign. It's also called a DNR . . ."

She was a woman with a job to do. She repeated her script exactly, like a telemarketer who had been coached by a lawyer. He listened wordlessly until she arrived once more at the critical question.

"Do you want to sign a DNR, Emerson?"

I could hear the cars and taxis rattling down Bleecker Street. A mundane accompaniment to a mortal decision. It did not escape me that, if I'd had that document, I would have been free. Yet he would rather do anything than face that piece of paper. Once again the slots made no sense.

"Emerson?" asked the nurse.

"I *don't not* want that," he answered miserably.

I found a carbon copy of the form, signed with his scratch marks, taped to the wall in his bedroom after she left. He was still propped on the bed pillows, but I wasn't sure if he was awake until he spoke:

"She's a death nurse."

"Did you make up that term?"

"No, she shook my hand and said, 'Hi, I'm a death nurse.'"

I was relieved to hear his sarcasm.

"What did she want?"

"I don't know."

I sat on his bed. "Did she tell you the same things Dr. Albas said, about the DNR?"

"Yes."

"And did you tell her you knew all that?"

"No." He stared up at me, his face etched with self-doubt. "Beth, would you have signed it?"

For a few minutes, I couldn't answer. I didn't know what to say or how to explain myself to him. During our conversations in recent weeks I'd had to silently acknowledge that, despite my own high regard for the state of being dead, the only death I knew was my own. The question entered my mind: What if the experience of death was fundamentally the way each person required it to be? In essence, this was possible—no more impossible than any other belief; in fact, it was a tenet of some belief systems and corresponded with the very existence of so many.

"What if there's something you want on the other side?" I suggested to him.

He gave me a blank look. "And what would that be?"

"Well, you talked about going to a cave that day, at Golden Hands. Or—I don't know. If your afterlife fulfilled your highest desire, what would that be?"

He looked at me now with curiosity, but this time he did not hesitate with his answer:

"Staying alive for another fifty years."

People named their heaven all the time. There was no reason to doubt them, no reason to assume that the afterlife they anticipated did not materialize just as they believed it would. There was a change in state, that much was beyond question. After that? Perhaps those who expected to sleep for eternity would continue to sleep, and Emerson had always counted himself among them. But now he had named a different heaven, as paradoxical-sounding as it was. His version of heaven was what had happened to me: I had survived death. He could have his heaven, I realized—another fifty years on earth, maybe more—by taking over my life.

I became distracted with this thought, exciting and slightly frightening as it was, like stepping into the racecar with him. But in any belief system there was a point when everything came down to faith, and this was what he lacked. He had long ago dismissed the pronouncements and traditions of the major religions as legends. Beyond this, he professed no curiosity about less mainstream beliefs concerning the afterlife—what he called "pseudo–science fiction." As he'd insisted in our previous conversations, his faith encompassed nothing beyond his last breath. Still, faced with his dejected expression, I couldn't help wishing he would consider an expanded view of his own situation.

"What if some part of you wasn't going to be part of your death?"

"What do you mean?"

Before I could lose my nerve, I began to tell him about that night at the hospital with Dr. Forza in 1969, describing the events around my resuscitation in more detail than I had to Hélène Moreau, but omitting the complications I had experienced, for I had no desire to upset him.

He listened attentively, like a child being told a ghost story, without a sound, his hands resting on the blanket over his legs. Encouraged by his interest, I went on to explain what had happened as best I could.

"And now I'm here. Some—something—must exist in both states," I concluded, "or there would have been nothing for them to bring back. Anyway, that's how it was for me. You can choose whatever metaphor you want."

He considered this. "I can choose my own afterlife?"

"What if you could?"

Instead of answering, he asked me to turn on the television, where the Death Watch continued on all the network channels. He pulled his knees up to his chest and turned away. "I hate the way the news isn't real hard news anymore," he said.

How many times had I read or heard about people passing over the threshold and then coming back? How many dramatic reenactments had I suffered through on TV? With each overlit, Vase-line-smeared account came a renewed frustration, a sadness at the way those shabby dramatizations turned death into a cliché.

Maybe because I have the soul of an archivist, my experience of death was echoed in the sensations I came to feel whenever I entered a magnificent museum or library. In the silence, the immense silence of those vaults, there was not a nothingness but an encompassing orderliness—a clean, systematic transfer of data, the movement from artifact to archive. And within the vast halls of that ancient, etheric library resided the great metaphysical archive, the record of every thought, action and utterance impressed upon the ether. The immortal being of every human being. It was more than complete. It was the absence of any lack. In this perfection, the experience of peace was total. I cannot say what my feelings were, for I had no sense of myself as a separate being. There was nothing to fear, no plot to fulfill, no sense of a single record or piece of information missing. Everything that could ever be needed or desired was present.

Except.

Dr. Forza stepped up to the table.

Then all that beauty was gone, and I was caught between two metal rails, drowning in a transparent plastic tent filled with oxygen. My lungs burned for air, but the body's reflex was harsh, ratcheting itself up from the hospital bed to draw it into my chest. It was this part that I had not described to Emerson or Hélène Moreau. It was this part I did not enjoy revisiting.

I swam up from the depths to swallow a burning gulp of oxygen like seawater, face to my knees, disoriented by a searing bolt of pain, then crashed back down.

That was my first new breath. Each breath was like that: Stunned, confused, I ratcheted up, drowned, burned. For eight, then twelve, then fifteen hours . . .

It went on for three days, a battle between air and water in my lungs that sent me in and out of consciousness as bruises began to spread on the back of my arms and my abdomen continued to contract, wrenching me up and down in the bed like a wind-up toy in obedience to the body's command to breathe at any cost.

Life was not simple for me after Dr. Forza's moment. There was a cord for birth and one for death, but mine was not cut. In that plastic tent of torture, my death cord was unfurled, stretched, considered, but I remained attached to both sides. Dangling. Dead, then undead. In the doorway, bouncing back and forth from one side to the other. It was not a method of dying I would choose for myself again. I only know that what I experienced when I crossed the threshold was sublime.

9

Accession Number: BC 1996.3

The object is one of several photocopied pages, folded and stored inside the front cover of Emerson's notebook (ref. BC 1996.1).

ENG-300 Final Exam
Prof. Randall J. P. Miller
May 4, 1983

Compose a 1,000-word essay comparing the following two texts:

1) From *The Book of Disquiet* by Fernando Pessoa (b. Portugal, 1888–1935), translated from the Portuguese:

Anyone who lives as I do does not die: he just finishes, wilts, devegetates. The place where I stood remains without his being there, the street he walked along remains without his being seen there, the house he lived in is inhabited by a not-him. . . . let's call it nothingness. . . .

2) From *June 30th, June 30th* by Richard Brautigan (b. United States, 1935–1984):

Unrequited Love

. . .

"Everything's ending," Emerson announced.

He was sitting cross-legged on his bed, shredding pages from his notebook. He withdrew a printed sheet that had been stored inside the front cover—an assignment to analyze two pieces of text—and handed it to me.

"Read it, please."

He cocked his head and listened with evident satisfaction while I recited the morbid passages. Then, instead of ripping it up, he tucked it back into the notebook and moved on to shredding a piece of fabric—what looked to have once been a pair of boxer shorts.

"What are you doing?"

"I don't know." He tore the patterned fabric into strips and added them to the snowy pile on his blanket. "Here's my problem, Beth, with your ideas about an afterlife and surviving death, all these meta-narratives of liberation: Why is this happening to me?"

"It sounds like you're judging it as bad. If you don't label things as good or bad, then they just are."

I felt like a hypocrite even as I said it to his emaciated face, but somehow I believed it.

"I see."

He tore the fabric apart with quick snaps of his wrists, the way my father ripped model airplane parts from their frames.

"That's easy for you to say," he went on, his voice full of undisguised cattiness. "Your death was *temporary*."

"It had some lasting effects."

I watched him shredding the fabric. "Whose boxer shorts are those? They look like they've seen better days."

"No one's. Anymore." He ran his fingers through the shreds, then idly tossed a handful up over the bed. "Can you get rid of all this, please?"

I was carrying off the offending scraps when he asked, "What do you mean, 'It had some lasting effects'?"

I was unsure whether I should go further and tell him the feelings I had entrusted to Hélène Moreau. In the end she had accepted their validity. Now that I was sober, I wanted to speak with her again, to better work out my position on things. But there was no way to anticipate how Emerson might react.

"It's probably not going to make sense," I began tentatively.

"Try me."

"The thing is, I'm here. Except I don't feel like I'm supposed to be here."

"You're lucky to be alive!"

What was the point of trying to make him understand? How could he know how strange it was, when he had always been so sure of himself?

"Like I said, it's hard to explain."

My attempt to backpedal came too late. His reaction was as hostile as a slap.

"I want to do so many things," he wailed, "and I can't, because . . . You see me here"—he gestured to the bed, the portable urinal—"And you, you can do everything, and you—"

I hung my head.

"You're a freak!" he yelled.

"I know."

I had to choose my words carefully. He was a very sick man, struggling with an unknown that was at least partially known to me. I couldn't expect him to relate. At the same time, I had no way to justify myself to him. To end the discussion, I brought up one aspect of the situation that I hoped he could sympathize with.

"There's something you're not considering."

He scowled at me. "What?"

"I have to go through the dying part again."

His tone was much gentler when he asked, "Was it painful?"

"I'm not going to get into that."

"So it was." He seemed to regard me with more respect.

"I didn't say that," I protested. "I'm not getting into that with you. Everything isn't a contest, Emerson. Those were different circumstances. Your doctor is trying to help you make choices so you don't have to think about that."

I paused, wary of upsetting him, but he was nodding at me encouragingly.

I went on: "What I'm saying is, no one wants to die—people will do *anything* they can to avoid it. So, can you see how I don't feel lucky to have to do it twice?"

"I wouldn't do this again."

"Well—I will. I have no choice."

"I see."

The reality of the situation seemed to carry some weight with him. I was about to change the subject when he huffed, "But your alternative is being dead!"

"Yes, except I keep trying to tell you—dying is the challenge, not being dead. I didn't have a problem with where I was. That doctor did."

"But a doctor has a sacred duty—"

"To first do no harm. That might not mean resuscitating. That's why that nurse came to talk to you the other day. You saw the truth of this yourself, and you decided the same thing."

He gazed blankly at the DNR taped to his bedroom wall. "But you're here now."

"In a way."

"What about your policy about not judging things as good or bad?"

"Yes, so by my own policy, *I just am.*"

He shrugged and looked at me unhappily. I sensed he was still angry when he said, "You know, Beth, some people suck at saying goodbye. I'm probably going to be one of them."

I found Hélène Moreau cleaning paintbrushes at her desk in Penthouse B—one paintbrush short, I was well aware, courtesy of Emerson's theft. The pettiness of his crime made me feel all the more awkward watching her. I suspected she'd invited me there again because she continued to see me as a facilitator in her campaign for the Beacon, but her attention steadied me, whatever the motive. I'd never felt comfortable talking about my death, and our last conversation had been like smelling salts —beneficial, if somewhat unpleasant. She also struck me as earnest, however superficial her quest seemed, and while Emerson may have had the right to refuse her his property, he had stolen something from her.

She gripped a bunch of the newly cleaned brushes in her fist and ran them over a newspaper to blot them, leaving traces of dark, winding lines like tire tracks on a pavement. "How is Mr. Tang?"

I shook my head, mesmerized by the patterns on the newsprint. "His meds are jacked so high that he's been sleeping a lot. That's why I was able to come up here."

"What about your ulcer, Beth? The last time you were here . . ."

I walked out onto her balcony. There were no paintings to look at, just a flourish of pigeon droppings on the stone balustrade. Below us, a fresh Manhattan evening was in progress. An unbroken line of taxis shook in the summer heat, waiting to move east on 44th Street.

She joined me under the stone archway, carrying one of the paintbrushes and a glass of water. I accepted the glass from her.

"Beth, how are you feeling?"

"I came back because I wanted to ask you—I've been thinking about what you said the last time I was here, about my success finding homes for the things in his collections. I wish you would tell me why this car means so much to you. It would be—"

"It's embarrassing, Beth."

"All right. Except, I'm trying to do you a favor. Because he mentioned the car again the other day, and your offer."

"He did?"

"Yes. He brought it up himself. I was thinking—I could suggest that he consider it."

Her expression brightened with renewed hope.

"But I don't know what other options he's weighing. For all I know, he may have promised it to someone already. In his will."

"I see," she said, looking resigned.

"If there's a chance, then I think it would help if I could show him that your reason is worthy somehow. I couldn't say anything the other day because I didn't have anything to tell him. Actually, he doesn't even know I've seen you."

On hearing this, her expression flattened. She picked at the handle of the paintbrush, seemingly debating the issue with herself.

"Fine," she said at last, "I might as well tell you. I have nothing to lose, have I?"

I did not see any harm in exaggerating a little: "I don't know how much longer he'll be conscious."

"Fine," she said again, still gathering her resolve. "Well. Here it is. The simplest way to explain it, anyway." She poked at the damp bristles of the brush, stalling. Finally, she began: "Those little paintings of laundry—you saw some of them—"

She watched my face.

"They're the first things I have been able to do in many years."

She kept her eyes on me, considering my reaction, but I remained silent. After the hostility Emerson had directed at my own confession, I did not want to discourage her from saying more.

"It's been a very long time," she said. "I took the materials with me when I started this search."

"Search? You mean, for the Beacon?"

"Yes." Her eyes began to fill but she caught herself and said brusquely, "It was like a switch turned on."

"And you could work?"

"A little. It's . . . As I get closer to the car . . ."

It was then that she recounted her trip to Germany and her meeting with Manfred Zeffler at the world headquarters of AG, AG. Riding through the wooded campus on the company's shuttle bus, she'd passed the display of classic AG models dotting the hills like grazing animals, and at the sight of them, put out to pasture, something shifted in her. She became determined to make something new. It was an artistic impulse she hadn't felt in years, and as it washed over her, she silently renewed her vow to find the old Beacon.

"It's a strange business, making cars," she said. "Not like any other form of manufacturing. The products are filled with human beings. There's an intimate association—"

I mused on this: What is a vehicle but a private capsule? One in which the mundane errands and memorable adventures of a life are accomplished. By some alchemy, through this constant association, a mingling, a transmutation, can occur. In memories alone, a car is capable of encapsulating an entire life. Or more than one. I reflected on Hélène's situation and wondered: Do you possess a car, or does it possess you?

It was clear how much she had invested her hopes in finding it.

"So . . . did you use the Beacon to make your paintings?"

She looked uncertain as to how to answer. "Yes," she said finally. "Well, that was one car I used. There were others before that. I have been struggling, but now I am beginning to work on these little ideas. I am superstitious enough to believe that even more might be possible if . . ."

She didn't finish her sentence, halted perhaps by the thought of the alternative. Instead, she went on, "Arthur Quint has been so patient, and I give him nothing new. He's been far more creative than me, reviving old work, trying to organize shows. But it's been worse, to tell the truth, because now I have a witness to my difficulties."

I didn't know how to respond. I only knew how to save the things other people created. I had never created anything, let alone struggled with the pain of losing that ability. What's more, I recognized that she had not explained what the car meant to her—only her reason for wanting it. I wondered if this would be enough to persuade Emerson.

"How did you get the car in the first place?"

She bit her lip, considering the question. She worked her fingers over the tip of the brush, smoothing it back into a point as she unburdened herself: "There was a man. We met at art school in Florence. They expected us to spend our days in the studios at the academy, or in dead museums, painting like good bourgeois. I came to hate it. I worshiped Duchamp and others who were engaged with ideas and sensations, not antiquity. Then this gentleman and I were in a car, driving very fast, and I began to conceive of painting without paint. It was already several years after the war. So much of the countryside we drove through was still in ruins. My eyes took in scenes I urgently needed to describe. The sensation of speed fascinated me. I always thought I would remember it later, but I found that I didn't."

The trace of a smile appeared on her lips before she frowned it away. "His name was Alto Bianco," she confided. "It's bizarre if you know the Italian, because he was—is—a short man, and rather dark. We drove together, so many cars, all kinds. Then one day he made the Beacon appear, as if he had built it himself. He was an Italian boy, Beth. He did not have the slightest interest in British cars. But I had seen one on the road and I could not stop talking about it. I had never felt an attraction to a machine, and it amused him. Driving that car was quite an excitement."

"He was an artist?" I asked, unable to recall any work by the man.

"Oh, Alto's family took care of him. The truth is, he was a frustrated artist. It wasn't like it is now, when enough money can buy you a career. He wanted desperately to paint. But he felt he had nothing to say. He saw some of my work and became attached to me, like you would rely on a talisman." She considered this. "It wasn't always an honor. He showed up where I lived—a house with other students. He called me a whore for my 'artistic crimes.'"

"What crimes?" I asked with alarm.

She waved the brush in the air as if to dismiss the question. "Because I was wasting myself, he said. Not producing enough, when I could be . . . I told him to stop insulting me. Then he said he loved me because I never talked about my art. He believed he was brilliant, but he could not create anything new. He told me this often—he was putting his bets on me."

"You made the Speed Paintings."

"Yes. And it wasn't long before we parted." She regarded the brush sadly. "Everything we make is a struggle for expression. Do you succeed?"

"Where is he now?"

Her lips tightened. "We're not in touch."

With that, I sensed that her testament had reached its end.

"All right, I'll tell Emerson," I promised, already working out how to describe her plight to him.

"Oh," she said, looking distressed, "I don't know if it's enough."

"Is there something else you want me to say?"

She thought about this before she gave me an answer so precise, so cryptic, I forced myself to memorize it so I could repeat it to Emerson exactly.

10

I COULD HEAR EMERSON calling out frantically as I let myself into the loft. I hurried to his room, where Tisa was buzzing around him with a towel.

"We're fine, Beth," he protested when he saw me in the doorway. "Go away. Go back to wherever you've been."

He was standing at the portable commode, and I could see that he had missed and urinated on the floor. Now his body was drenched in sweat. Tisa dried him and got him resettled in bed while I retrieved the mop and bucket.

He watched me in silence as I bleached the floor.

"I was with Hélène Moreau," I announced flatly. "At her hotel. I've been talking with her."

I expected him to be furious, and I was prepared to suffer his wrath, if only to get the subject out into the open. There was so little I could do to make anything better for him or to relieve his doubts. To me, the Beacon had no meaning, but I knew it meant something to him and to Hélène, and intentionally or not, I had put myself in the position of their go-between.

He was sitting calmly in bed, surveying my movements. Tisa tried to take the mop away from me, but I fended her off, happy to have something to focus on while I spoke.

"I was trying to find out why she wants the car. That's what you asked her when we met her, right? And you asked it again after I talked to Arthur Quint. So I was getting an answer for you."

He appeared attentive when I paused in my mopping, but he said nothing.

"I think she's desperate," I went on, wanting to convey the extent of her professional difficulties. I recounted her visit to the Beacon Company's new owner in Germany and the turn of events that had led her to us.

"It sounds superstitious—she said so herself—but it's like she can't function without it. Not just in her art but her life. She wanted me to tell you—" I summoned the exact, peculiar words I'd forced myself to memorize. "She said: 'Tell him I'm trying to make something whole again, from my youth. Something pure, that gave me the greatest happiness.'"

The information appeared to have no effect on him. He remained impassive while I put away the mop and took a quick look through the medical supplies on his bookshelves to see if I needed to reorder anything the next morning. I was about to accept defeat and go to the guest room when Emerson spoke again.

"She said she's trying to make something whole again?"

I nodded.

He launched himself off the pillows, his voice ringing with fury. "That bitch!"

"What's the matter?"

His eyes were on fire, his lips quivering with indignation.

"I knew it. Beth, get the files in the office on the Beacon. And whatever's on my desk, any faxes—"

"Why are you so upset?"

"She's taking us on. She thinks she can beat me. She announced as much to you. But I'm going to get it."

"*You own the car,*" I reminded him.

"No, it's—get the files. Please."

I feared that the meds had eaten through his last tethers to reality. Still, at his insistence, I gathered whatever papers I could find and paged through them with him: a bill for a set of tires the previous summer, insurance forms . . . He seized on a piece of fax paper covered with a neat grid of typewritten German and some handwriting in English.

"Look at the part I underlined," he said. "That's the engine number of the Beacon I own. Next to it is the number on the car's chassis—what the body attaches to. And below that, someone from the Heritage Trust confirmed that they should match."

"I don't get it."

He frowned at my obtuseness. "It's not the right engine."

"But doesn't the car run?"

"Of course!"

"If it has the wrong engine, how can it run?"

He shook his head at my limited understanding. "Another engine of the same *type* can make the car run. That doesn't mean it's the original engine that was put in the car at the factory. And in this case, it's not."

"Why would the engine be different?"

"I have no idea. It was replaced for some reason. It's not easy to track down something like this. But I had a feeling when we met her. And now we know: She has it."

"Hélène?"

"Yes. That's why she wants the body, Beth. She's trying to put them back together herself."

I was having trouble picturing this. "I'm confused."

Emerson went on, "Or if she doesn't have the engine yet, she's looking for it. We need to—I need you to find out from the previous owners in this file if they know anything about the original engine. Where it went, if it's ever turned up anywhere . . . Ask them if they've had any contact with Hélène or know anything about her."

"You want me to spy on her?"

He nodded.

It was true, then: The plot of intrigue I'd dreamed up for myself to escape the strain of his care was more than an imaginary game. I cringed at the thought of Hélène laughing at me over her drink after I left the hotel bar—cringed at the confession of my awkwardness—as if she cared about my death, my life or my plot in any way. I imagined her concocting the sob story I fed to Emerson in order to persuade him to relinquish the car. I had started to trust her, bared myself to her, and now I was a little afraid of her. I didn't know what was more disturbing, her behavior or the seemingly ridiculous reason for it. But my duty to Emerson was clear.

"All right."

At his insistence, I began to read through the auction records and the copies of the title certificates from some of the previous owners. In one of the auction catalogues, I saw that the car had undergone restoration work in August 1974 and that in March 1992 it had gone to a restorer in England for a second, more thorough, overhaul at a cost of $23,000. At that time, the car was logged as having the "correct engine."

"That means 'not original,'" Emerson pointed out when I read it to him. "It's a replacement."

"So, wouldn't that mean the original engine has been destroyed?"

"Not at all. No, it could be in another car—that might be how she got it in the first place. She's probably displaying it on a pedestal in her studio in Paris, like a Duchamp ready-made."

He seemed pleased with himself for having suspected her all along. More incredible to me was the fact that he immediately looked healthier. He launched himself out of bed again, as he had done the night when Hélène first phoned, and handed me an envelope from his bookcase.

"And there's this, Beth," he said, falling back onto his pillow.

Inside the envelope was a color brochure showcasing a range of new AG automotive models. He directed my attention to the engraved card slipped inside:

You are cordially invited to celebrate
the relaunch of the Beacon Motor Company

A SPECIAL EVENT FOR COLLECTORS

26 July 1996   8:00 p.m.
The Zeppelin Museum
Friedrichshafen, Germany

I ran my fingers over the raised lettering. "This is a party."

"Yes. But it's a way to do research. For *you* to do research. All I can do is fax. Put yourself in my shoes, Beth. I'm tired of faxing."

He handed me the cordless phone next to his bed—a dying man with a simple request: "Why don't you book a flight?"

PART II

THE ENGINE

II

HOW DOES AN ENGINE become separated from the chassis? And by what means does it go on to drive another vehicle? Many different ways."

The gray-bearded gentleman spoke with an English accent. Like me, he was lighter than air — dressed in formal attire and eating hors d'oeuvres inside the gondola of a zeppelin suspended over the main hall of a museum in southern Germany.

The Englishman thought for a moment. "If it's a racecar and the driver leans on it too hard, the engine can blow up and need to be replaced. That's something!"

He clinked his champagne glass against mine.

"Or, if the force of a collision drives into the front fan, the generator, you might put a different engine in. The original engine probably goes to a rebuilder, to be sold as a replacement. Believe it or not, the more valuable the car, the more likely the engine is to get separated."

His name was James M. C. Cook, according to his badge, and he did not need to tell me he was a Beacon owner. Along with most of the other guests around us, he wore an ornate gold lighthouse pin on his lapel, like initiates into a secret club. I complimented him on his pin before continuing my interrogation.

"Do you know of a Beacon collector — an artist — named Hélène Moreau?"

He shook his head and stared ahead vacantly, stumped after having answered my other questions so easily.

"I'm trying to find out if she has the engine from a 1954 roadster. You've never heard of her?"

As I began to describe Hélène's Speed Paintings, he looked relieved to see his wife returning from the ladies' room. They excused themselves to go down one level, to the B deck, where the zeppelin's smoking lounge and passenger bar were located.

From the panoramic window I watched a projected lighthouse beam moving in a pattern across the walls of the museum, nervously wondering, as I had done on my flight to Germany, how I was supposed to fulfill Emerson's assignment there. I had tried to tell him: It was a party, not a research facility. I was surveying the crowd, deciding which corner of the room it would be best to wade into, when I picked out an oddly handsome man. I'd noticed him earlier, walking into the party. He had an alert, intelligent face. His brown hair was spiked into high, uneven points, casually offsetting the old-fashioned cut of his tuxedo. In line, on the way in, he had greeted the people behind me in French, then spoken with a passing woman in Italian, while a second man remained constantly at his side. The second man was larger and more homely, with a massive, cartoonish jaw that dominated the lower half of his face. I wondered if he was the bodyguard of the spiky-haired man. At least one of them smelled of a spiced after-shave — an aromatic, herbal blend that might have wafted down the hills of a Mediterranean island on a hot day, the notes of green shade mingling with a darker scent of cloves and burnt cinnamon. Now, from my lookout in the zeppelin, I watched the spiky-haired man move through the room, shaking hands like a politician, until the crowd swallowed him up again.

I shifted to another window inside the airship, a full-size replica of a starboard section of the Hindenburg, moored by long ropes to the walls of the building. The vessel swayed gently in the air currents rising from the circulating partygoers below. I closed my eyes, picturing Emerson in his bed and wishing he were with me, knowing he would be enjoying himself so much more than I was.

Something poked me in the arm and my eyes flew open. A man costumed in a chauffeur's uniform stood before me, extending a silver tray stacked with headsets.

"For translation," he explained.

Like the others around me in the zeppelin lounge, I selected my language and hooked the headset over one ear. On a circular stage below, a pokerfaced gentleman was introduced as the chairman of AG. He addressed the room in German, his words echoing through my headpiece in English, relayed by a male translator.

"When we are considering the future of the automobile, we ask ourselves: How will we power it, and how will it operate?"

As he spoke, tuxedos and evening gowns rustled toward the stage like metal filings around a magnet.

"What do you think the future will look like?" the executive asked the crowd. "Already we are approaching the year 2000, the turn of a new millennium. Market and regulatory pressures are pushing us—and will continue to push us—to seek alternatives to carbon dioxide–producing power trains. What is at stake? Let's start with countries like China and India . . ."

Someone passed close to me in the floating lounge. I guessed who it was as soon as I smelled the after-shave—that smoky mixture of cinnamon, cloves and green shade. He stood at the window taming the spikes in his hair, parting them to one side absent-mindedly with long fingers, graceful in their movements. He waved away the offer of a headset from one of the chauffeurs —he was apparently fluent in everything. The homely bodyguard did not appear to be with him any longer, and he watched the proceedings below with obvious interest—much more than I could summon for the dry presentation.

"In the coming years, our present business model will no longer be sustainable," the executive announced to the crowd. "You are here tonight to preview an early concept for what may be the first new Beacon in thirty years: a clean-burning Beacon. The natural twenty-first-century successor to some of the most refined and powerful cars in the world."

Cameras flashed around the room as the executive pulled the drape off a mysterious form crouched on the stage. I could not tell one car model from the next, but from my viewing position in the zeppelin, the new Beacon did not look particularly friendly. It did not look angry either, like so many of the cars I saw on the street. Down on the stage, the new concept appeared to be vaguely shaped like a camel's head in profile, raised higher in the back, with an inscrutable, technical face.

That smell again: cinnamon and cloves and green shade. Then I heard a male voice coming not through my headset but directly into my left ear. His voice.

"Have you seen a *proper* 135 roadster?" the voice asked. "The original—what this car is loosely based on?"

He had an English accent, not German. But his inflection was mixed with disappointment. And a trace of something else. I glanced at his nametag.

Jorge.

Spanish?

"Yes, I've seen one," I managed to answer. I didn't tell him it was a scale model on Hélène Moreau's desk.

Below us, the men in chauffeurs' uniforms were walking through the crowd with microphones, taking questions from the audience.

"Why would you start with a roadster?" someone asked.

"Obviously, we are not, as you can see," said the AG executive, sending a wave of laughter around the room. "We are reviving the *memory* of a classic R-135 roadster, but updated as an SUV for the future, with a realistic capacity for five passengers . . ."

Again I felt his breath close by my ear: "Cars like the original

Beacon were the reason why the world fell in love with the automobile."

His smile was inviting, wide, made wider as his lips curled in a soft ruffle, like ravioli. Up close, he looked to be not much older than me. Mid-thirties? But he had an air of authority unlike anyone I knew, except maybe Emerson. I attributed this to his unusual accent.

Down on the stage, guests began to swarm around the car. The man I now thought of as Jorge stood with his arms crossed, surveying the movements of the crowd as intently as a shopkeeper on Saturday morning. It occurred to me that *he* might be the best way for me to wade into my research assignment. He seemed to know enough people . . .

I ventured a step closer. "Is this your blimp?"

"This isn't a blimp," he said matter-of-factly, leaning in and pointing over my head. "It's a rigid airship. It has a structural skeleton, which you can see from outside this gondola—that is, if you ever decide to leave it and join the party."

I stared at him in surprise. Had he noticed me here earlier?

His lips ruffled into another grin. "But no, it's not mine," he went on. "A man named Count Ferdinand von Zeppelin developed ships like these in the early 1900s. I believe this is his airship."

"Is this your party?"

"No, not really. I'm here to make up for the sins of others, you could say. My father drove the original Beacon Motor Company into the ground. Pardon my rubbish pun."

"You're related to Beacon?"

He closed his eyes and nodded wearily. "My grandfather founded the company. And, as I say, my father ruined it. I'm helping AG revive the brand."

I looked at his nametag again. *Jorge Miguel Beacon.*

"Congratulations, Jorge."

"I'm called Miguel. My mother was Spanish, though I mostly

lived in England." He nodded to himself at the memory. "With my grandfather."

"These tags are so formal."

"What about you, Bethany? What brings you to this zeppelin? You're a collector, are you?"

"Beth," I said, covering the end of my nametag. "I'm here . . . I'm representing the owner of a 135-M from 1954."

He nodded again. "Someone with good taste."

"We found out . . . we don't have the original engine in the car, and we're trying to find it, if it still exists. I was just asking another gentleman here, another Beacon owner, about how the engine might have gotten separated."

"Quite likely it's lost. There are countless reasons why engines go. They even get nicked. Have you gotten in touch with the Heritage Trust in Schnell?"

"I think — the owner — was working on that. We know the engine number. We're trying to find out if an artist named Hélène Moreau has it. Or if it's in another car," I was careful to add.

He glanced at my nametag again. "I'd love to help you, Beth. If you want me to. Do you fancy some dinner?"

He was offering his help, *if I wanted it*. Would it be like stepping into the racecar with Emerson? I wondered if my exit would be more graceful as he led me across a short bridge connecting the zeppelin to a restaurant on the museum's upper level.

"Did you say you represent the owner?" he asked, shepherding me through a throng of waiters preparing for the dinner service.

"Yes."

A look of concern crossed his face. "Are you a lawyer?"

"No, more like an assistant."

"Why are you smiling?" he asked.

"I was just wishing that someone I know was here tonight. He would have loved it."

"I think once someone is gone from your life, they might as well be dead." He grinned at me oddly.

"Oh," I said with an embarrassed smile, "you're talking about romance. I wasn't."

"No, not necessarily. Though I suppose it applies to that, too." He pulled out a chair for me at one of the banquet tables.

"The difference with romance," I said, by way of conjecture, "is that the person is still out there—as far as you know. You have to live with the lost chance."

"You're a romantic," he said with evident satisfaction.

"I don't know what I am."

"I'm a romantic myself," he said. "I'm doing what I dreamed of, and I'm alone." He thought for a moment. "Though I'm not quite sure why."

I couldn't help laughing. His way of speaking gave him a strange charm. It wasn't only his accent, it was as if he were channeling someone much older, from another time.

"I find that hard to believe, Miguel—that you're alone."

"It's true," he said good-naturedly. "And your sympathy has been noted. Being alone *is* romantic, you know, in the sense of the love we think of as ideal. Or chivalric. It relies on having passed through a long state of immense frustration, don't you think? The greater your anticipation, maybe, the greater your awareness of love."

By his formula, my awareness of love should have been colossal. Miguel was starting to sweat, adding a new, pleasantly musky note to the others in his cologne. It hit me with the suddenness of a crush. Other diners were pouring through the doorways and seating themselves around us as a waiter appeared and filled our glasses with a yellow wine I could not pronounce, a dry Riesling, according to the printed menu card beside my plate. Before long, the room was a traffic jam of tuxedos and gowns. Two elegantly dressed blond women skirted past the table, eyeing Miguel, and as they made their way forward an older man stepped up and kissed the shorter of the two women, taking her by surprise.

"Alto!" she cried, gesturing to her friend. "Look, Iris, it's Alto."

The man in question was stout, nearly square; beyond that, all I could see of him was the back of his tuxedo and an extravagant head of wavy gray hair. I tried to get a look at his nametag, but now he and the taller blonde were embracing.

"I think most people get tired of being frustrated in love," I told Miguel, watching them.

"Maybe not," Miguel argued. "Maybe they cling to that state because they sense that when it's over they'll miss the anticipation terribly."

Hélène's Alto?

I wondered.

The man turned. He was at least sixty, maybe seventy, with olive skin hanging in thick ridges from his cheeks. His eyes were hooded, set widely beneath his temples like an ancient toad. When the woman released his arm, I zeroed in on the nametag: ALTO BIANCO.

I turned to Miguel, eager to point out the man and explain my predicament with Hélène Moreau, but he was half out of his chair again, shaking hands and introducing himself to the other guests at our table—a group that included some auto journalists from the United States, judging by their tags.

A few tables away, the blond women were seated on either side of Alto Bianco, like shining andirons around a weathered log. He clamped a cigarette between his lips and raised a lighter. Didn't the Hindenburg explode in a ball of flames? He spun the wheel. I flinched. Then a pair of silver tongs descended and deposited a ramekin of duck-liver parfait on my plate.

At my elbow, a man with a buzzcut and sharp blue eyes was interrogating Miguel.

"I remember seeing a Beacon roadster cornering when I was six years old. This new concept tonight—*a crossover-slash-SUV-slash-slash*. Where's the emotion? Where's the sexiness?"

Miguel extended his arms on the tabletop. "Well," he began hesitantly, "you're associating . . . sexiness with a specific set of design cues that are really . . . quite old at this point. So many of those came from when car design was in its . . . infancy." He glanced around the table. "Can we move past that now?"

When no one responded, I nodded in encouragement.

He turned to me and spoke more passionately: "The excitement for my grandfather and his contemporaries was in mastering natural forces with a manmade machine." He paused. "And they did this. They succeeded beyond their wildest dreams. But they were limited in their conception of speed—of progress, really."

"What's your interest in this, Miguel?" asked an elderly journalist with a white mustache and a rumpled tuxedo. "Why are you helping a bunch of Germans revive your English grandfather's company?"

Miguel silently debated his answer.

"Because otherwise someone else would do it," he said finally. "And the result would be worse." He scanned the faces around the table. "This concept you're seeing out there tonight is just a start."

"Power trains are the problem—not cars," joked a guest at the other end of the table.

"Isn't that like saying it's not the gun, it's the bullet?" another voice replied.

"Well," said Miguel, "what if I point a gun at you and it's a squirt gun, just water coming out? Like that fuel cell down there —instead of billions of tons of carbon pollution."

"I would prefer that," I volunteered.

"It's not just pollution and toxic emissions. It's spills, seeps, irreversible damage to habitats and climate patterns . . ."

I wanted to keep concentrating on what Miguel and the others were saying, but it wasn't long before I lost track of their conversation while spying on Alto, who was ignoring the women next to him and talking on a mobile phone. I tried to read his lips, at least to determine what language he was speaking. Could he speak

English? But his lips proved as unreadable as his cloudy eyes, fixed on some faraway point outside the museum's balcony.

I had to find a way to speak to him, even if I had to collar a translator, like Miguel, to help me. That didn't mean I knew what I was going to say, though. Was I really going to walk up to him and start asking about a woman he knew four decades ago? Someone he'd called a whore for her artistic crimes? That would not be a friendly opener.

There had to be some time to mingle after dinner, I reasoned. I glanced at the menu card. Shortly, we could expect the arrival of the main course: VENISON NOISETTES ON MUSHROOM ROYALE WITH CRANBERRY-PEPPER SAUCE, VEGETABLES AND SPAETZLE.

When I looked up again, Alto's seat was empty. I stalked the room, hopscotching visually from one table to the next while the others around me turned their attention to bowls of consommé.

"Hey, is there any wine left on your end of the table?"

"That's why roller coasters don't do it for me. Once you know the course, it's speed with no mystery . . ."

There he was, at another table, with a different woman. A brunette. Though she was seated, I could tell from the length of her torso that she was extremely tall. Her dark hair was braided into high coils; her cobra eyes were exotically frosted with blue eye shadow. She turned and presented a chilly expression to Alto, hunched listlessly beside her, glancing over his shoulder.

The waiters began to serve the main course. There wasn't much time for me to accomplish what I had come to do. As we ate, I considered that the journalists might know something about Hélène—a semifamous person who possibly owned a vintage Beacon, or at least the engine. I sat forward and announced:

"An artist I know said that speed isn't modern anymore. I believe she's a Beacon owner—Hélène Moreau?"

"Exactly," Miguel said, slapping the table. "It's not modern. Our whole concept of transportation is a holdover from a different world. How can we make it new again?"

A few faces looked up from their venison.

I wasn't sure if I was supposed to answer. "I've spent most of my life on trains and buses," I said with a shrug. "Or walking."

The journalist with the white mustache rolled his eyes at me. "People like to have some form of personal transportation, you know. We can't all be up on conveyor belts up in the sky."

Miguel reclaimed my attention by leaning in to me conspiratorially, his lips nearly touching my ear. "I know what speed is."

His sudden closeness and the bass notes of his voice combined to stun the normal function of my nerves. I could manage only a whisper: "What?"

"Speed is the antidote to memory."

I breathed in his smoky green smell.

"You feel these forces," he said, "but they're not real. One gives you the illusion of moving forward, the other backward."

I couldn't form a reply. I just wanted him to remain there with the lapel of his tuxedo touching my dress. I sat in silence, inhaling him, feeling his slight movements, the drag of the fabric of his jacket over my bare arm. Then, no doubt in response to my paralysis, he sat forward and resumed his conversation with a woman seated to his right, a reporter from *Intersection* magazine, who excused herself not long after, complaining that she had broken her heel climbing the rope ladder into the Hindenburg.

The waiters emptied more bottles of wine into our glasses.

"Miguel, you're showing a car on the turntable with a hydrogen fuel cell. So, is that your bet?" a reporter asked.

"Not at all. It's one idea. We are also looking at electric, of course—electric cars being one of the earliest forms of propulsion a century ago. One that was quickly obliterated by petrol—"

"The Betamax of its day."

He nodded. "But where does the electricity come from? Burning coal?" He shook his head. "I'm talking about broader, more integrated solutions. I want to look at all the options."

Someone bumped the back of my chair. I turned to find Alto Bianco's latest date striding out of the room, defiantly balancing her tall crown of braids. Once again, Alto was no longer in his seat. The conversation around the table buzzed in my head as I anxiously scanned the perimeter of the room for him.

"So it's hybrids, electrics and diesels for the next twenty years?" someone offered. "Then biofuels?"

"Think of it a different way," said Miguel. "What if, by that time, the sun or some other source were cleanly generating the power needed to produce hydrogen? You see, there are many ways it could go."

There was no sign of Alto. I was beginning to panic when my eyes finally came to rest on a slouching figure silhouetted against one of the windows. He was out on the balcony, his hands in his pockets, apparently watching the rain fall. Not smoking. Not talking on his phone.

"How many years of fossil fuels do we have left?" I asked.

"Less than a hundred."

"Nah, less than sixty."

"They lost at least eleven million gallons just on that Valdez spill—"

"We're doing hydrogen at this unveiling," Miguel insisted. "You noticed the zeppelin out there?"

The table erupted with laughter.

"Because the Hindenburg went over so well in its day!"

"It only took three days to cross the Atlantic!"

"As I say, we're exploring other things," Miguel said. "Maybe that's next year's press conference . . ."

He was still speaking when the man I had seen with him earlier reappeared at the table. My heart sank when, with a few words, he escorted Miguel away to speak with guests at another table during dessert: an impressively airy zeppelin cake. I hadn't taken more than a few bites when I looked up and saw that the balcony doors had been opened to cool down the room, but Alto's form no longer occupied the space.

Had he jumped?

The building wasn't that high.

I couldn't spot him at any of the other tables. People were beginning to stand now, blocking my sightlines. I picked up my things and pushed through the tangle of diners to look over the edge of the balcony. I saw nothing on the ground but puddles. Hurriedly, I took the stairs down to the main floor of the museum. There, in the midst of the empty hall, I abruptly came upon the man himself, standing before some type of technical display. On closer inspection, I saw that it was a car identical to the one I had seen onstage earlier, except cut in half, with its insides showing.

Alto Bianco appeared to be studying the bisected vehicle. I moved closer. I still didn't know what I was going to say to him, or how I was going to broach my questions. Then he glanced at me, scowled and spat some words in Italian.

"Excuse me? I didn't understand what you said."

"Oh, and you are from where?" he asked, switching to heavily accented English.

"What were you saying?" I asked, relieved to know that I would be able to converse with him.

He pointed to the flayed vehicle in front of us. "This car has no heart."

"No heart?"

"What runs it?" With one of his polished brown shoes he kicked at the display. "Is no engine there. Is some batteries and chemicals, *molto molto freddi*."

In spite of my wandering attention at dinner, I had been persuaded by the arguments for the new ideas being proposed. Had Alto Bianco missed the headsets earlier?

I began to explain: "What runs it is an experimental engine that doesn't burn fossil fuels, doesn't pollute."

Alto Bianco turned his bored, cloudy eyes on me. He coughed before resuming in his accented half-growl: "Let me 'splain something. An engine is made with the hands, an' I can take it apart with my hands. Hand to hand. Mano a mano."

To demonstrate, he removed his hands from his pockets and clasped them around mine. His grip was weak, despite the weight of the aged flesh. He searched my face.

"You see?" His eyes were ringed with desperation. "For me, I prefer the personal relation."

I flinched at the movement of his hands, damp as cutlets, and he withdrew them hastily and stuffed them back into his pockets.

"Is a human connection."

"It's a machine," I said, correcting him. "And you were talking about the heart. A car like this has a critical idea at its heart."

"This? I think is very bad. Is not a car." He kicked it again with his shoe. "Is a lab experiment."

"Okay, maybe it's research right now. But it's trying to solve some major problems," I argued, as surprised by my own passion as I was by his density. "Some new form—maybe not this exact thing, but some new way of thinking about things could allow us to have a future."

He shrugged, unimpressed, his eyes now well beyond bored, bordering on stormy.

"Future for who?" he demanded. "Not for me."

I was stunned by his selfishness. Then, out of nowhere, a devious smile appeared on his lips and he shrugged. "Anyway, no car is really valuable until it is personalized."

He seemed to be amusing himself with some private thought.

"What do you mean?"

"I have personalized many cars." He winked at me, and his face brightened by one less cloudy eye. "With female assistance."

A vision flashed through my mind of him in the getup of an unrepentant Mr. Toad—driving coat and gloves, goggles, cap —fresh in from one of his wild rides. As sleazy as his personalization sounded—who knew what bodily acts were involved?—I seized on it.

"If you've personalized so many, you must have a favorite?" I asked, steeling myself with the thought that I was there for Emerson's sake.

"I do," he said somberly. "Is long lost to me."

"It was a Beacon, obviously."

He dabbed at his lapel pin to remove a spot of cranberry-pepper sauce.

"Did you have any problems with the engine? Did it need to be replaced?"

"Never!" he roared. "This engine was perfect. *Bellissimo!*" He calmed himself enough to add, "*La macchina*—is not important, really. The woman—"

He turned from me as the dining room expelled a noisy crowd down the stairs. The two blondes who had been with him earlier emerged from the swarm, dragging a new man along. They linked arms with Alto, sharing a private joke, and swept him off to the smoking lounge before he could even say *ciao*.

Based on my previous observations, I calculated that he would grow bored of them again within the space of one cigarette. Ten minutes. Enough time for me to see if Miguel was free. I felt cheated that the other man had hustled him away after dinner. I climbed the stairs again and located Miguel at the far end of the dining room, shaking hands with another group lingering at one of the tables. I stepped out onto the balcony to wait, assuming Alto's former post, and it was then that I saw what he had been staring at earlier: A short distance away, a bright red automobile was parked strategically in the glare of an outdoor spotlight meant to illuminate the landscaping around the museum. It appeared to be a new car, shiny and expensive. A car that asked only one thing: to be admired. Was he hoping to show it to someone in particular?

Then, to my dismay, Alto himself appeared below in the light rainfall, shaking the kiss of a puddle off his shoe. His leather glove reached to pull open the driver's door. Before I could turn for the stairs, I heard the engine thunder to life, then the headlights flashed and he was gone.

I retreated from the balcony. Now what? I had learned nothing about the Beacon engine. Nothing about Hélène. Miguel appeared to be settling into an intense discussion at the table. The room had thinned of all but a few guests. I had no reason to linger.

I collected my coat and shared the guest van back to the hotel with some of the reporters from dinner. As the van bumped along the dark, wooded roads I asked them again about Hélène Moreau, determined not to let Emerson down. It turned out that a few of them had heard of her Speed Paintings, but no one knew anything about her ownership or interest in a vintage Beacon engine.

At the front desk, a clerk handed me my room key along with a brief, misspelled phone message. It was printed on a sheet of hotel stationery that had been art-directed with the flair of a prescription pad:

Hotel Bayerischer Hof
Lindau im Bodensee

D-88131 Lindau / Bodensee Seepromenade Postfach 11 26
Telefon 0 83 82 91 50, Fax 0 83 82 91 55 91

> *From: M. R. Son*
> *Please phone.*

Emerson wanted a report, that much was obvious. What would I say? I had flown thousands of miles and had nothing to tell him. It was an unimpressive display of my research skills.

The light rain had stopped, and now the night was clear and black. In my room, I leaned out one of the windows to look at the lake. Above the stone lighthouse in the harbor, a promotional lighthouse was projected onto the night sky like a sailor's happy hallucination. The reporters had been speculating about the number of prospective investors who had come from around the world for the event—I supposed the marketing had to be convincing.

I heard a soft scraping sound behind me and saw that an envelope had been pushed under the door. Inside was another sheet of the hotel's prescription pad with a handwritten message from Miguel:

> I'd like to help you with the engine. Please join me downstairs in the bar, if jet lag doesn't prevent you. —M

Something did. Was it the intimacy of his handwriting? The use of a single initial? His M looked almost like a W, like a child's scribble of a bird in flight. I imagined him standing at the front desk, requesting the paper to compose the message. There was no doubt it had been delivered by a bellman, yet the directness of those strokes of ink inviting me to join him raised an inner turmoil. I did want to see Miguel, but for my own reasons. I wanted to meet him in the bar and spend the night with him, and not because of the engine. I was alone in Germany with no sick employer, and I didn't care about some abandoned, wrecked, burned-out hunk of metal. But it was my duty to care about it, and a one-night stand was not going to get us anywhere. More likely, knowing myself, I would sabotage our only lead.

I didn't trust myself, it was that simple. I didn't call Emerson back either. Instead, I left my cell-phone number for Miguel at the front desk, along with the message that I welcomed his further assistance but I had an early flight.

12

I T WAS RAINING WHEN I landed in New York. In the taxi to Emerson's loft, I listened to a message on my phone from Miguel, repeating his offer of help. Now that I'd aired out my head at forty thousand feet, I regretted leaving Germany without seeing him. There were some journalists from the party on my flight home gossiping about how Miguel had been down in the bar until the early hours of the morning. He'd had a news clipping in front of him, weighted down protectively with his glass. He never refilled his drink, someone made it a point to add; apparently, he was more exhausted than drunk. As they discussed what he'd said, jokingly imitating his accent, I pictured Miguel reading from his clipping:

"The Lighthouse. Correction—*der Leuchtturm*. A light of guidance and help. Also, a warning of danger. I quote: 'In the terms of the sale, the auto giant AG committed to investment and production targets set by the British government in exchange for tax breaks and other considerations.' They got their deal, yes. 'A Beacon revival looked certain until last week, when, citing "economic realities," the Board of Managers voted to meet the agreed-upon targets by reviving the derelict Beacon facility in Lugborough for use by another AG automotive brand . . .'"

In two flights over the course of ten hours, I'd convinced myself that I had correctly put Emerson's desires above my own. Now I thought Miguel probably could have used some sympathetic company himself.

At the loft, Zandra informed me that Emerson had insisted on backing off on his morphine while I was traveling—he said it made him feel more in control. He was shaking with fatigue and suspense, staring up at me from his bed.

"You didn't call."

"It went so fast. Anyway, I didn't find out anything," I admitted, hoping to manage his expectations. I was beginning to suspect we were on a wild goose chase. "No one knew anything about Hélène Moreau or the engine. I talked to as many people as I could: collectors, journalists. But I met someone—"

He turned to Zandra and rolled his eyes. "Beth, do we have to hear about your romantic conquests right now?"

"Wait—I met the grandson. Of the founder. A guy named Miguel."

Emerson's face drained of its unripe color. "And was this your conquest?" he asked, his voice rising with alarm.

I looked to Zandra—in whom I had confided the unorthodox nature of my love life one afternoon a few months earlier, after she showed me photos of the X-rated birthday cake some girlfriends had presented to her.

"What have you been telling him?"

Zandra shrugged, self-consciously twirling the tiny diamond stud in her nostril. "Not as much as you think."

"No," I protested. "There was no conquest of any kind."

Emerson looked relieved.

"He offered to help us," I went on. "Well, me—he doesn't know about you, obviously. Just that I have an employer."

"How is he going to help?"

"I don't know. The party was crowded and we didn't get to finish our conversation. I need to speak with him again."

Emerson seemed hopeful at this news. "Good. That's good. And can you finish calling the owners from that file? Please."

"Yes, I'll do it this week."

"And try to find any restorers who might have handled the engine."

I left a new, more urgent message for Miguel, and I spoke with two former owners in the United States, starting with a man on Long Island who had owned the car in the 1970s. That is, I got as far as his personal assistant, who said there was no record of the Beacon's engine being changed during his employer's ownership.

The most recent owner prior to Emerson, August Browne, also lived on Long Island. He had owned the car from 1990 to 1995. From the languid rasp in his voice, I guessed that I had woken him from an afternoon nap.

"I don't have that car anymore. Sold it at auction. Same way I bought it."

"Yes, I understand, but . . ."

I knew from Emerson's files that the original engine had been replaced years before Browne acquired the car. However, the body had been fully restored in England while he owned it. There was a chance he'd saved some records. I was in the process of asking him about this when he began moaning over the ridiculously low price Emerson had managed to get the car for at auction. It was like a replay of Garrett's first unhappy Hot Wheels trade.

"I *gave the car away* to that bidder. Never again!" Browne vowed, not knowing how right he was. As he recounted the humiliation he had suffered, I watched the arc of a plane outside, a white line drawn across the sky from east to west, silently willing Miguel to return my call.

It was odd to be back at my desk again. I found myself flipping through my calendar, informally tracking my personal decline. I had to admit that the daily grind of life was flatter than ever, with only my duties to Emerson to shovel into the mill. A fine sawdust covered more and more surface area inside me, muffling everything. By contrast, Miguel's voice on the phone made me vibrate like a gong.

He explained that he had temporarily relocated to an AG facility in Los Angeles. "What have you been up to since you got back?" he asked.

I recounted my unsuccessful attempts to learn anything from the previous owners, as well as my new offensive: to contact restorers who have worked on Beacons, a much larger task. "The problem is narrowing it down to a geographic range," I said. "The engine could be anywhere."

"I can see why you'd be keen to check with restorers."

"I'm an archivist," I began, unable to remember how much I had told him at the party. "Restorers have been on my mind a lot lately. How to rehabilitate something, even a machine."

"Getting a car restored by professionals is different to doing it yourself," he pointed out. "You restore a car with someone to be closer to them. People do it all the time. I did it with my grand-dad. It's the same if you're modifying a car, or in a club, or racing with a team—it gives you something to work on together, like we are."

Like I was with Emerson.

I told him the engine number, and he promised to see what he could find out.

"What are you going to do?" I asked, meaning the engine search, but he must have misunderstood, because he said he was heading out to ride his motorcycle around L.A.

"Isn't that a waste of gasoline?"

"But I'm a beautiful driver."

For a week after Miguel's call, Emerson kept himself in remarkably good shape, mainly by cracking the whip at me from his pillow. An ecstatic seriousness had come over him since my return from Germany: He supervised my search for the engine with the fervor of a devout seeker, greeting me each morning with whatever requests or ideas he had dreamed up the night before, and keeping the parameters open beyond Hélène's possible ownership, though she remained his prime suspect. In the course of those days I placed ads in the Parts Wanted section of classic car magazines and undertook questionable tasks on his behalf, including posing as a potential bidder—as I had legitimately done for him a few times at photo auctions in the years before he got sick —to gain access to information. Still, we'd made no real progress until the afternoon I retrieved a new phone message from Miguel:

I have news—good, I think. Give me a call.

At Emerson's insistence, I got him settled on the extension in his bedroom, so he could listen in while I phoned Miguel from my desk in the office.

"I think it's here in L.A.," Miguel announced when he heard my voice. "The car is in a hangar out at the Burbank airport."

"The car?"

"With the engine you're looking for, I believe."

"Really? That's fantastic!" In my excitement, I knocked my stapler onto the floor. Emerson's response rang back immediately from the other end of the loft, in the form of three abrupt, celebratory bangs—no doubt executed with his open palm on the headboard of his bed. Or maybe they weren't celebratory.

"What do you mean, 'you believe'?" I asked.

"I haven't seen it," Miguel cautioned, "but I'm quietly confident that the engine you're looking for is in a 135 roadster going to the Pebble Beach Concours."

At this news, I thought I detected a groan from Emerson through the phone line.

"It's going to what?" I asked Miguel, concerned about Emerson's reaction.

"A Concours d'Elegance. It's a show of classic cars. Imagine an outdoor party—like a lawn party—but with antique cars and judges awarding prizes."

"Okay," I said, still confused. "And when is this event?"

"Next weekend."

Suddenly the loft erupted in a series of loud bangs. The ruckus went on steadily, like a war drum, no doubt a combination of Emerson's forehand and backhand on the headboard—echoing with a slight delay and at a diminished volume, no less threateningly, through the phone line itself.

Miguel was yelling now: "Can you hear me, Beth?"

At once the noise stopped. But it had done its job in communicating Emerson's anxiety. I wondered if he and I weren't becoming telepathic.

"Sorry, the neighbors upstairs are renovating their kitchen," I said, not untruthfully, hoping the noise sounded enough like workmen's hammers, which were presently silent.

"If you can get yourself to Monterey for that show next weekend, you should be able to see the car there," Miguel said.

"If I can get myself—?"

One extremely loud bang shot through the loft from Emerson's bedroom. For a split second I was horrified that he had thrown himself out of bed. I feared that he was crawling down the hallway on his belly, until I detected his nervous breathing through the line, listening intently.

"Next weekend?" I repeated. "Next weekend is a long time away. Isn't there some way I could see it before that?"

"Oh . . ."

He seemed to be thinking about this.

"Please."

"Well, I suppose I could suggest that you—or your employer? —speak with the owner here in L.A. before he moves the car up to Monterey."

"Yes, could you arrange that?"

"I'll try to set it up."

"Thank you," I said, waiting for an auditory clue from Emerson that there was something more to discuss, but it was Miguel who broke the silence.

"I have plans next weekend anyway," he said. Speaking more cautiously, he added, "But if you come out at the start of the week, I could go with you."

A muffled cry arose from the other end of the loft. I paused, wondering if anything was wrong. Then I heard the distinct sound of skin slapping skin: what could only be Emerson's hand connecting with Tisa's in a triumphant low-five.

When I got back to his room, Emerson said, "I'm going."

"I think we should ask Dr. Albas."

"Go ahead." He crossed his arms over his chest. "She's not going to stop me."

"Okay, but there are some things we have to consider. Things you're not taking into account. Your medicines, all your supplies." I looked up at the bookcase hopelessly, trying to envision the vast shelves of tubes and pills crammed into a suitcase.

"I just had a transfusion," he argued. "Again. We'll be gone for less than forty-eight hours. Tisa will come with us."

Tisa turned to him with a look of dismay.

"I had a feeling it wasn't Hélène Moreau," I told him, pleased that my trust in her had been vindicated.

"What are you talking about?" he snapped.

"Well, now we know the car is in L.A. She doesn't even live in America."

He shook his head. "You're being naïve. We don't know that she's not involved—by any means. It *sounds* like the owner lives in Los Angeles, but that's all we know. She could be storing it there with someone."

"Oh."

I had never considered the lengths a person would go for the sake of a car—either that, or he was reaching new heights of paranoid obsession. In this parallel universe, any magnitude of absurdity seemed possible.

In any event, he would allow no clemency for Hélène. "Even if you're right and she doesn't own the engine, please keep in mind that she still wants *my car*, Beth. Very badly. Let's not forget that."

To my surprise, Dr. Albas agreed that Emerson could travel to the West Coast, provided that we brought along one of the nursing aides, as he proposed, and that he stay no longer than two nights. She reminded me privately that his health had become noticeably more stable in the previous weeks—and she surprised me by admitting that he had already lived longer than she'd expected.

"Something is giving him enormous motivation," she suggested. "I'm not going to argue with it. I've seen people in terminal situations accomplish all kinds of things."

In the middle of our hurried preparations for the trip, as if I wasn't busy enough, Emerson gave me another research assignment. He wanted me to track down photographs of the interior of one of a group of Case Study houses in Los Angeles—Case Study House number 22.

"You've got a blow-up of it right there on your wall," I reminded him, pointing down the hallway to where a poster-sized reproduction of the original color print hung outside his office. It was a space capsule of a house, docked in the Hollywood Hills, one of the few photos he owned with a person in it, a man in a white dinner jacket, standing with his back to the camera. The man was frozen there in his own private heaven, gazing out at the lights of L.A. in the distance.

"I want to see some parts of the interior that you can't see there," Emerson said.

But before I could find the photos he wanted, he shifted gears and asked me to call someone he knew from his NYU days—now a location scout for a film company—and set up a time for us to see the house while we were in California. The most absurd aspect of the request: He wanted to do it on the day we landed.

"Don't you want to get a little rest after your flight?"

"No."

"Why don't we go the next day, before we fly back."

"No way. We land at ten in the morning. I can rest all afternoon. We're seeing it that day, and we're getting there before sunset."

I shook my head at his stubbornness.

"And Beth—we're seeing the Beacon the same night."

"Both?"

"We'll go straight to the car afterward."

"Don't you think that might be too much?"

He rolled his eyes. "Just because you like being cooped up inside all the time doesn't mean Tisa and I want to."

Tisa bit her lip and shook her head at me apologetically.

"It'll be fine," he promised.

Our plane from Newark took off before dawn. Emerson was asleep in the row behind me, shrunken down into himself and wrapped in his own blanket from home. Tisa monitored him from the next seat, dressed for the occasion more officially than I had ever seen her, in the white uniform of a professional medical escort, white shoes and a white baseball cap with the brim turned up, her arm reaching protectively toward him. In those early hours, when the sky was still inky and unreadable, I dreamed a man was coming to me out of the fog. Then he was coming to me out of the ocean, alongside a jetty where a ship was moored. He was tanned and his chest was bare. He stepped out onto a shore of black-stained sand, onto a roadway, a racetrack. He wore a racing suit, open to the waist and dripping with seaweed. A great barren coast stretched behind him, a landscape stripped of everything but a long spine of rocks and a lighthouse that stood empty and dark. In his hand, he carried a lantern . . .

I woke up hot, my neck jammed against the window.

Outside, the sky had grown clear, and a small rainbow floated beyond the wing of the airplane. Only it wasn't an arc, I saw when I refocused my eyes. It was a complete circle of colors: a rainball. It hovered over the desert, over the sprawling mass of hard brown geometries. The parched shapes on the ground roused my thirst, and on my way to get some water from a flight attendant I checked from Emerson's row to see if what I had observed had been an optical effect caused by some warping in my window. But the rainball was still there, riding alongside the wing. If the pieces of the rainbow could come together over the desert, I had to believe we could put something back together ourselves.

The hotel Emerson had asked me to book in West Hollywood was built in the style of a château, though my suite on the top floor was more like a prewar apartment in New York City, except for the view: In place of gray streets and taxicabs, room 76 overlooked a green slice of Laurel Canyon at the back and the grid of downtown L.A. along one side. I opened a window overlooking the hotel's orange and yellow neon sign. On a billboard nearby, basking in the glow of the neon, a shirtless man was lounging between a woman's legs in a fashion advertisement. He longingly stroked the woman's ankle: an oiled pharaoh brooding over a desert valley, his dark hair spiked into points. The woman's fingers were splayed suggestively across her mouth, and one of her legs was raised, kicking up an impossibly high heel. From my angle, her feet were the same size as her eyes.

"Ridiculous," Emerson said when I pointed it out.

"I want those shoes," I told him, trying as I said it to reconcile a passing erotic thought about Miguel with the hunched, wasted shape of my employer poking around my hotel suite. He was in the sitting area, testing the soil of a bonsai tree that was lazing on a bureau like a contented housecat.

"It's an old movie set in here," he said, surveying the vintage furnishings, the small kitchen and dining room, and a walk-in closet large enough to be a starlet's dressing room.

"I love it," I decided, trying to picture Miguel lounging on the old velvet sofa with me, this time not seductively, not like the brooding, oiled pharaoh, but doing what couples did every day: watching TV, talking, waiting for dinner to cook in the little kitchen . . .

As much as I loved my room, I hated Emerson's, across the hall —what must have once been a maid's room for the penthouse. The stale notes of a jazz number were coughing out of the radio when we let ourselves in. Immediately, I felt the refrigerated air pumping from a wall unit, and when he shut the door I nearly tripped over the single bed inside. The view onto Sunset Boulevard was screened off by sheer curtains. When I pulled back the curtain in his bathroom, I got the disturbing impression that the whole room was about to slide down the hillside.

I came out and found Emerson seated on the bed.

"The suites are a little nicer," I said encouragingly, lowering myself into the single chair next to him. "This must have been some kind of mistake. Why don't I ask the front desk to put you in a room like mine, or Tisa's, downstairs?"

"No," he protested, lying back on the pillow. "I want to be on this floor, across from you. I prefer a small room."

The space was so narrow, Tisa had to do a little dance to get by me when I let her in.

"Am I pale, Beth?" Emerson asked.

"A little."

"I can't go out," he said hopelessly.

I sensed he was going to cry.

"You need to recover from the flight," I said, silently cursing his aggressive schedule. "Why don't I switch your house visit to tomorrow?"

"No! No, it's like you said, I just need to rest. Just give me a few hours . . ."

Tisa worked around us in the little room to hook up his nutrition pack, and then we left him there to sleep while I took her downstairs to the garden terrace to get some lunch. Afterward, we ended up falling asleep by the pool, and by the time we changed and got back to his room Emerson was sitting on the edge of the bed, trying unsuccessfully to stuff his feet into his sneakers. No sooner had I said hello than he insisted I drive him to the Case Study House immediately.

"'Stime to go," he urged, slurring a little but full of renewed energy. "Theresaways traffic. Havtaget there by sunset."

I disliked chauffeuring him, because I knew he would have preferred to be the one behind the wheel, even in a rental car. And I was conscious that I drove without flair, as I had been instructed to do in driver's ed class, my only objective being to get where I was going without incident. Emerson couldn't help making cracks about the "lameness" of our car, particularly when we came shoulder to shoulder with fancier models, but to my relief he did not critique my performance as we shuttled from one traffic light to the next on Sunset. He seemed focused on his own thoughts, smiling to himself as we wound our way through the hot brown hills. I had to admit, glancing over at him, that Dr. Albas was right: He was rallying.

"You still haven't explained what we're doing here," I said as I followed the location scout's directions to an address that turned out to be nearly invisible from the road. "Are we meeting someone with photographs of this house *at the house?* Because that would be a first."

"No," he said, springing up and down in the passenger seat.

"Are you thinking of photographing the house yourself?"

That would be another first. I had never known him to commission photography, let alone shoot any pictures.

"No. But I am doing research, sort of."

"For?"

He inhaled audibly, irritated by my uncharacteristic nosiness.

I tried again. "What do you need me to do at this meeting?"

"Oh, I don't need you to do anything. I want to look at this house because I'm thinking of changing the kitchen in the loft."

"You're what?"

"Renovating."

The extent of his ambition astounded me. Until I remembered that he had been listening in on the extension the week before when I told Miguel that the upstairs neighbors were remodeling their kitchen. I'd never explained that they were only putting in new countertops and a ventilation fan. I considered telling Emerson this now, but I was afraid of giving him any more ideas. As ill as he was, he could not stand being outdone.

"The kitchen we're going to see has freestanding wooden cabinets," he explained. "They're like sculptures."

"I could have gotten you some books."

"I have all the books! I have the best photo ever taken of this house. And I'll get the interior shots I want, eventually."

I cringed at the reminder of my failure to obtain them.

"It's all right," he said. "You did me a favor. Because at first I just wanted the pictures. But coming here is much, much better."

We never used his kitchen, except to reheat things that he could barely eat. And given the intricacies of planning a construction project in a historic building in Greenwich Village, it was unlikely he would live to see a renovation completed. But it was clear that the plan had lit a fire in him.

The location scout had been inside the place enough times to be our de facto tour guide through what turned out to be a series of glass-walled rooms pitched dramatically over the hillside. In the kitchen, the scout pointed to a concrete slab under my sandals. "This floor radiates heat from the hot-water pipes underneath." His finger arched upward. "And on the roof there are solar panels. These kinds of ideas were being modeled in 1960—and way before that, even. You'd think they would have caught on by now." He shook his head. "In terms of cooling, this house has a couple of different strategies for natural ventilation."

Emerson had claimed to want to study the kitchen, so I was surprised when he barely glanced at it. Immediately after we arrived, he slipped behind me and limped off to another part of the house, leaving me to take the tour. But since the place had an open floor plan, I could see him the whole time. With evident determination, he cowboy-walked to the far end of the lounge area, to a vast opening where a glass wall was slid back, like an immense patio door, framing an endless stretch of evening. The sun was setting through the smog, and the view of Los Angeles was like outer space turned upside down, with a million twinkling galaxies floating in an endless grid.

Emerson was circling a spot in front of the glass as if he were looking for something he had lost. Measuring something?

The film scout and I stood watching him.

I could swear Emerson was acting out a stage play. There was another actor with him in the scene—in his mind, at least—and they seemed to be having a conversation. One he was clearly enjoying. As their imaginary talk grew more intense, I could see Emerson's face beaming with pleasure, his cheeks glowing with sweat. He was having the time of his life, bouncing lightly on the balls of his feet as he took in the view.

The scout called to him: "We're heading out to look at the pool. Coming?"

Emerson straightened his posture at the glass. The city was blooming to light at his feet. In that instant, the silhouette of his wasted form before that slice of infinity was the most gorgeous thing I could imagine. He had brought himself here to reenact some memory, I was certain. It stretched before him like an endless runway of lights promising to guide his ascent to the heavens.

His contentment was absolute—I felt it in myself through the strange connection we had, sensed the relief washing over him in his quiet poise. If anything was missing, it was only the knowledge that it could last.

I turned to the scout. "I feel like I've been here before."

"This house? You have. In about ten different movies."

"Wait—"

"Should I list them?" he asked. "Wanna test me?"

"No, it's not a movie. It's the Julius Shulman photograph. Of the man in a white dinner jacket. Looking out at—this."

"Ah. A classic."

"He owns a print of that photograph," I explained, tilting my head in Emerson's direction.

"A rare color print!" Emerson called back. He turned toward us with a beatific smile, then placed his hand against the glass and resumed his meditation.

At the evidence of his happiness, I practically floated around the pool area, around the virtual borderlands of an image that I'd walked past every day outside Emerson's office without taking much notice, surveying the scene now from different angles with as much satisfaction as my employer appeared to be experiencing, judging by his posture at the glass. He had brought himself there not for the kitchen at all, but for some private triumph—a victory over the difficulties of his degraded circumstances that he'd invited me not only to witness, but to share with him. We had come west to find an old hunk of metal, and now, through the workings of his eccentric life, I was standing inside a house of the future. Not logging photographs of it, or stalking a poster of it in his shrunken indoor neighborhood, but feeling for myself how it was to experience such a thing at full scale. It was infinitely more satisfying, I decided, to be inside the picture. It made me hungry for a future, for other new things.

I was standing by the pool, examining the wide, flat roof extending over the terrace, when Emerson hobbled out to join me.

"Cool, huh?" he said, staring up at a slice of the overhanging roof. "From this angle, it kinda looks like a dove." He held his hand out from his shoulder, imitating a wing, to demonstrate.

Shocked, I searched his face for a sign that he might know the significance of the words he had just spoken—words that had come from my mother's lips at the unexpected sight of the newly built TWA terminal when he was a baby, words his own mother had responded to. But I detected no recognition in his face, and without thinking, I found myself answering as his mother had done: "But the architect—he didn't live to see it."

This earned me a wistful smile from him, a smile that I thought cemented our bond at last as friends, not merely as employee and employer—until I realized he was only preparing to correct me.

"No, the architect of this house is still alive, though it's what, 1996? He's probably pretty old. I wonder if he comes swimming up here." He glanced longingly at the pool.

"Right," I replied, embarrassed. "I was thinking of another building."

"These houses—they're like the architects' brains. Pure ideas." He turned to me. "There's so much I wish I could do . . ."

"What would you do?" I asked gently, remembering how unhappy the conversation had made him the last time the subject had come up.

"What they did. Make something new. Think of a new way to make a house, and you can think of a new way to live. Brain becomes idea. Ideas become houses, cities, cars—wheels of progress. I don't have to be an architect. There are other ways." Far from sounding discouraged, he was reeling off the tenets of his own manifesto. "We're prisoners of old ideas, Beth. If we can make things new again, start with no idea of a house. Or a car. Or a city. It's like Eileen Gray said: We have to get rid of the old oppression in order to be conscious again of freedom."

He was looking at me, but his mind was somewhere else.

"People were ready to do that, once. What happened? What's

changed since then?" He reached out for the doorframe to steady himself and then started to walk away, lifting each foot with great effort.

"Hey, Emerson."

He was out of breath. "Hey," he answered.

"Are you planning to visit more of the houses in your collection?" I was a little afraid to know the extent of his ambition.

"I wish." He hung his head. "I'll be in there," he said, shuffling off to resume his vigil at the glass.

It was during those hours of ragged glory when the temporary peace he had forged with his body gave way. After carrying him for thousands of miles to the splendor of that sunset world, the blood he had absorbed during his last transfusion began to leak from his intestines like an overfilled sponge. By 9 p.m., he was curled into himself in his hotel bed while Tisa took a taxi to buy diapers. At 9:15, the hotel sent a doctor who proceeded to consult with Dr. Albas by phone. The blood loss was slow, he reported to her in that way doctors have of making things that look terrifying sound utterly matter-of-fact. Emerson would need another transfusion within a few days, but he preferred to have this done in New York. The hotel doctor advised against taking the red-eye that night, arguing that Emerson needed to regain his strength. Dr. Albas insisted he fly out no later than the next morning. As far as Miguel knew, my employer was coming to see the Beacon engine that night. I was trying to figure out if I should prepare him for the sight of Emerson when Miguel called to tell me he was running late. And by then, Emerson refused to venture even so far as the lobby downstairs.

"You've done this for me before, Beth. You know how to make an offer."

"But *you* wanted to be the one to find the engine."

He was right, of course. There was no way he should attempt to leave his room. Still, I cursed him silently for insisting on seeing the Case Study House when he could have been saving his energy for the main event of our trip. "It's just that you came all this way," I complained, arguing uselessly from disappointment. "You should be there. Not me."

"I've had my field trip," he said placidly.

He had sabotaged his own mission with an indulgence, and now he was calmly lying in his hotel bed with no trace of regret. He sounded much more concerned about the specifics of my meeting with Miguel.

"He's bringing you dinner here?" Emerson asked when I hung up the phone.

"Just some take-out," I said, wondering if he was trying to push me and Miguel together like some kind of matchmaker before I dismissed the thought as absurd. "He's still at work. He said he's starving. I assume it's so we can leave sooner to see the car."

"He's coming up to your room?"

I nodded.

"Call me when he's on the way up."

I moved to leave.

"Beth—"

I turned in the doorway. His expression was forlorn.

"Just get it."

It was after 10:30 p.m. when Miguel arrived at my room with an apology, a bottle of wine and two take-out orders of steak frites. In place of his green-cinnamon scent, I was greeted by a medley of cooking odors escaping from the bags in his hands.

"That smells delicious."

I moved aside to let him in. As he passed, I heard an almost imperceptible, plaintive groan from out in the corridor. When I looked back I was startled to see a pair of eyes peering out from the shadows across the hall. Eyes surrounded by the faint silvery glimmer of eyeglass frames. It was Emerson, not Tisa, peeking through the crack in his door, watching us.

At the sight of him lurking there, I felt guilty about the tempting odors of the food he couldn't eat, about having dinner with Miguel when I had sworn I would find the engine, and about the thought that had jabbed at me ever since I'd accepted Hélène's invitation to lunch: I was going to accompany Emerson to the end of his life—there was no question of that—but when the end came, I would go on, when he couldn't. I would outlive him, a prospect that felt as empty as the knowledge that I had already outlived myself. I looked to him across the expanse of hallway that marked our separateness, but the eyes peering back were no longer concerned with me. They were looking past me, intently studying Miguel, who was pulling his hair distractedly into spikes with one hand as he crossed the suite, swinging the bags of food in the other. Emerson's eyes softened as he watched Miguel unpacking the food onto the dining table, then widened in horror when I waved across the corridor to him. I mouthed the words *I'll get it,* to reassure him, but in response the eyes retreated, downcast, and the door clicked shut.

"I usually end up eating rubbish when I work late. This is actually pretty good," Miguel promised as we sat down in the little dining room. "My apologies about the hour. There's something we're working on . . ."

"It's all right. I needed the extra time. There was a problem earlier."

"A problem?"

"Just that my employer isn't going to be able to come with us tonight, to look at the engine."

"Oh, we're not going to make it out to the hangar tonight, Beth," he said, cutting intently into his steak.

"But—wait—" I pushed my food aside. "I'm not that hungry. I'd rather see the car. I'm probably going to have to fly back to New York in the morning. Everything's changed. Please, could we go now?"

He went on hungrily slicing off another forkful of meat. "It's pretty late, you know? I told the guy we'd be there by nine. I'll go if you want, as soon as we eat this. We can give it a shot. But I seriously doubt the guy's still going to be there at this hour."

He put down his fork and held out his arm to me, revealing a wristwatch nearly as big as my dinner plate. I could not deny it was legitimately too late. But knowing that didn't help.

"Tomorrow night we'll go," he offered. "I'll pick you up at seven."

Then, with a meditative frown, he realized he had not poured the wine. He disappeared with the bottle into the kitchen to find a corkscrew. I desperately wanted to walk across the hall and consult with Emerson about what to do, but my hunger for the food and Miguel's company kept me in my seat.

"I wish my grandfather could be here with us," he announced cheerfully when he returned with the open bottle.

"Did your grandfather visit Los Angeles often?"

He let out a laugh as he poured the wine. "God, no. I don't think he ever left the Midlands. He wouldn't even visit us in Spain. He was an Englishman to his bones. He said he would smear like wax in the sun." Miguel seemed to consider this. "Like his son did. But he would have been chuffed that someone cares so much about one of his engines."

I finally took a bite of my own dinner, and with a small shock I registered that Miguel had come to see me anyway, to have dinner, though he already knew we weren't going to make it out to see the car. I grew calmer as we talked, with him there next to me, relaxing at the end of a long day, as couples did all the time without thinking about it, maybe not even appreciating it. I was conscious of Emerson, just steps away, being tended to by an employee as his health was failing, then I remembered that I was his employee as well. My time with him had obscured my sense of being alone; now my solitude was as palpable as if Miguel had pulled it from one of the take-out bags in a Styrofoam box. I couldn't help wanting the dinner with Miguel to keep going, to happen night after night — not play-acting, as I knew I was doing, as it had always felt in the past, but in that real place on the other side of the glass. How long had it been since I had eaten dinner with anyone besides a home healthcare worker? A dinner that wasn't heated in Emerson's microwave.

Miguel's comment about his grandfather called to mind something he'd said to me at the Beacon party. "When we met in Germany, I told you that I wished someone was there with me," I reminded him. "And you said, 'Once someone is gone from your life, he might as well be dead.'"

"I wasn't in the best frame of mind that night," he said, shrugging off the memory. "Anyway, he is dead."

"But your grandfather's cars are still around," I said. "And they mean a lot to some people. Those guests at the party, I talked to some of them . . ."

"They're nostalgic." He looked uncomfortable with the thought. "Regardless of how much I respect my grandfather, my hope is that, before long, we can look forward to a different nostalgia."

I could not untangle the idea of looking forward to looking back differently. "What do you mean?"

"Well, a lot of people—and I'm one of them—have all sorts of personal associations with cars."

"Their self-image?" I suggested, recalling Emerson's damning assessment of our rental car.

He nodded. "Or their youth. All kinds of memories, feelings of freedom and power . . . Those associations get attached to one model or another, and the models change from one decade to the next. But the car itself—the basic machine—hasn't changed in a fundamental way since its invention. There are billions of people out there—every generation—with all these ideas attached to an outmoded template: what someone originally defined as 'a car' one hundred years ago. When you add it up, the nostalgia around this is immense. It's a real problem. But it won't always be."

I didn't know if I was misunderstanding him or if he was looking forward to some future event of mass extinction.

"Are you saying you want them all to die?"

"No—just the opposite. I want them to live *better*. If people like me do our jobs, the day will come when that original nostalgia will fade. It will be replaced by other associations, other ways of getting around. Completely new systems. By then, cars like the ones my grandfather built will have literally become inoperable, too impractical and expensive for anyone to drive." He tasted the wine with satisfaction, then seemed to reconsider. "The sad part —and I admit, it is sad—is that we'll have to admire the old models in museums. People will never know what it felt like to drive them." He stared into his wineglass, then met my eyes with a look of pained resignation. "Something always has to be sacrificed for progress."

I thought of Emerson, waiting in the next room for me to win him an engine that would eventually be as incapable of functioning as he was.

"It sounds like there won't be any gas to run them anyway," I said. "If you can get away from the traffic jams."

He sat forward. "I know my inheritance has a limited life span. I want to develop ideas the way the early pioneers did, but there was demand for what they were making. If we can't acknowledge certain problems, if people aren't interested in the solutions, I'm hurling them into a void."

I thought of Alto Bianco, derisively kicking at the bisected car in Germany.

Miguel stared at me intently. "This is my last chance to make a new Beacon, Beth. In any form."

In those hours at the table, as I listened to him talk about the potential for the future, the fragile shoots of many stray thoughts rose from my imagination and wove themselves into a fantasy of my own future. An intimate bond that was not familial and not forged out of duty, but a new plot, one I would tend to, and growing from it as solid as the trunk of a tree: a romance with Miguel. It was a reverie affixed, unreasonably perhaps, to nothing more than a polite gesture—a take-out meal offered in apology for a missed appointment—but one that took root that night nonetheless and began to grow in my heart as freely as a weed.

Emerson regarded me warily the next morning as I broke the news to him.

"You never went to see it?"

Tisa had knocked on my door to summon me, at his insistence. Now she was trying to work around us in the tiny room, packing up his clothing and meds for the airport.

"I waited and waited," he moaned. "I can't believe you didn't see it!"

"He fell asleep," Tisa said softly to me. "About half an hour after that guy got here."

"I knew he would," I said.

"Tisa said he was in your room for a long time," Emerson protested.

"We were eating dinner," I reminded him. "Anyway, everything got screwed up last night. It was already too late when he got here."

"So, when are you going to see it?"

"I don't know. I told him I wanted to check with my employer because I was planning to fly back to New York with you guys this morning."

"No! No way." He picked up a hand towel next to him and threw it at me. "We are *this* close. You've got to stay, Beth. Cancel your plane ticket—change it again, whatever."

I'd intended to leave with him in solidarity. I did not want to be away from him for even forty-eight hours, despite the fact that he was going directly into Dr. Albas's care on the other side. At the same time, I was anxious to see Miguel again.

"*If* I go to see the engine," I said, "he told me he'd pick me up at seven tonight."

"Good," Emerson said with a nod. "You're keeping that date."

"It's not a date."

"No. It's an appointment."

"I don't think the owners will be there," I said, secretly fearing that the owner would somehow turn out to be Hélène. "Miguel says it's a married couple. But he hasn't talked to them. He's been dealing with the man who looks after their collection—the head mechanic, basically. The owners agreed to let him show us the car as a courtesy, because we're affiliated with Beacon. Otherwise, they don't know why we're coming."

"Miguel's doing us a favor by not telling them," Emerson said. "Because if they know how much we want the engine, it could influence their asking price."

Apparently satisfied with this evidence of Miguel's competence, he reached his arms up expectantly, and Tisa pulled him to his feet to get ready for his flight.

"So, the car's for sale?" he asked, anxious to confirm my bidding position.

"Oh, no—not at all."

13

A CHAIN-LINK FENCE.

The sound of crickets.

In a disused section of the Burbank airport, the setting sun cast a blue glow over an expanse of weeds and crumbling blacktop. Along an aging stretch of runway converted into a private dragway, a crew of shirtless men in jeans hunched in unison, burning old rubber patches off the strip to make it new again. Tendrils of acrid tar fumes filled my nose and throat. Thick smoke from the rows of small fires obscured the men's legs. Their torsos floated on the burning stench, blown west across decades of fevered races, twisting in the evening wind with the light, cool scent of clover.

At the end of the access road, a quarter mile or so past where the tarmen worked, Miguel parked his loaner sedan in front of a private airplane hangar. One of the doors had been rolled back, revealing a small office at the rear, where a radio was warring with a television for dominance. A middle-aged man in a baseball cap and a denim shirt and jeans emerged from the office to shake hands with Miguel.

"Thought you were coming last night."

"I'd hoped to," said Miguel. "But it got quite late. This is Beth Corvid."

In the semidarkness, we drifted among the dozens of vehicles parked in formation across the square footage of the hangar. The walls were decorated with racing posters even bigger than Emerson's house portraits. The one in front of me announced a French race in 1947 with an illustration of snow-covered peaks done in bright, simple blocks of color. A red car—drawn like a cigar with crazily spinning wheels—was whipping around a sharp turn in a mountain pass, with a green cigar gaining from the rear.

Despite the frantic activity on the walls, the air around us was still, suffused with a concentration of curious odors: leather and dust and gasoline. It wasn't an unpleasant smell, but the smell of a certain age.

"I don't see any Beacons here," Miguel noted with some concern.

I followed his gaze across the hangar. With so many motionless, hunched shapes before me, I had the sensation of being in a morgue.

"Car's been moved out," said the mechanic, watching us in the dim light.

"What do you mean?" Miguel asked.

It was the first time I had heard him sound anything other than self-assured.

"A friend of Mr. Russell's had a trailer going up this afternoon with a few other cars. Had space—offered to take it." The mechanic chuckled. "Saved us some mileage on the odometer."

"Bollocks." Miguel pressed a hand to his forehead and shook his head apologetically. "That car was meant to be there for another two days."

He took a seat beside me at one of the wicker tables in my hotel lobby. As anxious as I was to phone New York and tell Emerson about the latest complication, I indulged my desire to talk with Miguel, as I had done the previous evening upstairs, until he'd finally said goodnight with a polite kiss on both cheeks.

The fact that the car had already been moved up to the event, several hours' drive north of Los Angeles, meant that I could not report a victory to Emerson, who was waiting by the phone. And when he learned what had happened, he would no doubt insist that I remain in California until I had secured the engine. With this thought came the hope of spending more time with Miguel.

"It's a setback," I allowed, unsure of how much more assistance Miguel was willing to offer. "But at least we know where the car's going to be."

The waiter passed Miguel a cup of coffee, followed by a bowl of brown sugar cubes.

"Can we go back to plan A, so to speak?" I asked. "Approach the owners at the event this Sunday?"

"You need an invitation," he said. "Tickets."

I hadn't considered this, but it did not seem like an insurmountable obstacle. "Can't you hook us up with something through AG?"

"Us?" he asked, dissolving a sugar cube in the coffee on his spoon.

My cheeks went hot with embarrassment as I recalled, when we'd first spoken of it on the phone, that he'd mentioned he had plans for the weekend.

"I was talking about my employer," I lied, wondering how I was going to sort out whatever I needed to do to get myself there. "I don't want to get into a lot of detail, but my employer is determined to get this engine, Miguel. I can't go back without it."

"I'll look into it in the morning," he offered distractedly, before raising my hopes again. "At least we have a few days to work out the arrangements. Because by now every hotel on the Monterey Peninsula will have been booked for months. Unless we sleep outdoors—"

"Camping?"

Since I was a child—since those nights in the oxygen tent at the hospital—I hated tents. I hated the feeling of cold earth under my body.

"What do you have against camping?" he asked, reading my face with evident amusement.

I shook my head. "I tried it once in college . . ."

"You say that like it's a drug."

"No, I tried it, and it was . . ."

Too late, I worried that I was endangering Emerson's interests as well as my own. But to my delight, he shifted onto the sofa next to me and leaned in conspiratorially.

"I just remembered something from school myself," he said. "Something I saw—probably the most useful thing I learned at that place, now that I think about it."

"What did you see?"

"It was a bird, a blackbird. It got into a hall where I was studying. Some students held the windows open, I opened one myself, but the thing couldn't find its way out. It kept flying back and forth from one wall to the other." He swung his hand like a metronome over the wicker table in front of us. "It couldn't change its schema. We tried to coax it the other way, but it got more and more panicked. It thought it was trapped, when the whole time it was free."

"Did it escape?"

"I'm afraid not, no." He frowned at the memory. "Broke its neck, I think. I put it in my jacket and buried it on the way back to my room." He reached into his jacket pocket, as if the broken body might still be found there. "That was at boarding school." He seemed to be balling his fist tighter inside his pocket. "After my grandfather died, my father—well, my parents . . ."

"You didn't live with them?"

"They were dead too."

"Oh—I didn't understand."

"I didn't either. They were like that blackbird, except they flitted between their drugs of choice."

I didn't know what to say.

"What I was telling you last night—what I'm trying to do with my grandfather's company," he went on. "It's the same problem, not changing the way we do things. I don't want that to happen to people."

I was moved by his earnestness. Except it was almost as if he wasn't speaking to me, but to someone who wasn't there — someone he cared about deeply but who he doubted cared for him. Someone who needed to be convinced.

"Were you at school in England?" I asked, wondering where the blackbird was buried.

"Other places too. Before that, home, as far as I was concerned, was at the factory with my grandfather. My parents were always off somewhere, with increasingly dodgy people. I preferred to be with my grandfather, taking things apart, learning how they were put together."

I thought about this. "The only way I ever found out how things were put together was after they broke."

"I miss him," Miguel said. He extracted the hand from his pocket, and I saw that he was holding a wallet. He removed a small color photograph and held it out to me shyly: Framed within the white border was an older man gesturing enthusiastically behind the wheel of a vintage car. At his elbow was the younger, excited face of Miguel, hanging on to whatever the man was saying.

"I keep him alive through his company. There's no way I would reject it or do something else. To avoid my father's fate, what I do is, I work all the time."

"How old were you?" I asked, pointing to the little boy.

"About seven or eight."

He nodded self-consciously and put the photo back into his wallet.

Our seating area in the lobby was lit by a floor lamp, circa 1930 — a bouquet of tiny round light bulbs under a fringed shade. The combined force of the diminutive bulbs produced a glow that was otherworldly, like the softness of a silent film. Remarkably, the light erased the worry lines on Miguel's face. I wondered what it did to mine: I was tired, I knew. And nervous.

Our legs were touching. I thought we might have kissed then, but he sat forward abruptly and pushed the wallet back into his jacket, saying he would have to make some calls about Monterey and would get in touch with me the next day. Our goodbye was a repeat of the night before: a polite kiss on both cheeks.

I lingered on the sofa after he left, unwilling to admit the evening was over until my eyelids surrendered to exhaustion, my head muddled by jet lag and anxiety. Outside my room, flapping around in my bag for the key, a picture came to my mind of Miguel kneeling in the grass with the broken bird, its quietly instructive life brought to rest in some damp, anonymous plot.

14

A WATERY SENSATION WASHED through my dreams, pulling me up out of a sea of twisting forms and metal curves, a locking mechanism sliding open—and with every breath came the sensation of air filling me up, pushing against my frame. My ears flooded with waves of sound, the mechanical song of an engine . . .

I woke to the melody of an old spiritual. It was nearly over by the time I got out of bed and traced the source to a car radio down on the access road, on the canyon side of the hotel.

I pushed open the window.

Swing low, sweet chariot, comin' for to carry me home . . .

Miguel's loaner sedan from AG was revving below, buffed and polished for a road trip. The echo of the spiritual ribboned through my head as we drove north that morning under the pastel sky, a blur of deep purple flowers spilling endlessly over the highway barriers.

"I like the way you drive. You don't confuse skill with frenzy," I told Miguel, grateful not to have to reach for the grab handles overhead or brace my knees to steady myself. "Normally—I mean, when other people have driven me—everything is so rushed."

He stared at the road. "Thank you, Beth. I'm a keen driver, as you might imagine."

At his request, we lowered the windows a crack. "I like to feel something of the road," he said. "Otherwise I might as well be riding in a lift."

A low roar filled the cabin, and I sank comfortably into the privacy of my own thoughts. During my last phone call to update Emerson, he'd expressed my orders for Monterey succinctly: "Be ruthless." I'd told him about the mechanic's convincing talk of a Mr. Howard Russell, who appeared to be the owner of the car, along with his wife, Sissy. "I'm not sure what you're dealing with anymore," Emerson said. "This could go a lot of ways. Anyway, I don't care who you're bidding against." I could hear him lunging forward in his bed. *"You're an attack dog.* Do you understand?"

My nervousness receded the farther north I traveled with Miguel. Once again, his presence put me at ease. I had the feeling that I belonged where I was, doing what I was doing. This alone was acutely abnormal, but then again, I was on the opposite coast, where the abnormal might be normal, and the more I was with him, the less outrageous my fantasy of being with him seemed. He had not left me to fend for myself with the engine, after all, for some reason that wasn't clear. Was it too much to hope there was some mutual attraction? It could not be a coincidence that my time with Miguel was increasing as Emerson's was growing shorter. The reality of Emerson's condition was never far from my mind. I did not know what his death was going to be like—how it would unfold or how I would handle it—but it was advancing on me like a widening fault line. There was a chasm cracking open at my feet, and I had no concrete to fill it with. I would have to build another foundation for myself after he was gone, and I was beginning to imagine one I wanted to build.

My thoughts were interrupted somewhere on Highway 1, almost to Monterey, when the car clipped an oncoming butterfly. It was a tiny death, one that might have slipped from my notice if not for the geographic coordinates of the windshield, which left the point of impact beyond the arching jets of cleaning fluid.

Mushroomy chunks of body and wings were still flaking off when we went through a wide turn north of Big Sur. The coast took a deep breath. The earth's belly dropped. Then the hills came into view again and everything felt more sunken: the road, the ranch houses, the brown hills and the Pacific extending endlessly on stretches with no haze, the palm trees slightly lower than the power lines, the streetlights slightly higher than the endless sprawl of red tile roofs.

We passed through Carmel, a town with no streetlights and, remarkably, no mailboxes, and continued out onto the peninsula, where the properties were more hidden, just glints of water and clay chimneys between slivers of green. The road twisted amid pine and scrub and cypress, and as we drove deeper into the forest, the odors of pine and wood smoke mingled with Miguel's green-cinnamon scent. I touched my hand to the stream of air coming in the window. Was this how Hélène had felt, driving in the Beacon with Alto? As if the past had not hurt and the future was going to be different? I was more content being on the road with Miguel than anything I could remember doing in the previous thirty years, except for those few hours earlier in the week, when I had seen Emerson standing at the glass in the Case Study House, caught up in his private reverie.

"So, tomorrow's the big day," Miguel said.

"It was today—for that butterfly," I joked, pointing to what was left of it on the windshield.

"The milky mark it's left there on the glass is interesting," he said. "A bit like an abstract painting."

I laughed. "You sound like a Futurist."

"Pardon?"

"I've been reading about these artists in Italy at the turn of the century. I'm doing a little research."

"I'm familiar with the Futurist movement," he said. "But —they killed butterflies?"

"No. Well, conceptually. They glorified violence as art. They glorified war, too, as the world's hygiene. They were militant. And misogynistic."

Miguel paused to consider this catalogue, then added gamely, "Weren't they ageist, too?"

I nodded, appreciating once again how easy it was to talk to him. Like talking to Emerson. "Right from the start, they imagined their own end," I said. "Within ten years they thought they would be obsolete. And they welcomed this, because they would grow old, they said. It was natural to them that they should be overthrown themselves."

He shot me a wry look. "Well, I wish they'd been right. But I doubt they really wanted to be forgotten. They wrote enough manifestoes."

We were having a conversation, I recognized, about something I was interested in. As people did. As couples did. On road trips together. I hated to think it might not continue past Sunday afternoon.

"They wanted to tear down museums—and libraries and art academies. They compared them to cemeteries!" I fumed, insulted by the implied denigration of large swaths of my profession.

"Well, we ruin them anyway, don't we?" said Miguel. "Through disregard, through policies of neglect. Or through conquest—when we bomb the treasures of some country, or claim them and divide them up . . . But the thrust of their program, as I understand it, was to create while looking ahead—not to worship the past. That was the essence, anyway." He concluded with a dismissive wave. "The anarchy, the politics, that's something else entirely."

Until then, I had avoided going into detail with him about the possible showdown I faced with Hélène, but now I sensed I could confide in him, and he was the only ally I had.

"Do you remember the artist I asked you about the night we met, at the party?"

He shook his head. "I spoke with a lot of people that evening. I'm sorry."

"It's all right. Her name is Hélène Moreau. She had ties to Futurism, according to someone at her gallery."

"I've heard of her. She did a lot with cars, if I remember."

"Yes, and we think she has something to do with the engine we want. Until I came out here on Monday, I was trying to find out if this was true. I've met her, actually. But—it's complicated. I don't want to speak to her now."

"I'm told by—" He paused. "I'm sure I've mentioned this, Beth. The car we're going to see is owned by a married couple, in Beverly Hills."

"Except you haven't met them. And we haven't seen the engine number. We still don't know if this is the right car."

He nodded as we turned into the grounds of the hotel, an upscale lodge and outbuildings bordering the golf course where the car show would be held. I was surprised when he said then that we were not guests of AG. Our hotel rooms and entry passes for the auto event were courtesy of a Swiss watch manufacturer, whose CEO, Miguel explained, was a friend from school. On hearing this, I was touched by his efforts, since he'd sounded so annoyed at first by the turn of events. The rich notes of a new perfume crept in from the gardens around the hotel. I watched with a twinge of longing as Miguel unloaded our suitcases, and I reminded myself there was nothing between us except his faultless courtesy and a promised errand for my failing employer. Emerson had already left a message for me with the front desk. I opened the envelope in the privacy of my room. His instructions for me remained succinct:

Certain victory.

I wondered if putting the car and the engine back together was all he felt he had to hold on to: an artificial race that he could run until the end, one last competition to distract himself from the nothingness he believed awaited him. Was it the engine or the chase itself that meant so much to him? I doubted I would ever know.

After a dinner spent talking over the schedule for the Concours the next day, Miguel and I walked the garden paths around the hotel. The night air sank and spread around us as it cooled, funneling thick wood smoke across the peninsula.

"Did you know," Miguel asked, recovering from a coughing fit, "that the carbon from basic household cooking fires is responsible for nearly twenty percent of global warming?"

"Do they teach you those statistics to divert the blame?"

He stopped abruptly. "What blame? Beth, we haven't made a new Beacon in thirty years." He shook his head with disappointment. "Don't you see? That's the problem."

"I wasn't thinking."

"All I'm saying is, this enormous amount of carbon pollution could be avoided if people could be helped to obtain better, more modern cooking equipment. We still need to cook."

"Sure. There's nothing wrong with cooking."

"It's down to the execution. It's the same with transportation. We have to look at everything."

"Is this what you do when you're joyriding around L.A. on your motorcycle, burning gasoline?"

I cringed at the rustiness of the flirting levers in my brain. Sparring with Emerson was not good training for a would-be coquette.

He cocked his head. "I'm not alone as often as I was when we met."

I wasn't sure what he meant.

"Being in L.A., of course," I suggested.

He nodded.

I shivered.

"It's mild tonight," he said. "Why are you cold?"

"Because I'm a ghost," I said with a shrug. "An obvious sign of this is when you can't retain heat."

Without warning, he took my hands to test them in the warmth of his own, a grip that was pleasantly rough, less pampered than I would have expected. I closed my eyes and imagined his touch continuing over the rest of my body.

"I see what you mean," he joked, moving to sniff around my hair and neck. "What's strange is that you don't have any smell, either."

I leaned in until my cheek was nearly on his chest. "You do. It's nice. What is that scent?"

"It's from England. It reminds me of —"

He stopped. Until then he had seemed delighted by my presence, but now he looked either confused or upset that our walking path had led to my room. We stood together a few feet from the door. He shuffled his feet. "So, Beth, why are you researching Futurism? You mentioned it in the car."

"Because of that artist I mentioned, Hélène Moreau. I've been reading about the whole movement in a book I brought with me. I have it inside . . ."

I didn't tell him how I had confided in her, and how I had begun to feel close to her, as I did to him. He was glancing around at the other bungalows as I pushed the card key into the lock. I left the door open behind me, and he followed me into the room.

"From what I recall, the Futurists had strong opinions on lust," he said, nodding agreeably as I lifted the book out of my suitcase.

"Yes. But they didn't define it very progressively. They used it to justify rape and all kinds of violence after military conquest. A lot of it is disgusting, really."

I sat beside him with the book, making an effort to counteract the disorientation I felt by continuing to speak in complete sentences. "But they did want to transform lust into works of art."

His long, muscular leg was pressed against mine on the sofa, his arm available to lean against. I settled back with him, lifted the book and began reading from one of the bookmarked passages.

"'Lust is a force.'"

"That's it," he said. A wide smile wrinkled his eyes closed. "Who said that?"

"This was the manifesto of Valentine de Saint-Point, writing in 1913. A female Futurist. One of the few."

"Go on," he said, nudging me with his leg.

"'Lust is for the body what an ideal is for the spirit—the magnificent Chimera, that one ever clutches at but never captures, and which the young and the avid, intoxicated with the vision, pursue without rest.'"

I stopped reading, wondering if I was succumbing to such an idealized force. Then Miguel's lips came to rest on mine, with a pressure somehow both delighted and perplexed.

15

A PALE CRESCENT OF beach spread before a low retaining wall off the fairway where the Concours d'Elegance was already under way in a light morning fog. Fifty yards offshore, in one of nature's quiet dramas, a lone tree leaned crookedly to one side on an outcropping of rock. Isolated, motionless but for the light breeze on its leaves, the tree stretched its branches past the rock where its roots were bound, reaching for a passing sea bird, for sunlight—for anything that might rescue it from its solitude.

"That tree is copyrighted," Miguel informed me as he sat down across the table at the terrace restaurant for breakfast.

I sensed immediately from those few impersonal words that he was back in his formal mode, the way he had been that first evening in the zeppelin.

"I recognize that tree," I told him. "There's a silhouette of it printed on the shampoo bottle in my room."

I hoped the mention of my hotel room would encourage him to comment on the fact that we had spent part of the previous evening there together. Even so, I wasn't entirely surprised when he said nothing.

We sat staring in silence at the futile, copyrighted tree, as if nothing more than a goodnight had passed between us in the hours since. It was not much more than that anyway, I reminded myself: His stubble was damp when our faces came together, his eyes closed in pleasure. His hand reached for me and I was brought closer to the muscular contours of his arms and chest. I settled into his warmth, encircled by his arm, learning the lines of his body through the fabric of his shirt and suit. I was sinking into that magical realm of escape, as fogged and private as the night air outside, when I opened my eyes for a moment and was met with an expression of mild panic. I can only attribute what happened next to that look in his eyes, for with an abrupt, robotic apology about the hour and the long day ahead of us—repeated unnecessarily several times—he'd pushed his shirttail roughly into the waistband of his pants and made for the door.

I omitted all this from the phone conversation I'd had with Emerson before breakfast. Now Miguel seemed intent on devoting the breakfast hour to an explanation of copyright from the legal perspective of the tree. It was a disappointing step back in our acquaintance, but nothing could suppress the rush of adrenaline I felt when we walked together out onto the fairway. By then, the early-morning fog had burned off, and the sky was brilliant with sun. Before us on the golf course stretched a larger-than-life version of my brother Garrett's Matchbox collection, a precision lineup on wall-to-wall emerald shag. Along the fairway, the crowd split and remixed itself around an array of white tents crowned with pennants flapping in the breeze.

"I feel like we're in a medieval tournament," I said, dropping my sun hat to my hip like a shield.

Miguel, dressed in a dark suit and a linen shirt, was busy reading the show program, holding the booklet at arm's length before him as he walked. A crash of static split the air, and then a male announcer's voice erupted from the chain of loudspeakers running the length of the fairway: "Ladies and gentlemen, the owners and exhibitors have spent countless hours preparing their cars for today's Concours. They want you to enjoy them, but the rule is 'Look, don't touch.'"

A tangle of blue blazers, summery dresses and sun hats moved through the automotive sculpture park as groups of spectators alighted like flies before one antique car or another. One of the first models to attract my attention was a 1954 Rolls-Royce Phantom IV, identified, like many of the cars, by a special license plate on the front. In the back seat, a woman in vintage costume was smiling wickedly, paging through a gossip magazine in her lap.

"This car was once owned by Princess Margaret," Miguel informed me, pointing to a royal shield affixed to the hood.

"I love the names of those cars," I said as we walked on, recalling a documentary on Rolls-Royce that Emerson had made me watch with him one lethargic winter afternoon. The model names drifted like vapor across my mind. "Silver Ghost. Silver Wraith . . ."

"Phantom," added Miguel.

"Silver Cloud."

"My grandfather worked at Rolls-Royce during the Second World War," Miguel said. "He was an engineer, one of the professions the government exempted from service at the front, because they were needed at home. But he fought on the back end, in the aero division, where they built Merlins. That's a kind of —"

"Engine."

"You've heard of them?"

"Yes." I regretted that I hadn't paid more attention to my father's air-battle narrations over the years. "Those engines were the heroes of the war. My father always talks about the Spitfires, the Lancasters."

Miguel nodded, but instead of finishing his story, he gestured with his program to the scene unfolding in front of us. A seagull had landed on a rock at the edge of the coastline, where a photographer was taking beauty shots of an elegant coupe, its paint and metalwork glinting in the sunshine. The hood ornament was a finely executed miniature of a stork in flight—one of the countless permutations of wings mounted on the cars and wildlife around us. As the photographer snapped away, the metal figurine and the live bird appeared to lock eyes in the precursor to some avian duel.

"There are two Beacon 135 roadsters here today," Miguel said, folding back the program. "I suggest we take a look at both of them." He flashed me an unexpected smile. "You never know."

The car we had missed seeing in Los Angeles was parked at the far end of the fairway, about a ten-minute walk from where we stood. The one we came to first was the bonus car: a green roadster with a tan leather interior.

A heavyset man dressed in a morning coat and a beret came forward and greeted us with an inquiring smile.

"Just admiring your ride here," said Miguel.

"Ever driven one of these?" the man asked.

"Oh, yes," said Miguel. "In fact, I'm in the market for one now. And I'm curious to know, does yours by any chance have a replacement engine?"

The man smiled with a trace of arrogance. "No. It's the original."

"Still running well, then?"

"Of course. When they built this car, they did it right. For one thing, it was built by human beings, not robots."

"Thanks for the information."

Miguel shook his head, smiling to himself, as we made our way down the fairway.

"What's your position on robots?" I asked, wondering if it would generate as much chatter from him as copyright law had done.

"Critical, for many things," he said. "With cars, for preassembly, components, paint. But what he was talking about, final assembly, it's still partially done with human hands."

He ran his own hand through his hair, coaxing the spikes to

higher points. "I think most technicians are proud of what they're building. That's not to say they wouldn't be more proud to build something cleaner."

The second Beacon was so striking in its position on the fairway that I spotted it from a hundred yards away. The pale blue body was parked at an abrupt angle to the coast, as if the couple who owned it had abandoned it there in a fit of ecstatic passion and run off together into the waves, leaving the car to gaze tranquilly at the Pacific.

As if Emerson were urging me on, I raced ahead of Miguel to reach the car first. But it hadn't been abandoned. What I found when I ran up alongside the Beacon was a boy seated on a lawn chair—he couldn't have been more than fifteen years old —dressed in what seemed to be the male uniform of the day: a navy blazer and khaki trousers with a button-down shirt and tennis sneakers. He was absorbed in reading the show program on his lap.

"Hi," I said.

He lifted his eyes as Miguel rushed up behind me.

"I'd love to show my friend the engine of your car, if you wouldn't mind," Miguel said, panting slightly. "I'm trying to get one myself."

The boy nodded impassively. "It's my grandfather's."

Nothing about his posture suggested that he had any intention of moving.

"Would he let you give us a quick look?" I asked.

The boy turned back to the program. "He's walking around. He'll be back at some point."

Miguel stared down the endless green expanse, swarming with people. "We'll try back later," he said with a disappointed smile. "You're good to look after it for him."

It was past midday when we retreated down the fairway. The sun was hotter now, the brown hills in the distance a hazy gray. A dozen speedboats were anchored in the cove, bobbing over masses of kelp as thick as the crowds hurrying across the lawn in search of food. In the hospitality area where Miguel had arranged for us to have lunch, we ate among hundreds of others on a crazy quilt of picnic blankets spanning the grass in front of the lodge. Above this lively tailgate party ascended the ramp to the winner's circle, an Astroturf arch rising from a profusion of white flowers. In less than an hour, I reminded myself, Emerson's engine could be crossing into that winner's circle. And for the hundredth time that day I silently wished he were with me and Miguel.

Another loud crackle of static split the air as an announcer in a baggy linen suit took his place at the podium in front of us. "We all love to talk about our cars in superlative terms," he began. "But today we are surrounded by some that truly deserve it! These cars are splendid."

Spectators surged at the balcony railings of the hotel overlooking the winner's circle, clapping gently so as not to spill their drinks.

"Ladies and gentlemen, I take pleasure in presenting more than two hundred of the world's premier classics. Exotic, unusual and breathtaking examples of automotive artistry."

Champagne corks popped on the lawn as the parade of elegance commenced with a collage of elaborate metalwork. The first car to make its way along the viewing lane resembled a marvelous tropical fish. "That's extremely rare," Miguel noted, pointing out one fact or another about each vehicle as the parade rolled by under the hot sun. To my delight, his arm and leg brushed against mine more and more frequently; he leaned closer in consultation as the announcement of the winners grew near.

"Some of these cars have been in restoration for years," the announcer remarked. "Of course the owners have passion, or they wouldn't do it. Their passion is shared by everyone who works on these cars—the mechanics, the metal-benders, the guys in the shop—God bless them!"

As each class was called, the winning cars crossed the ramp

driven by their owners: Karl-Heinz, Omar, Buck, Corrine, Jean-Claude . . . The Beacon's category was approaching when my eyes were riveted by an alarming sight. Was I imagining it, or was I looking directly at the back of Hélène Moreau's blond, bobbed head?

Almost as soon as I spotted it, the apparition of her coiffure disappeared into one of the hospitality tents across the grass. I excused myself from Miguel, trying to suppress my panic as I made my way through the crowd, leaping over and between picnic blankets like a dancer en pointe.

What the hell is she doing here?

You know exactly what she's doing here, Beth.

Spoiling everything, when I was so close.

The security guard at the roped-off entrance glanced down at my badge. "You don't have a pass for this tent."

I pressed closer to the rope. "I know that woman."

I pointed to what I assumed he could make out, through a crowd of at least fifty others in a shaded tent, as the bobbed back of Hélène's head.

"Can't help you."

The guard waved me to one side to let a small group enter the tent.

Be ruthless.

"What about that guy she's with, the guy with the bright yellow baseball cap?"

Whoever the blond woman happened to be, she was — according to one of the helpful guests passing into the tent ahead of me — drinking coffee with the chief executive of a French crystal company.

I was certain it was Hélène. Or was it? It was impossible to tell from the back, and the woman wouldn't turn. What if Emerson had been right all along? What if she was the real owner after all, using the other couple as a cover? Or was she there to get the engine herself and to mount it on a pedestal in her studio like a

Duchamp sculpture, as Emerson imagined? So soon after I had reveled in a sweeping sensation of triumph, victory could not have felt any less certain.

Then the Beacon's class was announced and I was forced to abandon my surveillance. I raced back across the viewing area toward Miguel, jumping through the field of blankets and bodies. When the announcer called the winners' names I leapt into the air.

"Howard and Sissy Russell of Beverly Hills, California!"

My heart leapt next, at the sight of the pale blue car advancing down the lawn at a jaunty clip. Then, to the sound of the audience's applause, Emerson's engine was rolling into the winner's circle.

"Nobody could believe these cars when they first came out," the announcer cried. "George M. Beacon won worldwide acclaim for his company's stunning roadsters."

At the foot of the ramp, the driver hit the throttle.

"Listen to that engine! A sound to die for, as you can hear. And one that rarely failed. Thank you, Howard and Sissy, for bringing it across."

The car passed us in the viewing lane, a prize ribbon fluttering from the windshield. I fell into step behind it. I could hear Miguel jogging in his brogues behind me, rushing to keep up as we followed the car back to its parking area on the grass. Once again I felt myself pulling ahead of him, straining to reach the car first. Even before the Beacon came to a stop I called out to the driver. "Congratulations!"

"I was just—going to say the same," panted Miguel, arriving on my heels.

The man I presumed to be Howard climbed out from behind the wheel. He pulled the ribbon off the windshield and dropped it onto the front seat.

"Sis, this is inside," he said, wiping his mouth.

He was tall and strangely muscular, or maybe it was just that he had a youthful body compared to his face: The sharply angled cheeks were sanded by wind and sun, framed by sideburns the same stark white as the hair peeking out from the sides of his baseball cap. He wore an impeccably pressed version of his grandson's outfit, with the addition of a necktie.

Howard glanced over at his car and broke into a wide grin. "It's something, isn't it? Hardly the most significant Beacon in the world, but it's something."

The grandson unfolded himself from his chair and announced that he was walking down to the winner's circle to watch the rest of the ceremony.

"How much time did you spend restoring it?" Miguel ventured.

"You never ask those questions," Howard protested. "Not about the time or the money. The truth is, I don't think about it. And I never keep the receipts—because a long time ago, I *did* keep the receipts, and I made the mistake of adding them up and dividing the total by the number of times I drove the car. I was so miserable, there weren't enough drugs to console me . . ."

I couldn't take my eyes off the hood of the Beacon. One pale blue sheet of metal was the only thing standing between me and Certain Victory.

"Even after years of therapy," Howard continued, "I keep buying cars."

"Let's drink to the Concours," said Sissy, offering around a tray of plastic champagne flutes. "Because anywhere else, people would be horrified by these things he's saying."

"To victory," said Howard, giving me a wink that reminded me uncomfortably of Alto Bianco at the party in Germany.

Miguel turned to Howard. "May I ask where you found this car?"

"The chassis was in Argentina," Howard said. "This was supposed to be the 'donor' car for another Beacon I was working on —a coupe. I didn't plan to restore this roadster, too, but one thing led to another. What can I say? I love them both."

"Howard's been restoring this car for as long as I can remember," Sissy said. She was a slender woman who I guessed to be in her sixties, with blond hair fluffed over the sides of a black tennis visor. Her freckles and the champagne flute in her hand made her look more girlish than sun-damaged. She turned to Howard. "There was that part you could never find . . ."

I tensed.

"A taillight," he said. "No, it wasn't hard to find. You just heard about it a lot when I was doing it."

They kissed.

"Sissy's into cars," Howard informed us.

"I admit it."

"This really was a golden age, wasn't it?" Howard said. "You look at the Beacons after this era and they're not as subtle."

"This was the cleanest sculpture," Miguel agreed. "May I touch it?"

"Sure. It already won!"

Before I knew what he was doing, Miguel took my fingers in his own, cueing a reveille of nerves at the base of my spine. I panicked for a split second: I thought he was going to make a lunge for the hood, but instead he gently placed my hand on the front fender. The curved metal was warm from sitting in the sun. His hand guided mine as our fingers spanned the length of the car, like blind children. The flow of the lines felt like a body bending backward, but stronger and more permanent.

"Miguel is affiliated with the Beacon Motor Company," I told Howard and Sissy, launching into the introduction we had agreed on earlier.

"My grandfather's pride," said Miguel, releasing my hand. "Destroyed by my father. As every Beacon owner knows." He shook his head. "Apparently there weren't enough drugs to console him either."

"I'm sorry," said Sissy, patting Miguel's arm sympathetically.

"It was a long time ago," he said, reassuring her with one of his ruffled smiles. "He took himself and my mother out in a blaze of glory. I'm pretty sure *they* didn't feel a thing."

Howard put a hand on Miguel's shoulder. "I know the Germans are involved now with Beacon. Sis and I got an invitation to some event. After being out of business all these years, you're going to build cars that don't pollute?"

"We're not building anything yet," Miguel said. "Unfortunately. But what you're talking about, what we showed in Germany, that was just one concept, to start." Suddenly his tone grew cynical. "To feed AG's publicity machine."

The three of them were huddled around their discussion like my father and mother with Garrett at the dinner table.

"No one's figured out the fuel," Howard said.

"That's right," Miguel said. "But that's only one piece. We're looking at how to integrate different forms of mobility. Forget the old idea of a car. Think about transportation more broadly . . ."

While no one was looking, I touched the Beacon again. The heat of the body sank into my fingertips. I felt for its dormant pulse beneath my own. Inches away, under the hood, lay a piece of machinery that could convert energy into motion, could generate power on an earth-changing scale. It had altered everything in the world in the span of its brief existence. I felt all the more tiny and ineffectual by comparison.

". . . and innovative energy policies," Miguel was saying. "The world's population is being compacted into dense urban areas. What if our forms of mobility changed entirely?"

Howard took a step back, visibly overwhelmed by the extent of Miguel's to-do list. "Well, the last Beacons in the seventies were terrible," he said, "with all due respect to your father."

Miguel let out a hearty laugh, apparently enjoying Howard's critical assessment. "No, believe me, my father would not have commanded your respect if you'd met him in the seventies. And probably not much before that either."

"But for Britain—Sissy and I lived there for a while—this is national culture. The marque may carry on, but where's the authenticity? They've moved the Heritage Trust to Germany, for God's sake. There's a bunch of companies doing these revivals—"

"You can forget about the World War Two order of things," Miguel said. "The industry isn't organized as much on national lines now. In many cases, that's not even desirable."

Howard smiled ruefully. "Tell that to the blokes in Lugborough who are out of work."

"Unfortunately, they would have lost their jobs anyway, because Beacon—as it was—could never have continued. My father had psychedelic visions, but he and his colleagues didn't have the vision to lead anyone into a sustainable future, let alone—"

I tapped Miguel anxiously. He looked confused and then, suddenly remembering my mission, he, in turn, tapped the hood of the car.

"Since we're going on about Beacons, Howard, could we show Beth here the engine? It was the most important part of the car to my grandfather. I'd love for her to see it."

Howard nodded and handed his champagne to Sissy.

I felt my stomach contract as he reached under the center of the dashboard for the hood release. But I knew what I was looking for, and where to look. Emerson had coached me thoroughly.

The announcer's voice clattered on through the loudspeakers. Howard propped the hood open. I stepped closer, filled with the sense that I was about to encounter something alive—a heart of metal. I expected for it to expand and contract and beat its way out. But the hunk of metal remained still.

I fixed my eyes on the block, behind the line of six cylinders. Stamped there, on a metal ID plate, I read:

ENGINE NO. 39212
BEACON MOTOR COMPANY, LUGBOROUGH, ENGLAND.
MADE IN ENGLAND.

Mission accomplished.

Miguel flashed me a smile. I turned to Howard, attempting to conceal my jubilation.

"And—how do you find this engine performing, in terms of speed?" I asked, hoping the question sounded less rehearsed than it was.

Howard's answer was interrupted by an unintelligible shout from Miguel, standing across from us on the passenger side of the car.

"I know—there's some engraving on the cylinder head," Howard said, chuckling. "Odd son of a bitch, isn't it?"

I followed Sissy over to where Miguel was standing.

Howard frowned. "We had someone translate it once. Said it was probably a joke between the mechanics. It doesn't affect the performance, I can tell you that."

I stood with Miguel, examining the arcs of thick lettering tattooed along the length of the engine:

HÉLÈNE, MI RICORDO.

"It's Italian," said Sissy.

"What does it say?" I asked Miguel. "I mean, I can see the woman's name . . ."

He dropped his gaze to the ground.

"It says, 'I remember.'"

Hardly realizing what I was doing, I reached out to touch the lettering. I was about to make contact when I felt a presence by my side, as if summoned by those words scarring the metal.

With a start, I turned to find Hélène beside me, her flat face inches from mine, leaning in to study the writing on the engine. She was smiling strangely, with her teeth clamped together. I was so alarmed to find her there in the flesh—she was the woman I had seen earlier, after all—I couldn't think.

I stepped back.

"The *engine* remembers?" I asked, discovering to my dismay that my voice was shaking. "Did you know that was there?"

She unclenched her teeth, then put her hand to her mouth and fell into a fit of laughter.

A look of uncertainty flashed across Miguel's face, then he joined her.

"He was a conceptual artist!" she shouted.

"We thought it was funny ourselves," said Howard, but he looked at Sissy in confusion.

"The bastard," Hélène muttered, laughing again through her fingers.

Spurred by Miguel, her laughter gathered force until it was finally punctuated with a single word. "No," she said. "No," she repeated, more softly, but whatever other words she intended to follow it were overtaken by a heaving breath that collapsed into sobs.

Miguel offered her his pocket handkerchief.

"A minute," she said.

She stepped away in the direction of the shoreline, leaving me stunned.

"What was that all about?" Howard asked, grinning at his wife in disbelief. He turned to me. "Is she with you?"

"She's an acquaintance," I managed to say.

I had to act fast.

I turned to Miguel and widened my eyes for emphasis. "That's the woman I mentioned to you in the car."

He was busy draining his champagne flute, unaware of the pressure I was under.

I turned abruptly toward Howard and Sissy. "I'm sorry I can't be more formal about this, or tell you as much as I would like to." I glanced around nervously for Hélène, relieved to see that she was still forty feet off, her shoulders shaking, Miguel's handkerchief pressed under her aviator glasses.

"Time is short," I said. "Shorter than I can explain."

Howard and Sissy were regarding me with curiosity.

"I'm here—I represent someone—a collector. Who wants

nothing more in life than for me to purchase this car from you. Right now. Please believe me when I say it's very urgent. I have to ask for your answer now. As you said yourself, the car has already won. Why not sell it? Mr. and Mrs. Russell—" I glanced from one face to the other. "Please. Name your price."

I knew it was a fool's bargaining technique—Emerson would never have approved—but there was no time for finesse. I had to trust my instincts.

Howard carefully lowered the hood of the Beacon back into place and bent to examine the grille, as if he were conferring with it on my offer.

"Fierce, isn't it? Strong," he noted, dragging a finger across the metal bars. "It looks like it could devour you."

"What do you mean?" Miguel objected, squatting next to him. He pointed with his empty champagne glass. "It's nearly heart-shaped, but a bit like a honeycomb—purposeful. It's a symbol of industry, not hunger."

"Miguel!" I pleaded.

Emerson had sent me as his attack dog, and I would spare no one. I sensed that Hélène would be back as soon as she could wipe the mascara smears off her pink lenses.

At the panic in my voice, Miguel stood. Howard followed.

In desperation, I took everything I had learned in my years of watching Emerson negotiate deals and boiled it down to the single most effective tactic I had ever witnessed.

"I'm paying cash."

"Well, I should expect so," said Howard with a chuckle.

"Name your price," I repeated.

Sissy put down her champagne glass.

Howard named his price. (As I bragged to Emerson later, it was even somewhat fair.)

"Done!" I cried ecstatically.

"This model is ageless, don't you think?" said Howard, shaking my hand on the deal.

Miguel was trying to explain to him the cultural impossibility of this when Hélène reappeared beside the car, and the jubilant grin on my face shrank back to nothing.

"Excuse me," she said. "I just—I want to say why I had such a strong reaction a few minutes ago." She gratefully accepted a glass of champagne from Sissy. She avoided my eyes as she went on: "You see, I used to drive the Beacon roadster that first housed this engine."

Miguel winced, finally understanding my plight. I mentally calculated the premium that her chosen bargaining technique would have cost her in a negotiation—except there weren't going to be any negotiations. She was the only one who was still unaware of that, but her presence unsettled me nonetheless. Who knew what she was capable of? It pricked my conscience knowing that the message on the engine held some devastating sentimental power —that was obvious from her reaction. But she had seen it. Even if she couldn't have the engine, she had won that much, and with this thought I hardened my heart against her. She had conned me with her feigned friendship. Now I only wished she would leave so I could celebrate Emerson's victory.

"Ah," said Howard, clicking his plastic glass dully against Hélène's. "The car you're talking about ran the Mille Miglia."

"Yes, in 1954. Alto Bianco drove—"

"He ran it with his wife," Howard informed Sissy.

"No, he ran it with me," said Hélène, breaking into a girlish grin. She tilted her champagne in the direction of the Beacon and introduced herself.

"Oh, hello," said Sissy. "You ran that race? We've always wanted to."

Miguel, in turn, offered his hand to Hélène. As he introduced himself and his connection to the Beacon Motor Company, my mind flooded with the memory of Alto's accented voice at the party in Germany, bragging to me of his many "personalizations."

Now Howard and Sissy were grilling Hélène about something to do with Italy.

"What are they talking about?" I asked Miguel.

"A road race. It's named for the one thousand miles it covers. It started in the late 1920s, but they stopped it a couple of times over the years."

"Why?"

"Accidents." He grimaced. "It's been revived again, though —same route, but different rules."

"I was in that Beacon for thousands of miles in 1954," Hélène was telling Howard and Sissy. "So you can understand why I was so delighted to see this engine. And why I am interested in purchasing it from you."

"Ah, I'm afraid it's just been sold, along with the rest of the car," Howard said good-naturedly. I silently thanked him for discreetly refraining from identifying me as the buyer. "And even if it weren't" —he faced Hélène and clapped his hand to his chest in mock horror— "I am hurt, deeply hurt, that you would want to chop up my Beacon for parts. After all the sweat and tears Sissy and I put into it."

"Sold?" Hélène put her champagne glass down on Sissy's tray, eyeing me suspiciously. Still, Howard confirmed nothing.

Sissy pulled off her tennis visor and fluffed her hair before turning sympathetically to Hélène. "You're the third person who's offered to buy it this week."

"The *third?*" I exclaimed.

"Yeah, a guy called about it yesterday," Howard said.

At this news, I turned to Miguel. "Was it you?"

"No," he said, smiling strangely. "Though I would have."

"I can think of who it might be—can you, Beth?" Hélène said softly. Behind her pink glasses, her eyes were swollen from weeping. They fell on me accusingly. "Do you recall the bidder's name?" she asked Howard.

"Some collector from the East Coast, wasn't it?" he asked Sissy.

"It was that television host," she said. "One of his Ferraris beat one of ours in the Greenwich Concours a few years ago."

"I wish you'd told me that sooner," Howard moaned to his wife. "If I'd known that, I would've quoted a higher price." He smiled at me mischievously, obviously just as pleased with the deal we had struck. "Anyway, it doesn't matter now, does it? We've been thinking about moving into the sixties anyway. Sissy wants a Ghibli."

"A Maserati Ghibli?" I asked. My mind raced back to the model car of Emerson's that my brother had so desperately wanted to possess.

"If someone has already made you an offer for this car, I would like to counter it," Hélène insisted, looking from Howard's face to Sissy's, leaving no doubt as to the seriousness of her intentions. She gestured with her champagne glass to the hood of the car. "As you can see, the engine has a great deal of sentimental value to me."

Clearly, she was doing a number on Howard, and I sensed he was starting to weaken. It was anyone's guess how the couple would respond to Hélène's tug at their heartstrings. But then again, she had tried a similar bid with Emerson and failed.

"You'll have to work it out with the new owner," Howard said, gesturing sheepishly to me. "As I say, it's just been sold."

"Just now?"

Howard nodded.

Hélène's knees buckled a little. I could not meet her eyes.

"I see," she said. "Oh. What a shame."

I prayed she would walk off — I could not even look in her direction — but she stayed put, and with a supreme effort of grace, she began speaking with Miguel.

"I was at the Beacon museum in Germany earlier this summer," she told him. "I saw some pictures of your grandfather. And I believe I saw a photograph of you with him, as a child. Yes? I'm sure it was you."

"We were very close," Miguel said.

"Do you have dinner plans?" she asked him.

"Oh, he can't—we can't," I interrupted, waving my arm in an effort to include not only Miguel, but Howard and Sissy and their grandson—now approaching down the lawn—in the gesture.

"Of course," Hélène said, glancing at Miguel.

Beth, you are an attack dog!

"I'm sorry," I said. My face was hot with shame and victory when I turned from her and, without lowering my voice, began to extract from Howard the details I needed to wire money to his bank account. I could hear her trying to make small talk with Sissy, but by the time Howard and I had agreed on when to meet for a celebratory dinner, she'd wandered off.

A late-afternoon wind had come up from the Pacific. The sea air smelled fresh and sweet. Miguel and I headed back to the lodge on foot. Crowds streamed around us to the exits, while a swarm of staffers proceeded to dismantle the hospitality tents with impressive speed. I paraded in triumph ahead of Miguel, kicking my feet through the snakes of long golden streamers in the grass around the winner's circle, silently rehearsing my victory announcement to Emerson—until I looked back and saw Hélène wandering down the fairway, half bent to the ground, her head in her hands. I told myself there was nothing I could do. She knew Emerson's situation; a dying man's wish spoke for itself. The situation she didn't recognize was her own. I could turn back and approach her. I could take her hand and tell her as sensitively as I could muster what Alto had admitted—bragged about: how he had been more or less tattooing the engines of women all over Europe. His form of conceptual art might then seem extraordinarily depressing. It was true, she had lost the engine. But she believed she was special to him—and wasn't that something? Wouldn't the truth about Alto's many "personalizations" make her defeat even worse?

Miguel turned to see what I was looking at and said, "That had to be a little rough on her, what happened back there."

Now it was my turn to be robotic. "I came to get the engine."

"I know," he said gently.

"I got it."

"It's just . . . a human connection."

"It's a machine."

"She ran a big race in that car. Someone memorialized it—her lover, obviously . . ."

"Isn't this the same nostalgia you were so ready to kill off a few nights ago?" I reminded him. "A little hypocritical, no?"

He pursed his lips.

Why was I insulting him?

"What's wrong, Beth? You seem a bit cross for someone who's just found her holy grail."

I stared at him mutely. Then the sunshine and the bottomless glasses of champagne swamped me, and I excused myself to make a phone call.

"Yes! We did it!"

Emerson's jubilant voice on the line was the antidote I needed. For a short time, hearing him revel in the happiness I'd brought him, I forgot about Hélène and Miguel.

Emerson called out the news to Brian, who was on duty, subbing that day for Tisa. "We got it!"

The evident pride in his voice more than repaid me for the victory celebration that my teenage self had been denied at the track so many years before.

"Can you hear this?" he asked. "This is Brian opening the champagne."

I heard a soft popping noise in the background and smiled at the commotion of his bed-bound celebration. I explained that Hélène Moreau had not been the owner after all, but he had been right to suspect her, because she had indeed been in Monterey and had openly made a bid for the engine. As Emerson presumably sipped his champagne—it couldn't have been more than a thimbleful—he put the phone on speaker mode and demanded that I recount to him and Brian in gory detail the slaying of the dragon Hélène. He was so happy with what he judged to be the satisfactory conclusion of her story that I didn't have the heart to tell him about the personal message to her that had been inscribed on the engine. What did it matter now?

"Congratulations," I said finally.

"I was wrong," he said. "I thought she had it."

"Well, you were right in a way—she did want that engine."

"But we won," he insisted.

"Yes. We did."

I would have preferred to dine alone with Miguel, but I didn't dare skip the prearranged date with the Russells. I had to babysit them in case Hélène reappeared and tried to scotch the deal. I approached the evening warily, conscious that Howard and Sissy might try to find out more about the bidder I was representing —I couldn't risk Emerson's anonymity. Since his father was a fairly public person, it helped that Emerson used his mother's maiden name, but I reasoned that people like the Russells probably collected art as well, and a few ill-considered hints on my part could unintentionally give away his identity. Fortunately, they had something else on their minds as our dinner turned into a late-night celebration around one of the fire pits at their hotel. The two of them were in high spirits, eager to toast the latest addition to their collection—a 1967 Maserati Ghibli—now that they'd sold the Beacon to me.

"They're delivering it in two weeks," Sissy said, embracing her husband and the full-scale dream that Garrett had been denied, even in model form. "I'm going to have to work out with a trainer to get the muscles it takes to drive it," she joked with Howard.

"You found the car you wanted in the past four hours?" I asked in astonishment, mentally tallying the combined weeks, months, perhaps years that Emerson and Hélène had devoted to the same task.

"Sure. Hell of a gas guzzler, difficult to drive, but it's a beauty," said Howard serenely. "Did you *see* the cars out there today?"

Despite the festive mood, my thoughts stubbornly refused to settle. In this respect I was grateful for the cover of their chitchat, which eventually led to speculation about how much I could charge Hélène Moreau for the Beacon if I wanted to resell it to her.

Sissy suggested: "Ask for six of her paintings."

"No, three," Miguel said, claiming to have a reasonable idea of the market value of her work.

"One quarter of her bank account," countered Howard, apparently reveling in my earlier invitation to him to name any price.

"That sounds like a lot—probably too much," said Sissy.

"Okay, one-fifth."

They went on steadily lowering the price, a ridiculous imaginary bargaining session that could not have been any more antithetical to Hélène's first meeting with Emerson. But I was only half listening, distracted by the overwhelming awareness that there was no real satisfaction in winning when I would soon lose Emerson. There was to be no satisfaction with Miguel either. He excused himself while I was saying goodnight to Howard and Sissy. This time there was no note under my door.

16

A SOFT GRAY SKY hung over the Pacific the next morning, merciful on my hangover. In deference to the pain I didn't talk much on the drive back to Los Angeles, and Miguel again said very little as he drove. I fell asleep, and by the time I woke up we were approaching the hotel on Sunset.

After I checked myself back in, I found Miguel out in the driveway in the idling sedan. I didn't want to say goodbye. And I was conscious that we hadn't really spoken privately since my irritated exchange with him on the fairway. I drew closer, wondering how to stall for time before he pulled away. He'd started something in my room in Monterey—the attraction wasn't mine alone—but at the same time, I could not dismiss his brotherly coolness. I hoped, despite my fears to the contrary, that he would suggest we meet again.

He was behind the wheel, staring down at the driveway.

"I enjoyed this, Beth," he said politely.

"Thank you for your help." I bent tentatively to give him a kiss through the open window.

He tilted his cheek to meet my lips, like a favorite aunt, and returned to his surveillance of the asphalt. "It's not expected, maybe, for me to say something like this, Beth, but . . . I've been thinking about it, and I think you and I—or our hearts, maybe —are quite similar. Do you trust me?"

"Yes." I was encouraged to hear him speaking so personally.

"I don't know if it's possible to trust another human being until you trust yourself. Which is hard enough to do."

"What do you mean when you say we're similar?"

He cut the engine and rested his hands in his lap. "I mean, why are you in California right now, Beth?"

"To find something."

"Yes, and in doing that, you're helping someone else. From what you said, your employer. Your friend? In any case, this engine seems to be someone else's quest, and you've adopted it. I do the same. I devote my life to something that you could argue ruined my family. You and I get some satisfaction out of this dedication, but is it really ours?"

"I don't know. I don't know what you're saying."

One of the valets called to Miguel to make room for another car pulling in. I walked alongside as he let the sedan roll a few feet down the driveway.

"I'm making sure my grandfather's company continues on," he said. "I tell myself it's so that Britain can retain a proud part of its history. And—I hope, anyway, in the near future—to manufacture something that could be enormously positive."

"You're doing something with your life."

He hunched over the wheel. "I like to think so. Most of AG's management doesn't, though a few others do. Or so my friend Lynford tells me."

He looked up, his eyes darting between me and the wheel like a hunted man. "That's me, anyway. And I think you're being driven by something else, too."

"I did get a feeling of accomplishment finding that engine. But what was written on it has to do with that woman Hélène. It doesn't answer some questions I have."

He stared at me.

It was like the moment of bidding on the engine all over again. I had no idea what would happen, but I knew that if I didn't act, the chance would be gone.

"If I hadn't been looking for it," I blurted, "I wouldn't have met you."

I leaned down to kiss him again, but the look of misery on his face prompted an instant retreat.

"I'm happy I could help, Beth. But right now I can't make this a more personal situation."

I didn't know how that fit with what he had just said about our hearts. For the first time, I felt that we were speaking two different forms of English. But I could not avoid his meaning: There would be no romantic plot for us, that was clear.

"I should go," he said.

"Do you have to get up early?"

"Tomorrow, for a meeting—I'm dreading it—with AG. But usually not so early."

He smiled tightly.

At the sound of the engine starting, my mouth filled with wet cement.

"You didn't have to drive up there with me this weekend," I managed to say, each word hardening on my tongue.

"As I say, I was happy to help."

A familiar desire to withdraw overwhelmed me. It was comfortable, but in a forlorn way, like sitting down by myself to a reheated dinner, as I would be doing after Emerson was gone. A twisting sensation wrenched my gut, like cylinders turning and tumbling, until a name shot through my mind. The car was starting to roll away when the shock of it freed my tongue.

"Wait—"

Miguel stopped the car.

I felt my cheeks growing hot. "I have to ask you something. Will you tell me the truth?"

"You just said you trusted me."

"You mentioned someone a few minutes ago, your friend Lynford. Did I hear that right?"

"Yes."

Was it possible? How many could there be?

I asked: "Do you mean the property developer—Lynford Webster—an American?"

Miguel seemed to brighten at the name. "Yes, he's doing a lot of projects in Asia. Do you know him?"

"No. I mean, I've heard of him. Is he involved somehow in Beacon's business, or in AG's business?"

Miguel shifted the car into park. "Pardon?"

I walked over to where he was stopped.

"Mr. Webster. Do you work with him somehow, Miguel?"

"Oh. Not really, no."

The sensation of heat sank and spread through my neck, chest and gut like the hot drops in a lava lamp. "So then, if you're not doing business together—sorry, what did you say?—you're friends?"

"Well, yes. I haven't known him that long, but we've recently become quite close."

"Why didn't you tell us that earlier?"

"Who's us?" he said with sudden annoyance.

The heat was concentrating in my gut now, bubbling there. "You're close?" I asked. "What do you mean? Like, he spends time with you?"

"Sure." He shrugged. "He's mentoring me, I guess you could say. Not formally. It's more like he supports me personally."

"He spends time with you and mentors you?"

How could the same man be so absent from Emerson's side?

"It's like I'm the son he doesn't have."

"The *son he doesn't have*? Did he say that?"

"More or less."

I had to stop myself from reaching out and slapping his face.

An improbable dream of my own may have furled and unfurled weakly around Miguel, but the anger I felt now was on Emerson's behalf. It was as if Emerson were inside my head, dictating the words straight to my vocal cords.

"Or is *he* the father *you* didn't have?"

Miguel lowered his eyes.

I leaned down to the window, fighting to control myself. "The rich father."

He refused to look at me.

"I have no idea what your game is. But I was wrong. I don't trust you. I don't want to hear from you again." I turned to leave. "Goodbye, Miguel."

"Beth—you trusted me."

Inside the hotel, I couldn't wait for the elevator, and I ran up the stairway to my room. I stood for hours at the window over-looking Sunset, staring at the lights downtown. But instead of marveling at the wonders at my feet, it felt as if everything wonderful was receding from me.

After the first licks of dawn striped the sky and the city lights melted into the early haze, I got on a plane to return to Emerson, who was receding from me himself, hour by hour, even as I approached, receding into the mysterious realm that I knew without question would claim him.

17

THE BLADES OF A traffic helicopter cut the pale sky over lower Manhattan like a rotary fan in a hot parlor, sending a brief, useless breeze wafting up the Avenue of the Americas. In the cobblestone mews between Fifth Avenue and University Place, I stepped through a flood of spent rose petals, blown down from the trellises in surrender to the heat—a trail of pink, yellow and white like a bridal carpet leading me to a moment of truth.

In Dr. Albas's office on University, where I had been summoned alone, she explained the choices Emerson faced. If he let himself bleed internally, it would be the most painless and humane choice he could make for himself. "He'll fall asleep," she said. "He'll slip into a coma and go gently. But if he continues to insist on being transfused like we've been doing . . . I have to warn you, Beth. His body will go into a kind of trauma . . ."

I had returned from Los Angeles to find Emerson subdued. Surprisingly so. I wondered if it was because the chase that had animated him so much in the previous weeks had come to an end. It worried me enough to grill the healthcare workers about anything he'd said or done while I was away, until Dr. Albas explained that she'd already told Emerson the same thing she'd told me. Zandra and Brian thought Emerson was weighing his choices. They reported that he'd kept his morphine suppressed intentionally again, so he could be clear-headed enough to follow the action as I called in from California. Now that I was back, his meds had been set at inflated levels to ease his discomfort, and he was doped out. In fact, he spoke little about our recent adventure beyond answering some questions I had about shipping the engine back to New York, apparently content to know that the restored car would soon be part of his collections. Infuriatingly, it was something I'd witnessed often after he acquired a photograph: He immediately lost interest in it.

"Let's go see the engine," I suggested to him one afternoon, when it would still have been possible, with some difficulty, for him to be escorted out for an hour or so. By then, the engine had been removed from the Russells' Beacon and shipped from California, and Nate, the manager at the Perry Street garage, was supposed to have it with the chassis somewhere, with the mechanics who were reuniting the two parts. I never asked where, because Emerson refused to go.

"I just went to L.A. I don't want to leave this apartment," he said, closing his eyes on any further debate.

I could not deny he was failing. By my observation, the elevated doses of morphine now operated like a bullet train, carrying him straight from wakefulness to dreaming. In his bedroom, propped up against the pillows, he moved his head from side to side like any other commuter—arms up, bent at the elbows—though he was not holding a newspaper, not holding anything, except in his own mind. Something of great interest to him. He held his fingers at chin level as if he were making a goalpost. He was not exactly asleep, and definitely not awake. He was seeing something, experiencing some kind of chimera.

Morpheus. Poppy to morphine. He was practicing the sleep of death, springing up and down on the silver cord, deliriously tired, while his brain went on sampling input from the outside: passing voices, doors opening and closing, the contractors upstairs working on the neighbor's kitchen . . . Like his books turning into medical supplies, one day of living equated to so little now: the phone ringing, my clogs clomping up and down the floorboards, Zandra's afternoon talk shows and the garbage trucks rolling through the Village with their brakes in a perpetual squeal.

I sat on the bed by his feet and wondered if his mind registered where he was, suspended between states, perhaps already moving between them. Death was a slide show projected into a sunny room. It was there the whole time.

When Zandra brought in Emerson's breakfast the next morning, he informed us that his sleep had been plagued by nightmares.

"Like what?" I asked, curious to know if I was sharing dreams with him, along with his emotions and stomach pains.

"I remember a little bit of one," he began hesitantly. "I woke up thinking I had to get ready for work. Then, you know—I don't work anymore."

He looked bewildered.

"You can always go to your office, Emerson."

"I know that now. But it ruined my whole day."

His lawyer arrived later that morning. Their meeting was brief, and as the day went on, Emerson couldn't settle into one position for more than ten minutes at a time. He hung his head miserably while Zandra and I sat on either side of the bed, rubbing his back.

"Do you want me to call him?" I offered.

"Who?" Emerson asked.

I paused, not sure how much I should say in front of Zandra. "He might be back from Asia."

"Press harder on the left," he commanded.

"I could leave a message."

"No."

"What if I asked Laurel—"

"Just rub my back."

"I hate to see you in pain," I said.

He shifted his hips, clenching his teeth with discomfort. "I'm wearing you out."

"No, only Zandra and Brian and the others."

Zandra reached over the bed and gave me a shove, but Emerson didn't laugh.

He bared his teeth and made a move to stand up, then settled back against the pillows. "Beth, I just keep thinking: What if? What if *this*? What if *that*? Is everything ending?"

"I don't believe it is."

"If I believed what you told me . . ." He turned to Zandra. "You know, the morphine doesn't erase everything."

He slept for a while, and for the first time since I'd returned from California, I had the opportunity to reflect on my behavior toward Hélène. Emerson had convinced me that she was our enemy, but now that he'd won, I could not stop thinking about the message to her on the engine. Emerson would not be beside me for much longer. The race had been a useful distraction for him, and he was presumably making the car more collectible by reuniting the original pieces, but this exercise was now drained of all enthusiasm. In the end, the engine and the car would have to go to someone.

"Have you decided what you're doing with the Beacon?" I asked him that evening, wondering if its fate was among the things he had discussed with his lawyer, Bruce Kingston, earlier in the day.

His posture deflated in the bed, just as it had when the taxi driver had reached the end of the circuit at Gray Hill. He seemed to stall on the question.

"No?" I asked.

He gave me a curious smile and shook his head.

At this, I decided to be up-front with him. "I didn't tell you this earlier—"

He looked up at me, alarmed. "Didn't tell me what?"

"When I was in California—"

"Did something happen with Miguel?"

I shook my head.

"You haven't said a word about him since you got back. Are you still in touch with him?"

"We found what you wanted," I said, feigning nonchalance. "There's no reason for me to be in touch with him."

He sank lower in the bed.

"Listen," I said, "there was something written on that engine when I saw it. Besides the numbers and things."

He stared at me, waiting for me to continue.

"It was a message to Hélène."

I paused.

"Her name was engraved on it, along with some words. In Italian. It said, '*I remember.*'"

I waited for this to sink in.

"I remember," Emerson said.

It was unclear whether he was repeating what I'd just said or he recalled the inscription himself.

"What do you remember?"

With visible effort, he pulled himself up a little and held out his right hand to me.

"Beth, will you do me a favor, please, and take a look at this hangnail?"

"You can't have a hangnail. You have the most well-cared-for hands in Manhattan."

I sat on his bed and squared his fingers to examine them: tiny, like a child's, tinged an unhappy shade of yellow. I had barely begun to examine them when he squeezed my hands insistently between both of his. Then I knew there were no hangnails.

He turned to Maria-Sylvana, who'd started her shift by unpacking a box of syringes. "Would you please make me a snack?"

"The usual?" she asked agreeably.

"With a little extra butter, please."

She went off to the kitchen and I sat with him, perplexed, holding his hands as gently as I could. I hated the look in his eyes, a look of desperation mixed with a trace of the adolescent scowl I had detected on the steps of the 42nd Street library—a skepticism that was unwilling to be reassured. I wondered how long he had known he would share his mother's fate. I wondered if he had ever been in love . . .

These were not new thoughts. They were things I had asked myself many times, but he was my employer, and I did not know how to form the questions. The last thing I wanted to do was upset him. More than anything, I wished he would have peace.

He squeezed my hands again, his grip stronger than I would have thought possible.

"Beth?" he asked when we were alone in the room.

"Yes?"

I waited to hear his final pronouncement on the fate of the Beacon.

"I can choose my own afterlife?"

It took me a second to register the change of subject, and then I realized he was referring to our conversation weeks earlier. I was immensely relieved to see the hope in his eyes. I considered answering him as he often answered me: with a book. I could go out to the hallway and find his volumes on Plato, and read to him what the philosopher had articulated on that topic at the end of his *Republic*. I could pull out other books—countless books—detailing every established belief on the subject: doctrines from India, traditions from ancient Egypt and other parts of Africa, religious teachings about resurrection and the afterlife stretching back for civilizations. But I sensed he no longer had the patience for such a recital, and I could not risk it.

"Well, what do you think all the belief systems represent?" I asked. "There are all kinds of ways to express the same truths."

He looked away, his hands still in mine. "I guess . . ."

"Is there some afterlife you *would* want?"

"I guess I thought it would be the Beacon. That I would go there."

I nodded.

"But that won't happen. I don't want that to happen, anyway."

"Emerson—"

He interrupted me. "I want to tell you something. First of all, I never drove that car before."

"The Beacon?"

"No. Horace's car. At the track that day. Because I would have warned you."

I was too surprised to speak.

His hands grasped mine more tightly now, wringing them miserably in his own. "I see that scar on your leg that you're always trying to hide, and I think, Why didn't I warn her?"

"Forget about that. It doesn't matter."

"But I know now—it won't be the cave, or the Beacon. Do you see?"

I shook my head.

"Where I'll go," he insisted. "It's the scar. That's where I'm going, after Omega."

With his hands gripping mine, I sat speechless. The scar he spoke of was within reach of both of us, but I never thought to show it to him or to reach for it myself. Not because it would have seemed foolish, indulging someone whose mind was addled by morphine. And not because I felt—as I felt later—that those three inches of skin would make for a barren heaven. After all, I had asked him to consider every possibility. And what was a scar, if not a gateway?

No, I kept still because I sensed something of that first euphoric pain I had experienced at the track that day so many years before. As Emerson went silent and stared at me, I felt an exquisite horror, as if his words were not just an idle wish or a morphine dream, but the proposal of a spiritual possession every bit as sincere as that red-hot metal had been.

"Yes," I said finally, because there was nothing else to say.

It was only when Maria-Sylvana returned with his tiny helping of macaroni and cheese that I managed to look away from his triumphant gaze.

He released my hands long enough to feed himself—four or five baby spoonfuls—but he insisted I stay beside him to hold the bowl. It sat between us in my hands like a cup sealing our pact as I watched him chew slowly, slowly . . . My eyes were closing with exhaustion when I felt the abrupt sensation of something crashing into my jaw.

"Thank you," he rasped through lips caked with orange cheese.

I scraped a clot of orange off my face, stunned that he had managed to make full contact with a kiss, even if it was on the side of my chin. Without another word, he leaned back against the pillows, and the morphine promptly shuttled him to sleep.

An early-morning breeze had come up after rain—cool and sweet, laced with the soft smell of mud from the streets running down to the Hudson. I retreated to the guest room, where I lay awake until the sky began to grow light, and then I gave up on sleeping. That must have been when I slept.

When Brian woke me up just after 11 a.m., Emerson was gone.

18

WE FOUND HIS pajama top abandoned on the fax machine in the office. A fax had come through in the night—legal papers. I collected them from the floor and dropped them onto his desk. The top left-hand drawer was open and Emerson's wallet was gone.

The shift change from Maria-Sylvana to Brian had taken place while I was sleeping. Since Brian was freshly on duty, I couldn't imagine how Emerson could have vanished before his eyes.

I looked to Brian expectantly.

He crossed his fleshy arms over his chest. "He asked me to wheel him down the hall to his office. Then he sent me out to the deli to get him an egg sandwich."

"What? He tricked you! Why didn't you wake me up before you went out?"

I ran for my clothes, with Brian following behind.

"I thought I was doing you a favor, Beth. You were zonked out! He was happy in his desk chair. I was gone for like fifteen minutes."

Someone had failed to observe a Primary Procedure.

We searched the loft again. There was no sign of him, except for the empty office chair by the front door. I went back to his desk and took a few minutes to read through the legal papers that Bruce Kingston's office had faxed—a clarification of some clause in Emerson's will about the meaning of the word *bequest*. Then, with no option except to pivot from one empty space to another, I started making phone calls with the text of the Standard Policy for archivists running through my head: *It is your duty to ensure that each object in your care can be found easily when required.*

Dr. Albas (her answering service promised to page her).

Bruce Kingston (in court).

Eric Dart, the conservator: "I haven't heard from him in months, Beth," he reported. "Let me know if I can do anything."

The location scout in Los Angeles, who didn't remember who I was at first, but said he'd let me know if Emerson tried to reach him.

Dr. Albas called in on the second line. She asked me to keep her posted.

"He might call you," I suggested.

She sighed with frustration. "I hope he does."

The specter of Emerson's father floated through my mind. And right behind it, the image of Miguel in the car outside my hotel, smug in Lynford Webster's friendship—his mentorship: *like a son.* Had Emerson sensed someone moving in on him? It seemed unthinkable that he would try to get himself all the way out to Burring Port, but, after he'd been missing for several hours, I phoned Gray Hill. At the sound of Laurel's clipped greeting, I tried to iron the desperation out of my voice.

"Emerson might be visiting Connecticut today. Has he stopped there by any chance?"

"I don't know anything about Emerson's schedule," Laurel said, sounding distracted. "Mr. Webster is overseas."

"If Emerson stops by, will you call? It's urgent."

I couldn't bear the thought of him making his way alone through the city. Then I reminded myself that Emerson was an adult and a free human being. Not my ward. On the contrary, I was there to serve his wishes. If he wanted to take a skeletal wander through Manhattan, what business did I have trying to stop him?

It frustrated me that I couldn't make his final days any better for him. I was stuck in the doorway myself, like Janus, the Roman god whose two faces greeted me every month on the letterhead of the International Council on Archives: one face looking backward, the other looking forward. What should be saved from the past? What will be needed in the future? Alpha and Omega. I didn't know which direction I was facing myself.

I left Brian to answer the office phones and headed down Bleecker on foot.

An object's location should be recorded at all times.

At Golden Hands: a brief disruption of business.

Not there.

I kept alert for any limping forms all the way back along Bleecker, then down to the garage on Perry Street.

Emerson's Quattro was parked there as usual, at the top of one of the ramps. I asked Nate if Emerson had been there looking for the Beacon, but he reminded me that the car was with mechanics, being reunited with the engine. Not that Emerson could drive anyway.

Taxi. I trawled the Village by cab, street by street.

Nowhere.

It is your duty as an archivist to ensure that each object in your care can be found . . .

But the only thing in my care, the only thing that was entrusted to me, could not be found. Like a creature stirring from a long hibernation, I had finally discovered in Emerson's employ something I could accomplish: to help him die. Now he had turned into someone whose life was in danger.

Back at the loft, I thought Emerson might have wanted to see some of his friends from prep school, or college. Beckett's brother Tom, for instance, whose thin lips I had eventually kissed to exhaustion when we ended up getting together briefly in college. I had no number for Tom, and it had been awkward when I'd seen him at a party a few years ago. But I could call Beckett. First I had to find my neglected address book, buried in one of my suitcases in Emerson's guest room.

Once she registered who I was, Beckett launched into the news of her pregnancy, already several months along. She was so excited about it that we were on the line for ten minutes before I felt comfortable changing the subject.

"Have you heard anything about Emerson Tang lately? Or has Tom?"

"Besides the shutdown?"

"The shutdown?"

"Yeah, he's snubbed everyone out. Tom hasn't heard from him in more than a year. Anyway, you would know more than me. Aren't you still working for him?"

I worded my response carefully. "My job has changed, actually. I haven't seen him in a while."

"Exactly."

"If you hear anything about him in the next day or so? I'm trying to reach him. It's important."

"Sure. What about you, Beth? You still living in the city? What's going on with you?"

"Nothing much. The usual." It struck me how often those words had been my magic pass to communicate the truth without prompting any more questions. As I was hanging up, I remembered to ask: "Oh—is it a boy or a girl?"

"We're going to be surprised!"

"Congratulations, Beckett."

I tried to imagine what it was like to be on her end of the life cycle, instead of the end Emerson and I were on. Dr. Albas had warned me that it was natural for someone at his stage to detach, to withdraw from all but the most necessary human connections, in order to grieve his own death. I knew Emerson had already detached from his old professional associations. He had even deaccessioned his friends. I don't know why I hadn't expected him to do it to me.

Brian combed the streets around the building on foot until his shift ended, leaving phone numbers with the shopkeepers and asking them to call us if they saw anyone of Emerson's description. Periodically, Brian came upstairs and offered to bring me something to eat. I was so angry, I couldn't look at him.

In spite of my doubts, I wondered if Hélène might have phoned Emerson again or had something to do with his disappearance. The last place I'd seen her was Monterey. Was she back in New York? I phoned Arthur Quint's gallery and got an answering machine. I dialed the Royalton Hotel. My heart stopped when the operator offered to put me through to her room—she was back, after all—but there was no answer. Had she kept the room while she was traveling? I tried phoning a few more times, until I reluctantly left a message asking her to call.

The only sensible course of action was to do more research into Emerson's possible whereabouts. But this would require me to violate his privacy—something he knew I would be loath to do. The sources of information I considered to be fair game were any papers visible on his desk and the contents of his office files, which we'd always shared, and I already knew those to be bone dry, unless he was visiting every museum and gallery in the Greater New York metro area.

The surface of his desk was an equally barren land for clues. It was partially tiled with CD jewel cases and otherwise littered with old receipts, legal documents and business correspondence that I had continued to place there for him as a courtesy in the previous months. At some point he had stopped reviewing them. Now it all needed to be filed.

I busied myself sorting halfheartedly through the stacks of paper, and with each page I filed, I fought the urge to pull open the drawers of his desk. I rid myself of the temptation by turning instead to the college notebook that Maria-Sylvana had dug up. Emerson had been so amused by its reappearance that he'd moved it to his night table. Several times he had asked me to recite some of the contents to him—in effect, he had already invited me to look at it. Nevertheless, I paged through it uncomfortably, not quite reading it, only scanning the lines for anything that might be relevant to his current whereabouts.

The early pages seemed to be filled mostly with quotations and arguments with himself—the explorations of a cocky college student. One lengthy section was devoted to what appeared to be research notes for a written assignment, as if he had interviewed someone for a business course. He must have produced a report or case study on the company being discussed, though I never found the typed paper. The businessman who was being interviewed (some pages had been removed, and the subject was referred to only as "he") sounded more confident than the one taking notes. Was it his father? Five or six ruled pages were filled with quotations from the interview, carefully transcribed in Emerson's spidery hand:

> – "It's a leader's job to keep things on track."
> – His fear—that he'll fail; credibility; reaching the next rung
> – learned to "deal with reality" (not avoid)
> – sense that the world was already doomed, and his generation would finish it off . . .
> – "if people believe that what I want to do can be profitable —in more than one way—they'll support it."
> X – (obstacles:)

I flipped through the pages, thinner with notes as they went on. But what was this? Near the back of the notebook—
About *me*.
There was no question. My name was right there.

Amid Emerson's sporadic jottings in recent years were his impressions of a conversation I vaguely remembered, around the time I'd begun working for him. He'd been in the process of replacing the cassette tapes in his music collection with new CDs. We'd talked about the pros and cons of converting his archival records to electronic data storage, versus continuing with my traditional paper system.

BETH's big argument: "We already know paper can last for at least 2,000 years, but CD data is expected to degrade within 400!" (she is so CONSERVATIVE! But she is a saver, of course. A conserver . . .)

And cloistered. She's a professional cloisterer! Does she ever go out?

Does she ever look ahead and think, something NEW could be BETTER??? And that some things are *not* worth saving?

It depends on the factors in each case—but why argue about changing something we already KNOW can be improved?

When there are options to be explored. Failure to make something new—this is even worse than—

Insulted by his spidery hand, I stared at the rest of the pages uncomprehending, unable to focus. I threw the notebook down.

How dare he insult me.

Amateur philosopher.

Since when was he such a creative visionary? *He* was the one who was obsessed with the past—with old houses, no less. *Old photos* of old houses. And an old car. All he did was collect old things. Rich of him to call me a saver.

Let the police save him.

When Tisa arrived for her night shift I called 911 and reported him missing. I was still furious. In contrast to my irritation, which sounded merely like panic, the dispatcher's voice was warm and friendly. I believed her when she said she was sorry to hear how upset I was.

"I'm telling you," she said, "most of the time it turns out that someone just went to do an errand and their family didn't know about it."

At this, my anger toward Emerson collided with impatience: "He doesn't do errands. His guts are turning to *liquid.*"

An electronic beep reminded me that my call was being recorded.

"More than ninety-five percent of missing people show up within twenty-four hours," counseled the dispatcher. "More than ninety-five percent. Odds are, your guy will too."

She instructed me to fax a clear, recent photograph of Emerson to the number she gave me. The problem was, I had no recent photographs of him, no photograph at all. After scanning the drawers and shelves in his bedroom, to no avail, the only place I could think to look was in his desk. The one place I had sworn to myself I would not look.

There was nothing interesting in it anyway, I discovered as I rummaged around the drawers now. Not even an address book. He had obviously scrubbed the place clean of his own memorabilia, probably a long time ago. The few photographs I found of him (including the one I faxed to the police) looked like college snapshots, featuring a lot of people I didn't recognize. The only item of interest I ran across was an undocumented artwork—an unframed watercolor on stiff paper that he had never given me to catalogue—isolated in the middle drawer of his desk. Protected there from the interference of stray pens and other paraphernalia was what looked like a child's painting. It wasn't unattractive —that was the best I could say for it. It was a vague depiction of an Asian face. The reverse side was marked with black ink, a design like a little crow with three legs. There was no paperwork with it, but the Standard Policy was clear enough regarding items of unknown provenance: *Poor documentation is not, in itself, a reason for disposal.*

I stared hopelessly at the little painting as the evening wore on, functioning in a kind of dead alertness, like my teenage years replayed. I hesitated to leave the loft in case Emerson appeared, but I thought a walk might help clear my head. It was becoming unbearable to sit hour after hour, alternating between anger and frustration. Sometime after 1 a.m., I left Tisa in the empty loft with instructions.

I crossed Bleecker and walked toward the river, wondering if I could sense him. I believed he was alive somewhere, but that didn't make me worry any less. He had no medications or painkillers except the morphine pump attached to him, and I could not remember how full the cartridge was. He had no idea how to check it—he didn't understand the intricacies of keeping his cocktail of meds monitored and refilled. Mainly, I prayed his morphine would hold out. Because if the cartridge ran dry, he would be rocketed into a hideous stratosphere of pain so instantaneous and debilitating that Dr. Albas said the most merciful thing that could happen would be for his heart to stop from the pure shock of it.

Though of course that might not happen. He could just be left, wherever he was, calling out in pain. The DNR certificate was taped to the wall in his bedroom. Without that document, it was possible he would be found and resuscitated into a vegetative state.

I ran back to the loft and put Tisa on one of the office phone lines. Together, we spent the rest of the night calling hospitals and police stations, using different names, hounding the admissions clerks of the emergency rooms for anyone of his description. But as I should have known, there was no one.

19

W HEN I STEPPED off the small elevator at the Royalton the next morning, the first person I ran into was
a policeman. Farther down the hallway, the door to
Penthouse B was already open. I walked in to the sound of someone retching.

On the landing I found a second police officer, with his hat off
and a walkie-talkie in his hand. He looked at me with a distinct
expression of embarrassment as another bout of heaving issued
from the bathroom.

Behind him, two men were lifting something long and flat. My
mind registered it as a stretcher. But it wasn't the stretcher I focused on. It was the black body bag on top.

"I offered them a bedsheet," said Hélène, appearing at the
bathroom door. She crossed the room and touched my arm tentatively, her face colorless behind her colored glasses. "The linens
are fine cotton. But these men have their own protocol, and they
insisted."

The black bag was made of plastic, stamped with a white figure eight, turned sideways.

Infinity.

From the drape of the bag, I made out the rough shape of two
arms, a chest, the sunken cavity between the hipbones . . .

I heard Hélène's accented voice again. Soft. Businesslike. "The police have been calling his office, trying to find you."

"I just got the message. I went back to the nail salon as soon as it opened."

"What?"

"I was looking for him."

"He was here."

I nodded.

"It was a shock to see him," Hélène said. "He was sweating when I opened the door."

"When?"

"This morning! Beth?"

I became conscious that my jaw was shaking. Somehow the mechanical system of eardrums, nerves and brain continued to register her words.

She looked different. Messy. She was wearing a man's crumpled shirt over capri pants, a shirt covered in paint, cracked blobs of red, hardened drips. Her easel was set up on the balcony, under the cloister.

"I thought you were on the West Coast."

"I returned from Monterey more than a week ago," she said.

"How did he know you were here?"

"I have no idea. He might have guessed."

"Did you know he was coming to see you?"

"No."

"He didn't call yesterday, or this morning, before he came?"

"No. The only message I had yesterday was from you. I was out."

"What about this morning?"

"No. He arrived, I offered him the chaise longue," she went on. "I helped him down. I went to the bathroom to get him some water."

"He was hyperventilating," said a voice behind me. "He shut down."

"He was having trouble breathing," Hélène explained. She spoke like someone who'd had to report terrible events many times, but dreamily, as if she didn't quite believe they had happened.

She moved toward me. "He might not have wanted you to see this, Beth. He was perhaps trying to protect you."

I felt some strangulation in my nerves, my head popping every few seconds like the individual sacs in a sheet of bubble wrap. In their own Morse code, they were stamping my brain with the information:

Omega.

Infinity.

Two men wearing bright blue rubber gloves were trying to get past me with the stretcher. With Emerson. I kept my place, blocking their way.

"Where are you taking him?"

"City medical examiner, on Fifth."

"And then what?"

"Then we write a death certificate and you call whatever funeral home you want."

"Let me come with you," Hélène said as the men nudged past me.

I shook my head, mute with confusion. I had more questions for her than I could possibly articulate. But the men were vanishing with Emerson. My only instinct was not to let him out of my sight.

I heard her calling: "I'm concerned about you, Beth."

My legs followed automatically as the crowd with the stretcher moved down the corridor. The hotel manager escorted us into a brightly lit service elevator, where the men in uniform and I arranged ourselves into a horseshoe around the stretcher in order to fit inside. As the elevator descended, my eyes traced the lines of the infinity symbol stamped above Emerson's chest, following it around and around like a racetrack.

"Why is that there?" I asked the man at the front of the stretcher.

He glanced down. "He's our eighth case this morning."

The faces around me resumed their surveillance of the ceiling.

"Did he really just show up here?" I asked them. "This morning?"

The manager nodded. "The doorman said he was very polite."

When the elevator opened again the manager led us to one of the unmarked exits at the rear of the hotel. No sooner had the police disappeared down 43rd Street than the men with the stretcher extended its folding legs and left Emerson just inside the doorway, sheltered from the view of passing pedestrians.

"We have to lock up our van on this street," one of them explained.

"Right back," said the other.

The unexpectedness of their departure left me speechless. I wondered if they were having a cigarette. It seemed like a breach of protocol, but I wasn't about to leave Emerson to find out. Alone with him now in the half-light, I stared down at the trough between his hips. The shape of his body was alarming. Was his head twisted to the side? One thing was clear: However Omega had occurred, he had avoided being delivered out the door of his own building on a raft of muddy take-out menus.

At the morgue, I functioned in a calm stupor, overcome by the signal-jam of emotions and questions running through my head. Where was he the previous day and night? And why was he at the hotel this morning? Hélène was his competitor, not his teammate, as I was. If he had wanted to see her so desperately, why hadn't he gone to the Royalton in the first place? Then I recalled that she claimed to have been out the previous day. It was true that there had been no answer when I phoned. Had he gone to see her earlier and failed? The thought led me back to my original question.

My speculation was overridden by administrative duty when

I was led into a room to identify the remains of my employer, archived in a metal drawer like one of his own photographs. It was but an intake of breath to identify him, to register the parameters of the crude storage system where his flesh and bones were temporarily filed, a system of archiving in which I could claim no expertise. His body did not disturb me—I saw it as an empty vessel. What haunted me was the pose: He was twisted like a Rodin bronze, his gums bared like a monkey's. A thought went through my mind as they walked me out of the room, a thought I would despair of repeatedly during the events to follow: that Emerson had crossed the threshold burdened by some agony I could not know.

Outside the room, an attendant offered me Emerson's eyeglasses, his leather jacket and the two items found in his pockets: his wallet and, hanging from a leather fob adorned with a golden lighthouse, what I could only assume was the key to the Beacon.

"It's in writing, Beth, of course," Bruce Kingston explained over the phone. "But he was also clear in his conversations with me that he didn't want any kind of funeral."

I sighed into the receiver. "I know. He said it was too Sleeping Beauty to ride in a glass station wagon filled with flowers."

Bruce confirmed that his office had contacted Emerson's father and faxed him a copy of the death notice they'd provided to the New York Times.

"Emerson's written wish was to be cremated," Bruce informed me.

"Yes, that's my understanding, too."

He cleared his throat. "It's prepaid."

"Did he specify what to do with the ashes?"

"No," Bruce said mildly. "We don't have anything on that."

"Did his father say anything about it?"

"Only that it was in your hands."

Like me, Bruce had received a telegram from Mr. Webster in Taipei. Mine came to me in care of Emerson's address:

Profound sadness. Thank you for working with my son's lawyer to carry out his wishes.

I took the slip of paper with me down Charles Street and crossed over to the river, unable to get past *profound sadness*. I walked long enough for my head to fill with the riot of gulls' screeches and wind. Contrary to the watery landscape surrounding me, I had the sensation of standing in a bombed-out field, and curling up from the blackened earth were the smoky tendrils of what was lost: Emerson, who had been true to his word and not said goodbye. Miguel, who didn't want me, and who had somehow slotted himself in as Mr. Webster's son even before Emerson was gone. There were no doctors to speak with; there would be no more nurses coming by. The home healthcare workers had already been assigned to new patients, as of that afternoon. Dr. Albas, Tisa, Zandra, Brian, Maria-Sylvana, all of them . . . gone.

Among the words of condolence from museum people that I found on the answering machine back at the loft was a message from Hélène, of all people, asking about the details of Emerson's funeral service. I stabbed at the buttons of the answering machine to erase her voice, but I was trapped when she phoned back that afternoon and interrupted me in the middle of another call.

"There's nothing," I informed her brusquely. "No funeral, no memorial." It felt good to shut her out. "It's over," I added for emphasis.

"How are you, Beth?"

"I'm here by myself, and I have someone on the other line."

"I'm sorry. If you'd like to talk . . ."

"I don't think there's anything to say." I was about to hang up when I heard my voice continuing, as if by its own will: "He was bleeding internally. You have no idea how hard it must have been for him to get himself to your hotel."

"I could see how hard it was for him, Beth. I saw."

"Why was he there with you? It was about that car, wasn't it?"

"Yes."

"What did he say?"

"Very little. There was very little time—we didn't exchange pleasantries. He was holding himself against the wall when I opened the door. I tried to help him sit down. I only saw it briefly, Beth, the expression in his eyes—his departure was already there. It was primal, this communication."

My jaw was trembling. I pressed the phone against my ear and swung my head to make it stop.

"But what I felt was love," she said.

"You felt what?"

"Love," she said. "His face was lit up like a little boy's. He said, 'We have the engine.'"

"The engine?"

"Yes. It was plural: 'We have it.' He wanted me to know you had won it on his behalf."

"He knows you were there in Monterey," I said, too embarrassed by what she was implying to say any more.

"He was proud of you, Beth."

I trusted nothing Hélène had to say, especially when it came to Emerson. But as much as I tried to disregard what she was suggesting, it saddened me to admit that the behavior she'd described was not incongruous. It wasn't enough for Emerson to have won. His final act had been to gloat over his victory.

The thought of it was so disappointing, I heard myself yelling into the phone: "I don't care about that car! I would rather have him here with me than the car."

"Of course," she said evenly. "So, wanting to bring someone back to life is not an impulse you are immune to after all."

I slammed the phone down, cutting off both Hélène and the other caller. The last thing I needed was to listen to her clever logic.

For days I did not leave the loft. The funeral home wouldn't have his ashes ready until Monday, and I was only planning to store them anyway, until I could figure out what to do with them. I drifted between the kitchen and the office, answering condolence calls from museum curators and other beneficiaries. I assured my parents there was nothing they could do; I honestly could not think of anything. Now that I was alone again, I did not want to see people or talk to anyone beyond what my responsibilities to Emerson required. Hélène did not call again or leave any messages, and I was grateful for her restraint. I assumed I would never see her again.

At some point I became aware that my ulcer pain was easing —due, I reasoned, to a release of stress. Within a few days it had nearly vanished. This physical relief was the only positive change in the immediate aftermath of Emerson's death. When the new week began, I found myself busier than ever as the first pebble dropped in an avalanche of paperwork related to his estate. What had seemed so simple once . . . Emerson's accountant, Wayne, called not long after, and when I had gathered all of the bills that had come through during the previous month they formed a small mountain on my desk. There were hundreds of checks to write and phone calls to make, faxes to send and death certificates to file with banks and insurance companies. Then the word could go forth from the great electronic bullhorn that another human being could be deleted from the program.

It was during that time when I was summoned by Emerson's lawyer to administer the proceeds of his trust—a significant sum that Emerson himself had assigned to beneficiaries before his death. Bruce Kingston passed a copy of the list across his desk to me: a total of three organizations.

"It's only a suggested list, Beth. As trustee, you can apply the funds *for such purposes and in such amounts as you may, in your sole discretion, determine.*" Bruce finished reading from the document and scratched the gray stubble of his beard, ruminating over something, before looking up. "That's a recent amendment. He made that change not long before he died."

I looked at the list of organizations. "I recognize the first one. It's a group that works for the preservation of Modernist architecture."

"Yes, that's straightforward enough. The second one, the New York State Division of Licensing Services—that one he's specified as a fund for licensed beauticians. Scholarship money for college educations. It also funds a literacy program."

"Oh?"

He nodded. "The idea here is a lump sum, dispersed annually. Albany will take care of administering it to the individual applicants."

"Emerson was well attended to by some of New York's nail technicians," I explained.

"Evidently," said Bruce. "And he is directing the majority of the funds to the third organization, Auxiliant and Co."

"What do they do?"

"Research, according to the prospectus."

"What kind of research?"

"Technology, from what I understand—what else is there?"

"It's a for-profit company?"

"Yes."

"And you're saying this is what he wanted? These three organizations?"

"This is his list."

"Fine. Let's do what he asked."

Bruce stared at the paper in my hand.

"It was always hard to read him, Beth, but that recent amendment says he is inviting you to contribute your judgment and discretion in handling his estate. It's as if he were asking for your participation—on an ongoing basis."

"Mine?"

"Yes, it says you will act *as him,* effectively. There's nothing to prevent you from stepping in and doing things differently. If you wish."

It was an unsettling thought, but more immediately unsettling was the fact that, in the documents Emerson had drawn up in great detail, the fate of the Beacon had received no special mention. By default, Bruce explained, the car fell into the catchall category of household items, including his appliances and furnishings—a hodgepodge that Emerson had bequeathed to me, along with his loft and the nominal amount of cash left in his personal bank accounts.

It was up to me to decide what to do with the Beacon, then. On hearing this, I had an unwelcome vision of Hélène's pink, swollen eyes turning away from me that afternoon in Monterey. A renewed sense of gloom came over me like the stench of rotting leaves. She had some right to the car, by her history, by what was written on the engine. It was this knowledge that had made me her proponent, once upon a time. But the restored vehicle was my victory with Emerson—the trophy of our last months together. As he had told Hélène himself, *we* had it. His quest to reunite the car and the engine had taken root in a desire I might never understand, but through it I had lost my separateness for a time. With a shock, I realized that when I had tried to argue in Hélène's favor—when I had asked Emerson if he was thinking about leaving the car to someone else—the other party all along had been me. Whatever it had meant before, the restored Beacon meant only one thing now. It was our shared accomplishment. My memory of him. I would never relinquish it.

I pressed my fingers to my eyelids and cradled my head in my hands, hoping Bruce couldn't tell that I was trying not to cry in front of him.

"Do you have questions about any of this?" he asked softly, as if I would disintegrate if he spoke any louder. "The organizations listed here aren't aware of Emerson's bequest, because they're set up anonymously. This would be an ideal chance for you to make changes, if you were considering any."

I didn't know anything about managing estates. I'd thought that being an executor would be a simple matter of paperwork, a morning's worth of signatures. Instead, Emerson had entrusted me with an enormous responsibility. I pushed my face between my palms, desperate to squeeze an answer out of my brain. When I looked up, Bruce was regarding me inquisitively.

"Do I have to decide today?"

"Oh. No, no," he said. "Not at all."

I let go of my cheeks and felt the blood filling my face again.

"Give it some thought. How you handle his trust—and when —is entirely up to you."

"How about, for now, if you set up some initial distribution to this list annually—in the percentages he instructed? We can talk about it again," I went on unsteadily, "after I've had time to . . . you know? Would that be all right?"

"Absolutely. And very prudent of you, Beth. You have a lot on your plate."

To judge from the charitable donation receipts I accumulated that fall, I kept myself busy for a time going through Emerson's medical equipment and supplies, organizing anything reusable for donation. I found it difficult to dress for each day. The constant silence in the loft unsettled me. Whenever I came back from an errand, I readily inhaled the odors that lingered there, the closest thing there was to Emerson's presence. Once the medical equipment had been cleared out I did what grievers have done for centuries: I tried to sort through his clothing and possessions, but I only moved them around; I could not bring myself to get rid of much. I was in the midst of reorganizing his closet when my brother called from London, wanting to gossip about Emerson's funeral.

"My friends from home are bugging me to get the scoop," Garrett said. "You're the only one we know to ask."

"There wasn't a funeral," I said, unable to mask the annoyance in my voice. To change the subject, I asked when he would be back in the States for a visit, but he wouldn't let it go.

"Wait—the Emperor had no funeral?"

"Nope."

"Don't you find that strange, Beth?"

"No."

"The Emperor didn't have an exotic car bearing him off to heaven? With a private orchestra serenading him?"

He continued his taunts like a schoolyard tyrant.

"Do you know why he went to NYU, Beth?"

"No idea," I answered impatiently. "Because he was smart?"

"Tom said Emerson didn't want to go to a college with tailgates."

"What are you talking about?"

"He hated it at prep school because he had no family to tailgate with." He corrected himself. "Well, no mother. But the old man never bothered to show up either."

Was this how he and his friends had treated Emerson? It was no wonder he'd changed schools.

"Go to hell, Garrett. You're lucky you have a family."

"It's . . ."

"What?" I asked, wishing I could kick him through the phone line. "Are you reliving your glory days on a car bumper?"

"No," he said, his voice deflated of bravado. "It just hit me . . . The guy's dead."

"Yes. And you're never going to get that model car you wanted from him."

I waited to see if his epiphany would produce any further insights, but he had already moved on.

"So. What are you gonna do, now that your job has been . . . eliminated?"

No questions, then, about how I was coping with losing my employer, how I might be feeling. I was so used to Garrett's tunnel vision that I didn't bring it up. I reminded myself: He worked for a bank.

"Mom and Dad keep asking me the same thing," I said, making an effort to sound upbeat. "I've got some savings."

He groaned. "Of course you do. Is there anything you *don't* save?"

When we hung up, I took myself to Golden Hands for sanctuary, my uneasiness growing with every step closer to the little salon. I half expected Emerson to be there in miniature at the window, climbing up to his imaginary cave on the tabletop mountain, spying on Li and the others. I almost walked back out again, unsure if I was ready to face them. But before I could turn around, Li herself came forward and greeted me with a slight bow. Her strong fingers wrapped around my own and drew me insistently to one of the silk-covered benches.

I didn't know how to explain to her what had happened. I dug around in my purse and showed her the photo of Emerson in college that I had faxed to the police. By her somber expression I saw that she understood.

"I thought *warm feeling*," Li said.

Wordlessly, with a sympathetic smile, she placed my hands inside a deep pottery bowl. She poured rosewater over them from a ceramic pitcher, the heavy gold cuff on her wrist shining regally in the low light. Because she had always tended to Emerson, her personal care was disconcerting to me, even more so when I saw Mei emerge from the back without a customer.

With delicacy, Li dried my hands and smoothed them with a thick, sweet-smelling lotion. She ran her fingers through mine, working them back and forth to release the tension. Then she led me behind one of the bamboo screens and helped me to get undressed and settled on the padded massage table. There, with a gentleness that felt like sorrow, she applied her hands to the consolation of my exhausted body. She rubbed oils into my skin, easing the muscles, as she had always done for Emerson. Did I smell like him, I wondered, as my tears sank into the padded table—did I smell like the death side? Yet something about the movements of her hands banished such morbid thoughts as soon as they surfaced. The tender pressure, her careful attention, telegraphed to my body that it was alive. And more than that, it was alive in the field of a touch that approximated love. Was this what Emerson had felt? That human touch seemed to be healing more than my stiff muscles. It was as if a new spirit—a more lively substance—were overtaking me, entering my tissues and nerves and heart and brain as Li's hands pressed and smoothed it all into place.

In Emerson's loft that evening, the breeze through the window was laced with the clean smell of detergent from the laundromat across the street. I lay for hours in my bed in the guest room, unable to persuade my body to give itself over to sleep. To exhaust myself, I got up and began moving the library of Easter Island back onto the shelves in Emerson's bedroom, where I knew the books would be better protected from sunlight and dust. With none of Maria-Sylvana's delicacy or flair, I cleared away some of the remaining tubes and syringes from one of the lower shelves, then wiped it clean and began lifting the heavy books back into place.

It must have been an hour or so later when I sat down on Emerson's bed to rest and then drifted off to sleep there, to the sound of traffic. Even now, I cannot be sure if the sensation came in the early morning or late at night, or if the time of its occurrence matters much. Try as I might, I could not see him or hear him, only sense him in a childish game of hide and seek, proud of his hiding place: one that was not to be found in the garage on Perry Street, or at the morgue, or at Golden Hands, but somewhere within my reach. Then I felt a twisting in my stomach, and I heard the roaring of an engine, about which I was not warned.

20

OW DOES THE SOUL separate from the body? And if it is reanimated, by what mechanism does it move on to inhabit another form? These were questions I couldn't answer, though I had journeyed to the realm of death. My stay as a child was so brief that I had obtained only a glimpse, and it was this glimpse that had left me searching, defining, cataloguing. Not just objects, but whole systems of belief. In time, I tried each one on for its beauty and fit. Like dresses, they were all alike to me in one way: not in form, but in essence. Different skins stretched over the same bones.

Yet as I came to learn after Emerson's death, there was an aspect of the subject that my inquiries had not taken into account. For at least one afterlife is decided by the living. It is the afterlife born of mourning. In this afterlife, the deceased is fused to the life of the griever, by day, by night, in thoughts and memories. The dead are carried off to work and play and home again. It is an afterlife named for the dead, but its duration and character are entirely reflective of the person who mourns.

At the time, I did not understand the nature of grief, how it molds itself perfectly to the griever. Mine was the grief of Chinese nesting boxes: One coffin-shaped box turned out to contain another, with brass corners and matching locks. And each successive box unlocked the next, unlocked memories and emotions about other deaths over the years—distant relatives, a pet, some teachers, grandfathers, a grandmother. Until a box inside those unlocked, and I was grieving my former employer more deeply than all of them, grieving something to my core. I was pulled into a strange landscape then, a terrain I had never crossed. I trudged through it, finding nothing to orient myself by. And the paradox: I wasn't alone. I was carrying the person I was grieving.

I worked woodenly alongside Eric Dart's crew as they handled the dispersal of Emerson's photography collection, completing the necessary paperwork and watching silently every evening as a little bit more of him disappeared with each insured, boxed and couriered photograph that went out the door. I could not recall ever having so little enthusiasm for my job.

It was a time of suspended animation. I had two apartments, but no sense of being at home anywhere; I had a good deal of work, but no employment. More than anything, I was chastened by the events of Emerson's final weeks. He had berated me for wasting the life he couldn't have, but his condemnation went beyond that. There were the comments in his notebook: I was a professional cloisterer, he said. I hid away. I could not deny it. I was hiding myself then.

I set up a ladder to haul more of his books back into place on the higher shelves in his bedroom. As I worked, I wondered what Emerson would have been doing there in his loft, instead of me. He would not have been able to lift the books, that much was certain; some of them weighed nearly as much as he did in his final days. I restacked them one or two at a time for as long as I could, and once again promptly crashed on his bed. I could not even recall sitting down. The next morning, I told myself it had been an accident, passing out on his mattress for a second time, fully dressed. But again the following night, I fell easily into a restful sleep on his bed. So many of his books had been reshelved that I decided I would stay there to read and then move to my own bed in the guest room later, but I never did. From then on I slept in his room, unwilling to give up the peaceful oblivion that always came within moments of my surrender to the pillow.

It was the old, irresistible force pulling at me, tempting me to give myself over to a merciful oblivion, where there were no feelings and nothing to think about. Awake, I felt what I lacked with unbearable immediacy—I lacked Emerson's company, our closeness. Hélène's observation taunted me: "So, wanting to bring someone back to life is not an impulse you are immune to after all." She was right; I wanted nothing more. Not sick, not with him suffering. His illness and all those months of decline were already fading, like my ulcer, while Emerson himself was coming into clearer focus as the outline of a giant hole inside me. It was the feeling of having your breath taken away—except it did not stop.

With the loss of Emerson came the hard echo of another loss that I could not identify. Awake, I contended with it like a kind of panic, hyperventilating some days with a brown bag over my head, enveloped by the comforting familiarity of paper. Asleep, I felt nothing, making it by far the preferable state. But I could not manage to keep myself submerged day and night. The nerves in my brain crackled with wakefulness, even as I prayed for more hours of nothingness.

I lay there running my fingers over the non-childproof cap on Emerson's bottle of sleeping pills—one of the few prescription bottles I had not dumped out and refilled with his ashes in a fit of organizing obsession one afternoon. To me, it was a logical form of storage: The books that had once filled his mind with their contents had been replaced on the shelves by his pill bottles, and now the pill bottles held his remains. I felt this process of re-duction needed a final step—a sense of completion—but until I could decide what that was, I filled the little orange cylinders and stacked them neatly in an empty corner on one of the shelves (though the amount of fine grit was surprisingly abundant, leading me to store the rest of the plastic bagful in his backpack, in place of his liquefied food).

I considered the sleeping pills in my hand, considered my father's question to me: *What's your game plan?* What was I going to do with myself? The question raced through my mind as I shook the bottle—more than half full. More than a month's worth of sleep, if taken in the proper dosage. Or, if taken all together, quite a different experience. I had hoped I could be squeezed into a slot, after all. I had tried . . .

But as I lay down on Emerson's bed, these morbid thoughts shrank back, as they had done under the coaxing of Li's gentle hands. They were run off the road by a more insistent demand: Before I could consider any course of action for myself, I realized that I had a more immediate duty to Emerson to fulfill. His wish had been for me to release myself from my cloistered cell, but I did not possess a plot for that story. And if I did not have a plot of my own, I would carry on with his. Hadn't I been shadowing him for years already? Taking him into myself, bit by bit? Wasn't that what he had proposed on the night he disappeared? I intuited my first instructions then, knowing what to do as clearly as if Emerson were whispering into my ear.

21

SINCE I AM WRITING this account as Emerson's archivist and my job exists in the service of him, I won't dwell on my itinerary during that time except to say that, before October ended, I gave up the lease on my apartment in Chelsea and emptied it out—an achievement that was possible only because it appealed to my sense of order. Not knowing what to do with Emerson's possessions gave me an unprecedented ability to part with my own. Like a prospector with a pan, I sifted through box after box of objects and papers. Stuffing my life with straw possessions was only a theory of existence, I now understood. It did not pan out in practice. So I reduced and cleared until I'd filled eighteen body-bag-sized trash liners with souvenirs and shredded paper, and then I stored what was left in the middle of Emerson's loft along with my tax files. I got my hair cut, another remnant of my old self that was easy to part with, because I knew it would simplify things, and I made arrangements for a management company to watch over Emerson's uninhabited loft while I embarked on something like the year abroad that I had not been able to afford on my college loans. Emerson had collected photographs of houses all over Europe, and they made convenient route markers. It was better than throwing darts at a map. Without a formal plan, I managed to see most of the homes in his photography collection. It was just as one of the women I met in Copenhagen, Anne-Mette, said later: I was never going to find a life for myself in those slabs of concrete. But visiting them kept me busy for nearly two years, until another Chinese box fell open and led me straight back to the Beacon.

When I first set out, I discovered that not all of the houses from Emerson's photograph collection were still standing, and not all of them were open to the public. Sometimes I could only view a piece of an exterior from a side road or a nearby hill. It was a fresh shock each time to see how a building had changed from the clean new images I'd memorized on Emerson's walls. Some of the structures had become unstable and were long ago sentenced to demolition. Others had been altered so much that their renovation was the equivalent of plastic surgery, rendering them all but unrecognizable on the street.

I was surprised to find that my recollections of Hélène were stubbornly persistent. It was hard to forget her when she had been so present in Emerson's final months, and the more I tried to untangle what had happened between us, the more confused I felt. I made it a point while I was traveling to visit some of the obelisk monuments she had photographed when, I now understood, she had been unable to make any other artworks. The obelisks kept her in my thoughts, and I suppose I hoped to resolve my feelings about her through them, just as visiting the houses made me feel that Emerson was somehow with me, as if he could experience what I was seeing and doing.

By my informal assessment, the ancient obelisks had fared better than the houses. The oldest of the stone monoliths had been erected thousands of years ago to honor Egyptian royalty who were, in the words of one inscription, *given life forever.* Heaven was a separate place, a yolk suspended in its own shell, and so the great needles of quarried stone, dedicated to the sun gods, were raised to pierce the sky. Each stood as a silent testament to the connection between the heavens and the earth. Like a dripping egg, the sun set, the sun rose. A soul died to the earth and was reborn. The obelisks had endured as emblems of this ancient hope.

In my travels I met some of the voices in the cafés, and I found the beds at the top of the long flights of stairs to be welcoming. I wanted to believe I had put mourning behind me. Then, one day, the innermost Chinese box fell open, and I was forced to unpack its tangled contents.

It happened in the summer of 1998, after I had gone to Helsinki to visit a home that the architect Alvar Aalto had designed and lived in with his wife, Aino. It was the first portrait on Emerson's wall, and one of the few remaining for me to visit. In the photograph, the humble residence was little more than a stone path and a wooden door. In person, too, it was a relatively simple place to live and work, the kind of dwelling that might look joyless to anyone who did not understand that joy is not a home furnishing. From Helsinki, I flew to Copenhagen, eager to extend my time away, half consciously chasing Hélène's shadow. Just as she had done herself as a young woman in that city, I rented a flat with afternoon sunshine—a luxury of a mere few hours on the darkest winter days. And when the time came to extend my tourist visa, the U.S. government cordially invited me to report to a Central Processing Center and put my fingerprints on file. It was a technician there, whose name I never learned—a woman who spoke lovely English, like all the Danes I'd met since my arrival —who unlocked the last Chinese box.

I had been functioning until then with the help of my old, well-rehearsed imitations of normalcy: I'd learned my way around the city and spent my days going in and out of the furniture galleries on Bredgade or trawling the city's vintage shops. Not much changed in the galleries from week to week, but some of the staff had become acquaintances of sorts, like Anne-Mette, who ran a little gallery off Istedgade with her sister Helle. Remembering how the home healthcare workers had brought brownies and cookies for me when I was stationed at Emerson's loft, I sometimes brought the sisters little cakes from a bakery behind Strøget, and answered their exquisite English with small talk in my rudimentary Danish. I crisscrossed Rådhuspladsen—the town hall square—and walked from the record stores around Ny Østergade to the bookstores around Blågårds Plads that carried some English-language magazines and books. As far as anyone knew (and as I assured my parents in phone calls), I had a plan: I was preparing for a new career managing collections of modern furnishings. Except it wasn't true. I was stalled there. Then I was called to the Central Processing Center.

I chatted with the Danish technician as she pressed my fingers against the glass screen of a computerized scanner. She kept cleaning the glass with an ammonia solution and sighing. I watched her scan my hand half a dozen times before she finally declared the results to be inadequate.

"What's the problem?"

She gestured to the screen. "You don't have any fingerprints."

I didn't think I heard her correctly.

"Sorry, what did you say?"

She said it again. Quite clearly.

I thought maybe she was joking, and said so.

She shook her head.

It was such an absurd pronouncement that I responded automatically: "Everyone has fingerprints—if they have fingers. What are those right there?"

I pointed to traces of fingerish marks on the screen.

She pressed a key and magnified the faint gray scattering of hash marks. "Not usable. This one—the best one here—is less than ten percent recognition."

"Okay, then. I do have some fingerprints."

"No, you don't. Each mark should be a clean loop, arch or whorl."

It was pretty the way she pronounced it: *hawhørl*.

"By your government's grade categories, these don't even qualify as partial. Look at mine."

She pressed the button to scan her own hand, and I watched as a bunch of textbook-perfect flowers of human identity bloomed on the monitor.

The contrast was instructive. Without exception, mine were barely distinct scratches, as if I had been tortured. They couldn't have been more suspicious-looking if I had tried to destroy them intentionally.

"How are yours so perfect?" I asked in dismay.

"Because I don't work for a living." She laughed with delight at her own social-democratic joke.

"Seriously," I pleaded. "I've never been fingerprinted for anything before. Why are mine gone?"

She shrugged, blissfully unconcerned by my distress.

I said, "Everyone knows that when you get a little burn or a cut on your skin, they grow back in the same pattern. They teach you that in science class. Unless you destroy them with acid or something—which I haven't."

"Sometimes they wear off," she said. "Like the treads on a tire."

It occurred to me that I had gotten more manicures in a single year than most human beings did in a lifetime. Though I imagined that would have made my prints impeccable.

"If I got my nails done a lot, would that strip the prints?"

The woman laughed again—harder than she had at her own joke.

"Can I grow them back?"

She shook her head apologetically.

"Do you use a lot of cleaning products?" she asked with some seriousness. "Do you handle a lot of paper?"

I could not begin to tally the forests' worth of paper I had filed in my years on earth, or the oceans of cleaning products and bleach we had gone through in Emerson's final months.

Reluctantly, I accepted this as my explanation, as did the U.S. government.

That night, I fought a solid mass of heaviness, like a roof fallen in. Before my visit to the Central Processing Center, if I had felt blank, it was only me who felt it. And so the shock of the technician's pronouncement was severe. Now there was evidence: I did not possess the markings of a unique human being. Inside the Chinese box she'd opened, down at the bottom of the silk lining, was a worm I had never routed, a worm curled like a question mark, calling me to account for my own existence.

The second anniversary of Emerson's death was approaching, and I could feel the extra grief leaking out. Once more I found myself wondering what he would have done with his life. I had walked and even slept in his shoes (we wore the same size). He was constantly on my mind, and I talked out loud to him more and more frequently. I'd carried him to see the houses he admired, but I could not say whether I was living up to my responsibilities to him, or to anyone.

I lived like an earthworm, taking the days in like dirt, turning them over and passing them out again. It was as if Emerson's death had just happened. I did not understand how grief could work on such a time delay. The tap behind my eyes would not shut off. Some days, the tears began as I showered in the morning and did not subside until I passed out at night. Later, I would make myself scrambled eggs or sit at a bar with Anne-Mette and Helle. I told them nothing.

Accession Number: BC 1998.1

Postmark: 16 September 1998
Received: 30 September 1998

The object is a notecard from Hélène Moreau, handwritten in black ink on cream-colored stock (the initials HM engraved in navy blue), forwarded from New York City.

Dear Beth, The first small exhibition of my new work will be held at Arthur Quint's gallery, opening on October 8th. I hope to see you there. Are you still enjoying New York? —H.

The arrival of this simple communication from Hélène had a complex effect. Maybe I shouldn't have wondered at this. After all, I had kept her in my thoughts. It was my lingering curiosity about her, some affinity I felt for her, that had given me the idea to stay in Copenhagen, where she had once lived. I mulled over the polite nonchalance of her invitation, in contrast with the distinct charge emitting from between the lines. Like the flashing light on a hotline, it rang with the news: She was working again.

The next day, I got out of bed when it was still morning and took the train an hour north, to Humlebæk, to the modern art museum called Louisiana, where there was a wing dedicated to Hélène's work. I had meant to go earlier. The morning was overcast but warm, and before I went inside I walked the grounds, my spirits lifting with the breeze running up from the blue basin of the Øresund, a busy sea lane between Denmark and Sweden.

Inside the museum, a guard directed me to the two formal halls devoted to the Speed Paintings. The first room was startlingly long, more like a light-filled chute, with row after row of the narrow canvases unfurled in great lengths along the walls. Hélène's paintings had appeared sterile to me in textbooks, despite their intellectual drama. But when I saw them in person, stretching through the tunnel, they came alive along the slashes —thick sheets of scarred canvas skin, smeared with mud and black grease.

I sat with them the way Hélène had sat with Gertrude Stein: not trying to make sense of them. The tongues of butchered canvas riffed in the climate-controlled breeze, saying something I desperately wanted to understand. These were not the simple cuts they appeared to be in reproductions. They were not clean. Everywhere, there were jagged flaps and rips, the suggestion of torn flesh, hair—the wooden stretchers of the canvases showing through like bones. All at once the violence overwhelmed me. The light-filled silence echoed with a breathtaking sense of disruption, of something whole ripping apart. There was no doubt as to the intensity of the force that created them.

I escaped the long gallery at the opposite end and found an upholstered bench in the next hall—technically an extension of the main room, except this second group of Speed Paintings was larger both in physical dimensions and in number. The canvases here were unmistakably different. The wall text explained that they were derived from the European racing circuit. There was a docent at one end of the hall leading a small group through the exhibit. I moved closer to listen in, but he was speaking Danish. As they cleared out, a second group filed in, led by a woman in a smart black suit addressing her group in English. Her arm swept the room.

"What you're seeing here is something very special," she said. "It's a re-creation of the finishes of the Grand Prix races in 1954, done after the season." She clasped her hands together and brought them to her chest. "These are considered to be the height of Moreau's achievement in speed painting. She persuaded top drivers like Ascari and Fangio to send their cars ripping past her canvases." The docent smiled. "Though the works appear to be abstract, most art historians consider them to be portraits. And this is all the more poignant when you consider many of the drivers in this period died prematurely." She indicated one canvas: "The champion Ascari, the driver here, died the next year, testing a car, just days after crashing at Monaco. There were other crashes during this time, and many other deaths, not only among the drivers: A crash at Le Mans left eighty-two *spectators* dead." The docent pursed her lips. "Some of the teams withdrew from racing for years. What's incredible, in retrospect, is that Moreau was so prescient. She wasn't yet twenty-one when she conceived the Speed Paintings. What you see here is a record of what it was to be young and fearless—she had that in common with the drivers."

As I studied the canvas surfaces filling the cavernous space, I further upgraded the docent's assessment of Hélène's accomplishment, for, compared to the paintings in the first hall, these struck me as a new set of works entirely. Brighter. Less torn and stained. The suggestion of speed was like a sword defiantly slicing past from present. The curled strips of canvas moved under the air vents, flayed—but still alive.

The drivers raced past: Hélène had made them painters. Soldiers had already painted the fields with their blood, the world had been devastated by years of brutal wars, and now the racers became painters of pure velocity, hurtling toward a future that promised something better. The torn canvases were war bandages. They were laundry on the line, at home, far from the horrors of the battlefield. And they were speed.

I made my way out of the room dizzily, rushing to get away from the authoritative voice trailing after me: ". . . This last painting marks the beginning of a long period of silence in Moreau's work. Except for a few follow-up canvases in the next decade, this artist, who showed such great promise—who was so closely associated with speed—became, in effect, creatively paralyzed . . ."

I sprinted through the first room to the exit, charging past the guard who had given me directions on the way in.

"You're leaving already?"

Anne-Mette said the same thing when I went by her gallery to offer her my houseplants.

Helle joined in her sister's teasing. "What are you going to do, look at more buildings?"

There was no way I could explain myself to them. I had failed before, and now my grief was only more complicated. When a lover was filling some lack, a day would come when you were forced to face the truth: He left. Or you left. Either way, there was an end. But if you are filling the hole with a person who is already dead, there is no one to stop you. Once again, I sensed Emerson asserting himself through me: In a city where all I did was walk or bicycle, I suddenly wanted to be in a car going insanely fast. For two years, I had been paying to keep the Beacon stored at the garage on Perry Street, and I had never once gone to see it.

22

THE LOFT ON Charles Street smelled clean—too clean; instead of fading, the chemical and medicinal fumes had only expanded their dominion during the time the rooms had been closed up. Before I'd left, the odors were a comforting reminder of Emerson, but now they made me anxious. Certain objects, too, found cunning ways to remind me of the medical interventions that had gone on there. I picked up an enameled pen from a tray in Emerson's bedroom, and with one twist the pen came apart in two pieces. I pulled the cap off a fresh refill, dropped it into the barrel of the pen and retwisted it. The action was eerily familiar, though it was something I had not done in years. Being in Emerson's bedroom again had activated some muscle memory. I could not think what, until I was signing a little card to put in a bouquet for Hélène's opening and I realized: Refilling the pen was very similar to prepping a syringe to clean Emerson's nutrition lines. I had done it dozens of times, except now I wasn't wearing rubber gloves and there wasn't a nurse standing next to me.

I opened the windows to air the place out and ate dinner with the *Village Voice* as my placemat, scanning the advance notice of Hélène's show, though to me it read more like an advertisement for Arthur Quint's gallery. The article was accompanied by a striking photo of Hélène: a black-and-white shot from the 1950s that I had come across several times in books, and again, at a greatly enlarged size, at the museum in Denmark. Even with road goggles in place of her aviator glasses, there was no mistaking the flatness of her face. She was driving an elaborate black car of Italian manufacture—what looked like a prewar model. Its grille was composed of a hundred shining arrows. Long steel needles shot out from the center of the wheels like the scythes on a Persian chariot. Hélène's younger body was frozen there in the speeding car as it approached the unfurled length of canvas, stretched and bound like a virginal sacrifice—her smile a fascinating collision of misery and elation.

I wanted to believe that the news of her having moved past her paralysis held some promise for me, like having a lucky bird coasting off the bow of my boat. But when I arrived at the opening that evening, I saw that I was horribly mistaken. Behind the pink lenses floated the eyes of a drowning victim.

Hélène was huddled on one side of the crowded gallery, in conversation with Arthur Quint and another man I recognized as an art critic for the *Voice*.

"What's the problem?" the critic asked her. "It's your own promotional photograph."

"Forty years ago," she protested. "And once again, it has been used for something unrelated."

"Everyone does it to her," Arthur Quint complained.

"I'm trying to get a new photo taken," Hélène said. "With a Beacon."

"But that picture is sincere," the critic argued. He threw his hands up. "No one knows what to do with sincerity anymore! It's become completely awkward."

When Hélène saw that I was standing beside her, she moved mechanically to kiss me on both cheeks, then pulled me into the crowd and, without another word of greeting or explanation, introduced me to a Mrs. G-C, from Lake Como in Italy.

"I visited some modern houses there last year," I informed the woman, shaking her jeweled hand as Hélène moved off with my bouquet to greet another guest. I stood self-consciously beside the Italian woman, surveying Hélène's new paintings: nominally seascapes, views off the coast of Morocco painted from high ground. Once again, as with her Speed Paintings, the vehicles themselves were absent. The canvases included only the suggestion of speedboats, all but invisible except for the churn of a wake—hundreds of wakes—blurring across the Mediterranean toward the southern coast of Spain. As I had read during my dinner, the *Voice* critic applauded the paintings for being "ironically traditional," with "a sixties color quality, like Pucci prints." He did not, however, consider them to be on a par with her early work. To me, the paintings stood in direct contrast to the color quality of the artist herself. It was as if the bright canvases had drained all the life out of her.

Still hoping to get a chance to speak with her, I accepted Arthur Quint's invitation to a gathering afterward at a bar downtown called Sybarite, a dark space filled with candles and Latin music, where I observed Hélène making spiritless attempts to entertain her guests. She looked, as my father would say, like the fight had gone out of her.

"Thank you for inviting me tonight," I said when I saw an opportunity to intercept her near the bar.

Without asking, she ordered me a vodka tonic from the bartender—the same drink she had once fed to me in the padded bar at her hotel.

"How are you, Beth? You've cut your hair."

"Yes."

She squinted, assessing the short layers. "*Très gamine.* It suits you."

"You seem different too," I said cautiously. "Thinner?" I didn't know how to phrase it politely.

"It's this suit," she said, brushing the sleeves with annoyance. "It's closely tailored. I had it made in Morocco for the opening."

The smell of her turpentine perfume and the taste of the cold vodka tonic transported me back to that springtime with Emerson. I handed the glass back without another sip.

She was studying my face, silently negotiating the terms of our détente. "What have you been doing all this time? Are you continuing to work in Mr. Tang's office?"

"I've got some obligations related to his estate," I answered, not untruthfully. In an effort to bridge the awkwardness, I told her about my tour of Emerson's houses during the previous years—an adventure she declared to be *super*. I chose not to mention the co-headlining Obelisk Tour, or the fact that I had shadowed her to Copenhagen and fallen into an existential coma there.

"I've been having a tough time without Emerson," I said. "And I'm not happy about everything that's happened between us, Hélène. It's hard to explain, but . . . I hope you understand: I'm not giving up that car."

She studied my face. "I have a theory that if you grieve once, fully, it's never so difficult again. I learned this many years ago, after my mother died. One death will take you so deep in yourself—" She gave me a watery smile. "Can you believe that what you feel is possibly . . . useful? It's the same with stretching a muscle. At some point it transforms. There can be strength in it."

I didn't know how to respond without offending her. From what I could see, she was grieving something heavily herself.

"What about you?" I asked. "How are things with you?"

"I've had more energy," she said. "I don't get a lot of sleep. I find myself thinking about Alto . . . When we were together, I created my best work." She shook her head. "I've tried to understand this . . ."

The ambivalence in her face was painful to witness, especially after a period of forty years. Something had obviously gone very wrong.

"You said you fought a lot."

"Searching for the Beacon was my therapy, Beth. Do you remember that?"

"Yes."

"But when I saw the engine by chance that day in California—"

"What?" The musical elisions of her accent were no longer familiar to me, and I wasn't sure I'd heard right. "Did you say 'by chance'?"

"Yes."

"What do you mean? How was it chance?"

"I was invited there by an old friend from when I worked with the professional drivers. I was trying to fall in love with him. Well, I didn't." She let out a small laugh. "I saw you running down the lawn. We had not spoken in a few weeks and so I walked over to say hello, and then—"

"You saw the engine," I said, voicing the one thought that had eased my conscience. "And now you're making new paintings."

She cleared her throat with a pained expression. "Except it's like a Wildean trick. My doctor says I've been choking myself in my sleep."

"What, you mean like sleep apnea?"

"No, apparently it's some . . ." She frowned. "I can't explain it. The medical terms confuse me. When I found that message from Alto on the engine—"

"You didn't know it was there?"

She shook her head.

"You weren't looking for it?"

"Oh, no!" she said with a surprised laugh.

"You bid on it."

"Of course. I was excited—" She stopped, troubled by some

thought. She took a sip of her drink and then her eyes met mine. "When I saw what he'd written . . . You know, for a long time I tried very hard to forget him. People say you have to move on, and probably many people do manage to, because they're realistic. You may not believe that after so long you can still feel the intensity of—well, when I saw the message there . . ." She lifted her glass again. "I can't stop thinking we could have been happy together."

I understood that, far from helping her, the sight of the old engine had only dragged her more forcefully back into the realm of nostalgia. A romantic memory was strangling her and had been for a long time. She'd said it herself: She was trying to put something back together, something from her youth, something pure that had given her the greatest happiness. I wondered if it hadn't been the same for Emerson.

I wish it had been generosity that caused me to do what I did then—and maybe it was, partly, because I sensed that I could offer her something. But I needed her to assist me just as much. She looked confused as I tried to explain this.

"You want my help?" she asked.

"Yes, well, I thought, while you're here in the city—later this week—would you like to go for a drive?"

There was the telegram. And there was Miguel's account of a friendship. Otherwise, I had not heard anything from or about Lynford Webster since the summer Emerson died. I hated confrontation, but I could not ignore the remaining duties I understood to be mine. There were some personal items of Emerson's, including his watches, that needed to be returned to the only family member I knew of. And there was the most personal item of all—Emerson's remains—which I had been instructed to dispense with according to his wishes, though, in his refusal to accept what was happening to his body, he had not spelled them out. I thought my questions about the Beacon might be answered in the course of carrying out these duties, if I could summon the nerve to ask them.

The morning after Hélène's opening, I reinstated myself in Emerson's office and dug out my old research into the classic-car restorers. Now that I had the clarity of mind to shift my focus to Connecticut, it took only two phone calls to identify the missing link as Martin McVane, the owner of a respected garage in Norwalk. The morning I planned to drop in on McVane, I reread one of the faxes in Emerson's file, from the Beacon Heritage Trust.

Accession Number: BC 1998.2

20 June 1996

Mr. Tang,

Thank you for your latest inquiry. I am happy to reply.

If the engine has been changed over time, well, that happens.

If it was raced hard or crashed, the engine and gearbox might go one way, the doors fly off the other way, etc. Certain models were always raced, but it does not make any difference really.

To your question: "What is the vehicle? The chassis or the engine?" The chassis is deemed to be the vehicle.

Respectfully yours,
Manfred Zeffler
Brand Steward

I smiled to myself. One of Emerson's urgent faxes that summer. He couldn't help himself from splitting hairs about what defined the actual car. Knowing Emerson, he'd asked in case we had failed to get the engine, leaving open the question of whether he, or, presumably Hélène, was the true victor. But I recognized that Zeffler's clarification meant something else: By design, the engine was intentionally separate. From the beginning, it was always meant to be changed or replaced. I digested this as I walked down Perry Street to meet Hélène at the garage. She arrived not long after me, by taxi, wearing a souvenir baseball cap from a Broadway show, her breath smelling strongly of coffee. Together with her aviator glasses and the bewildered expression on her face, she looked like nothing so much as a lost tourist.

Inside the garage, the manager, Nate, escorted us to a part of the building I had never seen. From across a polished cement floor, we approached a private bay at street level, filled floor-to-ceiling with a reflective car cover—a voluminous golden cocoon. In the shadowy garage, the shiny fabric looked like a cross between a carnival tent and a UFO.

"You keep the car under that?" I asked Nate.

Hélène turned to me. "When was the last time you saw it?"

"I haven't."

She stared at me in disbelief.

"At first I couldn't face it," I explained feebly. "And then I was traveling."

She walked ahead, huffing her disapproval.

Nate knelt down on the cement and began disconnecting several thick black wires snaking out from the enclosure.

"What are those?" I asked.

"Triple battery chargers."

"Sounds redundant," sniffed Hélène.

He rolled up the garage door leading onto Perry Street, and the sides of the tent shifted with the inrush of air. The great golden cocoon seemed to breathe. It frightened me to watch it. Then Nate detached a hose from the side and it began to deflate. There was a flash as he pulled the cover off the high fenders. A rustle of fabric unveiled the body: the sweeps, the curves, long and low, all of it painted the thick, creamy color of a vanilla milkshake.

Inside the open-top car, two narrow blood-red seats touched casually, shoulder to shoulder. A skinny metal gearshift reached up from the carpeted floor. Something beside it caught my attention: a heap of fabric. I didn't get more than a few inches closer before I cried out.

"What is it?" asked Hélène.

"That's his."

I was afraid to touch it, to pull it out. The two of them stared expectantly at me as I leaned over the car door and closed my hand around Emerson's cashmere blanket.

I half expected it to feel warm from his body, but it was cool, the soft fibers suffused with a dark, medicinal smell. Beneath the blanket I found an unpleasant collection of objects. Lurking there on the carpet were crumpled paper towels, wads of Kleenex and a glass jar. The jar contained traces of a burgundy-black substance that I knew without any further investigation had once been Emerson's urine.

"My God."

Nate brought over a trash can and took everything from my hands.

"He was camping in the car?" Hélène asked.

Nate shrugged. "One night."

I turned to him. "You knew he was here?"

He held up his hands in surrender. "It was his car, right? He was free to come and go."

"When I asked, you said this car was being worked on by mechanics somewhere."

"It was — inside this bay."

"Nate, he was *dying*."

"All the more reason he should have access, right? He owned the car. He was paid up . . ."

I wanted to keep arguing with him, not because I thought he was wrong, only to vent the stress, however belatedly, of those long hours of Emerson's disappearance. Until I spotted something else on the carpet: the paintbrush Emerson had stolen from Hélène. It was lying askew by the gas pedal, like a twig fallen from an overhanging tree.

Now — of all times — when the woman herself was standing a few feet away. There was no question I would cover for him.

"I hope the floorboard's not stained with urine or anything," I said. On the pretext of examining the carpet, I bent over and flicked the paintbrush out of sight, under the seats.

At the back of the car, two thin exhaust pipes shot out from the body, flanked by a pair of woefully inadequate-looking strips of chrome bumper. I backed away from the pipes and joined Hélène at the front. She was examining the grille's thick, intricate metalwork: a series of elegantly squashed hexagons crossed with shining bars. Affixed to the hood was an enameled lighthouse badge—a flat, stylized obelisk inside a diamond, half white and half emerald green. It was hard to reconcile those clean, bright geometries with the mess of Emerson lingering in the car on his last night alive.

"It's all set to drive?" I asked Nate.

"Yeah, yeah. Good to see it getting out and doing some miles."

"It's gorgeous," gushed Hélène. "Though I do remember wishing the seats were more comfortable."

Her proprietary tone irritated me. The idea of Emerson being there alone on his last night, perhaps in great physical pain, continued to haunt me, but another thought had been burning through me like acid since the morning he was found: He had spent his final moments with Hélène, not me.

I turned to Nate. "Does this car have an engine in it?"

He laughed.

"Does it?"

He laughed again. "Oh, yeah."

"Can you open the hood, please?"

"You can just start it up. You don't haveta go through that."

"I'd like to see it. Is it the new—sorry—the original one?"

"Yeah. Sure."

Nate wiped his hand on his jeans, then reached under the dashboard for the release. "When it came back from California, we got them together in time for him to go . . . camping."

Even before he had finished lifting the hood, I saw the lumps of metal. An engine. As foreign to me as a comet.

Hélène, mi ricordo.

Hélène moved closer, transfixed by the sight of the words engraved there.

"Thank you," I said to Nate, newly embarrassed.

He lowered the hood.

"Hélène will be driving it this afternoon," I informed him.

"It used to overheat in traffic," she recalled, holding her hand to her throat.

"You won't have any trouble," Nate said. "It's sweet. You need help starting it?"

"I'll be fine." She wrapped her fingers around the thin wooden steering wheel. She spent some time finding a comfortable driving position, wriggling her body on the seat until she seemed satisfied.

"You don't take a nap while you're driving these postwar cars," she told me. "They're a bit of work. It's not the friendliest to use — what's the expression?"

"User-friendly."

"Not at first, anyway."

"That's why I needed you."

She leaned back and smiled. "I'd forgotten how close this seat is. It was easier for Alto behind the wheel. He was shorter than me."

She came into softer focus for me then, as the glow of anticipated delight overtook her features. Then her tone grew serious.

"Beth, well, I did try to bid on the engine . . . in the moment. And I do regret this, considering the situation your employer was in. You're kind to give me this chance to drive it."

Her words moved me to silence. She knew exactly why I had asked her there: I needed her to chauffeur me and, in a sense, Emerson. I'd pulled all the prescription bottles full of his remains off the shelves in his bedroom and brought them, along with the rest in his backpack. She'd agreed to drive so I could scatter them, and then to accompany me afterward on an ambush of sorts, to try to get some information from the restorer, Martin McVane. I had kept the car from her for years, and now her humbleness made me see her again as the vulnerable woman I had first met. The thought of her stolen paintbrush there in the car, abandoned carelessly by Emerson, reminded me of her vulnerability all the more.

I reached down to place my bags by my feet and, while Hélène was speaking to Nate, I felt around under her seat until my fingers found the paintbrush. "Can I try the radio?" I asked, after I dropped the brush into my purse.

"We'll be happier listening to the engine."

I wasn't sure.

She moved her feet purposefully and the car's breath erupted around us.

"Oh—it's glorious!" she shouted.

I was glad I'd brought my Walkman.

She pressed the throttle again and the engine sputtered, then roared.

"Octane's a little high in the gas," Nate said, kicking the edges of the metallic cover clear of the wheels. "Nothing we can do about that."

"There's no seat belt," I said, looking to Nate.

"Nope!" He laughed, waving us off as Hélène, working the clutch, inched the car out of the garage.

She turned the wheel, the car curtsied to the left, and then we were rolling down Perry Street like a parade float. I wondered when she would floor it, but we were still on cobblestones and she seemed content to take her time, barely blipping the throttle, driving cautiously, as if she were ferrying a child to school.

I directed her around the corner onto Greenwich Street. The cobblestones turned to smooth asphalt, and we were floating. It was like being on a magic carpet, but the smells were warm, strange, mechanical. On the narrow streets of the Village the flower boxes in the windows were fringed with the first fallen leaves. The air felt close, caught behind the little glass windscreen, the odor of leather and dust mixed with a rubbery smell I assumed was the set of Dunlop tires Emerson had bought the first summer. The Beacon's engine was humming, and the morning was loud with the sounds of exhausts popping on West Street. I didn't watch the road that morning as much as I watched Hélène. Her paint-stained hands on the wheel. That smell, a feeling. Something mournful—of what? The car felt like old times. But Hélène's movements were alive with concentration and grace.

We cleared the city, the grass unrolling like spools of film along the sides of the road as Hélène systematically overtook the cars around us, connecting from one parkway to the next, heading north and then east. I'd already warned her that after we crossed into Connecticut, I was going to release Emerson's ashes. It was she who had given me the idea, when I'd recalled her invitation to go driving together two years earlier.

The eulogy I'd composed for him the night before sounded like a movie review, so I'd ripped it up and stuck a yellowing cassette tape into my old Walkman. It was one of the handful I'd found among the upgraded piles of CDs in his "Merritt Parkway Driving Music" stack.

Accession Number: ETW 1988.? and BC 1998.3

The object is a cassette tape:

Cocteau Twins—*Blue Bell Knoll*
October 1988
4AD Records; Capitol Records (USA)
35 minutes, 20 seconds

NOTES:
British legend holds that the bluebell's knoll (or "knell") is audible only to those who are approaching death.

"One journalist, in reviewing *Blue Bell Knoll,* went so far as to say, 'When you die, and then open your eyes, if there isn't music something like this playing in the distance, you're probably on your way to the wrong place.'"

Ref: Cocteau Twins, "Heaven or Las Vegas" press release, 1990
www.cocteautwins.com/html/history/history14.html

When we crossed onto the Merritt, I squeezed the Play button on my Walkman and the morning filled with the scratchy, tape-recorded roar of angels and the singing of the engine, and the glory of it drowned out everything in my head. I twisted off the top of the first prescription bottle—Ativan—and leaned back to catch the airflow. On contact, Emerson's remains leapt out from the little plastic cylinder. The light dust flew up and away from the next bottle, and the next, and the next. For miles the delicate nets of powdery grit flung themselves like confetti over the grass and trees, sailing off into the woods or tumbling past bridges and roadside stretches of wildflowers, where I hoped they would fertilize something.

I had taken a long ride with him, and now that his human dust was falling away, I let the sensation of speed fill me up again. I was happy it was too noisy to speak, happy to feel the vibrations of the car through my body as I had once done with Emerson. As Hélène had done with Alto. When I looked over at her, she was radiant.

In Norwalk, we cut through a series of residential neighborhoods to reach the garage of Martin McVane. When the car was moving slowly enough for us to hear the birdsong in the turning foliage, Hélène began to recount a driving holiday she had taken in the Beacon with Alto Bianco in the summer of 1954. She rolled her shoulders back and forth as she recalled that they had run through the Italian Alps and then on to Geneva, to a hotel on the lake.

"His hair was wild," she said, "as if a great wind had blown him into your presence. Later, we didn't treat each other well. But when we were on the road, we never fought."

My own reaction to the man had been so negative, I decided not to mention that I had met him in Germany two years earlier. Instead, I asked, "What attracted you to him?"

I was surprised by the forcefulness of her reply.

"We just wanted to go like hell!" she said with a sharp laugh. "Because we could! Because the war was over and we were alive." She tapped her fingers on the steering wheel. "I was very young. I'd had only a brief life before we met, and anyway, that was destroyed by the war. So much was . . . I didn't feel anything when we were driving—it was bliss. On the nights afterward, the echoes would come into my eardrums. I could feel the acceleration building. It was erotic. It was a revelation to me."

"Like when you step off a boat and you're still rocking."

She nodded. "The experience imprints itself on the body. But the sensation soon disappeared. I wanted to continue feeling it." She considered this for a moment. "I was maybe addicted."

"Do you still love him?"

"I think maybe he didn't need love. Or, he would not allow himself to receive a great deal of it. He was a man like a camel." She pinched her fingers in the air. "He could survive on a thimbleful."

It occurred to me that Alto's account of his many personalizations might have been an empty boast, nothing more than a macho show of bravado. His message to her might be the only one.

"What happened?" I dared to ask, as we reached Martin McVane's garage.

"It doesn't matter. Well, it does. But we're here now."

McVane must have spotted the car pulling up. We were still parking it when he approached. He was a solidly built man in his sixties with a shiny alabaster complexion that reminded me of raw cod flesh. His voice, or rather the way he spoke, was relaxed

enough when he said hello, but as he circled the Beacon he studied its every curve without uttering another word.

I introduced myself and Hélène.

"What can I do for you?" he asked, finally turning to us.

As we walked with him into the garage, I attempted to disarm
him by appealing to his ego. I'd come into possession of the car
recently, I explained, and I'd been told he was the best restorer in
the area.

"Don't you do work for Lynford Webster, in Burring Port?" I
asked.

"Sure. Used to. Years ago."

He'd almost taken the bait. I only had to make it a little easier
for him.

"What about my Beacon roadster out there? Remember it
from his collection?"

"Course. It's an unforgettable car."

I exchanged glances with Hélène. At various times I had imagined all kinds of histories for the car, especially related to Emerson's college years, but at the party after her opening, Hélène's
yearning had made me consider the landscape of Emerson's own
youth. My heart was pounding.

"Do you know when Webster got it?"

"Boy, let's see . . . Must have been 1960? Maybe '61. It was a
gift to his wife, the Chinese woman. He also gave her a white cat.
I never met either one of them, but I can tell you I met plenty
of that cat's hair on those red seats and carpets. She must have
chauffeured that animal around."

I didn't know what Emerson's mother was like. All I had was
a photograph and a bill with the Websters' name on it from La
Valencia Hotel in La Jolla, California, in December 1962, the time
of my mother's sighting of Mrs. Webster at the airport. Emerson had saved the items in his desk, souvenirs of what might have
been his first family vacation, as a baby. After that, she had lived in
Connecticut with her husband and son for three more years. Em-

erson, my parents—they said the woman must have been glad to put her past behind her, to move to a place where so much was open to her. But if she knew she was dying . . . I'd seen it myself with Emerson. Grief can make you pull away. Something fired in my gut.

"She died in this car, didn't she?"

McVane nodded evenly. "Hit a stand of oaks about three miles from here. Trees took it okay. They had a couple hundred years on her."

I glanced at Hélène, but she had her eyes squeezed shut behind her glasses.

"Was she alone?"

McVane nodded.

"And you got the car after that."

He pulled his lips tight. "Yeah."

"What did you do with it?"

"Webster wasn't interested in trying to save the car. The body wasn't that much trouble, really, but the engine was going to take a lot of work to rebuild. So I sourced a replacement engine and sold the car to a dealer on Long Island."

"What about the engine?"

"As I say, it was going to take a lot of work to rebuild it, and I was a one-man shop in those days. I sold it as is to a collector in Florida."

"Do you know what happened to it after that?"

"No idea. But that was one of the finest engines of its day. They were practically indestructible. I imagine it went into another body."

"It did. From Argentina."

"Huh."

"His son was trying to put the body and engine back together."

McVane smiled. "Was he."

Whatever else he made of this, I didn't care to find out.

In a kind of funk, I directed Hélène through the maze of

country roads to Gray Hill. She piloted calmly along the winding route, brooding on what McVane had told us: "It was crashed. He says the body wasn't any trouble to rebuild, but the engine was? The engine was put into another car—and the writing is still there? It's strange."

"I'm glad Emerson got the original engine," I told her. "But apparently it doesn't matter. I learned—officially, anyway—that the car is defined as the chassis. Not the engine."

"Who says this?"

"Someone at the Heritage Trust. Manfred Zeffler."

"I suppose that's what he would say. Bureaucrats thrive on official pronouncements. But I wonder if there isn't something more to a car. They tell you this in advertisements all the time, it's so trite—who considers? There's an energy to the movement of the wheels. Do you know the Sanskrit word for 'moving wheel'?"

I shook my head.

"It's *chakra,* a word that is also used to describe the energy centers in the human body. There's an energy in the composition, the movement, the metal . . ."

"Metal conducts."

"Yes, and we are talking about enormous pieces of metal."

"What about the engine?"

She thought for a moment. "Well, in the human body, the engine is considered to be the stomach."

I pulled out the photograph I had taken from Emerson's desk. Hélène glanced at it before turning her eyes back to the road.

"This belonged to Emerson," I said. "I assume it's his mother. The date is right."

The ruffled border of the little square snapshot was stamped with the year 1963. It showed a young Asian woman standing before a placid slice of coastline. She and Emerson shared a strong likeness, in the width of the nose, the curve of the forehead. The emulsion on the photo was cracked and her skin had a greenish cast, as if she were sunken in a pool. She held her mouth open, but no teeth were visible. Her skin was flawless except for a birth-mark, like a smudge, on her left cheek. "Do you think she killed herself?"

"Maybe some flowers can't be transplanted," Hélène sug-gested, glancing at the photo again.

I tucked it into his backpack along with his other personal ef-fects. It seemed the woman had not died of her illness, as every-one thought. Or had her illness played a part?

Hélène pursed her lips. "She could have been trying to feel some power over her situation, no? Speed is a false power, but once you feel it, it's addicting."

Did she die triumphant? I wondered. In the open car, the last lemony streaks of winter sun bleached by snow clouds, she would have felt the frigid air rush over her. Then the whir and buzz of the engine, dropping and building to a full-throated roar. With the twilight blooming around her, she pressed her foot down and opened her heart to the sky.

23

ALL THE SHADES were drawn at the house on Gray Hill, the long rows of windows neatly covered with buff-colored parchment. There were no people or vehicles in sight, no signs of life. Met with the absolute stillness of the templelike building, I cannot say I was entirely surprised when Laurel greeted us at the door with an apology.

"He isn't available," she said, her voice stiff with embarrassment. But her choice of words had already betrayed her. Webster was home.

"I don't have an appointment," I said, not hiding my unhappiness at the prospect of being turned away. "I was hoping I could be squeezed in."

Laurel was dressed in what I now understood to be her customary uniform of white tennis shoes, a pair of khaki pants and a clean white shirt. She stood before me with arms crossed, like a bouncer, her hands devoid of a wedding ring or other jewelry, her squat form obstructing the entryway as a breeze from an open window somewhere in the house sneaked past her, carrying with it the scent of furniture polish. As the odor filled my head, I felt a kinship with Laurel, who had evidently been cleaning and polishing things by herself, and who could no more answer for her employer's ways than I had ever been able to for his son's.

Her eyes dashed from me to the silver backpack cradled in

my arms to Hélène's face, fixed with apprehension. With a sympathetic nod, she disappeared down one of the hallways, returning not long afterward to say that Mr. Webster would join us in a few minutes. She ushered us into the study off the main hallway, where I'd waited in vain for him to appear on my previous visit with Emerson.

I rested the backpack on the desk. Laurel was regarding it with curiosity—or perhaps she thought I was taking liberties, placing my own bag there.

"These are just a few things that belonged to Emerson," I explained.

"Oh?"

"I wanted to ask his fa—"

To my distress, she began pulling Emerson's belongings out of the bag, then impatiently picked it up and slid the rest of the contents onto the desk.

"These are very personal things. I . . ."

She was opening the acid-free envelope I had sandwiched protectively between two pieces of cardboard.

"Oh, my goodness," she said when she'd extracted the stiff sheet of paper inside. A smile of recognition spread over her lips as she inspected the little watercolor painting I had found in Emerson's desk.

"Do you know anything about it? It's not documented in Emerson's collections."

"His collections, yes," she said with evident amusement.

"Do you know who painted it?"

I tried to imagine Emerson in his office, working to master Hélène's stolen paintbrush, but the vision dissolved with her next comment.

"Someone in China." She propped the painting up against the backpack. "It belonged to his father, who asked me to remove it from this room we're standing in, oh, at least twenty-five years ago. I wondered where it went."

Embarrassed by Emerson's petty thievery, I attempted a joke. "He obviously started collecting very early."

Laurel was studying the drawing. "This is his mother."

"I thought so. I wasn't sure. He mentioned a painting once, but he made it sound like his father had it. I'm sure he'll be happy to have it back."

Laurel was shaking her head. "Nope. Not his style."

"You mean, the style of painting?" asked Hélène.

"No, no," Laurel answered, unhelpfully, as Webster himself appeared in the doorway.

I hadn't expected him to be elderly. I had never advanced his age beyond the newspaper photos of him I had seen when I was a teenager. Facing him there in his study, I felt much older myself. His hair had turned gray-white, like dried concrete, though the long, unruly sideburns remained a stylishly contrasting black —dyed, perhaps, to match his eyeglasses. Behind the thick, round lenses, his eyes drooped at the corners like gigantic commas. His face was framed by the same large ears as his son's, the pendulous lobes sagging nearly to the top of his collar. He was probably younger than Hélène, but his general condition of drooping and flopping made him appear much less solid. Only his perennial slim-cut suit provided him with some much-needed structure.

"I met your son very briefly," said Hélène as she introduced herself. "I could see he was a fine man."

He nodded and turned to me with a cheerful expression. "What brings you here this afternoon, Bethany?"

"Beth."

"Yes," he said.

"I brought Emerson's things." I gestured to the watches and cufflinks that Laurel had left strewn on the desk.

"I haven't heard from you since that summer," he said. He picked up a remote control from the desk, waved it in the direction of a darkened stereo console, then, at the sight of the watercolor propped against the backpack, seemed to reconsider. He placed the remote back down softly on the polished wooden surface.

"I was surprised you sent a telegram when he died."

He looked at me curiously. "What would you have had me do?"

I didn't have an answer. It was an unplanned salvo. Before I could say any more, he spoke again, his voice deflated of its original cheer. "I have another question for you. Why do you think my son didn't want to see me, at the end?"

"What do you mean, didn't want to see you?"

"Just what I said. When he came here that summer, he asked for my advice on some matters relating to his estate and trusts. He no doubt told you?"

"I don't know what you're talking about."

He looked at me skeptically. "At any rate—" He paused, seeming to reorganize his thoughts. "He said goodbye to me that day."

"He said you were traveling."

Webster shook his head. "Not that much."

Could what he was saying be true? I considered Emerson's habits of privacy—his systematic withdrawal from people in those final months, his self-declared difficulty with saying goodbye—and came to the dismaying conclusion that what Webster was saying might be true. It was hard to comprehend, the truth being so complete a reversal of my own fears that day, when I'd worried that I would be elbowed aside and Webster would take over. But Emerson had not allowed it.

Webster stared at me, his face sunken with misery. "Why did he shut me out?"

I recalled what Hélène had suggested to me at the hotel on the morning he died. "Maybe . . . he was trying to protect you."

"From what? What could he protect me from?"

"His pain."

Webster considered this, then stood from the desk and began

to pace. "That day when he came here—you were with him, weren't you?"

"Of course. I brought him."

"And you didn't want to meet me."

"He never suggested it."

"Did you ask to meet me?"

"I didn't think to ask."

"I certainly did, but he put me off. He told me he'd legally designated you as his caretaker, his trustee. And you were in charge."

"Excuse me," Hélène said. "You understand theirs was a business arrangement?"

"Yes. He hired me to help him," I said, silently thanking her. "What, did you think . . . we were together?"

He sank back into his chair. "I don't know what I thought," he said. "I only knew he was saying goodbye. It was earlier than your goodbye, maybe, but that doesn't make it easier."

His candor took me by surprise.

"He didn't say goodbye to me," I said. "You thought he didn't need you?"

"He hired you as his caretaker. Do you see—nothing was obvious with him."

"I think he felt alone."

"He told you his feelings?"

"No. Well, rarely."

Webster eyed me more closely. "He told you why he bought the Beacon? Or why he was looking for the engine?"

"No."

"Even though, if we can be honest with one another, this meant more to him than all the other trouble you took on his behalf."

It was the most searing blow he could have delivered, intended or not. Emerson had deceived me, even made me think he wasn't interested in the car after the engine was restored. He'd left me worrying about him when he disappeared. He hadn't said goodbye. The thought of it burned behind my eyes. But Webster had brought up the search for the engine himself, and that took some of the sting out of the burn.

"You knew he was looking for it?" I asked. "Do you know why?"

He shook his head unconvincingly.

"I think he was looking for her." I moved to reach for the little painting behind him, but Hélène was regarding me sternly.

"What if he was?" asked Webster.

"Maybe he was looking for you, too."

He frowned. "The heart releases too slowly."

"What?"

"Something I've felt for a long time."

He hunted through the bookshelves around his desk for a few minutes, bunching his shoulders tighter the more intently he searched. As I watched him scan the low shelves, I recalled doing the same as a child in the new library he had funded in Burring Port, inhaling the sweet scent of adventure glued into the bindings. Finally he gave up on the book and turned to me.

"Rilke writes that it's the poet's duty to praise deserted women: the great lovers. What about the deserted men?" Softly, to himself, he went on: "I'm the one who's alone." He circled the desk in front of me. "I found out by chance that you were looking for the engine."

"From Miguel?"

I had not said his name in a long time; it almost hurt to pronounce it.

Webster nodded. "I was speaking with him about something else and he mentioned his affection for your cause."

"Emerson's cause."

"Yes. I came to that conclusion."

I spoke hesitantly: "The restorer, Martin McVane—we just came from seeing him. He said she . . . died in that car."

Webster shook his head. "Beth, if someone was going to put

back together what I had taken apart, it should have been me. And I didn't want it put back together."

"That was all Emerson wanted."

He stared past me, remembering something or weighing something. "His mother didn't die in that car. That's the truth. She did not."

"McVane told us—"

"He was trying to help me save face. He called here as soon as you left."

Webster hovered over me like a shade. I wondered if he might be preparing to confess some transgression, but he only seemed to grow more mournful as he spoke.

"I gave her that car as a wedding present. It was spirited, like her. You could say it was Emerson's first car as well. He was still in diapers when we took him for drives on this hill. I sat with him on my lap and put his hands on the wheel. We showed him the ocean down the road, the woods. Everything I hoped he would inherit—"

His voice faltered.

I glanced at Hélène. She was studying his face.

"I used to have to clean the baby powder streaks off the seats afterward," he said, smiling sadly. "He was still a toddler when my wife's health . . . She was weakened by what she went through before she came here: anemia, blood disorders, jaundice—you cannot imagine the number of medical problems caused by starvation."

Emerson's imaginary scene of his mother having her portrait painted—a lighthearted picnic on the river with her girlfriends—flared up in my mind and burned away to nothing as he went on.

"At the time, where she came from, there were degradations, moral compromises . . . She had friends, teenage girls like her, who killed themselves. She was fortunate, I think—she believed in what she was working for. She wanted what they were promised: a modern society without want, high-rise buildings with electricity and television . . ."

He turned to the watercolor resting against Emerson's backpack. "The boy she loved painted this." Webster picked it up and placed it carefully back in the envelope. "There was a legal age for marriage, even in the villages. They were sixteen—too young. They didn't marry, and it didn't last. Not because their feelings changed." He shook his head. "The boy was pulled into a group of other farmers to carve a slogan into the hillside, to greet Party members arriving for a conference. My wife, along with some other girls, was paid a week's salary to welcome the committee members. She still wore her hair in braids then. She counted the different dishes on the banquet table that night—more than fifteen of them." He tapped his fingers on the envelope. "The boy didn't come back from the hillside alive. When she found out, she managed to leave with one of the committee members who had given her a steamed bun from his plate.

"I suppose she still loved the other boy when I met her in Hong Kong. But I took her here, and for a few years she had . . . well, for all she had been through—" His face brightened. "She believed in progress."

That shining in his eyes reminded me of Emerson's fervor in the Case Study House in Los Angeles, though it faded as he continued his tale:

"When the hospital visits started, I saw she was shrinking from our son. He would try to play with her, or sit with her, but she was like a stone wall. One day that winter, it was sunny and I persuaded her to come for a drive. I bundled Emerson up. We had not been out for more than twenty minutes when the Beacon started to vibrate. I guessed it was a wheel coming loose. But there was no way to explain—by then, the car was bucking violently. I was braking to pull off the road when the wheel flew off.

"I managed to bring the car to a stop. We were together there. Unharmed—I thought. But my wife was . . . well, something in her had loosened like the wheel. She wouldn't respond. I sat with her by the side of the road, but it began to get cold as the sun dropped. I had to find the wheel and try to repair the damage. I was upset myself by then.

"As a patch to get us home, I borrowed a nut from each of the other wheels, and when I finished what I was doing, she was gone. I blew the horn and waited. Nothing. I started walking with Emerson. We covered a wider area of woods. A sickening feeling would not leave me. I would call her name and stop to listen, but it was empty."

He collapsed into his chair. "I didn't find her until it was nearly dark, by a stream that was partially frozen. She may have tried to cross it. I thought she was still catatonic." As if it had just occurred to him, he added, "She was dead."

Hélène tilted her head to the ceiling.

"I can't describe how it was to carry her back to that car with my son. The woods, the darkness, it was like another place. To see her there on the seat . . . During the famine, she'd watched people eating leaves, eating soil. And there was my son, clinging to her, trying to lick the mud off her face. Afterward, I couldn't bring myself to use the car. I left it outside, uncovered, let the snow and rain wash the mud off the seats. Emerson used to play around it—I don't know what he remembered. One day I called McVane to get it out of here. Every time I saw it, it might as well have been her. But no one crashed. Not when I owned it, anyway. I asked McVane to separate the pieces so that it would only ever be ours, whole, as a family. No one else's."

"He never dreamed you were the one."

"I was a young man," he concluded with an apologetic nod. "It was a romantic response, I suppose, to a situation that, by then, had lost all romance entirely."

He stood to scan the bookcases again, then turned back empty-handed.

"Like Eurydice, my wife died in a field. Except the snake that bit her was inside her. *She was as full with her vast death as a fruit with its sweetness.* I'm paraphrasing, but you understand, as Rilke describes Eurydice: She was completely content with her death."

I shifted in my seat.

"She was fulfilled by it. My wife wasn't afraid of what was beyond. After she was gone, looking back would have been the end of me. My son may have permitted himself to look back—that was his right. But I won't be persuaded to do it."

The way he described his struggle—wandering in the woods, carrying his wife—though he meant it literally, I recognized that he was grieving, perhaps only then, as he reluctantly admitted to us what he had endured. His droopiness, his difficulties . . . All my suspicions of his betrayal in befriending Miguel dissolved before the evidence of his pain. I wanted to offer him comfort, to hug him, but one look at him, turning away in his chair, told me it was out of the question.

"How I handled my life afterward . . . The thing about parents, as your friend Miguel can tell you, is that we don't always manage things to our children's benefit."

"Miguel is not my friend," I said. "I don't even know much about him. Did you tell him you had a son?"

I could not control the slight accusatory tone in the question, though I was well aware that I had not told Miguel anything about Emerson either.

Webster seemed to be searching for words. "It wasn't necessary."

"I thought your connection to Miguel might be related to AG's business. He denied it."

"He told you the truth. The one who has business with Miguel is you."

"What do you mean? I'm not interested in having anything to do with him."

Distressed that he might know about what had happened in my hotel room in Monterey, I felt myself rising in my seat.

Hélène put her hand on my arm and addressed Webster. "Obviously, she is confused. Could you help us understand?"

"You'd have to speak to Miguel about that. It's not my place to discuss it. What do you do, Beth?" he asked, now smiling kindly at me. "Do you have a job?"

I found myself mute with embarrassment.

"I do have . . . I am . . ." I reflexively reached for the scar on my calf. How could I explain that for the previous two years I had occupied myself largely by hitchhiking on his son's life? Rather than elaborate on the nature of my employment, I asked, "How do you know Miguel?"

"There was a Beacon event at a zeppelin museum in Germany a couple of years ago."

"You were there?"

"Yes. I am a former owner, as you now know." He turned to Hélène and smiled. "And I understand you are too, in a sense?"

She returned his smile but said nothing, maybe because she was conscious, as I was, that the car he never wanted to see restored was parked just outside the shaded windows.

"I was introduced to Miguel that night," said Webster, "like other potential investors. He told me he was on his way to Tianjin, where China's battery manufacturing is based. We talked for some time. He kept in touch with me. I offered to advise him on something he's been putting together with the Chinese, but he's very sharp—he didn't need that as much as someone to mentor him personally. He reminded me of myself." He paused. "I lost my parents when I was very young, like him. His mind and talents are different from my son's, but, without intending to, he's helped me reclaim something of a parental role I have greatly missed. Now, if you'll excuse me . . ."

"Of course," said Hélène.

I could see he was weary, but there was something else I had to ask him, on Emerson's behalf.

"One more question before we go."

He nodded.

"Where is she buried?"

"It's not marked. Not noticeably, anyway."

I had not scattered all the ashes. There was a small amount left in Emerson's bottle of CD cleaning fluid, which had ended up on his bookcase when one of the healthcare workers had mistaken it for a med. I pulled the bottle from my handbag as I followed Webster and Hélène across the back lawn of his estate, relieved that Webster had not marched straight out the front door and into the Beacon. As we walked I noticed, dotted around the property, great pallets of building materials and what looked like solar panels waiting to be assembled.

Webster pointed beyond them to a field where some parcels had been dropped like bales of hay. "That's hemp insulation," he said.

"You're remodeling?" I asked as we passed a parked bulldozer.

"The exterior, yes. And parts of the interior."

"Are you tired of living in the Robie's house?"

"Not completely," he said with a frown. "But if my ancestors taught me anything with that pastiche of a house, it's that if we're going to be modern, we can't live like people of the past."

To my surprise, our small procession merged with the path I had taken two years earlier on my walk around the grounds. At the foot of a hillock, Webster stopped and pointed. "Short climb. You'll see it when you get up there, where two stone walls come together. I wanted an inconspicuous type of shelter."

He excused himself, pausing first to kiss Hélène's hand. He made a comment I couldn't quite hear about the car they had shared, and then he moved to shake my hand, glancing hesitantly at the bottle in it before turning away with a somber wave instead. I watched his progress through the woods as he returned to the house. He never looked back.

The hill was the one I had climbed before, like an Indian burial mound. Despite its gentle slope, Hélène's breathing was strained by the time we reached the top. Above us, sunlight shot through a canopy of leaves, forming a dome of blinding gold. From the moment the paths had merged, I knew what I would find before me, and now Webster had confirmed what it was. The cave had been sculpted stealthily, extending behind the pile of loose rocks. A roughly triangular opening marked the point where two aging stone walls had collapsed. I had seen the rubble, but not the opening. Webster may have put his family's name all over public memorials, but this part of his grief was intensely private. Only a small metal plaque behind one of the walls, mounted inconspicuously on a flat stone, distinguished his wife's final home from the den of a family of foxes. I dropped to my knees, attempting to convince myself of the Futurist's argument that a tomb was no different from a museum or a library.

"Are you coming?"

Hélène's flat nostrils flared. "I don't think so." She seated herself on a cushion of fallen leaves to wait.

The air at the entrance to the stone cave was cooler, more humid than the air outside. It smelled alive, paradoxically, but there was no movement as I reached my arm in and struck Hélène's cigarette lighter. I saw nothing but the rough inner surface of the rocks, surprisingly clean—sections that must have been taken apart for the burial and then carefully rebuilt.

The cave was deep, but the entrance itself was not very high, requiring a belly crawl to pass through. I would have given anything so as not to put my body against the cold ground, but there was no other way in. I advanced like a snake, claws of moist dirt scraping over my stomach. When I was far enough in to clear the entrance, I flipped over and pushed my shirt tightly into my jeans.

The ground felt level under my legs, presumably where they had buried the coffin. I was lying on top of her. Emerson had said he would go to a cave when he died—the cave on the golden happy island—and I had convinced myself earlier in the day that the metallic tent at the garage had been his golden cave. He had slept inside it, across the Beacon's seats, on the night he went missing, returning by some animal instinct to the place where he had last been together with his mother and father. In his own way, he'd reunited them as a family, along with the car body and the engine itself. The jubilant currents of those childhood rides must have coursed through his memories. They had never lost their power.

Outside, under the dome of yellow leaves, Hélène was singing to herself in French, high-pitched notes that sounded to my ears like a lullaby. I recalled the architect Schindler's observation that caves were our first homes. Mothers are our first homes, I realized, my face wet with tears as I began to pat the last of Emerson's ashes into the dirt. It was this modest tomb that I had found him weeping over in desolation all those years ago.

Eurydice was fulfilled by her death—wasn't that what Webster said? She was satiated. Wrapped in her long burial clothes, she was already indifferent to the world of the living. She had moved beyond it, into death; she was content to stay. But the poet's alteration of the accepted version of the story meant something more to me: It meant I had not been content to stay. As my father had been trying to tell me in his own way . . .

I had so little memory of it, dipped as I was afterward in the waters of forgetfulness, the tips of my hands dragging through, erasing my fingerprints . . . I recalled the sight of the house numbers as I was brought out—clearly visible, black-on-white over our front door, nailed into place there long before by a father who'd wanted to be sure his family could be found quickly by an ambulance or a fire truck in the middle of the night. Dressed in the flannel pajamas I wore when they carried me into Webster Memorial, I was the last person to be contemplating mysticism in light of the evening's events. There had been some trauma, a dislocation. I was home, and then I was swinging back and forth over a threshold, like an infant in a bouncy swing. I reached another home not long after, in the absolute sense.

I was safe there, as if playing in the neighbor's yard just across the fence, and then someone was calling me back. I had almost stayed too long. I don't know where I was—I don't know how you could apply a *where* to it. What could have persuaded me to come back? I wondered if I would ever be able to answer, just as I wondered why Emerson had finally entrusted himself to me.

Alone in the cave, I called up for review the various afterlives in my archive, compiled over years of reading, until I recalled the concept of *Ibbur*—or impregnation—as named in the Kabbalah, in which the soul of the departed occupies another living person temporarily, in both body and spirit, often for the purpose of accomplishing a worthy task. This tradition collided abruptly in my mind with another that I had run across, in an account of some remote tribe—I could not remember where—whose people believe that when one of their own dies, the soul is too naïve at first to be given a new life, and so it must be chaperoned by the living until it is ready to choose a new one. It enters the body of a loved one then, and remains there for a time.

This is grief. A Westerner might call it possession, and fear it, for it implies the loss of self. But for the members of this tribe, to be possessed by the dead and carry the death to term is a badge of great honor, like a child growing inside, a womb carrying a fetus.

This was Emerson's use for me. It was then that grief revealed its power: I'd been closer to him dead than I had been to anyone alive. I could continue to live through him; I had the plot I'd long desired—his. But it came with a price. I would never know what my own life could be. I was as hesitant about that as he had been of his own death.

He'd carried me as I'd carried him. Now his afterlife in me had reached its full term. Somewhere in the maternity ward of Webster Memorial, a new mother like Beckett was welcoming a being into the world. I had to do the opposite and let him go. It was the kind of pain Mr. Webster had known, a grief he still struggled with—what my mother had prayed I would never feel. Weightless in the cave, I felt the commotion in my belly, something trying to move through as I attempted to end my old, unended conversation with Emerson.

In the beginning, we were sailors . . .
Water was the road of our adventures for thousands of years, straight from the womb . . .
Did you prepare for your birth by feeling scared in the womb? Of course not. It would be absurd.
Death is no different.
Formless into form.
Form into formless.
Who can say you are not a being, even now?
Here, in my thoughts. In my heart . . .
When we were sailors, we believed the earth was flat. Then adventurers went off in their ships and gave their testament, piecing together another truth. They passed from this life still unsure themselves, but in time, beliefs changed.
You are not going to sail over the edge, Emerson. No, not in death either.

24

OUTSIDE THE BURRING PORT station, I sat in the car watching Hélène wipe a dusky constellation of bug matter off her glasses with the front of her T-shirt. She'd driven us there, and I intended to put her on a Metro-North train back to the city before attempting to drive myself down the road to my parents' house.

"The train is coming now?" she asked, moving to climb out of the driver's seat.

"No. Not for a few minutes yet."

"Could we rest here?" she asked, falling back. "That was strenuous today."

"Of course. You don't have to wait on the platform."

Without the camouflage of her glasses, the sadness in her eyes was plain to see. I tried to make conversation with her, but every subject I could think of shrank into a stream of mundane babble. I had not anticipated this moment, when I would have to take the car away from her again. There had been no way of knowing how it would be. It seemed she had not come to terms with some lingering grief.

I could believe now that reuniting the car and the engine had given Emerson a final peace. But he had known, by the end, that Hélène was just as possessed by its memory. Even if he did relish his victory, it seemed cruel that his last act had been to taunt her.

Was that worth the effort of dragging himself all the way to her hotel?

The truth entered my mind then, wholly formed, as if my brain moved aside for another sensibility to make itself heard: Emerson had left the paintbrush in the Beacon on purpose.

He couldn't write. What simpler, more portable symbol of Hélène could there be? The brush was as good as an arrow pointing to her, in case he failed to reach her hotel. He had even left it on the driver's side. He had brought together the two things she needed to work: her missing tool and the inspiration she needed to use it.

"Hélène," I began, grasping that Emerson had never intended the Beacon for me at all. "I don't completely understand what this car means to you, but I think Emerson wanted you to have it."

She turned to me with a look of uncertainty.

I pointed to the key hanging from the dashboard. "When he went to your hotel that morning, that was in his pocket."

"It was?" She regarded me with tense, questioning eyes.

I remember.

"Oh!" she cried, reaching a hand tentatively toward the key.

"What did you say he told you that morning? 'We have it.'"

"I thought he meant *you* and him."

I shook my head. "He went there to give it to you."

She reached for me across the seat, managing to grab the fingers of my left hand in an impassioned shake. "Are you certain? This must be very difficult for you, Beth."

"No, it's not. He wanted you to have it."

The tears in my eyes blurred the outline of her pink glasses. She hugged me now in earnest.

"Thank you. Oh."

Up close, embracing her, I felt relief, then thought: Just as her quest was being fulfilled, mine was starting again. It wasn't that I was alone; it was that for a time I knew something different. Unknowingly I had rehearsed intimacy with Emerson for years, the glass wall shrinking and becoming more portable until it fell away. He had given me a taste of something, and I wanted it again; a deeper connection, as I had once envisioned in another form with Miguel. But I still could not decipher Webster's words—that I was the one who had business with Miguel.

The Metro-North train glided to a stop at the platform in front of us, and Hélène gave me a questioning glance.

"If you're going to drive this back to Manhattan, I need you to drop me off at my parents'," I said. "It's just down the road."

She turned the key in the ignition. When she spoke again, her tone was more businesslike. "I want to be clear. My original proposal still stands, Beth. I am offering to purchase this car from you, or from Emerson's estate."

"I am his estate." I directed her out of the station, thinking how disappointed Howard and Sissy Russell would be to know that I wasn't going to make one red cent on the car after all. "It's a gift," I insisted. "His lawyer's office can help us with the paperwork. And please, don't thank me. It doesn't have anything to do with me. He wanted you to have it."

There was no more awkward silence after that. She spoke excitedly on the way to my parents' house, working through her schedule and determining how quickly she could wrap up her business in New York. Her plan, seemingly hatched there and then, was to register herself and the car to rerun the Mille Miglia in Italy the following spring. It turned out that she had stayed in touch with Howard and Sissy Russell, and she intended to invite them to stay with her in Italy while she practiced for the road race.

"You'll come for the race too?" she asked.

"I'll try," I said halfheartedly, picturing Webster's stooped back as he walked away from us that afternoon. Was he alone tonight, reading his book of Rilke poems? "*Loss.* How do you tolerate so much loss?"

I meant it rhetorically, but Hélène answered.

"At first, I couldn't," she said. "I remember . . . Well, I was seven when we were told that my father was killed. Eventually we got the news about my brother. He was too young to be a soldier, but he joined the Resistance. It continued like that."

"It must have been very hard for you."

"Well, I was alive, and they weren't," she said, keeping her eyes focused on the road. "Was that all right? I didn't think so."

"You didn't think you should be alive?"

She shook her head.

"You were a child," I said. "That's a child's response."

"It might have been. When I went away to art school, to Italy, it helped me a great deal." She glanced at me. "I permitted myself, with maturity, to change my mind."

"Did you ever live there again? After Alto?"

She sighed. "Not for any length of time. Though I love that country. And I hated the destruction Mussolini brought to it. Hearing that man speak today about what his wife went through in China . . ." Her voice trailed off. "What people have been put through in the name of progress. Even so, I am not political, though there are some who accuse me of it."

"I heard something once—" I began, recalling Arthur Quint's seemingly well-rehearsed denial of her political motivations.

She narrowed her eyes. "What?"

"Just—"

"Fascism," she said flatly.

She drove on with her jaw clenched, and I wondered if she would say anything more. "There was a connection," she said finally.

I looked to her, waiting for her to continue.

"But I had no idea how much."

The gallery assistant, Katya, had known something after all. "I'm familiar with the Futurist movement," I said.

"Yes, well, that happened thirty years before I was born," she said dismissively. "But there were other links, coincidental."

"What links?"

"The cars I used, the time I was working in—so many things exist as traces in the paintings. Some say Fascism because I used many Italian cars, and Mussolini's government propped up the auto industry in Italy after the First World War, when those cars were built. His influence, shall we say, helped many of the companies survive at critical points. But it was the same across Western Europe. People were hungry, there was no work, like your Great Depression here. There was a healthy interest in supporting a promising industry with passion and talent behind it. This fascination with aerodynamics, speed, it caused a kind of glorious madness. Everything seemed open. The newness of the technologies and the materials—it inspired advances in art, music, literature, architecture . . ."

She steered the car through a corner.

"There were already concours in Europe, and the Fascist Party made a special effort to promote those kinds of events, to present cars as fashionable. Also racing—it had been a sensation since the twenties." She seemed to rise to the memory, before adding: "And this was how the Reich demonstrated its technical prowess. Hitler was obsessed with racing. He promoted it heavily. He set workers to building the autobahn."

She glanced at me miserably. "*Everyone* fell in love with cars. I was as mad for speed as the rest of them—for the freedom and all it promised. The engineers like Miguel's grandfather believed in that promise. And it was overtaken by ambitions far more brutal than they could have imagined." She paused. "Can you think how it must have been for them? Everything they built was used for war."

I realized then that this was a story I knew—one my father had taught me inadvertently through years of battle scenarios. After Hitler invaded Poland and the war spread, the workers in factories across Europe, and later the United States, found themselves, as they had in the First World War, applying a generation's worth of advances to military vehicles and munitions: engines used as weapons, engines for tanks and jeeps and fighter planes, defended by more engines, like the Merlins that had powered the Spitfires to victory. The capacity for destruction was unprecedented as engines pursued one another through the sky, dropping bombs that destroyed much more than the auto factories themselves.

Hélène nodded as I spoke. "Can you blame Miguel for wanting to make something new? Destruction comes with creation, advances—I find these things uncomfortable to reconcile, though the truth was there in my paintings."

My mind filled with images of the museum halls in Denmark: torn canvases that recorded the force of speed for what it was, an irreversible rupture. Out from the jagged rips flew a century's worth of evidence that what had once been revolutionary needed to become more evolved. Out from the rips flew Miguel's blackbird with its lament: Still, we demand nothing new.

I directed her along a series of small streets, reflecting soberly on these revelations, until we crawled to a stop in front of my parents' mailbox. One glance at the house told me that my mother and father were in the kitchen eating dinner—I could see the light shining at the end of the hallway through the darkened living room. I forced a smile, dispirited at the prospect of watching Hélène drive away. I was gathering my things to climb out of the car, wondering again how to say goodbye to her, when she touched my arm.

"There's something else. Something personal. Alto's family in Rome—"

She seemed to be studying my face, assessing my trustworthiness before continuing:

"They were Fascists, Beth. They supported Mussolini. Before and during the war. Among their gestures of loyalty, the Bianco family gave over their fleet of grand cars to the Duce and his officers."

"What do you mean, gave them over?"

"Permitted the use of them—like you would pay protection money. All of their fine coach-built cars were used for . . . the business of the Fascist Party, and this favor managed to protect their collection of motorcars through the war. While living people weren't protected." She paused. "That rumor you heard about me. It's because my Speed Paintings collaborated with them also. With the ones who were responsible for the death of my father and brother, and the horrors suffered by so many others."

"What are you saying?"

"Alto's father—in truth, he was a sadistic man—he decided it would be amusing to tell me the history of his fleet, or I might not have been burdened with this knowledge."

With a chill, I sensed what she was trying to say. "You mean, those are the cars you used to make the Speed Paintings?"

"The earliest ones, yes."

"But you didn't know."

She was shrinking beside me in the seat, curling into herself like a nautilus.

"I knew."

I was too confused to speak.

"The war was over. The lives were lost. I had to decide: What was the greater action? I used them. I worked with whoever I needed to in their circle to do it."

She searched my face.

"For me, the car was the paintbrush, you see. A very costly one. I had no money, no way to obtain those materials. This was how it began . . . The first ones, they were anti-painting, anti-aesthetic. They were pure rage."

"What if his father was lying, just to upset you?"

She turned to me with pitying eyes. "He showed me photos, Beth."

"Photos?"

"The one he especially treasured was from 1938, before the war. It was a black car, with a grille like a hundred arrows. There in the back seat was Mussolini. Beside him was Hitler, riding through Rome on a state visit. It was the first car I used."

My mind returned to a comment she had once made—she had kept many of the early paintings, and then given them to the museum in Denmark. Paintings more savage than those in her later racing series, as I had sensed when I saw them all together. She had flirted with destroying them, as the Futurists had once prescribed.

She twisted her lips. "In my nightmares I am driving those animals . . ."

I didn't know what to say.

"But I don't forget. And I can't forget. There was a photo taken of me in that car for *Life* magazine, recording the making of a Speed Painting. It has followed me for forty years. Every opening, every article. When I see it, I can't tell you the grief that pours in."

"But you made artwork . . ."

"Does that redeem something? I hope so." She touched the dashboard of the Beacon. "This was the first car I used that wasn't tainted. It has always been separate."

Alto's message to her on the engine seemed to have more than one meaning. "Does this have something to do with what happened between you and Alto?"

She curled down tighter into herself.

"But he was practically a child during the war, like you," I argued, unsure why I was defending him. "It was his family's crime, the crimes of a regime. Wasn't he the one who brought you this Beacon?"

She nodded. "If you can see that, then . . . Beth, maybe I don't know you well enough to say this. But I watched you with that man Miguel, in Monterey. I saw you cheer with him when the car received its ribbon—you were so alive. And when I entered that circle around the car I could tell he was protective of you. I don't know what happened, but from what was said earlier, with Mr. Tang's father, it sounds like something about him is bothering you. I would suggest you find out what you don't know. I learned some things about the Beacon company when I went looking for this car, and I can tell you: Miguel's parents squandered nearly everything he could have used to build his future. But something remains. Some courage, some desire to progress. Miguel seems to remember enough from his grandfather to try."

I leaned over and hugged her delicately.

"I know something now about Alto," she said as I climbed out. "About love, he said: You have to believe you deserve it. He didn't believe. But all this time, I thought I failed. And it wasn't true."

My mother sat across from me at the empty kitchen table, mending a pair of biking shorts. I watched her pull a thread from her sewing box, an old cookie tin manufactured to look like Wedgwood china. The pale blue tin was ringed with marble-white figures, a miniature scene of goddesses, cupids and hounds. In the center of the lid, two women in togas leaned over a man collapsed on a rock, his wings folded—was he asleep, or dead? One woman touched a hand to his shoulder, the other extended a long branch to his wing, as if to say, *We are not the same, but we are not separate.*

Even in that faux-porcelain tableau, there was no escape from grief, I decided as I followed my father through the house after dinner. At the door to his workroom, he paused with a sense of occasion, allowing me to take in the scene. Before us, the Battle of Britain was in full swing, the air thick with wings. A mechanical flock of Spitfires was diving and soaring its way to certain victory.

"Imagine what it would have been like up there." He gestured to the blue ceiling with its picturesque scattering of storm clouds. Beneath the painted sky sat Garrett's old desk, nearly covered

with a sprawling papier-mâché reconstruction of the Cliffs of Dover. I spotted an unfinished plane on one of the workbenches. "Is
this another Spitfire?" I asked, picking it up.

"Careful," he said. "This part here's not dry. The key with
painting is patience." He directed my attention to the backlog of
aircraft waiting to receive their colors. "It's tempting to rush it,
but you'll end up with fingerprints in the paint if you hold pieces
that aren't fully dry. That's what makes the difference, Beth. You
can always tell an amateur—there'll be fingerprints in the paint."

I bit my lip, considering whether to say anything.

"I don't have any fingerprints."

"Oh?" He glanced down at my hands with mild curiosity.

"No. I found out when I was living in Europe. Mine are missing."

He chuckled.

"I'm not kidding," I protested. "The government almost didn't
extend my visa. I don't know if it's funny."

"No, it's odd," he said. "But it would give you a huge advantage in painting models."

"It's like I don't have a mark of my own—like you, like other
people."

"You'd probably want to keep a damp sponge next to you anyway, to wipe off any glue that gets where you don't want it to.
Like the glass canopy on the fighters . . ."

As he went on talking, the wind through the attic windows
kicked up a sharp perfume I always associated with him, with
home, filling my mind with a lost memory from the hospital: my
father smelling of craft glue, singing quietly to me in the skinny
night-lighting of the hospital room.

He was busy wiping a stray smudge of glue from the canopy
of a German fighter plane when I asked him the question I had
never been able to answer.

"What happened to me that night? In the hospital."

His shoulders flinched. He gazed at the plane in my hands. Then he rested the one he was holding on a piece of newspaper and sat down beside the Cliffs of Dover.

"What do you want to know?"

"When did you know I was dead?"

"In the hospital."

"What happened?"

He studied the cloudy sky on the ceiling as if examining it for defects. "You turned blue."

"And then what?"

"Then I had to call your mother." He shook his head. "I had to tell her . . ."

"Where was I then?"

"They moved you into a special room with oxygen, to try to work on you—I had to stay outside. That's when they called the priest. They were trying to get tubes into your lungs. To remove the fluid that kept you from breathing. No one could do it. Everything that happened that night—it was harrowing." He paused. "I was brought to a police officer, there in the hospital, and he questioned me."

"What?"

"Well, they had to determine what happened before we got there, to make sure that your mother and I hadn't done anything wrong. I told him how we called the doctor when you spiked such a high fever—we didn't understand how serious it was."

I waited, then—waited for him to admit what I had always felt.

"You were dead, honey. Your life was over."

His face, his expression. I see them still, as if frozen in chunks of amber—those primeval archives—the flecks of his eyes caught forever in the very emotions they exuded, looking out, flightless, from the exquisite prison of memory hardening around them.

We both knew what had followed in the next hours and days,

when they had finally let him into the room where I was kept in a plastic oxygen tent. For a time, the door between life and death was held open, and I bounced back and forth over the threshold, tentatively attached to both sides. For as long as I lay in that tent of torture, they did not know whether I would slip back, slip over again for good. It would have been so easy to surrender to that sublime peace.

Why did I fight it?

Like a gift, the words of Mr. Webster's poet offered themselves to me. "Love has led me here," sang Orpheus. He sang it to Death, to bring his Eurydice back.

I felt it then: my father's hand against the plastic, pressing through the tent. Mano a mano. His hand against mine. In those long hours, what was closest was love. It was no sacrifice of mine to be alive. It was only selfish. I had wanted more time, with him, with my mother and brother. And I had fought for it, just like Emerson.

My father stood then, beside the Cliffs of Dover, and reached for me, as I had wanted to reach for Mr. Webster. We stood together under the frantic sky, and when we pulled away again, he was hunched in uncertainty, his eyes brimming.

"I know how lost you've been, Beth. And it's hard to stand by because . . . I see what you're going through, and I can't help thinking—" His voice broke. "That's what you spared your mother and me."

A purpose could take surprising forms, I recognized, ones I'd never thought of. Maybe we weren't supposed to know all our purposes. Maybe that's why I'd felt so lost.

After a few minutes he straightened his shoulders. Then, as if surfacing from a deep dive, he said: "If they hadn't revived you, that would have been it—for me. I would have followed you. Do you understand?"

I remembered then the question that Emerson had asked me once. *When you die, do you even know how it ends?* And now my father was telling me the plot: It would not have spared him either. And when he'd followed me, my mother's plot would have changed irrevocably as well. And then? Without her husband and child, how would the plot have ended for her? Alone, with Garrett asleep in his bed . . . I imagined the suffering Mr. Webster had gone through after losing his wife and child, the grief that Miguel and Emerson had known following the deaths of their parents, and I did not want to know any more of that plot. My father had done the only thing he could: He'd put his hand against the plastic, reaching for mine. He had stayed by my side, night after night, and it had not come to be.

Now he sat before me, his face full of self-questioning. I wanted to tell him, but I couldn't explain, that the darkest stretch of the trail through grief obscured what more and better life may be beyond, for I was only just emerging from it myself. In the cave that afternoon, a birth into death and one into life had been accomplished. I had carried Emerson's death to term, and, crawling into his mother's tomb, I had undergone that difficult labor. I did not want to say goodbye to him, but I understood: The death cord had to be cut. Two engines could not fit into the same body.

25

WHEN I CLEANED OUT Emerson's office and vacated his loft, I saw that the records and papers were like a warm blanket around me that had become full of moth holes over time. The archivist looks forward, looks backward, but there is so much the records cannot explain. Emerson's afterlife was how my own came to be written. I traded a plot in the ground for one that continued after both our expiration dates had passed. Was it possible for me to leave him completely behind? No more than anyone could resist memory.

Though I'd deleted Miguel's number from my phone years before, I could not completely dismiss him from my mind. One afternoon the following spring, when a crew of motorcyclists came joyriding down Bleecker Street, I took to heart the only piece of advice Hélène had given me and phoned the headquarters of AG in Germany. Miguel was traveling to a charity event at the New York International Auto Show later in the week, I was told. I realized that if I wanted to see him, all I had to do was purchase a ticket.

I was nervous that April afternoon, pushing through the door of Golden Hands. I almost walked back out again, but I was encouraged to continue inside by my conviction that getting a manicure for a party had always been Mei's great hope for me. After seeing how much Webster had aged, it was less of a shock to find that Li's hair had gone completely gray. Li showed no signs of remembering me. With a polite greeting, she left me in the care of a younger woman in an orange sweatshirt. I scanned the faces on the wall of framed licenses for Mei, but she was nowhere to be found.

The new woman rubbed the moisturizing lotion into my arms sloppily, let the cream stray onto my shirtsleeves. Silently, she buffed my nails with a vigor bordering on violent, finally mentioning that she was majoring in material sciences at Columbia. "Metallurgy," she explained with evident pride, renewing her assault on my nails with the buffer. "I know the best angles and pressure for polishing."

After questioning her for a few minutes, I understood that she was a beneficiary of one of Emerson's trusts—one I was supposed to be evaluating, along with the trusts for the preservation of Modernist architecture and the technology company Auxiliant —all of which I'd neglected after Bruce Kingston arranged the annual payments. My nails did have a bright sheen, I noticed as the girl stuck her head back into a textbook.

The Javits Center that evening was hot and crowded, but even without the superior viewing platform of a zeppelin I found Miguel easily enough. He was dressed in a white dinner jacket and black tie, standing six feet above the floor of the main hall on a revolving display devoted to Beacon. Beside him stood the man with the headset who had been with him at the event in Germany —a PR person of some sort, I realized as he led Miguel over to speak with a group of guests sipping cocktails. I climbed onto the platform and made my way to the outer edge of their circle.

"The revived Beacon Company is going to be working with private and governmental partners to explore new systems for clean transportation," Miguel was saying. I noticed that he'd dropped the word *Motor* from the company name. "The Chinese are building high-speed rail, investing heavily in clean technologies and beginning to secure the supply stream of key raw materials for producing green energy," he went on. "The opportunity here is for us to . . ."

Parked on the turntable beside Miguel was a new Beacon prototype: a long, low vessel in silver, a refinement, apparently, of the earlier theme. I inspected it, keeping to the back of the crowd until it disbanded. Then I detected the spiced notes of Miguel's aftershave, and I knew he was behind me.

"What are you doing here?" he asked with a confused, ruffled smile.

I handed him my camera. "Please, take my picture with it."

He stepped back and took a shot, then greeted me with a polite kiss on both cheeks.

"How have you been, Beth?" He smiled again, examining my face. "You seem different."

"Hair, maybe . . ." I wasn't sure what to say. I gestured to the machine beside him. "What's this one about? I heard someone say it doesn't have a real engine."

"It can roll," he protested. "It's here to demonstrate a concept. One vision of the near future, anyway. This car runs on electricity, and it can also be driven straight onto a high-speed electric train with charging points inside. The idea is that you would be able to plug in and recharge your vehicle while the train carries you a long distance. Then you'd have it for shorter drives at your destination—all with no emissions along the chain if the electricity comes from clean sources. It can even be charged by the sun. Look—there's our tribute to the solar gods."

He pointed up.

A reproduction of the lighthouse from the Beacon logo towered over the stage. I saw that it had been altered—remodeled at the top and painted to resemble a golden obelisk.

"It always amuses me what the marketing people come up with," said Miguel. "Would you like to sit in the car?"

He helped me lower myself into the driver's seat and then got himself settled on the passenger side. He pushed a button in front of me. "This is our future vision of the old 'provisional cover,'" he explained as a transparent roof closed over us. "It's fitted with next-generation solar cells."

As the canopy closed, the sounds of the convention center went mute and we were on a turntable, spinning silently.

"Are you having a good time?" I asked him.

"I'm never having a bad time—as my father used to say."

It was the first time I had heard him mention the man without sounding angry.

"I'm well." He nodded confidently. "A bit more settled these days. I wasn't in the best frame of mind when we met that summer, but I'm good now. Happy, actually."

He leaned in.

"What about you, Beth? I've wondered how you were doing. I almost called you last month, when—well, but you banished me two years ago in L.A." He turned to me with a chastising grin.

He was teasing me, I could see, but I couldn't deny it was true.

"It's happened to me before, you know," he said.

"It has?"

His grin faded. "And I lost a pair of boxer shorts in the bargain."

I laughed at the idea of this. "What?"

"I'm serious."

"How did that happen?"

He shook his head dismissively. "Have you ever met someone, and you realize, not until much later, how critical they were to your future? You can't know it at the time, except that something about them strikes you. You remember where you stood when you met them, what you said.

"I did," he went on. "I met someone like that. And I could see he had the ability to accomplish things. I had no family . . . I was lost. It woke me up, talking to him. It turned out he'd lost a parent, too. He encouraged me. Talking to him made me define who I wanted to be. Now I'm here—" He gestured with amazement to the convention center, the golden obelisk looming over the stage. "And I have no idea what happened to him. We had a plan together . . . for . . . this."

Miguel looked out the window. The PR guy with the headset was hovering outside the car. I worried that he would interrupt us, as he had done at the dinner in Germany, and I prayed he wouldn't, because I thought I was beginning to understand something.

Miguel's arm was resting on the console between us. I tapped his sleeve. "Your dinner jacket reminds me of a guy in a photograph—inside a modern house in L.A."

"Yes, I know the photo you mean. It's a Case Study House."

"It's a cool place," I said. "I went there once."

"I did as well," Miguel said. "The party I just mentioned. That's where I met him."

"Who?"

I could smell a dry, leathery nervousness on his breath.

"The guy I was talking about."

There was an underwater roaring in my ears, momentarily deafening my other senses as a memory surfaced in my mind. When I'd rejoined Emerson inside the Case Study House that August evening, I had been ready to tease him, to ask him why he hadn't worn his dinner jacket like the man in the picture—when I saw he was trembling.

"Just felt like standing there," he'd said, attempting to sound casual.

"It's a perfect night," I'd replied, deciding not to give him a hard time.

"It is," he'd agreed. "It's the night that's always happening, and is always going to keep happening."

I faced Miguel. "I have to ask you something."

"You want to marry me," he joked. "What took you so long?"

"That's not funny. I wish you would explain—" I wasn't sure where to start, or what he knew. I sensed that I had to feel my way carefully, one mystery at a time. "I just wonder—what happened that weekend, in California?"

"What happened with you?" he countered in a tone of friendly debate. "We were saying goodbye, and then you were having a go at me about my friend Lynford Webster. A good man, as far as I can see."

"I'm not upset about him anymore. I misunderstood something. I'm talking about before that. With us."

"We found the engine."

"No, in my hotel room."

"I was conflicted."

"About what?"

I could tell he was uncomfortable. I wanted to speak plainly, to let him know how much our brief association had helped me, like the friendship he'd described earlier. But I could feel the wet cement pouring into my mouth again, hardening there, as if to stop me from revealing how vulnerable I felt. I tried to talk through it, as difficult as it was. The words came slowly. And not as intended. "I know we'd just met. Maybe I shouldn't have hoped that it . . . but . . . we spent part of a night together. You told me our hearts were similar and asked if I trusted you. And then you said you didn't want to make our relationship more personal."

He pulled at the points in his hair. "Beth, have you heard about that woman you bid against in Monterey? The artist?"

"Hélène Moreau? What about her?"

"She died last month. That was when I almost called you."

"What?"

"When you didn't say anything earlier, I had a feeling you might not know."

I was too stunned to speak. I'd been occupied for months cleaning out Emerson's loft and office. I'd heard from Hélène only once since she drove the Beacon away, when she'd mailed me a volume of Rilke poems as a gesture of thanks, with the Royalton message slip from Emerson inside. I had been considering getting in touch with Bruce Kingston and investing some of the funds from Emerson's trust to start an archive for her. I thought I would try to track down the photographs in her obelisk series and collect them in Emerson's name—Anonymous. Now she was dead. I understood immediately that I was not sad for her. The sadness of death was an affliction reserved for the living, not those who were already gone.

Miguel shifted in his seat. "She was in Italy with Howard and Sissy Russell, believe it or not. Practicing to rerun that race."

"I know. In the end, I—well, my employer—let her have the car with the restored engine."

"I heard that," he said. "I saw Howard not long afterward, at a Beacon event."

"Did she crash?"

"Oh, no. She died in her sleep, more or less—though from what Howard said, it was a bit more violent than that phrase normally suggests."

Outside the car, people were milling around the stage, leaning down and peering at us through the glass.

He turned to me. "Do you want to hear something strange? Howard said that before they got to Italy, she had that bit of writing buffed off the engine."

"After all that, she erased it?"

"All what?"

I tried to reconcile the Hélène I had known with the thick-headed man I had met in Germany, scornfully kicking the new Beacon with his brown leather toe.

"I'm glad she did that," I said. "But I wish she'd gotten to run her race."

"It may be just as well. It's not the same now as in 1954. It's very technical."

I hoped that her erasure of the words meant that she'd come to terms with her memories and regrets. I wanted to keep talking about her, to help me wrap my mind around the news that she was gone, but I was aware that he had used Hélène to change the subject.

"A few minutes ago," I said, "when we were talking, you said you were conflicted about me. Why?"

His jaw tensed. "It had never happened to me before."

"What?"

He seemed to be working the answer around in his mouth with difficulty, as if he were battling an influx of wet cement himself. Then all at once his face softened. "Beth, I'm . . . I'm in a relationship. It was very new that summer. Completely new, in fact—for me. Because, I'd never had one. Not what most people would consider one, anyway. And that night, I came very close to cheating on her."

All around me, faces were pressed against the transparent canopy, trying to get a look inside the car. I smiled back dumbly, glancing from eyes to teeth to hands as he began to explain.

"I felt close to you," he confessed. "It's strange. I went through a difficult time before I met you. Like I was saying earlier, when I was getting serious about reviving Beacon, I mapped out a plan with that friend I mentioned. I mean, where do you start, to start a company again? He was the one who got me thinking about the kinds of things I'm doing now, way beyond what my grandfather was doing. Not devoting effort and energy to what we already know can't be sustained, when so much more is possible. I had some ideas of my own, but he had this way of drawing me into a bigger picture. I hadn't spent that much time with anyone since my grandfather. At some point, he let me know that he had other feelings for me, that he was attracted. I couldn't reciprocate. But I didn't want any change in the plans we were working on. He was a brother to me. I told him this."

"What did he say?"

He shook his head. "When he didn't return my calls, I wrote to him—for quite a while, actually."

"How long?"

He thought about this. "Four or five years."

"*Years?*"

"I was shut out. That may have driven me more than anything. I had to get serious about the plan, sell the marque to AG to raise seed money. Each step, I did it to prove to myself — to him — that I could do it, and I did. On my own. Because he vanished."

"With your boxer shorts?"

He shrugged, and I had no doubt: another one of Emerson's petty thefts.

"I still miss him. I've lost so many people I cared about . . . That summer, just before I went with you to Monterey, I met this woman in L.A. I was ready for something . . . I don't know. I wanted to give it a chance. I didn't say anything to you that night because — what would I say? We hardly knew each other." He sighed. "I was sick of one-night stands."

I kept my eyes averted. "I know what you mean."

"That's what I meant when I told you I couldn't make it more personal, not then, anyway. I was drawn to you, Beth. Maybe we could have talked more, later. But you banished me." He grinned again at the word. "It was frustrating, but it also made things easier."

While he talked, I tried to navigate a scramble of emotions — about myself, about Emerson, about Miguel. I recalled the interview notes in Emerson's notebook, the ones I'd read on the night he went missing, realizing now that it was his record of a conversation with Miguel, still very young and already intent on his comeback.

Emerson had risked his heart, but not fully.

"How long ago did this guy vanish?" I asked Miguel.

The time frame he gave was not long before Emerson hired me, years before he was noticeably sick. He'd retreated into photographs, other people's concrete visions of the future, rather than test the limits of Miguel's affection for him. I wondered if that was something else he'd inherited from his mother, by default, a kind of vicious cycle where one loss creates a fear of others until certain intimacies are no longer possible, even when they're most needed. Like Hélène, he must have preferred the illusory perfection of memory. He must never have intended to keep the appointment to see the Beacon that night in Los Angeles, but he had drawn so close, traveling there for a last glimpse of Miguel from across the hall. He'd watched from a distance as their plan took shape and followed the progress in letters that went unanswered, asking Lynford Webster for advice on how to fund the venture—even, in a sense, bequeathing his own father to Miguel. He hadn't abandoned Miguel. He had been looking after him the whole time.

Miguel was regarding me quizzically.

"I have to ask you," I said. "Does AG have anything to do with a company called Auxiliant?"

He looked shocked. "No! Thank God. And I hope they never do."

"What do you mean?"

"Auxiliant is a completely separate company. How did you know about it, Beth?"

"I don't really. I just heard something about it and I'm trying to find out more."

He glanced around. Despite the fact that we were sealed inside the car, he lowered his voice. "It consists of me and a small team that works with me. And a few investors. Most of the investors were recruited at that event in Germany. We're buying back the rights to the Beacon marque from AG. We can't announce it for a few months, until the lawyers are finished. The production of Beacons—in a different sense—is going to be reinstated in England on the site of my grandfather's factory. Also in China and one or two other countries."

"I was told Auxiliant did research."

"We do. We organize and fund research, through much bigger partnerships. The idea is to develop clean technologies, and some parts of them will be branded under the Beacon name. It's nothing like AG's business model. For the past few years, it's been a kind of skunkworks within AG, with the management's knowledge, but no meaningful funding."

I had to tread delicately. I needed to know if my understanding of Emerson's true will was correct. "So the investors you mentioned, they've been backing you?"

"No, their participation is quite recent. It's taken nearly two years to put together the buyback offer. That night at the zeppelin event I thought it was hopeless. But not long afterward, when I turned thirty-five, I started receiving money from a trust, blindly."

"Blindly?"

"My grandfather," he said with a sudden smile. "It had to be. Except I don't know how he managed to hide even fifty pence from my parents. He was . . ."

He bowed his head. When he spoke again, he was more composed.

"We have the *ability* to make something new. Not just new: better. People not caring—that's what's frustrating."

"You're brave to try," I said, recalling Hélène's words.

"But it's expensive to be brave. And I'm poor. It's only the proceeds of that trust that have been keeping me on life support."

My heart seemed to be beating in my throat. I knew now what Webster had been alluding to when he said I had business with Miguel. But it was more than the funding I controlled.

All around us, the faces staring into the car seemed to be waiting for me to speak. I fought to keep the identity of his benefactor from rising off my tongue. I understood that Miguel had been grieving when I met him in the zeppelin, grieving not the loss of his grandfather and his parents, but Emerson. Miguel had been the one to find the engine for him. For that, and for so many other reasons, he deserved to know the truth.

"Your grandfather," I said, "he's—"

The interior of the car seemed to shrink around us. What had

Webster said when I'd asked him if he'd told Miguel he had a son? *It wasn't necessary.*

For all his losses, Miguel had managed to gain some forward motion. He had opened himself up to intimacy and, left with nothing, rehabilitated far more than his family's name. He was proud of having done it on his own. If I resurrected Emerson's ghost, wouldn't it only drag him back into those woods of grief he'd been finding his way out of? I'd watched it happen to Hélène.

I glanced nervously behind us, expecting to see that dark place looming in the rear window. But it was clear.

"Your grandfather—"

"What about him?" Miguel asked, watching me with anxious eyes.

I realized I was shaking. "He must have loved you very much."

Was there any air in the car?

"How do I get out of here?" I asked, groping for a door handle. I looked around—there was nothing.

Miguel threw his arm across my seat as my mother used to do when she hit the brakes, as if she could stop me from marrying the windshield. He touched a button to retract the roof, and the rubber-scented air of the convention center washed over us.

The man with the headset was waiting for Miguel on the passenger side. I climbed out and crossed to where they stood. "It was so much quieter inside the car," I said, accepting a goodbye kiss from Miguel on each cheek.

"Yes," he said. "But is that a plus?"

A woman with heavily bronzed skin pushed past me to get a closer look at the Beacon. She commandeered Miguel for a tour of the vehicle as another man, sweating heavily under the lights, took the microphone and introduced himself as the company's technical director. "Men and machines cannot coexist without some cost to the natural world," he told the passing crowd. "The question is not 'What kind of car do you want to drive?' It's 'How do you want to live?'"

I crossed the stage, searching for a cell-phone signal. When I got through to Bruce Kingston's office, I made an appointment for the following week, to talk about managing the trust in order to give the beneficiaries the maximum amount to work with. As Miguel said, who knew what was possible? I didn't need to start a new archive for Hélène just now. The living were the archives of the dead, I decided, though I hadn't counted myself among them until I came into Emerson's employ.

I'd said goodbye to the old Beacon two years before, and as I left the stage I ran my hand over the new one, wondering how many others had done the same when they were building it, shaping a new idea of the future.

"Excuse me, miss? Please don't touch the car."

It was the man with the headset. Trying to be polite.

I withdrew my hand. "Look—no fingerprints."

He stepped closer to examine the paint. "What's that right here?"

I could see why he would have thought so.

Some round spaces. Blanks, really. A filmy impression of palm sweat and grease—a souvenir composed of skin cells. If nothing else, it indicated where someone had been.

ACKNOWLEDGMENTS

Some exceptional people underpinned the early development of this book. I remain especially grateful to Carolyn Eastberg, Anthony Champa, Geoffrey Precourt, Susan Smith Ellis, Robert B. Smith, Sarah Barth, Courtney Barth, M. C. Boyes, John Lineweaver, Maggi Tinsley, Carlo Armani-Tinsley, Andrew D. Miller, Jennifer Weissman, Bern Caughey, Mark Cunningham, Todd Knopke, Josh Poteat, and Michael Mrak. I am deeply grateful to four collaborators whose support and talents were vital to the book's realization: Andrew D. Miller, Euan Sey, George Hodgman, and literary agent William Clark. My gratitude to Marcel Cornis-Pope, Christopher Wilson, Marita Golden, Tom De Haven, Alan Filreis, and the late Maureen Duggan-Santos and Nora Magid, for their advocacy and intellectual generosity. Thanks to all those who provided support or technical input, particularly Jonathan Welsh, Frank Markus, Jim McCraw, Todd Lassa, Dorothée Walliser, Cara Forgione, Jennifer Champa Bybee, Robin Kimzey, Richard Backer, Robyn Dutra, Inge Hoyer, Jonathon Keats, Joe Richardson, Kari Nattrass, Julie Claire, Tom Bouman, Amy Goldwasser, Susan Armstrong, Melissa Dallal, Natalie and Larry Welch, Jean Tierney, Cathryn Drake, Faith Wascovich, Fred Kanter, the Unboundary autocross team, and Houghton Mifflin

Harcourt, especially Jenna Johnson, Johnathan Wilber, and Larry Cooper. I am grateful to the European Translation Center and the House of Literature in Paros, Greece, for providing a residency during the revision of the manuscript, and to the Virginia Commission for the Arts for an earlier writing grant. Special thanks to Dan Ross, Yorgo and crew, and to the designers and many professionals who shared concepts, roads and route maps—for your MOBILITÉ, AMOUR ET CURIOSITÉ.

Sources and References

The second Rilke poem referenced by Mr. Webster is "Orpheus. Eurydice. Hermes," originally published in *New Poems* by Rainer Maria Rilke, 1907, 1908; an English translation can be found in *The Selected Poetry of Rainer Maria Rilke,* edited and translated from the German by Stephen Mitchell, Vintage International, 1989.

The poem "Unrequited Love," named in Emerson's notebook, can be found in *June 30th, June 30th* by Richard Brautigan, Dell Publishing (a division of Random House, Inc.), 1977, 1978.

The quotation by Mike Nichols in the second epigraph appeared in an article by Joan Juliet Buck in *Vanity Fair,* June 1994.

Grateful acknowledgment is made of the following works, which provided helpful historical context and are recommended for further reading: *Mao's Great Famine* by Frank Dikötter, Walker & Co., 2010, and *Italian Sports Cars* by Winston Goodfellow, MBI Publishing, 2000.

Thanks to Mike Robinson at Bertone for his observation, "It's expensive to be courageous," paraphrased in the novel; to Michael Borum at CocteauTwins.com for his kind assistance; and to Frank Rinderknecht and Rinspeed, whose "UC?" concept car of 2010 served as a functional reference for the second (1999) Beacon prototype.